"You've seen me in a swimsuit. It's not a big deal."

He couldn't stop his eyes from roaming over her bare skin and that valley between her breasts. When he met her gaze again, he didn't see desire like he'd hoped—he saw uncertainty.

"You must've really hit your head," she joked, but the smile failed to meet the expectation of the joke. "You've never talked like this before or looked at me like…like…"

"Like what?" he murmured.

"Like you want me."

"I know exactly what I'm saying and what I want, Piper." He purposely let his eyes drop to her mouth as he slid his hand up and over her bare shoulder. "You know how special you are in my life and how much I value our friendship."

"Then why are you looking at me like you want to kiss me?" she whispered.

* * *

To Tame a Cowboy is part of the Texas Cattleman's Club: The Missing Mogul series:

Love and scandal meet in Royal, Texas!

TO TAME
A COWBOY

BY
JULES BENNETT

Published in Great Britain 2013
by Mills & Boon, an imprint of Harlequin (UK) Limited,
Eton House, 18-24 Paradise Road, Richmond, Surrey TW9 1SR

© Harlequin Books S.A. 2013

Special thanks and acknowledgement to Jules Bennett for her contribution to the Texas Cattleman's Club: The Missing Mogul miniseries.

ISBN: 978 0 263 90490 1

51-1113

Harlequin (UK) policy is to use papers that are natural, renewable and recyclable products and made from wood grown in sustainable forests. The logging and manufacturing processes conform to the legal environmental regulations of the country of origin.

Printed and bound in Spain
by Blackprint CPI, Barcelona

National bestselling author **Jules Bennett**'s love of story-telling started when she would get in trouble as a child and would tell her parents her imaginary friends were to blame. Since then, her vivid imagination has taken her down a path she'd only dreamed of. And after twelve years of owning and working in salons, she hung up her shears to write full-time.

Jules doesn't just write Happily Ever After, she lives it. Married to her high school sweetheart, Jules and her hubby have two little girls who keep them smiling. She loves to hear from readers! Contact her at authorjules@gmail. com, visit her website, www.julesbennett.com, where you can sign up for her newsletter, or send her a letter at PO Box 396, Minford, OH 45653, USA. You can also follow her on Twitter and join her Facebook fan page.

First I have to thank Charles Griemsman,
editor extraordinaire, for his cheering and guidance
as we worked together on Piper and Ryan's story.

Second, to Shannon Taylor. *Thank you* doesn't cover
all you did to help me. From reading my rough draft to
talking me through scenes over the phone to making
sure I had my cowboy "lingo" down correctly. :-)

And last, to the other amazing authors
in this continuity. I had a blast swapping scenes and
getting inside your heads for a bit!

Prologue

Twenty Years Ago

Piper Kindred was so sick of being snubbed by the girls who thought the only things worth talking about were their lip gloss shades and where they got their new outfit. She was also sick of being disrespected by the boys who didn't quite know how to handle her so they just ignored her.

Where did she fit in? God, she hated school. Even the third grade sucked. She'd switched schools so she didn't have friends yet, but seriously, if this was how the rest of the year would go, she'd rather be home riding her horse or learning to rope. School was overrated anyway.

Especially considering that at recess for the past two days all she'd heard were brats mocking her. Today was no different.

"Look at her belt buckle."

"What kind of name is Piper, anyway?"

"Dude, did you see that clown hair?"

Piper rolled her eyes at the annoying kids trying to get on her nerves. It was working, but she'd never let them know it.

She'd heard enough crap from other kids about her name and her wardrobe. So she liked plaid flannel and cowgirl boots; she was Walker Kindred's daughter. Didn't they know he was a legend? Morons. Didn't even know her father was pretty much a celebrity.

And the hair comments they kept tossing her way? Yeah, there was hardly a day that went by she didn't have to hear something about "carrot top" or "finger in a light socket" or "Bozo the Clown." So it was red and curly. To be honest, she liked being different from all these other stupid kids.

"Don't let them get to you."

Piper spun around on the playground. A boy at least a head taller than her stood with his thumbs hanging in his belt loops. He had a head full of messy dark brown hair and the brightest blue eyes she'd ever seen. And he was wearing a flannel shirt. Obviously they were the only two cool kids.

"I'm not letting them get to me," she told him, lifting her chin in defiance. "I don't care about those smelly boys or this dumb school."

He laughed. "My name is Ryan Grant. Thought you could use a friend if you were tired of playing alone."

"Yeah, well, I'm not. Those losers have no idea how awesome this belt buckle is," she told the boy. "My dad got it for me when he won the PRCA title last year."

The boy stepped forward, his brows raised. "Your dad won the PRCA title?"

"Yeah."

He shook his head. "You don't have to lie to make friends."

Piper shoved her hands onto her hips and glared at the annoying kid. "I don't have to lie at all because my father is the coolest man ever. There's not a bronc he can't ride."

Okay, probably there was, but still. Her dad was the coolest and he got paid for riding and being a cowboy. Could any of those other loser kids say that?

"What's your dad's name?" Ryan asked, obviously still skeptical.

"Walker Kindred."

Ryan laughed. "You're lying."

"I don't care what you think. My name is Piper Kindred and Walker is my father. Like you know anything about the rodeo anyway. You probably don't even know what PRCA stands for."

"Professional Rodeo Cowboys Association," he shot back. "And I know who Walker Kindred is."

"Then why do you say I'm lying?"

"Because, well…you're a girl. I've never seen a girl who knows about the rodeo."

Why were boys so dumb? For real?

Piper sighed, so ready to be done with recess and get back inside where she could just concentrate on her schoolwork and get another miserable day behind her.

"Whatever," she told him, rolling her eyes. "I don't care what you think if you're going to be just as stupid as the others."

He crossed his arms over his chest and grinned. "Okay, since you got to ask me a rodeo question, I get to ask you one. I bet you can't answer it."

Piper had had enough. She clenched her fist and plowed it into his nose. When he landed on his butt on the blacktop, she loomed over him.

"I don't have time for jerks who think I'm lying," she told him. "I've grown up around the circuit. Walker is my father and if you have any more stupid things to say, I have another fist waiting on you."

Ryan shook his head and came back to his feet. Surprisingly, he was grinning.

"You pack a mean punch, even if you are a girl."

Piper eyed him. Apparently that was a compliment.

"You wanna hang after school?" he asked, holding his hand to his nose then looking at it to see if he was bleeding.

Piper figured they'd just made some sort of bond so she nodded. "Sure, but don't think just because I'm a girl that I don't know everything about the rodeo."

Ryan laughed. "Wouldn't dream of it, Red."

She sighed and headed toward the double doors as the bell rang for them to go back inside.

If the worst he called her was Red, he might just become her one and only friend.

One

Piper Kindred did a double take at the black sports car. Her heart sank, bile rising in her throat. No, it couldn't be.

Oh, sweet mercy. There was no way this massive accident would have no casualties. Wreckage lay crushed with mangled pieces across the median, shattered glass scattered along the stretch of highway, a black BMW on its top and a large tractor-trailer on its side, blocking both lanes of traffic.

As a paramedic, Piper had seen plenty of wrecks, fatalities and gut-wrenching scenes, but nothing settled fear as deep within her as seeing the familiar car that was so often in her driveway…the car that belonged to her best friend, Ryan Grant.

The ambulance barely came to a stop before Piper grabbed her heavy red medical bag, hopped out and hit the ground running. The warm November sun beat down on her back as she ran toward the chilling scene.

The medic in her couldn't get to the victims fast enough. The woman in her feared what she'd uncover once she reached Ryan.

Once closer, she squatted in an attempt to see the inside of the vehicle. A wave of relief swept through her the second she realized the car was empty. Okay, so he wasn't trapped, but what was the extent of his injuries?

Sirens blared in near surround sound between the police, ambulances and a fire truck trying to assist the wounded and clean up the mess.

Piper tried to keep her eye out for Ryan, hoping she'd see him sitting in the back of an ambulance with just an ice pack on his head. But her duty was to assist where needed...not to seek out those most important in her life.

As she moved closer to the tractor-trailer, where the majority of the cops seemed to be congregated, she noticed numerous Hispanic people huddled together. With disheveled clothes, scraggly beards and various cuts and bruises, Piper couldn't help but wonder what they were all doing at the scene of an accident involving only one semi and the car of her best friend.

Piper ran to the group of obviously injured men and women. Some were crying, some had their heads dropped between their shoulders and some were shouting Spanish slang even she didn't understand because of the rapid rate, but she could tell they were angry and scared.

As Piper passed two uniformed police officers she heard the words *illegal* and *FBI*. Yeah, this was so much more than an ill-fated accident. By the number of uniformed officers scouring the area, it looked as though these people were not here legally.

Moments later she heard other officers discussing how so many stowaways were hidden in such a small compartment in the back of that semi. This situation was beyond what Piper was used to. Her job right now was to assess and treat the victims, not to worry about the legalities of this mess.

"Where do you need me?" she asked another paramedic who was examining a man's leg beneath his torn pants.

"The truck driver was pretty shaken," the paramedic told her. "He's sitting in the back of a squad car for questioning right now. No visible injuries, but his pupils were dilated and he did say his back was hurting. Seems he was driving this illegal group and he had no clue."

Piper nodded, gripped her bag tighter and headed toward the squad car closest to the overturned semi. Sure enough a trooper had his forearm resting on the roof of the car as he leaned in and listened to whatever the man seated in the back was saying.

"I swear I had no clue what was in the back of my truck. Please, you've got to believe me," the driver pleaded. "I was just trying to get into the other lane and that car came out of nowhere. I didn't see him at all."

According to the man's story, he was completely innocent. This was a mess of epic proportions and not something a few questions would solve. But all Piper needed to do was to assess the man to see if he needed to go to the hospital or if he could continue being questioned.

"Officer, may I please check him out?" Piper asked. "I understand he has back pain."

The officer stood to his full height and nodded, but didn't move too far away. Often medics and cops worked together. Being a first responder required teamwork and so far she'd never had an issue with any cop getting in the way of her treating a patient at the scene.

Piper leaned in and saw a middle-aged man with a protruding belly hanging over his faded jeans, a dirty, bushy blond mustache with matching beard and nicotine-stained fingers.

"Sir, my name is Piper and I'm an EMT. I was told your back is hurting. Can you stand?"

He nodded and slid out of the car as Piper backed up. When he came to his full height, he winced, grabbing his lower back—whether for show to get the officer's sympathy or because the pain was indeed real, she didn't know. Yet again, not her place to judge.

"If you'll come this way, we can set you in the back of an ambulance. You may want to go to the hospital just to make sure nothing else is wrong, but I can get your vitals over here."

"I appreciate that, ma'am."

As she led the man toward the nearest empty ambulance, her eyes scanned the crowd for Ryan. Had he already been taken to the E.R.? Were his injuries life-threatening? The unknowns were killing her.

She knew a life flight chopper hadn't been dispatched to the scene, so that was a mild comfort. Not only for the fact Ryan didn't need a medevac, but that none of the others involved in the accident did, either.

Another ambulance arrived on the scene as Piper assisted the truck driver into the back of a vacant one. When fresh paramedics hopped from their emergency vehicle and made their way toward the group of injured people, she jogged back over to assist.

But froze in her tracks as one head lifted and a familiar set of dark eyes met hers. He was amid a group of Mexicans, but this man… She knew this man.

Dear God. How could this… What the hell…?

"Alex?" she whispered to herself.

Piper took off at a dead run and stopped beside Alex Santiago. Her bag dropped at her feet as she held her breath.

Was she honest to God seeing the man who'd disappeared months ago without a trace? Could it truly be him?

The man glanced up at her, holding his hand over his eyes to block the glaring afternoon sun.

My God. It *was* him. The hair was a shaggy, unkempt mess and the scruff on his cheeks and chin indicated he hadn't shaved in a few days or even weeks. But this was Alex… The man who'd been missing from Royal, Texas, for months.

The man most people assumed had become a victim of foul play, maybe even at his best friend's hand. But here he was, living and breathing.

"Alex, what on earth are you doing here? Where have you been?" she asked, eyeing the knot on the side of his head.

He winced as she slid her fingertip over the swollen bump. "You must have me confused with someone else. My name isn't Alex."

Piper's hand stilled above his head as she leaned down to look him in the eyes. She was pretty sure she knew what her friend looked like. Just because she hadn't seen him in months didn't mean she was clueless.

She looked closer. Um…yeah, this was Alex. If he didn't think he was Alex, then he'd hit his head too hard in that crash. But at least he was alive.

"Your name is Alex Santiago," she told him, making sure to keep her eyes locked on to his, waiting for a spark of recognition from his end.

His brows drew together and he slowly shook his head. "I've never heard that name."

"Then what do people call you?" she asked, worry growing deeper with each passing moment.

Alex's eyes searched hers; he opened his mouth, closed it and sighed. "I don't…remember. That doesn't make sense. How could I not know my own name?"

"You have a good bump here on your head," she reminded him as her eyes traveled down to the wrist he cradled in his other hand. "Looks like you may have broken your wrist."

He glanced down and simply nodded. Piper worried

shock may be setting in. Between the accident and the apparent memory loss, she had no doubt Alex was shaken.

"Let's get you to an ambulance and see what the doctors have to say once you get to the hospital," she said gently. "I'm sure you'll remember you're Alex Santiago in no time. I'm Piper Kindred and we've been friends for a while. Can you at least tell me how you got into that truck?"

Piper lifted her duffel bag, helped Alex to his feet and held an arm around his waist when he started to sway. "Easy," she told him. "No rush. We're only going to that ambulance a few feet away. Think you can make it or should I bring a gurney?"

"No, I'm okay."

She didn't quite believe him so she kept him leaning against her side as she led him to the waiting ambulance.

"Go ahead and lie down on that cot," she said as she assisted Alex into the back of the vehicle.

"Do you know where you are?"

His blank look added to the sickening feeling in her stomach.

"We ready to roll?"

Piper glanced at the other EMT on the scene. They might as well go without her because there was no way in hell she was leaving without at least seeing that Ryan was okay…and to tell him of miraculously discovering Alex.

"Go ahead and take him. He's got some memory loss so he doesn't know his name. Make sure the doctors are aware this is Alex Santiago and he's been missing for months. I'll go inform an officer because Alex was the subject of an ongoing investigation."

Turning her attention back to Alex, Piper offered a warm smile. "You're in good hands now, Alex. I know you're confused, but I'll be at the hospital as soon as I can to check on you."

Continuing to hold on to his wrist, Alex leaned back on the gurney. Piper closed the doors and tapped the back to inform the driver he was good to go.

With several paramedics now on the scene, Piper felt comfortable going in search of Ryan.

After searching frantically, running through the chaos, she found him next to the road on the other side of the over-turned semi. Her knees weakened with relief at the sight of Ryan whole and upright. He was a good bit from his car, so she had to assume the officer had taken him aside to get his statement.

But glancing at Ryan and actually talking to him were two different things. He looked fine, but looks, as she'd discovered numerous times over the years, could be deceiving. Internal injuries were nothing to mess around with and could prove fatal even when a patient looked perfectly fine.

Added to needing to know the extent of his injuries, she had to tell him about the mind-blowing discovery she'd just made.

Alex Santiago was alive. Their friend who had been missing for months was alive and on his way to Royal Memorial Hospital with an obvious broken wrist and some memory loss. But he was alive.

But, my God, what in the world had he been doing in the back of a semi-truck filled with illegal Mexicans? So many questions whirled around in her mind. She had no idea what the hell was going on, but she knew Alex was probably scared and confused.

As Piper moved closer, she noticed Ryan holding on to one of his sides. A trooper was jotting down notes and nodding as he took Ryan's statement. Piper closed the gap, but stayed a few feet away, waiting for him to finish.

The sight of him with a slight bruise over his right brow

and his hair even messier than usual made Piper want to throw her arms around his broad, muscular body and squeeze him to death for scaring her. But he'd probably laugh at her if she got all misty-eyed or mushy right now.

She'd seen this cowboy compete on the rodeo circuit countless times. She'd seen him get knocked around, bucked and nearly trampled, but nothing had terrified her more than the sight of his totaled car.

The trooper stepped away and Piper inched closer on still shaky legs.

Ryan caught her eye and offered that crooked smile. "Hey, Red."

That smile could melt the panties off any woman… and it had according to rumor. But Ryan was her friend so her panties had stayed in place over the years. Though she wasn't blind—her bestie was the sexiest cowboy she'd ever laid eyes on.

With that dark, messy hair usually hidden by a black Stetson and heavy-lidded baby blues, yeah, Ryan Grant was one very fine-looking cowboy and he did some mighty nice things to a pair of well-worn jeans.

"You need to be seen," she informed him, raking her eyes over him to look for other visible injuries. "And I won't take no for an answer."

"I'm just sore and banged up a little, that's all." He reached out, grabbed one of her shaky hands and squeezed. "You look tense. I'm fine, Piper."

"You will be checked out because you'll want to come to the hospital anyway when I tell you who I saw."

Ryan shrugged, hissing and grabbing his side again. "Who?"

Piper's eyes darted down to his ribs. "If they're not broken, they're bruised, so you'll be going straight to X-ray when you get there, big boy."

"Who did you see?" he insisted.

All joking aside, she leaned in and said, "Alex."

"Alex?" he repeated. "Alex Santiago?"

Piper nodded. "He was in the back of that semi."

"Piper…" He eyed her as though she was the one who'd hit her head. "Alex was in the truck?"

She merely nodded, crossing her arms and silently daring him to argue.

"How in the hell did he get there?" Ryan asked.

Piper nodded toward another ambulance and guided Ryan toward the open back. "He doesn't remember."

Ryan, still holding his side, put his foot on the back step. "He doesn't remember how he got into the semi?"

"He doesn't remember anything," she whispered. "He didn't even know his damn name was Alex when I was talking to him. He didn't recognize me and he was totally clueless."

"Damn it." Ryan glanced around at the group of Mexicans being tended to by EMTs and talked to by the cops. "He has amnesia?"

Piper shrugged. "I honestly don't know. He had a good-size knot on his head, but that could've happened from the accident. He's on his way in the squad I came with, so we'll catch a ride with another. Right now I think we both need to get to the hospital for multiple reasons."

"I don't need to get checked out, but I'll appease you only because I want to see Alex for myself."

Piper studied him, as if she could see beyond the surface and actually make an official diagnosis.

"You all right?" he asked. "You look a little pale."

Piper caught his worried gaze and smiled. "I'm fine. And if the doctors give you the go-ahead and release you, I'm going to kick your rear end for worrying me to death when I saw your overturned car."

Ryan's wide, signature smile spread across his face. "There's that Piper love. Come on. Let's get to the hospital."

"Oh, God, Ryan." She held a hand on his arm before he could step into the back of the ambulance. "What about Cara? Someone needs to call her."

Piper couldn't even imagine what Alex's fiancée, Cara Windsor, would think when she was told he was alive. Piper was stunned and thrilled, but she was worried about how extensive this memory loss was.

"Let's get the facts from the doctor first," Ryan suggested. "We can't have her running all in there in hysterics and shock. We need to prepare her for this and have concrete information."

Piper nodded. "I agree. Let's get to the hospital. And while you're getting checked out, I'll find out Alex's status."

"Red—"

She held up a hand. "The fact my heart rate is still out of control after not knowing if you were okay or not gives me the right to override anything you say. Now get your butt in and let's get to the hospital."

Two

"Nothing broken."

Piper stood inside the thin white curtain separating Ryan's cubicle from the rest of the Emergency Room.

She crossed her arms and smiled. "Anything else you want to tell me?"

Ryan shrugged. "Not really."

Narrowing her eyes, she stalked forward. "Keeping the bruised ribs and concussion to yourself?"

Busted.

"I'm fine," he assured her. "Nothing a little over-the-counter pain meds won't fix or a good shot of my grand-pa's bourbon. A cure-all, he always claimed."

Piper rested her hands on her hips, pulling the buttons across the chest of her cute little EMT uniform. Damn, but she was pretty when she was angry or about ready to light into him like some mother hen.

"You have a concussion, Ryan. No drinking."

"You medical types always take the fun out of healing."

As he'd intended, she took his joke and rolled her eyes with a hint of a grin.

"Seriously, I've had way worse getting bucked off a horse."

"You're staying at my place tonight," she told him, pointing her finger at his chest. "No arguing."

As if he'd turn down that invitation. Piper wasn't only his best friend, but a friend with whom he'd always wanted more. Yeah, he may have a concussion from that accident, but he wasn't dead.

He'd never pursued anything beyond friendship with her for a couple of reasons, the main ones being he was always traveling and she'd never shown any interest in him on an intimate level.

Added to that, her father had been a rodeo star and he'd heard Piper swear on more than one occasion that she'd never, ever fall for a cowboy.

But he was home now and ready to see if something beyond friendship could exist.

"Fine, I'll let you pamper me. But only if you'll make that chicken soup I love so much."

Piper threw her arms in the air and sighed. "Don't milk this, Ryan."

He laughed and extended his hand for her to take. She moved closer and he wasn't about to mention the trembling he instantly felt when they connected.

"Tell me about Alex," he said, stroking her palm with his thumb. "What are the doctors saying? Did you call Cara?"

Piper eased a hip onto the edge of his very narrow, very thin E.R. mattress. "The doctors are still unsure as to whether or not the amnesia was caused before or during the accident. He has old bruises, so he was in a fight or some other accident before today. His wrist has several breaks and he'll be going to surgery soon to repair that. More than likely they'll either do a plate or at the very least pins."

Broken bones were reparable, death was not. Ryan couldn't even believe that Alex was here after all these months of wondering what had happened—whether he'd run away or been the victim of foul play. But now he was back and hopefully this amnesia was short term so he could explain just what the hell had happened.

"What about Cara?" he asked.

"I just checked with the nurse and Cara has been notified. I'm sure she's on her way."

"What did they tell her?"

Piper looked down at their joined hands. "That Alex was found alive, but he'd been in an accident. He has some memory loss and a broken wrist."

"She's got to be worried sick," Ryan said.

"I can't even imagine."

"When can I get out of this bed?" Ryan grumbled. "I want to go see Alex and I think someone should be with Cara when she arrives. They're going to need their friends."

Piper nodded. "Dr. Meyers said you were free to go as long as someone stays with you overnight. I assured him you would be in good hands."

Ryan only wished he'd end up in her hands. But, alas, Piper would never see him as anything other than her best friend. Even if she did have deeper feelings, the woman was stubborn and because her father had pretty much abandoned his family to dominate the rodeo circuit, Piper would never turn to a cowboy for any kind of a relationship beyond friendship.

And that left him out, considering he'd traveled the circuit for years and now intended to open a school for children to teach them his love of rodeo. The new ranch he'd purchased a few months ago just outside town had a vast amount of acreage, perfect for teaching young children the basics and allowing them to progress to higher levels of learning all in one location.

But as much as he loved his sprawling new ranch, he

was more than willing to go to the small bungalow Piper was renovating.

"Let's get to Alex's room," he told her as he eased off the bed, concentrating on his movements so he didn't get dizzy, stumble and cause Piper to have him admitted. "Is he still in the E.R. or in his own room?"

"They just put him in a room and they're going to do the surgery in a few hours once the surgeon is available and up to speed on what happened. They have to be careful with the anesthesia because of his head trauma."

Piper slid the curtain aside with a swish and took off down the hall toward the elevators before she froze and turned back to him.

"Sorry, Ryan," she said as she waited for him to catch up. "I'm so used to going at lightning speed, I wasn't thinking you're probably sore."

"I'm fine, Red." Though he wasn't going to object when she slid her arm through his to guide him. Not that he needed it, but he appreciated her care. "I've been through worse with my job."

They reached the elevator and rode up in silence. When the doors slid open, he let Piper take the lead because she knew the hospital better than he did and he wanted her to think she was actually assisting him in walking, though he really wasn't in all that much pain except for the ribs.

"He's in the last room on the right," Piper said as they rounded the corner. "Should we both go in or just one at a time? I don't want to bombard him or overwhelm him since he won't remember us."

Ryan held on to his sore side. "He's already talked to you and I don't think I'm that intimidating."

Piper nodded. "Just don't pressure him about details. The doctors said the memories need to come naturally and not be forced."

Ryan pushed the door open and gestured for Piper to enter first.

"Hi, Alex," she greeted with a warm, kick-in-the-gut smile. "I wanted to check on you and I brought another one of your friends."

"The police just left," he told her. "I didn't know if they were going to let visitors in or not."

"I'm sure visitors are fine," she told him, stepping aside so Alex could get a look at Ryan. "And I'm sure in no time you'll be mobbed. You've had a lot of people worried to death about you."

Alex's dark eyes darted from Piper to Ryan, then back to Piper.

"Do you remember him?" Piper asked hopefully. "You guys are in the Texas Cattleman's Club."

"Sorry." Alex shook his head. "I'm afraid I don't."

"It's okay. I'm Ryan Grant."

Ryan stepped toward the bed and still couldn't believe his eyes. Alex truly was here. He was banged up and in desperate need of a haircut and shave, but the man some feared dead was actually alive.

"I think we should also tell you that someone else is coming to see you," Piper said. "Cara Windsor."

Ryan watched Alex for any sign of recognition. But nothing. Not a blink, not even an eye twitch.

"She's your fiancée," Ryan stated. "But if you're not ready to see her, that's fine. She'll do whatever you want."

"I felt she deserved to know you were alive," Piper told Alex.

Alex leaned his head back against the stark white pillow. "Damn it. This is frustrating. I don't even recognize my own fiancée's name? What the hell happened to me?"

Piper patted his uninjured arm. "That's what we'll find out. Don't push it, Alex. The memories will return. The doctors still aren't sure if the memory loss is long or short term, but we will do everything we can to make sure you get your life back."

"Would you rather we ask Cara to stay out right now?" Ryan asked. "Visitors are up to you. Whatever you're comfortable with."

Alex brought his tired gaze back to Ryan. "No. No. If seeing her will help trigger something, I'm all for it. Does she know about my condition?"

"The nurse who called Cara filled her in." Piper slid her hands into the pockets of her navy work pants. "I'm sure she'll be here anytime. Is there anything you want me to get you? How's the pain?"

"The wrist hurts, but it's tolerable since they gave me some pain meds when I got here."

"Have you had any spark of a memory?" Ryan asked, coming to stand at the end of the bed.

"Nothing. I keep waiting for something... Anything." Alex glanced at Piper. "So my name is Alex..."

"Santiago," she supplied.

"And I have a fiancée?"

Piper nodded. "Cara Windsor."

Ryan waited, but thankfully Piper didn't mention any more about Cara or her father who wasn't too keen on the idea of his baby girl's engagement to Alex.

Alex may be a venture capitalist, investor and new member of the most elite men's club in the U.S., but being a member of the Texas Cattleman's Club still didn't mean he was good enough for Cara...according to her father anyway.

Alex looked at Ryan. "And you say we're members of some club?"

"The Texas Cattleman's Club," Ryan confirmed. "Do you recall any of the men there? Chance McDaniel or Gil

Addison? Chance is your good friend and Gil is the TCC president."

Alex ran a hand down his face. "I don't know either of those names."

Frustration hung heavy in the air and Ryan's heart ached for his friend. So many people cared about Alex and would want to help him through this tough time, but would Alex want a bunch of strange faces all up in his business right now?

"Oh, God."

At the veiled whisper, Piper and Ryan turned to the door to see Cara—pale face, hand covering her mouth, eyes wide. As if she realized there was an audience, she dropped her hand, straightened her shoulders and moved in with slow, easy steps, all the while never taking her eyes off the patient.

Ryan watched as Piper stepped aside and made room at the edge of the bed for Cara. Cara started to reach for Alex's hand, but stopped as if she remembered he had no idea who she was to him.

"I can't believe this," she said, her voice thick with emotion. "I've prayed for so long. Wanted to believe you were okay, but not knowing…"

Alex studied her. "Cara?"

"Yes." She held up her hand, the one showcasing an impressive diamond. "I never took it off, never gave up hope."

Ryan stepped around the bed and tapped on Piper's arm, nodding toward the door.

"We're going to let you two talk," Piper told Alex and Cara. "It's good to have you back, Alex."

He smiled and nodded, but kept his eyes locked on Cara. Hopefully seeing the love of his life would spark something that mere friends couldn't conjure up from whatever depth of suppressed memories he had.

"Call me if you need anything," Piper whispered to Cara.

"Can I talk to you for just a second?" Cara asked.

Piper nodded and stepped outside the doorway.

"Is there anything you can tell me about his status?" Cara pleaded.

"All I know is that he was found in the back of a semi in a hidden compartment with a group of illegal immigrants. The doctor isn't sure if his memory loss is from the accident or something that happened before. That's really all I know."

Cara let out a shaky breath. "Thank you for being here for him until I got here."

Piper reached out and squeezed Cara's hand. "I know we don't know each other that well, but please, if you need anything at all, I'm here. It's no comparison, but Ryan was in the accident, too, and seeing him there really shook me up. I can't imagine how you're feeling. So if you need to talk, cry or just vent, I'm here."

Cara's smile reached her watery eyes. "I appreciate that, Piper. More than you know. And I may take you up on it. I need to get back inside."

Piper gave her a brief hug and watched Cara go back on the other side of the privacy curtain just inside the door. Seconds later Ryan walked out.

Ryan closed the door to give the newly reunited couple some much needed privacy.

"Did you see his face?" Piper asked. "He looked so lost, so confused."

Ryan leaned against the door and stared up at the ceiling. "I can't even imagine what he's feeling. But they're strong. Cara will help him through this."

"But what if he doesn't remember and he doesn't love her anymore?" Piper asked.

Glancing back down, Ryan shook his head. "That won't

happen. Alex is stubborn and a fighter. He won't give up until he finds his way back to us…and Cara."

Piper looped her arm around his and tugged him away from the door as she started walking down the hall. "I hope so. But for now, they have each other and I plan on getting you home so you can rest."

"And while I rest, you'll make that chicken noodle soup?"

Piper glanced up at him, trying to hold back a smile and failing. "Only because I'm so thankful you're alive and I know how much worse you could've been injured. But don't expect this every time we're together, big boy."

"Wouldn't dream of it, Red. Wouldn't dream of it."

Three

Piper got Ryan settled on the couch, remote in hand and feet propped up, before she went to make his precious soup.

Wasn't that just like a man? Fondling the remote, reclined in a cushy chair and waiting on supper? She smiled as she headed to the kitchen. For some reason catering to Ryan didn't bother her in the least. She knew he was no slacker when it came to work. The man was iconic in the rodeo circuit and now he was working his butt off trying to get a school open for children to learn the tricks of the trade. Piper was proud of her best friend and if the man wanted chicken noodle soup, then that's what he'd get. And she'd throw in some homemade bread just because she was still so relieved he hadn't come out any worse for the wear from that scary accident.

The look of despair on Cara's face kept filling Piper's head. Cara's world had been turned upside down months ago when Alex had disappeared and again today when Cara discovered he was alive…but he wasn't the Alex she knew and loved.

Piper was grateful Ryan was in her living room, fully aware of everything and everyone around him. Not that Piper and Ryan had the romance Cara and Alex did, but the bond she shared with Ryan was the most secure relationship she'd ever had…and stronger than most marriages.

Sighing, Piper focused on the task at hand. She was thankful that when she cooked, she planned ahead and froze things. She pulled open her freezer drawer and took out the chicken and stock she'd cooked and frozen just last week.

In no time the kitchen smelled wonderful and homey, nothing a scented candle could provide.

The TV blared in from the living room and Piper smiled. He was watching bull riding and cheering like some men do with football or basketball. Her Ryan was bulls, horses and broncs all the way, baby.

She rested her palms on the edge of the granite counter and sighed as she closed her eyes and thanked God for so many things today. First, she was beyond relieved that Alex was alive and, for the most part, unharmed. Second, she was grateful nobody had been killed in that horrendous accident. But more than anything, she was beyond grateful Ryan was okay. Not only was he okay, he was dominating her television and recliner, and that was just fine with her.

If she ever decided to settle down and marry, Ryan Grant held all the right qualifications. Oh, she'd never put the moves on her best friend. That would be weird… wouldn't it?

She'd be lying if she didn't admit she used to wonder "what-if," but Ryan never saw her as more than just one of the guys. So that was the role she stuck with.

Besides, even though he had stepped aside from the rodeo circuit, he still had that thrill for adventure and danger in his blood. She couldn't live with that, not again. She'd spent years watching her mother suffer while her father chased danger on the circuit. Injury after injury, her mother swore she couldn't handle it anymore.

And finally one day, she didn't. They'd divorced and

Piper had rarely seen her father again. She refused to do that to herself or her future children.

So, while she may be looking for a man just like Ryan Grant, there was no way she could make him Mr. Right. But having him for a friend was one of the best things that had ever happened to her.

"Hey."

She turned to see Ryan, arms crossed over his chest as he leaned against the doorframe. Sweat beaded on his forehead.

Of all the times for a heat wave to sweep through Royal, Mother Nature decided now would be a good time. What happened to the cold spell they'd just had last month?

"Sorry about the air," she told him. "Remodeling your own house can save a bunch of money, but there are certain drawbacks. I'm hoping to have the system put in next week. That's why I keep the blinds down and fans on in every room. I also wasn't expecting the temperatures to get back up to Hades levels this time of year."

"I'm good," he told her. "I'm more concerned about dinner."

He smiled, but all Piper could think about was how he'd been flipped in his car only hours ago. Yet here he stood in her kitchen joking about the heat and dinner.

"You okay?" he asked.

Piper offered a smile. "I'm fine. Just slaving away in here while you do nothing. You were supposed to be resting in there, you know."

He pushed off the frame and eased toward her in that easy way he moved, but she figured he did it now so she wouldn't catch on to the fact he was still dizzy.

"I'm resting," he assured her.

"You're in the kitchen—that's not resting." She looked

up at him when he came to stand within inches. "I can't pamper you if you won't let me."

"Is that what you're doing?" he asked with a crooked grin. "Pampering me?"

"Not if you don't get your butt back in that recliner," she insisted, hands on her hips. "Now get out of my space so I can work."

"You're trembling, Red."

"It's out of anger," she lied. "You need to be relaxing."

He stepped forward, she stepped back. They danced until she backed up against the countertop.

"I think you're finally coming down from the adrenaline rush of your workday," he told her, holding her gaze and invading her personal space. "I think you're in here thanking God about Alex, about me."

She narrowed her eyes. "You know me too well."

He grinned, placing a hand beside her hip as he swayed slightly. "Yes, I do. And that's how I know your trembling and feistiness stems from relief. You know how this day could've ended."

Piper closed her eyes, an attempt to block out the initial images she'd conjured when she'd arrived on the scene... especially when she'd spotted his car. She'd have nightmares about that terrifying sight for weeks.

"You have no idea what went through my head when I saw your car," she whispered. "I couldn't take the time to single you out, I had a job to do and it nearly killed me."

Ryan brought up his other hand to stroke her cheek and she realized he'd wiped a tear away. She lifted her lids, found him studying her face as he eased closer.

"Nothing can keep me down, Red. I won't go out in something as trite as a car accident. I've been through a lot in my years and a flipped car is nothing."

Piper inhaled, taking in Ryan's masculine, familiar

scent. He stood so close and, not for the first time, Piper admired that stubbled chin and jawline, those broad shoulders and full lips.

Damn, she shouldn't be admiring her best friend's lips, no matter how kissable they looked.

"It's that danger you crave that scares me, Ryan." She valued their relationship and that she could be brutally honest with him. "You're so laid-back, so carefree. But when it comes to adventure, you live for it. Do you know how broken I'd be if I lost you?"

Those lips turned up as he shrugged. "Don't worry about me. I know my limits and I know how to remain in control."

His eyes darted to her mouth, then back up to her eyes as he inched forward. This time she knew he wasn't reacting from the concussion and swaying. He had genuine lust lurking in those baby blues.

"This is just both of us coming off adrenaline," she whispered. "Nothing more."

"Maybe. Maybe not."

His thumb stroked across her bottom lip and Piper forced herself not to slide her tongue out and taste him.

The timer on the oven beeped, making her jump.

She stepped aside, causing Ryan to move, as well. He shoved his hands into his pockets as if he didn't know where else to put them.

"Dinner is almost ready," she told him, yanking a drawer out to grab a pot holder. "I'll bring it to you."

She silently pleaded that he'd go back into the living room because if she turned back around and he was still there looking at her with those heavy-lidded hungry eyes, she feared she'd succumb and take what she thought he was offering. And, dear God, she'd die of humiliation if she ended up giving in only to find out he hadn't wanted intimacy.

How in the hell had they come to this point? Was it the adrenaline or had today's accident been a wake-up call? Surely he didn't feel that way toward her. They'd been friends for years and he'd never tried taking it to the next level.

But the desire in his eyes said he was ready. If this wasn't just an aftershock from the accident, she had to consider a whole new angle to their friendship.

No matter what, Piper knew she needed to keep her emotions under control. She couldn't get romantically involved with Ryan. Being best friends was as far as she could allow her heart to go.

She still had a sinking fear that he would get bored with being home for good. She knew him well enough to know that if he got restless, he'd head back out on the road, leaving her staring at his taillights.

Ryan closed the bathroom door and turned around to… Oh, for the love…

Could he not catch a damn break? First he wasn't steady on his feet because he'd hit his head, then he'd nearly kissed his best friend and now this? Come on.

Lingerie everywhere. Every damn where.

Red lace, yellow satin… Bras, thongs, silky-looking nightgowns. Of course she hung this up to dry. And of course laundry day was the day he had to stay with her.

Well played, Fate.

As if that damn near kiss in the kitchen wasn't enough to have him cursing his overactive hormones, now he was faced with the very intimate undergarments Piper slid into after a shower or before bed.

He couldn't help but imagine peeling that bright blue thong down her long, toned legs.

Who knew Piper kept such a beautiful secret beneath flannel, T's and well-worn denim?

Ryan rested his hands on the edge of the sink and stared at himself in the mirror. What the hell had he been thinking rubbing her lip like that? He knew she was leery of trusting people. After all, he'd been in her life since she'd punched him in the face in grade school for accusing her of lying about the rodeo. Of course, once he'd finally believed her dad was *the Walker* Kindred, Piper's cool status had skyrocketed. They'd been near inseparable since.

So why had he taken such a dumb, careless risk with her?

Ryan sighed, reaching to turn on the faucet to splash some cold water on his face. He'd taken a risk because he'd always wondered what that sometimes smart mouth felt like, tasted like.

Oh, they'd shared pecks on the cheek and countless hugs over the years, but Ryan fantasized about peeling back another layer, finding that hidden sexuality.

He'd been on the road so much, he'd known it wouldn't be fair to her to start a relationship. She'd lived through enough comings and goings when her parents were married. No way would Piper want to have a part-time boyfriend. But it was hell always coming home between circuit tours, seeing her, hanging out with her and not touching her.

And because they were best friends, once he'd had to hear about the night she'd lost her virginity to some schmuck who hadn't deserved her, let alone something so sacred.

Ryan splashed his face once more with the refreshing water and used the small white hand towel to dab it dry.

With his face buried in the terry cloth, Ryan inhaled her sweet, jasmine scent and groaned.

"Damn."

He was pathetic. On the circuit he could've had damn near any buckle bunny he'd wanted but, despite what the media had portrayed, he truly wasn't a man-whore. He'd had many lonely a night when he'd wonder about Piper... Wonder what she was doing or who she was with. Wonder if she was falling in love with some local cowboy who only dressed the part but played it safe or if she was cozying up with someone even calmer like a teacher or a banker.

He'd spent much of his time on the road wondering what his best friend was doing back in Royal without him.

And admitting that to even himself was a big step. For years he'd fought the growing attraction, thinking the emotions stemmed from her being the only woman he was that close to with whom he'd never slept.

But Ryan knew different. He knew Piper was special, which meant she deserved someone special who would treat her right and be the man she needed him to be. A man who would stay grounded and give her the stable life she'd always craved.

"You okay?"

Piper tapped on the door and Ryan pushed away from the sink, which he had to grab on to again because quick motions like that weren't the smartest move to make.

"I'm fine," he called back. "Be right there."

After I get my libido and dizziness in check.

He took a deep breath, wincing at the pain in his side from his damn bruised ribs. He opened the door and turned the corner, only to find himself tilting. Or was the hallway moving? Either way, before he could get a hand to the wall, he went down. Flat on his face.

"Damn it."

Piper came rushing around the corner. "Oh, Ryan. What happened?"

She squatted to take his arm and humiliation set in. Really? Was this necessary? Did he have to be coddled by the woman he'd rather be seducing?

Surely the sight of sexy lingerie hadn't caused all the blood to rush south.

"This damn concussion made me dizzy," he told her, coming to his feet. Slowly. "The last time I had a concussion, I was laid up in bed for two days."

Piper wrapped her delicate arm around his waist and smiled up at him. "And I'm sure you had some cute little buckle bunny keeping you company and playing nurse."

Ryan laughed as she led him back to the living room and into the recliner. "Nope. Just my partner, Joe, and he complained the entire time."

Above him, Piper propped her hands on her flared hips and lifted one perfectly arched brow. "I know how those hoochie mamas are. Not only are you a big name, you're smokin' hot. You should've demanded someone who looked better in a skirt."

Ryan laughed so hard, he had both hands on his side trying to suppress the pain. "Smokin' hot? You think it's wise to call me that after what almost happened in your kitchen?"

Piper shrugged. "You've seen yourself, Ryan. Don't deny it. I can admit when I think someone is sexy and there's nothing wrong with stating the truth. As for what *didn't* happen in the kitchen, I already told you, it was just adrenaline."

Ryan held her gaze, waiting on her to look away because they both knew she was lying. Adrenaline had nothing to do with the near kiss. A kiss he could practically taste.

"Stay right there," she ordered. "I'll bring you a tray with your food on it. Do you need another pain pill?"

"I'm good," he said, shaking his head. "I'll tell you if I want one later."

Her eyes narrowed. "Don't try to be macho. If it hurts, no one has to know you needed something to take the edge off."

Ryan leaned his head back against the cushiony chair and laughed. He knew exactly what would take the edge off. Unfortunately he feared she'd give him a black eye if he mentioned it.

"Whatever that smirk is, I know your mind has wandered into the gutter." Piper bent down, pointing in his face. "Don't think I don't know how your dirty little brain works."

Grinning at her, he shrugged. "And that's why you're my best friend. You know and you still love me for it."

Piper rolled her eyes and went back into the kitchen. Ryan didn't even try to look away from those swinging hips. The woman was going to be the death of him.

Unless he actually got her into bed. Because if that day ever came, Ryan knew they'd set each other on fire with all this chemistry suddenly simmering between them.

Four

Okay, so sleeping naked wasn't an option, but damn it was hot in here. Ryan had gone all the way down to his black boxer briefs, put the large box fan blowing right toward the bed and he'd kicked off all the covers. Even the ceiling fan on high wasn't helping.

Of course, it wasn't just the heat that was bothering him; it was the damn woman who insisted on pampering him. While he loved a little bedside manner now and again, he'd prefer it with a little more petting and kissing and a hell of a lot more naked skin than his nurse had showed.

Ryan tried to get comfortable, but his damn side was killing him and that embarrassing fall he'd taken earlier in the hallway hadn't helped. But he wasn't about to mention that to Piper. She'd rush him back to the E.R. for more X-rays. Surely she had some over-the-counter pain meds. Maybe that and an ice pack would help.

If she only knew half the injuries he'd had over the years, she wouldn't be so worried about a few bruised ribs and a concussion.

He glanced at the bedside clock. Nearly midnight and he hadn't heard anything in the house for a while. More than likely Piper was sleeping in something satiny, sans sheets and blankets to stay cool, with all that silky red hair spread across her pillow.

When she tapped on his door, Ryan jerked up in bed. Damn ribs had him wincing and clutching at the sheet like a baby. Obviously she wasn't resting.

"Come on in."

He had no idea what he expected her to be wearing when she stepped in, but booty shorts and a skimpy tank both in the color of a pale blue was not it. Would he have welcomed her in had he known she was wearing so little? Hell, yeah. Even if he didn't have permission to touch, he would look and capture mental picture after mental picture to use for future fantasies.

How pathetic could he be? In his defense, he usually only saw her in that ugly work uniform or denim and boots. Though he did admire her in a nice pair of fitted jeans and those sexy cowgirl boots she wore. Now if he could just get her to wear them with a little skirt or something to show off those long legs. And her pajamas did cover more than a bathing suit, but still…

"I brought you an ice pack and some ibuprofen."

With all his fantasizing, he hadn't even noticed she carried a bottle of water and ice pack in one hand and three pills in the other.

"I assumed you wouldn't come ask for anything." She set the water on the bedside table and handed him the pills. "So here they are and we can pretend you're still macho and repel pain, but humor me, take the pills and use the ice pack."

Ryan laughed, popped the pills into his mouth and took a long swig of water. He needed it to replace the saliva that had all dried up when his best friend and her smokin' hot body had sauntered in.

"To be honest, I was just thinking of getting something for the pain."

"Let me look at your ribs," she told him, easing down on the side of the bed. "I'll try not to poke too much."

While most women who wanted to get up in his business tended to tick him off, he found Piper's gentle hands and caring nature sexy and appealing. She was certainly no buckle bunny with blatant sexual advances. Piper wasn't a woman who needed to throw herself at a man to gain attention, nor did she need a man to complete her.

But that didn't mean he wouldn't try like hell to get her attention. This was new territory for him, but after seeing passion flare in her eyes in the kitchen earlier, he was confident in his quest.

Piper Kindred had been independent since she'd bopped him in the eye in the third grade and as the years had moved on, he'd respected her more and more.

But now his feelings were growing beyond respect, beyond friendship. And now that he'd retired from the circuit and was closer to opening his own rodeo school, the thought of settling down appealed to him more and more. *Piper* appealed to him more and more. He'd have to be damn sure he wanted to cross over that friendship line and take her along for the ride.

As she slid her hands over the tattoos covering his torso and side, Ryan resisted the urge to reach out and move a wayward curl that had slid down over her eye. Instead he allowed his gaze to journey down to the vee of her cami. The thin material did nothing to hide the outline of her nipples. And those dainty straps could be snapped off with one expert flick of his fingers.

"There's still some swelling," she murmured. "But the ibuprofen and the ice will help with that."

She glanced up at him, and he was totally busted for looking at her chest.

"Are you serious?" she joked with a smile. "You're checking out my boobs?"

Ryan shrugged. "You put them out there."

Piper rolled her eyes. "I sleep in this, you moron. Besides, you've seen way better racks on the hoochie mamas that chase you all over the circuit. There's not a lot here to see."

"Listen, I'm a guy," he countered. "You should be worried if you'd walked in here like that and I *didn't* stare. Boobs are boobs and we want to see them all."

"Yes, I know. Any hint of skin around the chest area and you guys instantly quit blinking and your mouths fall open."

Grinning, Ryan took the ice pack she held out. "We only do that with attractive women."

"Oh, please." She laughed. "Besides, Ryan, we're best friends. I'm like one of the guys."

"Not from where I'm standing. You're all woman."

With no effort on his part, his tone had changed. His voice had deepened, his smile had faded. Yeah, he wasn't kidding about her not being just one of the guys. Yes, she'd grown up around cowboys and now worked with mostly men, but she was far from a guy and all that silk and lace hanging to dry in her guest bath proved his point.

"You've seen me in a swimsuit," she reminded him, her voice softer. "It's not a big deal."

He couldn't stop his eyes from roaming over her bare skin and that valley between her breasts. When he met her gaze again, he didn't see desire as he'd hoped, he saw uncertainty.

"You must've really hit your head," she joked. "You've never talked like this before or looked at me like...like..."

"Like what?" he murmured.

"Like you want me."

"I know exactly what I'm saying and what I want, Piper." He purposely let his eyes drop to her mouth as he slid his hand up and over her bare shoulder. "You know how special you are in my life and how much I value our friendship."

"Then why are you looking at me like you want to kiss me?" she whispered.

"Because I do."

She didn't back away, but her body froze beneath his touch. The dead last thing he wanted to do was to scare her or to make her uncomfortable. Unfortunately he'd managed to do both.

His plan of seduction needed a bit more work. He wasn't used to being the one chasing. If he didn't botch it, this could be interesting.

Ryan dropped his arm and eased back into his propped-up pillows. "Thanks for the pills and the ice."

Her brows pulled together. "So you get all worked up and then…nothing?"

Shrugging, Ryan grinned. "I've been worked up before, Red. Now get out of here before I take what I really want."

Deep green eyes widened, but she just nodded as she came to her feet. "Good night, Ryan. I'll be in periodically to check on you."

He swallowed, afraid that if he opened his mouth, he'd beg her to stay, to crawl beneath the sheets with him and see just how far they could push their friendship.

But in the end he watched her go, and waited for the door to click shut before he groaned out his frustration.

Thank God his injuries weren't worse. There was no way he could stay here long term and not want to try his hand at playing house with his very sexy, very intriguing best friend.

And he'd been scared that retirement would be boring.

* * *

Mercy. Someone had beaten him with a two-by-four…
or his car had flipped and pinned him. Either way, Ryan
nearly whimpered when he crawled—yes, crawled—out
of bed the next morning.

He'd been thrown from a horse countless times. But
normally he'd soaked in a tub of hot water and have a
nice rub-down after to help ease the pain that would inevitably set in.

But asking Piper for a rub-down last night would've
only ended one way…with all their clothes off.

Padding down the hallway toward the kitchen, Ryan
rounded the corner. At the small kitchen table, Piper sat
with papers spread around her and her hand holding her
forehead up while her other hand scribbled something.
A tall oscillating fan sat in the corner, rotating back and
forth to stir the air.

"Piper?"

She jerked, dropped the pencil and sent it rolling off
onto the tile. "Ryan? You okay? I didn't expect you up
this early."

Her eyes ventured down his body, heating him even
more. Okay, if she didn't keep her eyes up, she was really
going to get a sight. He was barely holding it together as
it was, considering she sat there in that damn flimsy pale
blue tank. The outline of her nipples mocked him just as
it had last night.

"I couldn't sleep, but I'm usually up early anyway."

"I know you cowboys are notorious for being early ris-
ers, but I was hoping you'd rest a bit more."

Piper came to her feet and damn that silky outfit looked
just as sexy this morning—more so since it was all rum-
pled against her body…not to mention how sexy that satin

looked lying against dewy skin. Yeah, the heat was taking its toll and he was reaping the benefits.

The curves of her perfectly shaped bottom taunted him. Ryan flexed his hands at his sides and called on his every last ounce of willpower.

She bent to retrieve the pencil and the top gaped just enough to give him even more to fantasize about. He looked away because, God help him, if he kept looking at her he was going to forget she was doing a good deed for him and totally swipe those damn papers off her table and lay her down and…

"Are you in a lot of pain?" she asked.

"Yeah." His tone sounded like sandpaper, but he couldn't even get enough saliva to swallow. "All over."

She tossed the pencil onto her pile of papers and moved across the room to open a small cabinet. She removed a bottle and popped the lid, shaking out three pills.

"Let me get you some water." She handed him the medicine and pulled a bottle of water from the fridge. "You probably need to keep some ice on those ribs, too."

While she busied herself getting his ice pack, he watched her turn into a paramedic right in front of his eyes. She was always putting others' needs first and it was apparent he'd interrupted something she was working on.

"What are all the papers?" he asked, nodded to the mess on the table.

Piper moved to his bare side and gently applied the pack. "Oh, it's nothing. Just the glamorous spreadsheets my life has been condensed to."

"What the hell do you need a spreadsheet for?" he asked, walking over to take a glance.

"I like organization," she explained. "I can't focus on my renovations and the budget if I don't have it laid out right in front of me."

Ryan fingered through a few sheets before he turned back to her. "I've told you I will gladly foot the bill for someone to come in and finish this. You don't have to drag out the process of fixing up your house."

Crossing her arms over her chest, Piper lifted her chin. "Are we seriously going to get into that again? I know you have a concussion, but surely you recall me not only saying no to your first offer, but hell no."

Ryan propped his hands on his hips, a little more than pleased when Piper's eyes drifted down. She quickly brought them back up to meet his gaze, but she'd looked enough to puff up his ego where she was concerned. Yes, he'd planted the seed and now he just needed to keep her sexual curiosity up.

"Listen, Red…" he started. "I know you have this stubborn pride, but I can afford to help. Why won't you let me? Pay me back as needed. That's fine if that's how you want it. But for heaven's sake, at least let me send someone to fix the air-conditioning."

Before I die from watching sweat trickle down that tempting valley between your breasts.

"I told you it will be installed in a couple of days."

"I can have someone out here today."

Piper rolled her eyes. "Quit steamrolling my life."

"'Steamrolling'?" he repeated. "I'm trying to make you more comfortable."

"Really? Comfortable? Is that what you call it when you undress me with your eyes like you did last night and then admit you want to kiss me?"

Ryan raked a hand through his bed-head and sighed. "Piper—"

"Seriously, Ryan." She cut him off. "I want to chalk this up to your concussion, but I need to know what's going through that head of yours."

He moved forward, knowing he walked a fine line, but he loved a challenge. "Maybe I'm seeing my best friend in a new light. Maybe I find you more appealing than I ever thought and maybe since I've moved back for good, I find that spending more time with the one person who knows me best is just what I need."

Her eyes locked on to his, silence enveloped them, and the only noise cutting through the room was the faint ticking of the fan as it rotated.

"Ryan…" she began. "What you need is more rest because you're obviously delusional if you think we can be anything more than friends. Get that thought out of your head."

"Fine." For now. "What are your plans today?"

"I want to visit Alex, but at some point I need to run by the clubhouse. I'm supposed to replace the medical equipment in the day-care facility, but I need to see how bad the damage is. Some may be reparable."

The fact that some jerk had vandalized the Texas Cattleman's Club's new day-care facility because they didn't want women or children around was absurd. It just proved a narrow mind was behind last month's break-in.

"Need me to come along?" he offered.

"No, but you're more than welcome to come to the hospital with me if you'll put your Romeo moves on the back burner."

Ryan mock bowed. "Your wish is my command."

She twirled around and headed down the hall. In no time her door shut and he assumed she was putting clothes on. Shame that.

Ryan ran a hand down his stubbled face and grinned. There was no way he could get the thought of her and him beyond friends out of his head. He'd just gotten cozy with the idea, and the prospect of seducing his best friend was growing more and more appealing by the minute.

Especially since she'd pretty much thrown down the gauntlet. She should know him better than that. Didn't he always accept a challenge?

Ryan laughed to the empty kitchen. Retiring from the circuit and moving back to Royal was the best move he ever made.

Five

Piper drove her truck to the hospital, with her passenger pouting the whole way over the fact she'd refused his offer of money or help with her renovations.

First of all, she'd already told him no. She was more than capable of building her house with her own two talented hands and her meager savings. Yes, it would take longer, but the satisfaction she got in the end from knowing she'd done it herself would be well worth the tears, sweat and sad bank account.

Second, how in the world could she concentrate on anything when Ryan had looked at her in a whole new light last night? She'd tried to play it off, even joke about the concussion, but Piper wasn't naive or stupid. Ryan was developing feelings for her that she wasn't ready for and might never be.

Okay, so maybe he wasn't just pouting about the money.

And yes, at one time she'd wondered what-if… But the fear of losing him as a friend had overridden any lustful feelings she'd conjured.

He'd looked so damn sexy lying in her guest bed with his chest bare and the tattoos showing along his side, his pecs and one arm. Ryan Grant was truly a work of art and she might have taken her time in running her fingertips along his well-defined muscles.

"Do you think he's regained any memories?" Ryan asked as they pulled into the parking lot at Royal Memorial Hospital.

"I hope, but there's really no way of knowing." She found a spot surprisingly close to the front doors. "With his scans showing both old and new head injuries, we have no idea just what the hell he endured during those months he was missing."

Ryan sighed. "Hopefully he'll remember soon, not only for his own sanity, but for Cara and Chance."

"I know. I hope when Alex recalls what happened, that those who accused Chance of having anything to do with this come crawling to him for forgiveness."

Piper hopped out of her truck. The mere thought of Chance McDaniel, Alex's good friend, having anything to do with his disappearance was ridiculous...at least to her it was. Just because Chance and Cara used to date was no reason for Chance to try taking Alex out of the picture permanently.

Chance was an upstanding citizen, and he might still have feelings for Cara, but the man was honorable and loyal. No way would he have had Alex kidnapped.

Piper and Ryan moved through the hospital's double doors as they whooshed open. Silently they rode the elevator together and headed toward Alex's room. Tension was going to be high whether his memory was back or not. So many people were waiting on answers and watching him closely for any sign of recognition.

When they rounded the corner, Piper saw Cara at the end of the long, stark white hallway on her cell and dabbing at the corners of her eyes with a tissue.

Obviously not good news.

Piper glanced at Ryan. "Why don't you go in and see Alex? I'll wait out here and talk to Cara."

Ryan slipped into the room and Piper waited while Cara finished her call and slid the phone into her pocket.

"He still has no memory?" Piper asked, pulling Cara into a warm embrace.

"No. And Zach just left. He didn't remember his own business partner." Cara sniffed. "But I thought for sure he'd remember me...what we shared."

Piper held her friend until Cara eased back, dabbing her eyes once again.

"I'm sorry, Piper."

"Don't be sorry for me," Piper insisted, sliding Cara's honey-blond hair back off her forehead. "I'm willing to lend my shoulder anytime and I'd say if anyone deserves a good cry, it's you."

Piper couldn't imagine the emotions swirling through Cara. The woman, engaged to the love of her life, had had him taken away, and now that she had him back, had discovered he still wasn't fully hers. The nightmare for Cara continued.

"It means a lot that you care so much," Cara told her. "Alex and I both need support right now."

"Of course you do and I'm happy to be here for you," Piper replied with a smile.

"I brought some pictures this morning," Cara said, looking down at her wet tissue. "I thought seeing the happier times we shared would trigger something. But he just stared at them with a blank face and then he apologized to me. I had to step out here. I refuse to break down in front of him. He needs me strong."

"You're stronger than I could be." Piper squeezed Cara's slender shoulders. "And his love didn't die, Cara. It's still in there. We just need to give him some time. No one knows what he went through, so the doctors aren't sure how to deal with it."

Cara nodded and raised her head. "Do I have mascara under my eyes?"

Piper smiled. "No. You look beautiful as always."

"I doubt that. I'm an ugly crier, but I've been holding it together in front of Alex. Can't have him thinking I'm some sort of weak woman."

Piper laughed. "Honey, you are anything but weak. You've been through a lot these past few months. It's certainly understandable that you'd be upset now that he's back with no memory. Even Alex would understand if you had a breakdown."

Cara shook her head. "I won't break down in front of him. He needs me to help him through this. And that's exactly what I intend to do."

"Are you ready to head back in or do you need a moment?" Piper asked.

"I'm okay. He'll be happy to see someone besides me again."

"Oh, I wouldn't bet on it," Piper said, holding the door open for Cara to enter.

Alex lay in the bed, his arm now in a cast from the surgery he'd had the night before to repair his broken wrist.

With his hands in his pockets, Ryan was across the room, half sitting against the windowsill. His eyes darted to Piper and she couldn't help but feel whatever they'd started last night was far from over. The man could hold her in her place with simply one heavy-lidded gaze. How did he have such a hold over her after a few honest words? His words should've scared her to death, but instead they'd excited her. Aroused her.

God, she was in trouble here. Her stomach had never fluttered over a man before and she was even more out of her element because her hunky best friend was causing those flutters.

"Hey, Piper," Alex said, offering a brief smile. "I just told Ryan that you don't have to feel like you need to be here checking on me all the time. I'm sure you have a life. Besides, I've had several visitors. Apparently, I know a lot of people."

Piper nodded. "And all of them are worried about you. Did the doctors say anything about your amnesia?"

Alex shook his head. "I had a CAT scan, but they can't tell from that. All it showed was multiple head traumas."

"It'll come in time," she assured him, praying she wasn't lying.

"Not soon enough," he told her. "I can't imagine what you all went through."

His eyes sought Cara. The muscle in his jaw ticked as his eyes filled. "What she's been through because of me is killing me."

"I'm fine, Alex," Cara assured him. "Just concentrate on getting better. I'm not going anywhere."

Piper's throat clogged with emotions. These two were going to fight their way back to each other. As she glanced across the room, Ryan was still looking at her. The tension, the love, in this room was almost more than Piper could take.

She could not get wrapped up in that emotion called love. Look what it had done to her mother. The woman had had a marriage she'd always dreamed of to the love of her life, yet it hadn't been enough. In the end, it hadn't held together the bond of marriage.

But as Piper watched the chemistry between Cara and Alex, she couldn't help but pray that love would be enough here. These two deserved happiness, deserved to find their way back to each other.

"Is there anything we can get you guys?" Ryan asked.

"Cara, have you eaten today? Piper and I can stay while you go out for a bit."

Cara waved a perfectly manicured hand. "Oh, no. I'm fine."

"I'm fine, too," Alex declared from the bed. "I don't need babysitters."

Cara bit her lip as if to fight off tears and Piper wanted to comfort her. But Piper also understood pride was a very sacred emotion and Cara wanted to be strong in front of Alex.

"I'm sorry," Alex murmured. "It's just hell being here, not knowing what led up to this and knowing I've hurt so many people."

"You didn't hurt anyone." Ryan spoke up. "You may have developed amnesia before you vanished and wandered off. Or someone could've had a hand in your disappearance. If that's the case, then whoever is behind this is the one who hurt so many people. You just happened to be a pawn in someone's sick game."

The list of suspects was short, but Piper didn't want to believe anyone she knew and trusted could be so cold and calculating. She knew the police were thoroughly investigating everyone in Alex's life.

She was sure Chance couldn't be behind Alex's disappearance. It had to be someone else.

Alex had recently been elected into the elite Texas Cattleman's Club and most people were excited to have him as a member. Cara's dad hadn't been too thrilled, but Piper didn't think that would be grounds to have someone kidnapped. But who else could it be?

"Will you promise to call one of us if the doctors say anything more?" Piper asked Cara.

"Absolutely." Cara stepped forward and hugged Piper, whispering in her ear, "Thanks for being here."

Piper squeezed back. "I wouldn't be anywhere else."

"Alex, it's really good to have you back, man." Ryan eased around the side of the bed. "Please have Cara call me or Piper if you need anything at all. No matter how small."

Alex nodded. "Thanks. That means a lot to me."

Piper turned and nearly ran into a woman dressed in a dark gray suit. "Oh, sorry."

"No problem." The lady smiled. "I'm Bailey Collins from the Texas State Police. I've been assigned to investigate the case involving Mr. Santiago."

"I wasn't aware the state police was coming in on this," Alex chimed from his bed. "Are there leads I'm not aware of?"

Bailey's eyes darted around the room. "I'd like to speak with you alone, if I could."

"Absolutely," Piper said.

"I just need to talk to Alex for a few moments."

"We were just leaving," Ryan stated, taking Piper by the arm and leading her out the door.

"I can step outside, too," Cara added. "Take your time, Ms. Collins."

Piper and Ryan moved out into the hallway and waited for Cara to close the door behind her.

"The cops have been questioning him quite a bit," Cara told them. "They must really be onto something if they called the state investigators in. I hope they can get to the bottom of this really fast."

"They will," Ryan assured her. "We just need to support Alex and pray he gets his memory back soon."

"Do you need anything before we go?" Piper asked.

"I'm good." Cara smiled and patted Piper's arm. "You two go on. I'll call if there's any change."

Ryan hugged Cara and turned toward Piper. She slid

her arm through his as they walked away. Once inside the elevator, Piper leaned over and kissed his stubbled cheek.

"What was that for?" he asked.

"Just for being you. For being so sweet and for being alive after yesterday's accident."

His brows pulled together. "You're still shaken up over that, aren't you?"

She stared at the descending numbers above the door. "More than I wanted to admit."

Ryan kissed her on the top of her head. "That's for caring so much, Red. You'd be lost without me."

Piper laughed, elbowing him in the side. "Shut up."

Ryan gasped and grabbed hold of his ribs. "Wrong side, Red. Damn, you got them."

Piper jerked around to see him smiling.

"Kidding." He laughed. "My other side is the one that's hurt."

"I'm going to poison you next time you whine at me to make chicken soup," she joked. "Don't scare me like that again, you jerk."

Her threat didn't hold much merit considering she laughed her way through it.

He laced his fingers through hers as they stepped off the elevator. "Wouldn't dream of scaring you again."

Several days after the accident and Alex's reappearance, Ryan stepped into the Texas Cattleman's Club and took in a deep breath, which was getting easier as his bruised ribs healed.

The fact that he was now a member of one of the most elite men's clubs in all of Texas never failed to thrill him. He'd traveled all over the country competing and winning titles some cowboys only dreamed about. Since retiring and moving back to Maverick County six months ago, he'd wanted so badly to settle, to start planting roots here. What better way than to be part of a century-old club?

He'd made a name for himself on the rodeo circuit and he'd made a crap-load of money through wise investments, and he was accepted as part of this elite few.

The club was more than one hundred years old and for most of that time had seen few changes. That was, at least, until a new set of members took hold of the reins and decided to update the facilities with a tennis court and a child-care center—after they'd allowed women to become members.

And it was those decisions that had some of the long-term members sitting up a little straighter in their seats and complaining about the changes taking place to their club.

But Ryan was on board with change.

Ryan passed the old billiards room, which had been turned into the child-care facility and was now being repaired after last month's break-in. Ryan headed to the meeting room, eager to talk to the others to get their take on Alex's return.

Ryan greeted the other members as he stepped into the room. Only five days ago Alex had been discovered and Ryan knew this meeting would be like no other they'd had thus far. Most of the other members would be excited to have Alex back.

Chance stood against the wall where various hunting plaques and trophies were displayed against dark paneling. Next to him was Paul Windsor, Cara's dad. The two men were in deep conversation about something and Ryan would bet his entire ranch that something was the return of Alex Santiago.

Paul had made it no secret that he wanted Chance and Cara to be together. But Cara's heart belonged to Alex...

At least that's how it had looked each time Ryan had seen her at the hospital. You couldn't fake that emotional bond.

Within minutes the members were seated around the table. The club president, Gil Addison, stood at the head of the long gleaming table and called the meeting to order.

"As I'm sure you all know, Alex Santiago was found alive a few days ago," Gil stated, looking around the table. "I went to the hospital yesterday to see him. He's suffering from amnesia. The doctors are still unsure if it's short or long term."

"So far he recognizes no one and even names aren't ringing a bell," Ryan interjected.

Paul Windsor grunted. "I haven't been, but I hear the prognosis isn't good."

Ryan listened, not a bit surprised that Paul hadn't visited Alex. Paul was one of those high-society men who felt no one was good enough for his little girl. Added to that, Alex didn't come from money—he was a self-made millionaire. Paul Windsor turned up his nose at nearly everyone, but at Alex in particular, since the younger man had his sights set on Cara.

"Actually, he was just released from the hospital and the prognosis is neither good nor bad," Ryan countered. "The doctors aren't sure if this is long-term or short-term memory loss. They're all just taking it one day at a time."

"I visited him." Chance spoke up. "He's frustrated, but he's confident he'll get his memory back. The doctors are telling him to take it easy because of the trauma to his head, but you know Alex."

Several men around the table chuckled, but Paul continued to look put off.

"Cara is pretty confident, too," Ryan added. "She's hardly left his side."

Paul's frown deepened and Ryan couldn't help but smile

inwardly. Ryan wasn't one to stir trouble, but he really didn't care for Paul Windsor. The man was arrogant and tried to rule everything and everyone by looking down his nose at them and pointing his finger, expecting people to ask "how high" when he told them to jump. Not only that, he was a notorious ladies' man and, if Ryan's count was accurate, was now searching for wife number five. That poor woman.

"Yes, Cara has been spending a great deal of time with him," Paul all but grumbled. "But you know Cara, she'll do anything to help people. I'm sure she's spending so much time with him because she wants to help jog Alex's memory."

Chance jerked his head toward Paul, and Ryan felt like he was caught at an intense tennis match with his head bobbing back and forth.

"Cara is fragile and I'm not sure she can handle all the pressure," Paul went on. "I imagine this will take its toll on her."

Ryan nearly rolled his eyes at Paul's inaccurate statement about his daughter. But when he glanced across to Chance, the man seemed intrigued as he leaned forward on the table, eyes on Paul.

"Cara is a strong woman," Chance supplied. "But this whole situation could break the strongest of people."

Ryan kept his mouth shut. He'd seen Cara, spoken with her, and he'd never seen a more determined woman... except Piper.

But, as much as he hated to admit it, Paul and Chance were right. Cara had endured a great deal of heartache, and Chance had been a source of comfort for her in Alex's absence.

Still, Ryan had seen Cara's face when she'd stepped into that hospital room for the first time. There was love in her eyes, worry and fear had been evident, as well, but Ryan thought for sure Cara and Alex would work through this.

Even though he knew never to try to get inside the female mind, Ryan couldn't help but wonder if the lovely Cara Windsor had feelings for both men.

"Alex will likely be returning to the meetings next month," Zach Lassiter said.

Ryan glanced to the end of the table where Zach sat. The self-made millionaire shared a downtown office with Alex, and Ryan knew Zach had been worried sick about Alex. They all had.

"I invited him today," Zach went on. "I offered to pick him up, but he wasn't feeling up to it. Not that I blame him… I was just thinking it might jog his memory if he was surrounded by people he used to know."

"No need to force him to come back," Paul declared. "We can carry on without him for now."

Ryan wished Paul wouldn't be so blunt about his disdain for Alex, but Paul was blunt about everything. From women to business, Paul Windsor made no secret that he always got what he wanted. And if he didn't like you, he also made no effort to hide his feelings.

As the meeting continued, Ryan couldn't help but think of Cara and Alex at the hospital. Was Cara just there out of guilt or obligation since they were engaged?

And he couldn't think of them without thinking of the way Piper had watched the reunited couple—the hope in her eyes, the soft smile that had lit up her face.

Piper might say that she had no intention of falling in love or becoming a wife, but that woman couldn't lie worth a damn. Her actions spoke volumes and it was what she *wasn't* saying that intrigued him.

Six

Piper pried the edge of her crowbar behind the next shingle and tugged until it came loose. With her gloved hand, she picked it up and sent it sailing in the direction of the small Dumpster she'd rented for this very fun occasion.

Some women chose a day at the spa; Piper chose to spend her time getting sweaty with manual labor.

Ripping off shingles before applying new? Yeah, this was just a blast. Even more so because the previous owners hadn't removed the other roof before applying this layer, so Piper was in a double bad mood. But she was eager to see her new roof installed because she'd chosen dark brown dimensional shingles that would give her little bungalow more proportion and character.

So she got excited about roofing…that didn't make her less feminine. Did it? Just because she knew her way around a ranch, had grown up wearing dusty boots and flannel as opposed to frilly dresses didn't mean she was any less female. She liked to do her own work and didn't care about the sweat and the mess.

It would be all worth it in the end…if she made it that long. Mercy, this was hard work. Piper was starting to believe that she actually worked harder on her days off than she did when she was helping to save people's lives.

Tires crunched over dirt and gravel and she glanced

over her shoulder to see who was visiting her. She should've known. Ryan was nearly her only visitor. She had a few friends, but Ryan was like the proverbial house-guest that never left. He always showed up unannounced and she loved it. Loved that they were so comfortable with each other that her house seemed like his and vice versa. Granted he'd only been back six months from the rodeo circuit, but she was at home at the ranch he'd purchased on the outskirts of town. The sprawling eight-thousand-square-foot mansion was exquisite, and the expansive lands made it the perfect place for him to open his rodeo school.

Ryan opened his truck door. "What the hell are you doing?" he asked the second one dusty boot hit the ground.

Piper kept her back to him as she pried loose another shingle. "I'm icing a cake," she called down.

"Don't be sarcastic," he yelled back.

"Then don't ask stupid questions." She tossed the shingle into the Dumpster and went to work on another. "I have another crowbar if you're here to offer your services."

"I don't have time to offer services, but I'll do the whole damn thing this weekend if you'll come down."

She laid her crowbar on the roof and eased toward her ladder. After she safely stepped onto the ground, Piper whirled around, jerked off her work gloves and crossed her arms over her chest.

"You know I'm renovating this myself and you know I need a new roof. Why are you acting all angry? Is it because you actually saw me doing the manual labor or you're afraid I'll screw it up?"

Ryan sighed. "I'm not worried you'll screw it up. You're too much of a perfectionist. I'm worried you'll get hurt. There was no one here and if you'd fallen, who would've helped?"

A bit touched by his fear for her, Piper smiled. "I'm

fine, Ryan. I've lived alone for a long time and I'm used to taking care of myself when I get hurt."

Ryan shook his head, then reached out to shove aside a stray curl that had escaped her messy ponytail. "You shouldn't have to worry about taking care of yourself."

"Because I'm a woman?" she mocked.

"No, damn it, because I care about you."

He glanced up at the roof, rested his hands on his narrow hips and sighed. His black cowboy hat shielded his eyes from the afternoon sun, but she knew those bright baby blues were taking in her work and in his mind he was calculating how he could fit this into his schedule so she wouldn't have to do it.

"I can be here on Saturday to help you with this," he told her. "I'm busy the rest of the day, and tomorrow I have a couple things in the morning to take care of."

"I work all day on the squad tomorrow," she said, refusing to allow him to take over. "I'm off Saturday. I'll probably have it done by then."

Ryan's eyes came back to hers. "Why can't you just take my damn help? You've been like this the whole time I've known you."

Piper laid a hand over her heart as if to ward off any hurt from seeping in, but he'd take her gesture as sarcasm, which was safer for her. Doing things on her own had been all she'd ever known. Depending on anyone else was never a good idea. Being let down hurt way worse than being alone.

"Then if you know how I am, why do you continue to argue?" she asked, raising her voice. "I bought this house with every intention of working on it myself. I want to do the labor so I can be proud and prove that I can do something. I'm talented when it comes to this, Ryan. Why do you keep trying to intervene and take control?"

Ryan's shaded eyes leveled hers. "I just want to make your life easier, Red. That's all. I'm not trying to take over or to run your life. I only want to see you happy."

"I'm happy when we don't argue about ridiculous things." Piper stepped back, shoved her gloves into her back pocket, jerked her ponytail holder out and smoothed all her hair back once again and secured the band.

"Listen, I'm sorry I yelled," she told him on a sigh. "I'm tired, sweaty and stressed. I shouldn't take it out on you."

"Then let me finish the roof for you or call someone who will."

"No." She shook her head. When would he get it through that thick skull of his? "I've got it."

"Stubborn as ever."

"Said the pot to the kettle," she murmured.

Piper turned and started up the ladder again. "If you're not here to help and you just came to throw insults, then go. I have work to do."

She didn't look down and didn't even glance back when she heard him bring his engine to life and pull out of her drive.

Yeah, even though they were best friends, they argued like an old married couple.

Piper laughed at the image. No way in hell would she ever marry a cowboy.

Besides, didn't he know she'd never take help unless it was an emergency? She could handle this on her own just fine, thank you very much, and if she chipped a nail doing it, well, she'd carry on and not worry about it.

Piper picked up her crowbar and got back to work. Frustration and anger was the perfect combo to put into demolishing old shingles. Because it was either concentrate on renovations or think of how sexy Ryan had looked all angry and dominant.

She didn't want to find that Neanderthal attitude of his appealing but she couldn't help it. Ryan truly cared for her, and she believed he wanted to see her happy, but she also knew he was developing feelings for her. If she kept letting him sink into every corner of her life, soon he'd want more and then what? Would they move in together? Marry?

Piper cursed when the crowbar went sliding because she wasn't concentrating. She reached out, careful of her balance, and caught the tool.

Ryan and any hormones either of them had flaring up needed to go to the back of her mind. She had to concentrate on one thing at a time.

Ryan walked around the perimeter of his recently installed fence where he hoped to train eager riders with his new horses. The men he'd hired to put the fence in had done a remarkable, efficient job.

Tugging on a few posts, Ryan was more than satisfied at the work. He'd paid a hefty sum for a speedy project and he wasn't disappointed.

Dirt and dust kicked up over his worn boots. Ryan propped a foot upon the bottom rung of the gate and looped his arms over the top as he looked out onto the fields. He couldn't wait to get Grant's Rodeo School kicked off in the spring.

Ryan was working with a man he'd met on the circuit who did some PR for events. Soon they'd have brochures and flyers to pass around to surrounding towns and mass mailings to send to various rodeo organizations.

The late fall sun beat down on him and Ryan adjusted his Stetson to shield his eyes. This new chapter of his life was both exciting and a little nerve-racking.

He was ready to settle down and start on another stage of his career and personal life, but he wasn't sure where to go beyond this school. At least, he hadn't been sure when he'd first come back, but now he was starting to see a clearer picture. He knew he'd wanted to have a more stable, calm life. Joining the Texas Cattleman's Club and teaching kids to ride was a great start, but Ryan knew as amazing as both those things were, he wanted more. Call him greedy, but he didn't care.

Piper had been the one constant in his life all these years. She'd been his best friend, his therapist, his inside-joke person at parties. They shared a bond on an intimate level that most couples never even tapped into.

He hadn't been joking or messing around when he'd discussed kissing her. The pull between them was stronger than anything he'd ever imagined. Ryan wanted to explore this newfound chemistry. Piper may be scared—oh hell, he knew she was even if she wouldn't admit it—but he wouldn't let anything happen to their friendship.

Yes, he was a guy and he was attracted to her in a "more than friends" way, but he wouldn't let their relationship fall apart over one roll in the sack. Yeah, he definitely wanted more.

Ryan stepped away from the gate and started back toward his house. He wondered if she'd like to help him with his school. She more than knew her way around horses and the rodeo. And she'd be a hell of a lot prettier sight than any other cowboy he'd hire.

Stepping through his back door, Ryan hung his black hat on the wooden peg. Crossing to the center island, he grabbed his phone and checked it for messages. One missed call from Piper, but no voice mail.

After their little argument yesterday, he wondered if she was calling to apologize for being so pigheaded. More than likely she wasn't. Knowing her, she was calling to hear *him* apologize.

Ryan tried her cell only to get her voice mail. Without leaving a message, he hung up and slid the phone into his pocket. She was at work, so maybe she didn't have time to answer or she had it turned off.

She usually took a lunch break about halfway through her shift. Ryan glanced at the clock and figured if he booked it through town, he could surprise her. She needed more surprises in her life. She needed a man to step up and be a man. She needed to see herself as a woman and not just as one of the guys.

When Ryan pulled into the lot where the paramedics usually parked, he didn't see Piper's truck anywhere, but he went inside anyway only to be told she'd taken a personal day off.

Heading back out to his truck, Ryan was really confused. Piper never took a day off work. Ever. The woman would crawl on her hands and knees to go to work to help save lives and make people comfortable.

He tried her cell again, but still no answer. Worry settled deep, especially with the whole Alex kidnapping still unsolved—at least Ryan assumed something illegal had transpired, especially since the state police investigator had been called in.

Ryan drove straight to her house where her shiny black truck was parked on the brick drive beside her little bungalow.

Ryan took the porch steps two at a time, rang her doorbell and opened her screen door himself when she didn't answer soon enough to suit him. The main door was locked so he used the key on his ring. Yeah, they were that good of friends. When he'd moved back permanently she'd given him a key.

Worried at the sight he'd enter into, he moved cautiously. When he rounded the corner to the living room, he found Piper on the couch, stretched out and asleep... wearing the exact same thing as yesterday.

He moved closer, surprised for so many reasons. Piper never napped, never called off work and never wore the same clothes two days in a row.

Then he saw a cord sticking out from under her back and bent to inspect. Heating pad.

A bubble of fury started within him, but he suppressed it until he knew what exactly had happened. Other than the obvious that she'd been hurt, he decided to keep his mouth shut until he had more information.

"Hey, Red," he said softly, tapping on her shoulder. "You're sleeping the day away."

She moaned, wincing as she tried to move. Her eyes opened and blinked several times as she tried to focus on him.

"Went by your work. They told me you took a personal day."

Her hand went to her head and she nodded. "I did."

"Care to tell me what happened?"

"Actually, I'd rather not," she said around a yawn. "I'm not in the mood to hear 'I told you so.'"

Ryan rested his hands on his hips. He could approach this one of two ways: he could be that sarcastic, snarky friend she probably expected or he could show some compassion and help her with whatever it was she needed. Being still a little sore from his accident, he understood her grouchy mood and not wanting to be chatty.

He eased down onto the coffee table and grabbed her hand. "I have officially deleted 'I told you so' from my vocabulary. Tell me what happened and where you're hurt."

Piper rested the back of her hand across her forehead and stared up at him. "I swear, if you say one word, I'll take my tool belt and use each and every one of those tools on you in a very unpleasant way."

"You're stalling, so it must be pretty bad."

Staring up at the ceiling, she sighed and closed her eyes. "This stupid house is only thirteen hundred square feet. I know exactly what I want it to look like and I know what to do to get it there. But when I have stupid screw-ups like this, I can't freakin' finish the project if I'm hurting myself."

"Red…"

Her eyes met his. "Right after you were here yesterday I fell off the roof."

"Damn it, Piper." Fury bubbled within him. "And you're just now telling me?"

"Actually, I called. I didn't leave a voice mail because I assumed you'd just see my number. But I'm fine." She turned her face to look at him and even offered a slight smile. "I'm a professional, remember?"

She started to sit up, winced and held on to his hand, a true sign she was hurt. But he didn't say a word. No need in saying "told you so" when she knew perfectly well he'd been right.

But he'd take being wrong any day over seeing his friend hurt. And he wasn't going anywhere until she was better. Best not to mention that to Little Miss Independent.

"Do you need to be seen?" he asked.

"No, no," she assured him as she shook her head. "Nothing some heat and rest and Motrin won't help. It's just a nuisance."

"What can I do?"

"Nothing. I was just calling earlier to tell you, but I didn't want you to worry."

Since she'd sat up, they were nearly nose to nose as he leaned in toward her. "Not worry? You fell off your roof,

Piper. You're obviously in a lot of pain and you don't want me to worry?"

"I fell off the lower part that's just over the porch," she told him, rolling her eyes. "I wasn't up on the main part."

"Don't downplay it. You didn't fall off a curb, damn it." He ran his gaze over her arms, which had a few bruises and scrapes; apparently the landscaping and bushes had caught her fall. "Take off your shirt."

Piper jerked her head back, pulled her brows together and said, "You've got to be kidding me. You go from attempting to kiss me the other night to wanting me naked? If you think I'm that vulnerable because I'm down—"

"Shut up and take your shirt off so I can see how badly you're hurt," he said, raising his voice over hers. "Can you just do one thing I say for once? Let me take these next few minutes and make sure you're okay."

"I told you I was."

Damn insufferable woman. Couldn't she just let her tough exterior down for a few minutes?

"Then humor me and let me see for myself." He purposely softened his tone because Piper was a sucker for gentlemen. It was when he yelled that she felt challenged and got her back all up. "You can barely sit up on your own, so I know it's more than a little discomfort."

She hesitated, still holding his gaze and Ryan refused to back down. Not this time. She needed to see that he was dead serious about taking care of her.

"Would it make you feel better if I took my shirt off?"

Piper rolled her eyes, but made no move to remove anything. Why did he find her stubbornness and independence so damn attractive?

"You can either take it off so I can see, or I'll do it for you." He offered her his sweetest smile. "I assure you, I won't be gentle."

Her eyes widened as her hands went to the hem. Slowly, agonizingly so, pale skin was revealed until her torso was covered in nothing but a silky lace yellow bra. Damn, how could he have forgotten about that lingerie fetish she seemed to have?

He'd seen the woman in a bathing suit for crying out loud and he was her best friend. But there was something about Piper being half naked and vulnerable that brought out the caveman in him. He wanted to pick her up, take her to bed and spend the next several days examining her injuries, making them feel better.

Ryan's gaze remained on hers as he reached out to slide his hands over the dark purple knot and bruise over her side. Goose bumps instantly dotted her skin and Ryan practically felt the tingle all through his own body.

Damn, maybe this had been a bad idea.

Too late now.

Way, way too late.

Seven

Piper closed her eyes. She wasn't used to being on the receiving end of such treatment. And the way Ryan's fingertips were gliding along her rib cage had her fighting hard to maintain her composure, to remain in her seat and not throw her arms around his neck and let him claim that kiss he'd tried for the other day.

Apparently injuries made them both horny because she was having instant flashbacks to raking her hands over his torso and the heat that had met her gaze.

"Ryan," she whispered, opening her eyes to find his face even closer than she'd first thought. "I—I'm fine."

His eyes traveled from her face to where his hand was sliding just below her breast. Suddenly the pain wasn't her first thought.

"I need to see your back, too."

She lifted her knee onto the couch and twisted her body. Ryan's gentle touch along her bare back was just as potent as when he'd been examining her front. Those fingertips may be on the surface, but she felt that contact all the way to her heart.

"How bad does it look back there?" she asked, thankful her voice didn't crack.

"Looks like you fell off a roof." His hands continued to slide softly over her skin. "You have one hell of a knot and bruise. Are you sure you don't feel like anything is broken? Shouldn't you have an X-ray just to double check?"

Piper eased back around and smiled. "I'm pretty sure I'd know if something were broken. I hurt, but not that bad. And today is the second day, so it's sorer."

His eyes held hers and Piper wanted to lick her lips, she wanted to smooth her couch-messed hair away from her face, but she did neither. She sat there, waiting on Ryan to say something, to do something.

She didn't wait long. His strong hand came up and cupped the side of her face and she couldn't help but lean into his touch, his strength.

"I can't keep denying this between us," he whispered.

Her mouth opened, anticipating his touch, his kiss.

Ryan inched closer, his mouth a breath from hers. "This is insane."

"Yes," she agreed.

"I'm going crazy wondering what you taste like."

Now Piper did lick her lips because she wanted this kiss more than she realized...or at least more than she'd been admitting to herself.

"What if this is a mistake?" she whispered, hating that her fears had been spoken aloud.

"We've made mistakes before. I prefer to take the risk so I can learn from mistakes," he told her. "But I have a feeling this risk will have a huge payoff."

He didn't wait for her to find another reason to stop. Ryan knew what he wanted and he'd waited long enough... nearly twenty years in fact.

His hands slid over her smooth cheeks as his fingertips slid into her curls and, before she could finish her gasp, his mouth was on hers.

And thank God he was sitting because to have this

woman in his arms in an intimate way after all this time made his knees weak. Warmth spread throughout his body as he coaxed her lips apart with his tongue. His hat flipped off his head and onto the floor.

She was on the same page because she met him thrust for thrust and her arms wrapped around his neck as she scooted closer.

Ryan slowly slid his lips over hers, wanting to memorize every single part of them, wanting to know exactly how she tasted and how soft she was. He wanted to know what turned her on, what buttons to push to drive her crazy.

He knew her as a friend, but he wanted to know her as a lover.

Careful of her hurt side, Ryan eased his hand down the other side of her torso, dipping in at her delicate waist and then back up to the lacy edge of her bra.

"You shouldn't be this sexy to me," he murmured against her mouth. "I shouldn't want you the way I do. God help me, I have no willpower with you."

Piper's head tipped back, exposing that long, slender neck. He took full advantage and kissed his way down, continuing a path until he reached the top of one breast.

He paused because he was pretty damn sure he'd go all the way, but he didn't want to scare her or to make her regret anything later.

His thumb stroked just at the bottom edge of her bra, slowly slipping between the wire and her breast. And that little tease of skin against the tip of his thumb made his zipper even tighter than it was before.

"This…this shouldn't go any further," she told him, breathless.

Ryan didn't remove his hands, didn't back up, but he did nod. "My mind knows that, but other parts of me think it hasn't gone near far enough."

A slow smile spread across Piper's swollen, wet lips. "I'm still reeling from the fact that my best friend wants me and is one hell of a kisser. Can we just stop right there for now?"

He leaned in, captured her lips for another brief kiss and sat back. "If you think I'm a hell of a kisser, that leaves me hope you'll want more. I'm good with leaving you wanting me."

She laughed and playfully shoved at his chest. "You're hopeless."

"I was thinking horny, but hopeless works, too."

With one last sultry glance, Piper reached for her shirt and struggled to put it back on. Ryan took the garment from her hands and slid it over her head, careful when she had to lift her arms.

"What can I do to help?" he asked. "Other than take your mind off the pain with incredible bouts of hot, sweaty sex?"

Easing back down onto the heating pad, Piper offered a smile. "Tempting as your poetic words are, this body cannot handle too much of an aerobic workout tonight."

Ryan came to his feet and propped his hands on his hips. "Okay, then. Point me in the direction of the next project that needs attention. I'm here, might as well do something."

"Other than the roof, I need to yank out those kitchen cabinets. I ordered new ones, but they're on back-order, so I do have a little time."

"Did you get that dark mahogany finish you fell in love with?" he asked.

Her eyes closed as she sighed and settled farther into the couch. "No. They were way out of my price range. I ended up getting a dark wood finish, but they are a cheaper model and brand."

Ryan glanced down at his fierce little warrior. The woman truly believed she could do all and be all. Why didn't she ever ask him for help? Just once he'd like to be the one to come to her aid without begging her to let him.

"You know I would've been more than happy to get those new cabinets for you."

Her lids flew open and green eyes met his. "You're not buying my cabinets, Ryan. That's ridiculous. You have a school you're paying through the nose to get started and you just bought a massive home. Besides, this is my little house and I love it. I'll love it with cheaper cabinets just as much as if I'd had the expensive ones. They all hold dishes and food the same way."

He knew she wasn't some pampered diva who wanted the best of everything, but he'd seen her face when they'd been looking through the sample catalog she'd brought home from the store. He'd seen how she'd froze the second she turned on to that page, how she'd stroked the picture with her fingertips.

Most women went that crazy over diamonds or fancy clothes, but his Piper was just as happy wearing her flannel, with some killer lingerie beneath. She didn't ask for the best in everything and she'd already cut enough corners with this renovating project. Now she was sacrificing something that she truly wanted because she was practical and hadn't been able to justify that extra expense.

"So the roof and the cabinets are the pressing matters?" he asked.

"I know you want to do something while you're here, but don't. Seriously." She held his gaze, pleading with him. "I'll get back at it tomorrow."

Like hell she would. But his mama raised a gentleman before she'd passed unexpectedly, so he was going to keep his mouth shut.

"I'm just curious," he told her, holding his hands up in defense. "I wouldn't dare try to overtake your project. Besides, my own ribs are still sore. Just thought if you had something small to do."

He'd not let on that he wasn't too sore that he couldn't put a dent in her kitchen or her roof. Either job would be fine for him to start tackling, but if he started now, then she'd get up and insist on helping and then she really would end up hurt.

A slight smirk flirted around that mouth he'd just sampled. "What do you say we have some lunch and not discuss all these renovations that still need to be done?"

"Tell me what you want to eat and I'll bring it to you."

"I can get up." Piper sat up and shook her head. "That pain pill is kicking in. Besides, the more I move, the more it will work the soreness out. There's only so long I can lie on that heating pad. I've probably lost five pounds in sweat since last night."

Ryan's eyes ventured to her chest, then back up. "At least you didn't lose it in the places that matter."

Piper came to her feet and smacked his chest. "You're such a pervert."

"Honest," he corrected. "I'm simply honest."

Piper sat in one of the chairs of her mismatched set in the kitchen. Ryan was prying off the countertops and setting them out the back door...much to her protesting.

"I wish you wouldn't go to so much trouble, Ryan."

He put the final piece out the door and came back in, wiping sweat off his forehead. "If I thought it was trouble, I wouldn't be doing it. And even though you griped and complained, I still want to help. I couldn't just go home and leave you here in pain. Besides, if I'm here making sure you don't overdo it, I might as well get some work done. The sooner this kitchen is back together, the sooner you can make real meals again. I'm selfish."

They'd enjoyed simple ham sandwiches and chips for lunch considering her stove was unhooked and the dishwasher wasn't installed due to the new cabinets coming soon.

And he'd sweetly convinced her that he could start the demolition of the old cabinets and if he began hurting he'd sit down. Weren't they a pair? Both stubborn, both hurt… But she'd butted heads with him long enough. She knew he truly wanted to help so she'd allowed him this small victory.

"I knew you had an ulterior motive," she told him.

Crossing the kitchen, Ryan opened the fridge and reached in to pull out a beer as he had done so many times before. Piper liked how comfortable he felt in her home. She'd never had another man in her house with whom she felt this comfortable. Ryan had always just been part of her life; she truly wouldn't know what to do without him.

He leaned against the cabinet and took a long, hard pull from the bottle. Piper admired the view of her best friend without his shirt, how his muscles flexed without any effort from Ryan. The man simply had to shift and those muscles put on quite a show.

When he licked his lips after his drink, Piper swallowed and tried to ignore that she had been taken off guard earlier with how toe-curling that kiss had been. She knew her best friend could kiss, because she'd heard talk from some ladies, but she'd never, ever, thought he'd kiss her in that way or that she'd be nearly on her knees because of the intensity of it.

"Want to bring it out in the open or just let it keep replaying in your mind?"

Piper's eyes met his and, damn him, he was grinning because he knew what had been running through her mind.

"How do you always know what I'm thinking?" she asked.

He shrugged, took another drink and sighed. "Call it a gift. I just know you better than you know yourself."

Piper rolled her eyes. "All right, Mr. Smarty Pants. What was I thinking?"

"You were thinking how you wished you would've ravished my body earlier instead of calling it quits."

Piper laughed. "Not hardly. Try again."

"Oh, you're right, that's what I was thinking." He set his beer on the top of the fridge and crossed over to her, bending and blocking her meager breeze from the fan. "You were thinking that the kiss we shared was more than you expected. You're wondering if we're going to do it again or if you should press your luck. Maybe it won't be as great the second time."

He took her hands in his, pulling her to her feet. Their faces were mere inches apart and Piper did her best to keep her breathing steady though her heart was beating rapidly.

"You're afraid to admit to yourself that you enjoyed it and you wonder what would've happened if we hadn't stopped."

Piper's eyes held his. "I'm pretty sure I know what would've happened."

"Doesn't matter that it didn't," he whispered. "One day it will."

Gone was the gentleness from earlier. Ryan gripped her arms, tipped her toward his chest until she landed against him, and then he claimed her lips.

Being trapped against such a strong, hard chest was no hardship and being in Ryan's arms somehow felt…

perfectly right. Every part of their bodies lined up where it should, making that image of the two of them in bed even more believable and real.

Just the thought of where he promised they'd end up sent a shiver down her spine. One part of her wanted to explore beyond these kisses, but the other part worried the door to friendship would slam and they'd never get back this bond they shared.

But right now, with his hands holding her firmly in place, his erection pressing into her belly and his mouth making love to hers, she almost didn't care about crossing into unchartered territory with Ryan. She almost didn't care that he was her best friend and the closest thing to family she had.

Then she remembered he was a rodeo man. A true cowboy. He had the itch in him to chase adventure and go from one arena filled with screaming fans and danger to the next.

Just like her father.

And while these kisses were totally off the charts and had her fantasy life shifting into overdrive, she knew she could never fall in love with a cowboy. There was no way she could live the life her mother had tried to put up with. And there was no way Piper could tame a cowboy.

Once that thrill of adventure entered their blood, it never left. Could Ryan really and truly be done? He was opening a school, so Piper knew he was serious about staking roots here for the long haul. But what if he grew bored? What if he needed that adrenaline rush that only the rodeo could provide?

For right now, Piper slid her arms around his waist and allowed his kiss to take her to another place. A place where they were just two people acting on this new attraction... not two people destined for heartache.

Because as scared as she was that he may decide to leave again, she couldn't deny the fact she was getting in deeper with her best friend.

Eight

"You don't have to stay, you know."

Piper pushed off the wooden porch with her bare toe and put the swing into motion. Ryan lounged across her chaise on the other side of her porch.

"I know," he told her, tipping up his cowboy hat to look at her. "I want to. Nothing else to do."

Piper laughed. "You always make me feel so appreciated. I'm so glad I rank just above nothing else to do."

"You know you also rank above castrating cattle, so don't act like you're at the bottom of my priority list."

Taking a small throw pillow from her wicker swing, Piper launched it across the porch, hitting him in the chest. The swift move made her back ache, but it was worth it.

"You've got such a smart mouth." She laughed.

"You wouldn't have me any other way," he murmured.

Still smiling, she eased back onto the swing and enjoyed the soft evening breeze. "No, I wouldn't."

For a moment Piper let the tranquility of the evening wash over her. The crickets chirping in the distance, the starry night, the warm breeze blowing across her porch. She loved having a swing out here to just sit in and reflect at the end of the day.

True, her home might still be in disrepair, but it was coming along and she was going to be able to be proud of herself when all was said and done. And the A/C was going in tomorrow afternoon. Thank you, God. Because if she had to keep seeing Ryan strip out of his shirt, mop his forehead with the garment and have his pecs flex beneath beads of sweat, she may very well die from want and lust.

"Do you remember when we'd ride our bikes past here?" Ryan asked, breaking the silence.

Piper glanced out to the sidewalk that stretched between the road and her yard. She could practically see the younger versions of the two of them peddling by. His bike had been blue and black and hers had been red with a horn. She'd loved riding up behind him and squeaking that loud thing. He'd jump every time. The trick never got old.

"I do remember," she said with a smile. "I believe I told you one day this house would be mine."

"Even back then you saw the potential in this place. I never knew why you loved it so much."

Piper shrugged, toeing off the porch again. "I always thought it looked cozy, homey. I wanted a house that I could feel loved in and this one always had toys in the yard and a mom or dad swinging up here. It just seemed like the life I wanted."

"And now?" Ryan asked. "What life are you looking for now?"

Across the porch, her eyes met his. "I wouldn't mind that life now. Though with my crazy work schedule and my time off spent here, I'm not sure the dating scene is going to happen for me for a while."

"You work too hard."

"That's because some of us aren't high and mighty celebrities making money from the rodeo circuit."

Ryan tossed the pillow back at her. "I'm not a celebrity, Red. I'm just a man who's opening a school on my ranch. I'm ready for the simple life."

Piper hugged the pillow to her chest. "You may be ready for the simple life, but I know you. You're laid-back and easygoing, but you have that reckless, adventurous streak in you from your rodeo days. If they called and asked you to come back, don't act like you wouldn't jump at the chance."

"I want a life like my parents had." His words instantly took her back to their childhood. "I want the love they shared before her death, before my father let guilt eat him alive. I know love exists. I saw it firsthand and it would've lasted forever."

Piper swallowed the lump in her throat. Ryan's mother had been killed in a car accident when his father had been driving. Piper had never seen a more distraught, broken man in all her life. The guilt, the depression, all had taken a toll on him and he'd ended up dying of a massive heart attack when Ryan was a senior in high school.

Piper knew that was another reason Ryan had been so hell-bent on getting out of town. He was running from the painful memories. And he'd buried himself in the circuit until that was all he knew, all he lived for.

"Are you sure you're not getting the itch to travel again?" she asked. "You've been home six months. That's a record for you. What about when the holidays are over? Will you be bored?"

Ryan shook his head. "I'm too busy here to be bored. I've retired for good."

Yeah, her father had, too. Twice. And all these years later that scar tissue on her heart was still deep.

"I'm not him, Piper."

She glanced up as Ryan shifted to sit on the edge of the chaise. "Whatever you think the similarities are between me and your father, my loyalty to you isn't one of them."

"It's just hard to get past how similar you two are."

Ryan came to his feet, rested his hands on his hips and stared out at the full moon that lit up the night. "You know I've never left you. Ever. I've never deserted you when you needed it. And I never intend to."

Piper sighed. "I know. I'm sorry. I'm just in a mood today. Between this house and my back being sore, I'm just a mess."

He glanced over his shoulder, throwing her one of his sexiest smiles and, like every other woman on the receiving end of that seductive grin, her insides quivered and she couldn't help but smile back.

"You're not a mess. You're allowed to be bitter about your father."

"True, but I shouldn't take it out on you." Piper slowed the swing and came to her feet, crossing to stand beside Ryan. She slid an arm around his waist and leaned against his strength. "I know there's nothing about the two of you that's comparable. You're loyal, honest and dependable."

Ryan's soft chuckle vibrated against her, so not helping her current state of battling just how sexy her best friend was and how her growing attraction was scaring the hell out of her.

"You've described the perfect dog," he replied, wrapping his arm around her shoulder.

"You know what I mean." She swatted his rock-hard stomach. "You're the one person I can always depend on. What we have is much stronger than family or most marriages, even."

"Which is why we are a perfect fit."

"Are you back to sex again?"

Ryan turned her toward him and grinned. "I'm a guy. Everything is about sex."

Piper laughed. "Well, I'm not sure if you've noticed, but not too many guys do the whole sex chat around me."

Ryan's arms cupped her shoulders through her flannel shirt. "That's their loss. I not only know what you wear beneath this heavy shirt, I also know what's inside you. Any man who doesn't appreciate what you have is a complete fool."

Piper studied his face. Nothing about those heavy-lidded eyes or that perfectly shaped mouth indicated he was teasing or joking.

"Then I must've dated fools," she murmured. "And how did we get on the topic of my sex life?"

Ryan brushed her lips with his. "Because I want to be part of it."

Piper gasped as Ryan turned that nipping playfulness into full-fledged attack. His hands slid down to her denim-covered rear and pulled her against him. Mercy, he was already aroused.

He started walking back toward the chaise. Piper had no choice but to follow. Well, she had a choice. She could either follow him or break this amazing kiss that had her lighting up on the inside. There was no way in hell she was going to stop this staggering assault on her senses.

Without breaking the kiss, Ryan eased onto the chaise, bringing Piper down to straddle his lap. His hands slid to her waist, holding her steady as she adjusted to the new arrangement.

The intimacy of this pose was not lost on her. She could feel him between her thighs as his hard torso pressed against her. His mouth continued claiming hers as his hands moved up her back, beneath her flannel.

She was so glad she'd grabbed a shower after he'd stopped by. She may not have fixed her hair nor done anything above and beyond, but she was out of yesterday's clothes and she was clean.

"Ryan," she panted against his mouth, "what are we doing?"

"Making out." He kissed along her jaw, down her throat and moved his hands from beneath her shirt to start working on her buttons. "Don't worry, I won't let this get out of control."

Piper would've laughed, but his talented hands were moving inside her shirt to her aching breasts. Out of control? They'd both let this get out of control the moment they made the conscious decision to kiss and stroke each other.

And making out at nearly the age of thirty sounded so…pathetic. Surely there was another word that didn't sound so juvenile.

But even if they'd gotten out of control, she didn't care because her body had taken over and she had no clue what rational thought was anymore.

There was no way in hell they could turn back now, but this intimacy between them was moving faster than she was comfortable with. Even though they'd been dancing around this topic for days, she still saw him as her best friend and she wouldn't give up that friendship for a quick roll in the sack.

His tongue traced the edge of her bra. Okay, so she was quite comfortable with that and maybe their trip in the sack wouldn't be so quick. The man certainly was taking his time in driving her insane with desire.

Piper arched her back because, well…she still had no control over her body when Ryan's hands and mouth were on it. And there wasn't a woman alive who could blame her. He was her best friend, he'd never deliberately hurt her and he was hot, hot, hot with a capital H-O-T.

His mouth remained on her breast as he continued to undo the rest of her buttons. When he slid the material aside, he circled his hands around her waist.

Those rough, callused palms gliding against her smooth skin provided that extra bit of friction she needed, craved. God, what would it feel like to have those hands all over her?

Piper gripped his shoulders and pressed her knees against his thighs as he moved one hand to cup her breast and then raked his tongue over her nipple.

"Ryan," she whispered, "we're on my porch."

He lifted his head and grinned. "I know."

She wasn't into PDAs, and this went way beyond that, but she didn't have any neighbors too close and shrubbery around her porch was shielding them.

Added to that, if they had to stop to go inside, she'd die. This felt too good, too right.

When his hand moved to the button of her jeans, Piper froze. "Ryan?"

"Shh. It's okay. I know you're not ready, but I want you to feel. I want you to see how right this is." He unfastened her pants, slid the zipper down and whispered, "Trust me."

She'd trusted him her whole life and now was no different.

"Lift up a tad."

Piper rose onto her knees, but dropped her forehead to his as she watched his tanned fingers slip inside her panties. She held her breath, waiting for that moment when he'd fully feel her and she him.

"Don't tense on me now, Red."

Piper closed her eyes as he parted her, sliding one finger, then two between her folds and slowly working back and forth. Before she knew it, her hips were moving, her heart was racing.

"You look beautiful," he whispered.

Her eyes locked on to his as he kept that slow, steady rhythm against her core. She tilted her hips faster, needing more and not sure how to ask for it. This wasn't weird and she didn't want to start begging and make the moment awkward.

"No hurry here," he told her. "I could touch you, watch you, all night."

"Ryan…I…"

"I know."

He cupped the back of her neck and captured her lips as his fingers moved over her, then finally in her. Between his mouth and his hand, the assault on her body was too much and the inner fight came to an end. No more trying to hold out because she was worried about their friendship. Nothing could stop her from taking this moment he was so freely giving.

Piper moaned into his mouth as her body spiraled out of control. Bursts of light flashed behind her lids; her entire body vibrated and shook as the climax slammed into her.

Ryan continued to stroke her even when her tremors ceased. Piper didn't know what to do now, but she knew there was no doubt they were headed toward sleeping together.

And she was starting to wonder why it had taken her so long to see this may not be such a bad idea.

Nine

Piper wiped at her damp cheeks, cursing herself as she turned into her drive. After all these years as a paramedic, she really should be used to seeing death. But no matter how many times patients died en route to the hospital, Piper took each death personally.

There were always the what-if and if-only moments. The question of what if she'd arrived sooner… If only those cars had pulled aside when they'd seen the ambulance coming through instead of waiting until the last minute, in turn slowing them down… Timing was crucial during a call and today's patient had not had time on his side. Piper knew no matter how fast they might have arrived, more than likely she wouldn't have been able to save his life. But she was only human and guilt consumed her with every death.

Especially today's patient. A young father who had been complaining of chest pains while running and suddenly collapsed. The look of horror on the wife's face as she'd clutched their baby to her chest would haunt Piper for a long, long time.

Life wasn't fair and Piper was damn sick of bad things happening around her. Alex still hadn't regained his memory, but he'd been out of the hospital for a few days. Hopefully being back home on his own turf would trigger something.

Cara was nearly attached to his side and Piper knew the woman was barely holding it together, clinging to a thin thread of hope that the old Alex would soon emerge and they could go back to the happy couple they once were.

The front of Ryan's truck stuck out from the back of her house. What on earth was he doing parked on the grass behind her house?

Piper pulled right up in front of the garage and grabbed her purse. As she walked around the side of the house, her back door was propped wide open and Ryan's signature heavy-metal music was blaring out into the yard. He obviously had a warped mind if he considered that yelling music.

But she had her favorite bands and he had his. Heavy metal was by far his favorite type of music and Pantera was his all-time favorite band.

Music was one area they definitely did not agree on, but if that was the man's only flaw, well then, she had a true winner on her hands. Good thing she didn't have too-close neighbors.

She stepped into her kitchen and her purse dropped to the floor with a thud. Ryan jerked around, smiled and reached over to turn down his radio.

"You're home earlier than I thought," he told her, resting his hands on his narrow hips. "I was hoping to be finished here."

Piper didn't know what she wanted to stare at more: Ryan with his shirt off, sweat glistening in each and every dip and crevice around his pecs and abs, or the brand-new cabinets he'd installed.

And not just any cabinets, but the ones she'd wanted originally. The crazy-expensive ones she'd denied herself because they were way out of her budget.

As if her emotions needed another hit today. Piper's

tear button was pressed again and she cupped her mouth to keep from making a total fool of herself. Her damn quivering chin was a dead giveaway and she was such an ugly crier with a red, snotty nose, puffy eyes and blotchy skin. Yeah, she certainly wasn't turning any heads with that frightening look.

"Red, it's just cabinets." Ryan crossed the room and took hold of her shoulders, forcing her to look at him. "I didn't mean to make you cry. I thought you'd be excited."

Piper shook her head, taking in a deep breath. "I can't believe you did this, Ryan. It's…it's… Why did you change the order?"

He shrugged. "Because this is what you wanted."

Damn it, she wanted to be upset with him, but how could she when his sole reason for doing this was to make her happy? His reasoning was so simple, so selfless. And that's exactly how he'd been his whole life from the moment he'd walked up to her on the playground so she wasn't lonely or uncomfortable. Even when she'd hit him, he'd stuck around to make sure she was happy.

There wasn't a selfish bone in Ryan Grant's body. Plus, he caught her at a weak moment and she didn't even have the energy to be angry even if she wanted to.

"These were expensive," she insisted, stating the obvious.

He shrugged. "I only shelled out the difference in what you had already put down for the others. You paid for most of these, if that makes you feel any better."

Her eyes drifted over his shoulder to the new mahogany cabinets. Even without the countertop in place, they were stunning and really made her little bungalow's kitchen look classy.

"They're perfect," she told him, bringing her gaze back to meet his. "I'll never be able to thank you."

"I didn't do it for thanks. I did it because I care for you and I want to see you happy." He studied her face and frowned. "Want to tell me what had you in tears before you came home?"

Piper stepped back, wiping her face again and trying to paste on a convincing smile. "It was nothing."

Resting his hands on his narrow waist, Ryan cocked his head. "Piper, you can't lie to me, darlin'. Tell me what happened. Is it Alex?"

"No, no. I talked with Cara last night and he still hasn't regained his memory."

"Something happen at work?"

Piper turned toward the cabinet and slid her hand along the smooth door. She moved to the window above where the sink would be installed and stared out at her meager backyard.

"We lost a patient on the way to the hospital," she told him. "He was around our age. He had a wife and a new baby."

"Damn."

Piper turned around and leaned back against the edge of the cabinet. "It happened just before my shift ended and I thought I'd come home, soak in the tub and get my cry out of my system. I didn't know I'd have company."

Ryan closed the space between them, cupping her cheeks. "I'm not company, Red. If you want to get that cry out, go right ahead. My shoulders are strong. I can handle you."

Piper resisted for all of a second before Ryan just pulled her against his hard body. She wrapped her arms around his waist and rested her cheek against his warm, bare chest.

"Quit always trying to be so damn strong, Piper." He stroked her back, then reached up to pull her ponytail free. His hands slid through her hair. "I don't need you to put up a front around me, ever. Just be yourself, let it out. No one has to know you had a moment of vulnerability."

Yeah, but she would know. Unfortunately she just couldn't keep the emotions bottled up any longer. Piper let her buried sobs rise to the surface. She clutched Ryan's back, her forehead resting against the middle of his bare chest.

She inhaled his masculine scent and didn't care that he was all sweaty. She needed to draw from his strength, from his affection.

"You should've seen her face," she cried. "His wife was holding their baby, her eyes held hope, but I knew he wasn't going to make it. I couldn't even look at her, Ryan. I'm a coward. I knew he was fading and I wanted to get him into the ambulance before we lost him. I didn't want her to see that."

"You did what you could."

Piper sniffed, her body shook as more sobs tore through her. "I couldn't do a damn thing to save him. Now that baby will grow up with no father and his wife is all alone."

Ryan knew that right there was the main reason this patient had hit her so hard. Even though her father hadn't passed away, he was gone from her life and she still felt that void. Piper had never had closure, had never been able to fill the gap he had left in her heart. The only things she had to cover that hole were years of bitterness and anger.

"You can't save everyone," he told her. "You're human. Only God controls who stays and who goes."

Piper slid her hands around, flattened them against his chest and lifted her face to look at him. Ryan wiped the pads of his thumbs across her cheeks and held her face firm between his palms.

"I'm sorry I fell apart on you."

Ryan smiled, nipped at her lips. "I'm not. I like knowing you want to lean on me for comfort. I want to be here for you, Piper. For everything."

Couldn't she see that? After all these years, couldn't she see that he was ready to settle down now, that he was back for good? That he was finally ready to sow permanent roots?

"What happed to the A/C installation?" he asked, hoping to take her mind off work.

"Sorry, they had to reschedule. I'm so used to it now, I didn't think. You worked all day in this heat?"

He shrugged. "It's Texas. I can stand the heat."

Her shining eyes held his and Ryan moved in closer. Slowly, so slowly, in case she wasn't ready for his intimate touch. But he had to taste her, had to show her that she was special, that she was cherished even when she was vulnerable…especially when she was vulnerable and let that guard down.

He slid his hand across her cheek, beyond her ear and to the back of her head, pulling her in toward him.

"Stop me," he whispered, warned. "Stop me from doing this again."

"I can't."

Yeah, neither could he.

Ryan stole her lips and just like the other times he'd kissed her, a wave of perfection consumed him. Perhaps this was the woman he was meant to settle down with. Perhaps this woman who'd been in his life since childhood and through school and the wild ride on the circuit was the one who would stand by his side until he was old and gray.

Piper's arms slid around his neck as she toyed with the damp ends of his hair. Her soft moans filled him as his tongue danced with hers.

Allowing his hands to travel down her back, Ryan cupped her rear and tugged her against his hips so she could see just how she affected him. This was beyond friendship and, if he were honest with himself, they'd passed friendship well before they'd kissed the first time. They'd passed it the instant he'd moved back, considered her naked and in his bed, then imagined her never leaving his side or his new ranch.

Ryan took a handful of her shirt and tugged it from her work pants. He needed skin, her skin. That soft, delicate, satiny skin that always felt so amazing beneath his roughened hands. He wanted that goodness, that near innocence she could bring to his life. And he wanted her to see just how special she was.

Moving his hands around to her belt, he unfastened her pants when she gasped his name.

"What's wrong?" he asked.

Her eyes locked on his as she panted and licked her moist lips. "I—I…"

She closed her eyes, shaking her head, and Ryan eased back from his grasp on her disheveled clothes. Whatever she was about to say, she was right.

"We can't do this." He smoothed down her shirt and took a step back, ignoring the devil on his shoulder telling him to take what his body craved. "You're vulnerable and I'm horny. That would make for a really bad wreck in this relationship."

Piper laughed. "That's one very blunt way of putting it."

"Have you ever known me to be any other way?" he asked.

She adjusted her belt. "No, I haven't. That's why I admire and care for you so much."

Ryan watched as her shaky hands refastened her belt and he knew they needed to get out of this house, away from the temptation of being alone with their jumbled emotions.

"You up to going out tonight?" he asked.

Her head popped up and she grinned. "What did you have in mind?"

"We could go to Claire's."

Piper's smile widened and Ryan felt the kick in the stomach that had been associated with that potent action.

"I'd love to. That's exactly what I need."

"I have a few things to do over at the school first. I had some men working on a new barn today and I need to catch them before they leave. But I can be back in a few hours." He smacked a kiss on her cheek. "Try to leave the flannel and jeans in the closet. 'Kay, Red?"

Rolling her eyes, she turned to head toward her room. "Lock the door behind you, slick."

Whistling as he headed to his truck, Ryan knew that even if Piper came out for their date in her most worn plaid flannel, holey jeans and beat-up work boots, he'd still be thrilled to be seen with her at the upscale restaurant in Royal. He never did care too much what people thought. They were going to talk whether you wanted them to or not. He always figured if they were talking about him, they were leaving others alone and he had thick skin.

He was anxious to take Piper to Claire's. They hadn't been to the restaurant before together and he wanted to start staking his claim, barbaric as that may sound. He wanted Piper to get used to the idea that he was putting down roots in Royal and he intended for his life to intertwine with hers. Forever.

Ten

This was absolutely silly.

Piper stood in front of her mirror wearing only a lacy black thong and matching demi bra. Yeah, this was as pretty as her wardrobe got because nearly everything in her closet consisted of flannel or denim. She had a couple of dresses, mainly because so many people were getting married lately, but she wasn't going to wear a dressy dress to Claire's. Though the upscale restaurant's romantic ambience called for something above plaid flannel, being overly dressed just to eat dinner simply wasn't her style.

She sighed and glanced at the clock on her bedside table. Ryan would be back in about thirty minutes looking all freshly showered and sexy as hell. The man could wear anything, throw on his Stetson and look like he'd just stepped off the pages of a calendar featuring hot, hunky cowboys.

Piper went back to her closet, hoping something had changed since the last time she'd peeked in there.

Fingering plaid shirt after plaid shirt, she stared at the few dresses she owned. The bright blue was her favorite because it was simple, but it was also very striking and she really didn't want to call attention to herself.

Her eyes moved over the black one and she paused. Black was a nice "I want to blend with the crowd" color.

She yanked the sleeveless dress from the hanger before she could change her mind. While she hated dresses, she didn't want to embarrass Ryan. He was taking her out to keep her mind off of her terrible workday…and probably so they could get out of the confines of her steamy house where the sexual tension had settled into every nook and cranny.

Was he classifying this as an actual date? Was he trying to go beyond friendship and make things more intimate? So many questions, so many worries.

But for tonight, she wasn't going to analyze everything to death. No, really. She wasn't. Piper vowed to herself that she would enjoy Ryan's company and this was no different than if they were grabbing a piece of pie at the Royal Diner. This time they would just be dressed up, eating steak and using the cloth napkins at Claire's.

She slid the dress over her head and groaned when her curly hair sprang from her shoulders. Could she be any more clichéd? Curly red hair and green eyes with a fuller figure. She wasn't a supermodel-thin blond…she was just curvy and curly.

As she looked at the black dress, she started to wonder if she just looked like a witch. Yeah, this wouldn't do. Yanking it off, she tossed it onto her unmade bed and went back to the closet. She found a dress in a Kelly green that matched her eyes and prayed she wouldn't look ridiculous in it. The thing still had the tags on it because she just knew another of her friends would get married soon.

At this rate she'd have to start housing her dresses in the guest-room closet because she was accumulating so many. She wasn't much of a dress girl, but a small sliver of her enjoyed dressing up for her friends' weddings and bridal showers.

The sleeveless wrap dress looked much better, she admitted as she tied the satiny ribbons at her waist. But she refused to be one of those women who tried on every stitch of clothing in her closet and claimed she had nothing. This was Ryan; he wouldn't care what she wore.

Now for the shoes. Work boots were probably a no. Other than those and a few tennis shoes she worked out in, she had one pair of dressy sandals that had a low, very low, heel.

She slid into the silver sandals and threw on earrings before she tried to tackle her hair. That was always a losing battle. But with the elegant restaurant, she opted to pull her hair back as opposed to going in looking like she just finished her shift as a circus clown.

The good thing about the curls was they made for a cute messy bun at the nape of her neck, which she secured with a heavy silver clasp that had been her mother's. That was one piece of jewelry she would never part with and often wore even with flannel and denim. She always felt a connection with her mother.

By the time she'd applied a bare minimum of makeup and a little more gloss than usual, her front door opened and shut. Ryan's boots clicked down the hardwood in the hall.

"You still in the shower, Red?"

"Don't you wish," she called back.

When he whistled she turned from checking her purse on the bed to see him leaning against the doorway. His eyes raked down her body and took a slow, leisurely stroll back up.

"If you keep looking at me like that we won't get out of this bedroom," she joked, hoping he didn't pick up on how nervous she was all of a sudden.

"That would be fine with me," he told her. "You look

hot. Care to torture me further and tell me what you're wearing beneath that dress?"

"Black lace."

Ryan's eyes closed and he sighed. "I asked for it."

Laughing, Piper slid her purse strap over her shoulder and headed to the door. "Come on, big guy. We need to get out of here before we miss our reservations."

"I'd rather move toward the bed," he grumbled.

That made two of them, but someone had to keep their wits about them and for now it looked to be her. Though the heat in his heavy-lidded eyes made her tingle in places she'd never tingled before… So what would happen once they got into bed?

She smiled as she moved down the hall. Yes, there would be a when, not an if. She'd resigned herself to the fact she wanted to sleep with her best friend. She wanted to know him on a deeper, more intimate level, but she wasn't sure if she was ready yet.

As she reached for the knob of her front door, strong hands came up to grip her shoulders, spinning her around and pinning her against the door. Being trapped between a hard panel of wood and a hard panel of…well…

"You're not fighting fair," he murmured as his lips hovered over hers and his hands held her in place.

"I wasn't fighting at all," she chided.

His eyes darted to her mouth. "That's what makes this so bad. You're not even trying and you're driving me out of my ever-lovin' mind."

To know she had that much power over Ryan warmed her, made her feel like the vixen she never knew she could be.

"You're looking pretty sexy yourself, cowboy," she told him.

A crisp black dress shirt pulled across taut, broad shoulders. And he'd forgone the Stetson and just settled for that sexy, messy bed-head he wore so well.

"Did you get to talk to the guys about the new barn?" she asked.

Ryan's lips tipped into a grin. "Trying to distract me?"

"Just trying to stay focused so we can get to the restaurant."

"Yeah." He sighed. "We're ahead of schedule and I'm ready to start bringing in more livestock."

A lock of dark hair fell over one bright blue eye. Piper slid her fingertip across his forehead to move the strand aside.

The muscle in his jaw ticked, his nostrils flared, and Piper's body tightened in response.

"Are you sure we can't stay in?" he whispered, eyes on her mouth. "I don't want to think about the school or anything else. Just you. Us. And whatever these feelings are."

The man was more tempting than Satan himself, but she had to take this slowly. Over twenty years of friendship couldn't be thrown aside for a few hours of sweaty passion. She had to think long term here.

"You make it hard to be strong for both of us, Ryan." She tried to make light of the situation, but soon...soon she would let down her guard and her own emotions would come flooding out. "Just give me some time."

"Baby, we've known each other for so long, what's a few more days?" He grinned, his eyes meeting hers. "You're worth waiting for, but that doesn't mean I can't give you, and me, something to think about."

His lips moved softly over hers, lightly at first, then he coaxed hers apart with his tongue. His mouth was firm yet tender, and Piper nearly melted against him. She knew what he was doing. Seduction at its finest and Ryan Grant was the president of the club.

Ryan leaned into her a bit more. From torso to knees they were connected with only the thin barrier of their clothing. Damn material.

Piper nearly lost her mind with want, with need, but Ryan pulled back and smiled, the same smile he used to throw at cameras when he was asked about the circuit. There was love in that smile and Piper was going to have to think about what that meant.

"You ready? I'm starving," he told her. "I hope you can keep your hands off me tonight."

Piper smacked his chest and turned the doorknob behind her back. "I'll try to resist and let you have a nice meal without me molesting you."

"I can make sacrifices anytime you feel like molesting me, Red. You just say the word. Hell, I could probably eat my steak, drink my beer and enjoy your molesting all at the same time. I'm good at multitasking."

The warm evening air greeted them as they stepped onto her narrow porch. "That's such a guy answer."

"Babe, I'm all guy. And when you're ready to find that out firsthand, you let me know."

He moved by her, opening the door of his full-size black truck.

When she gripped the armrest on the door and put her foot on the running board, Ryan cupped his hands around her rear end.

"Need a spotter?" he asked.

Piper glanced over her shoulder to see him squatting, smirking and staring up at her. "Get your hands off my butt, slick."

"Just trying to help a friend."

His hands remained until she swatted him. "You're trying to cop a feel, pal."

"I don't know what you're talking about. Simply help-ing you get into the truck."

Piper climbed in, by herself, and stared back at him. "I've climbed into this truck, and my own, for years. You've never offered to *spot* me before."

"A guy can't decide to just help without being ridi-culed? I'm hurt."

Ryan closed the door to her laughter and Piper crossed her legs. This was going to be one very interesting "date" if he kept up this playful flirtation. She liked it.

Ryan was going to die. He couldn't handle this any-more. The romantic ambience of Claire's with its crisp white table linens topped with fresh floral centerpieces and tapered candles… Between all of that and the damn wrap dress just begging for him to peel off of Piper, he didn't know how he was going to make it through the rest of dinner.

Thank God their steaks had arrived and he was able to concentrate on the big slab of meat and not the vee of that material that crossed between her breasts.

How could he possibly even think of ordering dessert when he only wanted to taste what sat across from him?

"You're going to get us thrown out of here if you don't quit looking at me like I'm a piece of chocolate cake."

Ryan grinned. "It's a shame you're not."

"You need a new topic, cowboy. I'm well aware of where your mind stands, but can you think of something else to focus on? Your new school? Alex? Anything?"

"I suppose." Ryan shrugged. "The school is coming right along and I have some teenage boys who are helping and getting the hang of how things will be run. I'm hoping to hire them to help the younger kids and at the same time train them a bit more and get them ready for the circuit. There's one in particular that has potential."

"That's great." She beamed. "You'll be awesome at this, Ryan, I just know it. Having a rodeo school for kids is perfect for you."

Ryan loved her smile, and it warmed his heart that she was just as excited as he was about the project.

"Any more from Alex?" he asked, trying to stay off the topic of his hormones and the fact she was sex on a stick tonight.

"Cara didn't return my call earlier, so I haven't heard anything." Piper eased forward, resting her elbows on the white cloth. "I hate to bother her all the time, but I care for Alex and I worry for her. I don't want her to feel like I'm just neglecting her."

"Cara has so many friends who care for her. She's overwhelmed, but just the fact you called tells her you care. She'll be fine, Piper."

Piper smiled. "See, you went ten whole seconds without flirting or talking about sex."

"I'm trying."

"I know something that will kill your...personal issue," Piper said. "I have to go replace the emergency equipment that was destroyed in the break-in at the clubhouse's day-care center. I didn't get there the other day."

"That still pisses me off. To vandalize where children will be watched and cared for all because some insane person doesn't want women in the club? It's too late to change that, so let's just move forward and stop creating more of a mess."

"That's why you're so awesome." She smiled. "You don't agree with those who believe women have no place at the TCC. I think it's a great thing and the day-care facility is brilliant."

"Any idea what you have to replace?" Ryan asked, taking a long pull of draft beer from his pilsner glass.

"I was told there are several first-aid kits that were damaged and the CPR cart. The entire lock cabinet was shattered, too. I told them I would get everything in order so the safety inspector can come finalize the area."

Ryan watched Piper's delicate hand as she used a fingertip to circle her wineglass. Those hands had saved lives, held on to loved ones who were in fear; they'd lassoed horses and even helped bring foals into this world. His Piper was one very intriguing, diverse woman and he couldn't wait to feel those hands on his body.

"I thought that was you two over here."

Ryan turned as Piper did and saw Dave Firestone and Mia Hughes approaching their table. Dave was Alex's business rival and his beautiful fiancée, Mia, was Alex's housekeeper. A little conflict there, but they were making it work. The newly engaged couple stood hand-in-hand and Ryan was so happy that they had worked out their problems and were now headed down the aisle…like so many others in Royal lately. Engagements were becoming an epidemic.

"You look beautiful, Mia," Piper exclaimed with a wide grin across her face. "Are you two celebrating anything special other than being engaged?"

Mia patted Dave's arm. "Being engaged and the fact Alex is home. We're trying to pin down a date for the wedding right now."

"Have the police contacted you again since Alex was found?" Dave asked.

"We talked to them at the site and then I went down the other day to tell them all I knew," Piper said.

"Nathan Battle stopped by the ranch several days ago," Ryan said, mentioning his friend, the sheriff. "I just hope they catch the bastard who was behind that. Nathan was pretty thorough when he and I talked. And since he and Alex are friends and he's invested, I know he won't rest until he gets to the bottom of this mess."

Dave wrapped his arm around Mia's waist. "At least we can move forward with the wedding and not feel like someone is missing."

"Have you found a dress?" Piper asked.

Mia's smile widened. "I did and it's perfect."

"What color are your bridesmaids' dresses?"

"I'm thinking of going with a neutral so the flowers really pop, but I'm not sure."

Ryan watched as Piper's face lit up at the wedding talk. She may think she wasn't bride material, but Ryan could totally see her in a long white gown, all that fiery hair spilling down her back.

He shook the image off. Was he really and truly ready to be the man at the other end of that aisle?

"I'm really happy for you guys," Ryan told them. "Would you care to join us? We were just about to order dessert."

"Oh, no." Dave shook his head. "We've already had the chocolate cake. We're actually thinking of having them do our wedding cake, so we wanted to sample it again."

"The sacrifices he makes for this wedding," Mia joked.

"You sure you don't want to sit and visit?" Piper asked.

Dave and Mia met each other's eyes, their smiles widened.

"We really need to head home," Dave said, not taking his eyes off Mia. "But it was great to see you two out and looking so cozy. Maybe there will be another engagement soon?"

Piper's mouth fell open, but Ryan just laughed. "We wouldn't want to steal your thunder, pal."

As the happy couple walked away, Ryan glanced back to Piper who was glaring at him.

"You let them think we're here on a date," she said between gritted teeth.

"Why not? We are."

"But they don't need to know that."

Ryan reached across the table and took hold of her small hand. "Listen, you better get used to the fact I want you. Not just in bed, Piper. I want you in my life as more than just a friend. If that scares you, then join the club. I scared the hell out of myself when I finally admitted it, but I won't live my life scared. I want us to be seen together in public as a couple."

He eased forward, tugging her until she was leaning across the table, as well.

"And also get used to the fact that one day, very soon, you'll be in my bed and we won't be done after just one time."

By the time they left and were headed back to Piper's house, Ryan was beyond sexually frustrated. Seeing her curves shift beneath that dress, knowing that bow on the side was the only thing holding it in place was driving him completely mad.

But because this was his Piper, he wouldn't push it. She was a very independent woman, very strong-willed and when she wanted something, she'd come after it with everything in her. He couldn't wait to become the prey instead of the hunter.

Ryan pulled into her brick drive and killed the engine.

"I'll walk you in."

Of course, by the time he got around to her door, she was already out.

"I would've gotten the door for you," he told her, taking her hand and leading her up the wide walkway.

"I'm capable of getting out of a car, Ryan."

He turned back to her, the moon casting a soft glow around her and the streetlamp highlighting one side of her delicate face.

"I know what you're capable of," he murmured, moving in closer. "I know everything about you, Red. But you need to know that this is moving into the territory of dating and I plan on doing more for you. You deserve a man who will treat you like a lady and not just as one of the guys."

"You treat me like one of the guys," she retorted.

Ryan squeezed her hands and grinned. "Trust me, I don't think of you as one of the guys. And maybe it's time I treat you better. You shouldn't always have to be seen in flannel and work boots, Piper. You're a lady and I know you wear very ladylike things beneath those work clothes. Why not showcase that a bit more?"

Piper shrugged. "I don't know any other way. I'm comfortable in my work clothes."

"Well you're a knockout now and you look comfortable." He eased in, letting his lips glide gently across hers. "You're not feeling out of your element, are you? All dressed up and on a date with me?"

Her lids fluttered closed. "No. I feel…"

"What?" he whispered. "What do you feel?"

Piper tipped her face up toward the moonlight. The column of her neck combined with the deep vee of her dress made for some very sexy skin exposure and damn if his hands didn't itch to stroke every inch and then follow through with his tongue.

So he did.

With the tips of his fingers he started between her breasts where the material met, then slid them up and over her throat and around to her jawline. Easing down, he opened his lips and followed the path until he got to her jaw, then he moved around to her waiting lips.

Piper opened for him, surprising him when she took hold of his face between her hands and stole the control right out from under him. Her body eased against his, her lips took everything he was offering. Slender hips bumped his and his pants grew even tighter. Seemed like every time he was around her lately he was hard as a horny teenager.

She groaned slightly and eased back, still framing his face in her hands.

"You make me forget that I'm supposed to be the strong one here," she said, licking her moist lips. "You make me want things that I know I shouldn't. But you make me also wonder what this would be like. Would we be better? I can't imagine anything better than what we already have."

Ryan reached up, taking her face in his hands, mirroring her actions. "I *know* we'd be better. I know it because I wouldn't allow this relationship to go anywhere else but up. I meant it when I said I was here for good, Piper. I know you're scared because of your dad—"

"Ryan—"

"No, you will listen," he told her, pulling her face closer and looking into her eyes. "I care about you on a level I didn't know possible. Don't compare me to a man who shut you out and only remembers you a couple occasions per year. I know more about you than he ever will. And I damn well care about you more than he ever did."

Piper closed her eyes. "You're so good for me, Ryan. But that fear is just part of me. I've never lived without it."

"Then maybe it's time you started." He kissed her hard then eased back. "And when you've conquered that fear, I better be the first to know."

Without another word or a backward glance, Ryan made the hardest decision to date. He marched to his truck and got the hell out of temptation's way because one more look from Piper's misty eyes and he would've gotten all soft on her.

And that would've pissed both of them off.

Eleven

Piper pulled into the TCC clubhouse parking lot and sighed. She was not looking forward to teaching the day-care workers CPR or fixing the vandalized equipment.

Her mind was still on Ryan Grant and last night's promising kiss and touching words. He was putting it all out there, laying his emotions and heart on the line. The man never knew fear, never considered failure. He'd always been that way: careless, free and courageous.

But he'd never been hurt, never had the stability of life ripped from beneath him. He'd always known what he wanted and he went after it full-force.

And apparently he had his sights set on her.

Nerves settled low in her belly as Piper started up the sidewalk toward the clubhouse. The large single-story stone building with its slate roof was very masculine, very eye-catching. Until recently it had been an all-male bastion, with membership off-limits to women and children not welcome at all.

Such a shame that now when the club was getting with the times and allowing women to join, some members found it necessary to fight overturning the archaic rule.

Piper stepped into the clubhouse and took a left toward the new child-care facility. Perhaps some of the disgruntled men were grouchy because the new day care took the place of the old billiards room. Oh, well, wasn't her job to judge, only to fix the equipment and help the staff get certified in CPR.

When she stopped in the manager's office, a petite blonde sat at the desk muttering to herself and working on what appeared to be a spreadsheet.

Piper tapped the back of her knuckles on the doorframe. "Excuse me."

The lady with a short blond bob jerked her attention toward Piper. "Oh, sorry. I was lost in thought. Can I help you?"

"I'm Piper Kindred." She stepped into the office, extended her hand. "I'm the paramedic who is supposed to replace the equipment and certify some of the day-care workers."

The woman shook her hand. "I'm Kiley Roberts, the new manager. So great to meet you."

Kiley had soft brown eyes and a kind smile. Piper could easily see her working with children and putting worried parents at ease.

"I stopped to look at the equipment the other day, but I missed you," Piper said. "Is this a good time to get into the facility? I came early since we're not scheduled to do the certification for another hour."

"This is perfect." Kiley came to her feet. "Come on back."

She punched in a security code and the locked door to the facility clicked open. "I straightened that room up after the police went through it, but I am not sure what all needs to be replaced."

Piper gripped her heavy duffel full of supplies. "I'll figure it out."

"Are you a member here, too?" Kiley asked, flipping

on the light in the small utility room where the medical equipment was stored.

Piper laughed. "No. I have too much on my plate to get involved with this he-man, she-man battle."

"Oh, I've already heard from both sides about the women and children. I'm not sure why some of the male members who voted against it feel the need to vent to me, but I listen. Most times when people complain, it's just to get their emotions off their chest and then they feel better." Kiley smiled. "But arguing and complaining about it now seems a bit silly."

Setting her black bag down, Piper unzipped it and pulled out basic first-aid kits. "It's only a matter of time before the dissenting members come around. Besides, I think the few women who are members are strong and it's only a matter of time before more come aboard."

"I agree," Kiley said, easing a hip onto the small desk in the corner. "Is there something I can help you do?"

Piper studied the damaged kits and decided to toss them all. No need in keeping items that were probably no longer sanitary.

"Actually, you can keep me company," Piper said. "Unless you'd like to get back to that spreadsheet."

"Believe me, I love my job, but spreadsheets were created by the devil."

Piper laughed. "Tell me about yourself. Do you have any kids of your own?"

"I have one." Kiley's smile widened, her eyes sparkled. "She's two and her name is Emmie."

"Two years old?" Piper asked, raising a brow. "You must have your hands full."

"I do, but in a good way. She's my world."

"Is your husband a member of TCC?"

That bright smile faltered, but Kiley recovered. "I'm

divorced and he has nothing to do with Emmie. So, no. He's not a member."

Way to go, Piper. Would you like salt and a napkin to go with that foot you just shoved in your mouth?

"Sorry," she said.

"No worries. I'm better off without him."

Piper nodded. "My parents are divorced and my mother always said the same thing. Times were hard for her—for us—but I know we were better without my father than we would've been with him."

"I won't lie, being a single mother isn't easy, but I'd do anything for Emmie. I've just never understood how anyone could walk away from a marriage, let alone a child."

Piper swallowed. She'd always wondered the same thing.

Silence settled in as Piper exchanged the first-aid kits and put the old ones in her bag to dispose of later.

"What about you?" Kiley asked after a bit. "Is your husband a member of TCC?"

"Oh, I'm not married."

Kiley shook her head. "Are we two of the select few in Royal who aren't engaged or already married? People are hooking up around here like crazy."

Piper laughed as she locked the cabinet and gathered her bag. She and Kiley stepped into the hall.

"There are a few single women left, not many though," Piper told her.

Men's voices filtered down the hall. Piper and Kiley turned toward the entryway where Josh Gordon stood chatting with another TCC member.

"That's one of the members, Josh Gordon," Piper pointed out. "I'm not sure of the other man's name. I think he's fairly new."

Piper didn't miss the way Kiley's back and shoulders instantly stiffened, her eyes focused on Josh. Interesting.

"Do you know Josh?" Piper asked.

Kiley jerked her head around. "What? Oh, no."

"He's one of the members who isn't keen on the idea of women and children on the premises."

Kiley crossed her arms over her simple white shirt. "Really? I assume he's single then if he's not interested in the equal rights."

"Yes. Also one of the few single men in Royal." Piper glanced at her watch. "I have to go grab some more things from my car for the CPR class and for the cart in the medical room. I'll be right back."

Kiley smiled. "I'll be here."

As Piper walked away, she caught Kiley's eyes going back to Josh. There was a story there. Piper didn't know what, and it wasn't any of her business, but something about Josh did not sit well with the cute new day-care manager.

Piper took her bag to her truck and pulled out another duffel with items for the CPR class. The last thing Piper needed to do was to get involved in someone else's personal issues. God knew she had enough of her own.

She knew Ryan and there was no way he was going to allow the sexual tension between them to die down. He wouldn't shy away from it the way she might try to. That man would tackle it head-on and Piper had a feeling if she didn't hang on for the ride, Ryan would bring her along anyway. His charm alone was very potent.

Two days later Piper set her purse on the newly installed granite countertop and smiled.

She shook off her damp arms. The rain beat hard against the kitchen window and she wondered where the sneaky home renovator was. She hoped he didn't think because they were growing closer that it meant he needed to go above and beyond on her home. She definitely didn't want things to start getting awkward here.

Ryan came through the doorway from the front of the house. Hands on his hips, brow furrowed, he asked, "You like?"

It had been a day from hell because she'd had to work almost four hours extra when a new hire had decided *not* to show up. Piper really hated that her emotions were all over the place from stress. Plus, when it came to Ryan, her emotions had not found solid ground and she didn't know how to feel. Damn female hormones.

"I understand why you finished the roof when I hurt myself," she started, feeling tears burn her eyes. "I even let the cabinets slide because I'm shallow and I was thrilled I had the upgraded ones. But yesterday you laid the tile for the shower and floor in my bathroom and today I see my front door was installed."

"So why is this a problem?" he asked. "Because you wanted to do it all? Piper, you've done an insane amount of work on this house. I just wanted to help you and I didn't have anything pressing to do today. The school is ahead of schedule. I worked there this morning and there's nothing I can do until the inspector comes in a couple of days anyway. Spending my spare time here keeps me busy."

Piper shoved the wayward curl off her forehead and tucked the strand behind her ear. Damn crazy hair of hers. As if she needed something else to bother her today.

"You look like you had a bad day," Ryan observed, studying her face. "Why don't you come into the bathroom and help me with that tile design behind the new vanity. After that little piece is done, that room will be finished. Would that make you feel better?"

Piper smiled, forcing herself to be happy he was so handy and understood her love of hard labor, too. "I suppose, but only if I get to control the tile cutter."

Ryan extended his hand and guided her toward the bathroom. "I wouldn't have it any other way."

Piper stepped through the doorway to her master suite bath. The blue glass tile for the open shower sparkled. He'd just begun the backsplash above the sink and she could already picture the beauty.

"I'm so glad I went with the brighter blue in here," she told him. "It's so hard to tell from those itty-bitty samples, but this is gorgeous."

Ryan's hand slid around her waist as he tugged her close. "Sometimes you need to see the whole picture, but beauty normally comes from something small and builds over time."

Piper eased back to look over her shoulder. "Are you getting deep on me, cowboy? I'm just talking about a bathroom."

"Maybe I'm talking about you." He kissed her nose, swatted her butt and stepped around her. "Now quit trying to get me out of my clothes and get to work in here."

Laughing, Piper stepped over the tile saw and moved toward the work area. "I think we both know I wouldn't have to try to get you out of your clothes. They'd just fall off if I said the word."

"Oh, what a glorious day that will be," he said with a wide grin and sigh.

The house shook as thunder boomed and the lights flickered, but came right back on.

"Time for a storm," Piper told him. "The sky was pretty black and that rain really cut loose as I was walking in the back door."

"We need the rain, but I hate storms."

Piper laughed. "I know you do. You're living in the wrong state, you know."

Ryan shrugged, picked up a small, patterned piece of uncut tile and measured it next to the wall. "I wouldn't live anywhere else. I love this town. I knew when I wanted to settle down and make a permanent home, I wouldn't go anywhere else."

"Even with all those places you traveled to?"

"Royal is still the best place on earth." He set the tile down on the counter and looked her in the eye. "Best scenery I've ever been exposed to."

"Ryan, you aren't playing fair."

A naughty grin kicked up one corner of his mouth. "I'm not playing and I never claimed to be fair."

"You're wanting to settle, you claim, so why are you pursuing me?"

Nerves settled in her belly because she wasn't sure she was ready for the answer he would give. This was moving too fast, or perhaps they'd been headed this way for years and she was just catching up.

"Maybe I haven't considered anyone else. Maybe I want to know what a relationship with my best friend would be like." He moved closer as the lights flickered once again. "Maybe I believe that we could have something special, something beyond what we both expect or imagine."

Piper swallowed, holding his gaze. "What about love?"

Ryan froze for a second, then raked his hand down his face. "Piper, you know I want marriage and the whole thing my parents had. I know they were a minority when it came to eternal love, but I'm not sure that's what I feel right now. All I can do is move forward and hope that's what happens. I can't guarantee anything and I'm not making promises."

Piper reached up, cupped his cheek and stroked his dark

stubble with her thumb. She knew he didn't love her, not like a man would love a woman romantically. He loved her on a friend level and that was fine because she herself wasn't sure about that intimate degree of love. Did it even exist? Certainly not for her parents. So how would she know if she was making a mistake if she and Ryan moved forward?

"I can't think about settling down, Ryan. I like my life. I enjoy my work, fixing up my house, hanging with you and watching our friends fall in love and marry."

Ryan reached up, grasped her hand and squeezed. "I'm not asking for wedding bands here, Red. I just want you to know I'm not going anywhere and I plan on seducing you at every opportunity I get. If anything else comes into the mix, then that's icing on the proverbial cake."

Shivers raced through Piper as another loud rumble of thunder shook her old house. The electricity flickered once, twice and finally died.

Silence surrounded them; darkness enveloped them as they stood still holding on to each other.

"Looks like no work for us," he murmured. "I think fate just handed us a prime opportunity."

Piper inhaled Ryan's familiar scent as fear was replaced by certainty. This was the one man who knew her better than anyone. Why shouldn't she let him possess her body, as well? She'd slept with two men in her life, neither of whom she had feelings half as strong for. Ryan was it for her. No, she wasn't ready for marriage or kids, but intimacy with the one man who always made her feel safe and cherished, and treated her like a lady would not be a wrong decision.

"I'm tired of being strong for both of us." She searched his eyes, praying she was making the right decision. "I'm

tired of analyzing this to death and I'm tired of this achi-
ness I feel when I'm around you. I can't handle it anymore."

Ryan slid both hands around her face and into her hair,
pulling her closer. "Piper, I don't want to pressure you. Be
sure about this. I'm demanding and I don't want you to
regret this later."

"I'll have no regrets," she told him, knowing she
wouldn't. "I want you. I want what's started between us.
I know you in so many ways, but not the most important
one. I want to know more, Ryan. Show me more."

Ryan's lips came down fast and hard on hers. He
claimed her as he never had before. His tongue thrusting
in and out as his hips aligned with hers had Piper moan-
ing and gripping his shoulders.

Rain beat down on the house, thunder rattled the old
windows. Storms had always been sexy to her. The in-
trigue, the careless manner in which they came through,
the loss of control. Much like sex.

The ambience couldn't have been better scripted for
their first time. With their playful bickering through the
years and the way they'd met, with her quick punch to
his face as kids, the thunderstorm sweeping through was
almost nostalgic, like Mother Nature echoing their own
stormy relationship.

Perhaps Fate had planned this whole evening. Who was
she to argue?

Ryan gripped her shirt and tugged it from her work
pants. With little finesse, he jerked it apart, sending the
tiny buttons flying across the room, spattering as they hit
the wall, the floor. Piper didn't care that he was in such a
hurry. She knew the need he had because that same urge
burned in her, stronger than she ever thought possible.

"Wish I'd worn something a little more feminine," she
told him.

Hunger stared back at her. "I don't want you any other way, Piper. Always remember that."

Strong hands encircled her waist, his thumbs stroked along the underside of her breasts across the lacy edge of her bra.

"Perfectly feminine," he whispered. "Perfectly mine."

As shivers raced through her, Piper went to work on his pants. In no time Ryan had released her, shucked his work boots and jeans, leaving his glorious body in only black boxer briefs. Seeing this man in swimming trunks was hot, but this was downright scorching with his erection trying to spring free out the top of his boxers. Ryan Grant should pose for one of those hot, hunky cowboy calendars. The world really shouldn't be deprived of seeing this tatted-up bad boy in nothing but his Stetson and snug briefs.

"I wish I could see you in the light," she muttered. "I feel cheated."

"Surely you have candles."

Piper started to turn away, but Ryan caught her arm.

"Take off your pants. I want to watch you walk away so I can see everything I've been wanting for months."

"Months?"

Ryan nipped at her lips and whispered, "Years."

Piper had no idea she'd held such control over him and she knew he wasn't just saying this. Ryan had had his fair share of buckle bunnies, but he'd never flaunted it and never acted like his ego had become inflated because of it.

And the fact that he could have nearly any woman he wanted and he'd wanted her for so long only made her all the more anxious to be with him.

Piper unlaced her work boots and kicked them off, shoved her pants around her ankles and kicked them aside, as well.

Even in the dark, Piper could see Ryan's eyes widen as

they slid down her body. Anticipation swirled inside her, sending shivers shooting throughout her body.

"You better hurry up if you want those candles," he told her, his voice husky.

Piper turned toward her bedroom where she had a large fat candle on her nightstand. She grabbed it and the matches in the drawer and hurried back, careful not to bang her toe on the end of her bed. The darkness could be sexy, but bashing yourself before foreplay could even begin would not be a turn-on. They'd had enough injuries between them.

When she turned, Ryan stood in the doorway, then moved toward her. Apparently this intimate party was getting started.

Piper set the candles on her dresser and lit them; the room soon basked into a soft, radiant glow.

Ryan eased forward, sliding his hands around her waist, then to her back, and dipped his fingertips in the top of her lacy panties.

The gentle light from the flickering candle set the perfect scene and she could so appreciate his body all the more. The ink that swirled around his left pec and up over his shoulder intrigued her. She'd never given the tat much thought before, but now she found it sexy, alluring, as it stretched across his taut muscle.

"Seeing your panties hanging in your bathroom a few weeks ago nearly killed me, Red. I instantly imagined what you'd look like in them. I knew you'd be smokin' hot. But even my imagination didn't come close to reality."

Roaming her hands up his chiseled biceps and over his shoulders, Piper smiled. "I'm glad you're not disappointed. I don't want this to be awkward, Ryan."

His hands moved into her panties and cupped her bottom, jerking her toward his erection.

Ryan's shadowed face inched closer to hers; he licked his lips and hoisted her up off the floor. Piper wrapped her legs around his waist, her arms looped around his neck. His chest hair tickled her breasts.

"I've waited so long for this," he whispered. "I want to memorize every moment, but mostly I want to be inside you. I want to know how you feel around me. I want to see you lose control again and know that I'm the cause of your recklessness."

Who knew her best friend had such a sexy bedroom voice? And who knew he'd had these thoughts about her for so long? Had she missed the subtle hints or had he kept his emotions and fantasies hidden on the inside?

"Then why are we still talking?" she asked. "Take what you want, cowboy."

His wide smile melted her and she sank her fingers into his messy hair and pulled his mouth against hers.

With only their underwear separating every aching part, Piper rocked her hips against his as her tongue swept inside his mouth, seeking more contact. She just couldn't get close enough.

Ryan walked backward until her back hit the wall.

"I want all of you, Piper," he murmured against her lips.

Sweat dampened their bodies.

"Since the fans won't work without electricity, maybe a cool shower will help us."

Piper grinned against his lips. "I doubt we'll cool off, but the thought of getting you naked and wet is one of the best ideas you've had."

"I try." He laughed.

He eased her down his body until her feet hit the cool tile. She slid out of her panties and unclasped her bra, flinging it aside. When she glanced back up, Ryan was watching her, his lids heavy, his gaze on her body as if he were looking at her for the very first time.

"The word *want* seems like such an understatement right now," he murmured. "Crave, desire, hunger for…"

Feeling a bit more flirtatious, she was naked after all, Piper held her arms wide. "Then take what you want, Ryan. I'm not afraid. Once won't be enough and I can't guarantee slow or gentle."

His eyes came back up to hers. "If you knew what I want from you, you would be afraid."

"There's nothing you can do to scare me away," she told him, easing closer. "I know you, inside and out. And if you'd shut up, I could get to know you a whole lot more."

In one swift move, Ryan lifted her up walked into the newly renovated bathroom. Thankfully she'd washed the dust out of the shower last night so she could see the tile work.

Holding on to Piper, he stepped over the small tiled edge into the wide, open shower with nozzles on each of the side walls. This was one area she'd refused to skimp on and, man, she was so glad she had put in the extra cash for this luxurious, oversize shower.

Water slid over her body as Ryan reached up and tugged on her hair. Piper stepped aside, pulled the rubber band loose and flung it out of the shower. Ryan took both hands, shaking out her day's worth of sloppy ponytail and tilted her head so her hair became soaked from the spray.

Closing her eyes, Piper relished the moment of being held, cherished, pampered and even loved by her best friend in a way she never thought possible. There was nothing awkward or weird about their coming together. If anything, being naked in the shower with Ryan was a level of perfection she'd never experienced in her life.

Piper held on to his arms and lifted her head. Water

dripped into her face and Ryan eased down, using his lips to capture the droplets on her forehead, her cheeks, her lips. Cupping both breasts, he sank to his knees and kissed her flat stomach.

"I've never seen a more beautiful sight," he said, looking back up at her. "I'd stay on my knees forever for you, Piper."

Damn, why did he have to say things like that? She didn't want the whole of forever to enter into this. She wanted sex. That's all. She didn't know if this would work and bringing another complication into the mix made her uncomfortable. For now, she needed to concentrate on the fact that she was about to make love to Ryan.

Before she could reply, he kissed her stomach again, his hands roaming down her waist and settling at her hips. Instinct had her spreading her legs wide, placing her hands on his wet, muscular shoulders.

Ryan kissed her belly button and made a path down until he was at her center where she ached the most. Strong hands gripped her hips as he kissed her inner thighs, one agonizing inch at a time.

Piper looked down, wanting to see him, knowing the erotic image they made, and the knowledge of what he was about to do turned her on even more. This was a giant step beyond making love and she couldn't do a thing to stop him. She'd lost all control over this situation—perhaps she never had it to begin with. Ryan literally held her in the palm of his hands.

He used his thumbs to spread her apart and he took no time in gliding his tongue across her. Piper's knees nearly buckled, but his hold on her hips tightened as he made love to her with his mouth.

Easing back, Piper rested against the tile next to the pulsing spray. She needed more, so much more, but she didn't know what or even how to ask. Every part of her screamed for release, yet she didn't want it to end too soon. She could hardly control herself and she wanted to remember this moment.

As if Ryan knew what she needed, he slid a hand down her leg and took her foot, placing it on the small bench along the back wall of the shower. Exposed as she was, Piper felt sensations she never knew were possible with her body. She'd certainly never experienced anything like this before.

Her hips pumped; her hands went into Ryan's hair, his shoulders, anywhere she could reach because the turmoil her body was going through was driving her insane. She needed… She didn't know what she needed. Faster, slower, harder. Something to make this ache subside.

Ryan eased a finger inside her and…yes. That was it. Piper jerked her hips against him as her body tightened and the climax slammed into her. Ryan continued his assault with his mouth and hand until her shivers ceased.

But when he looked up her body at her, Piper heated all over again.

"You're the sexiest woman I've ever seen," he told her, coming to his feet and leaning his full length against her body. "I can't wait, Piper. I need you now. We can do slow later."

Later. She liked the sound of that. One word held so much promise and the fact they were just getting started sent thrills of excitement through her.

The flickering of the candlelight combined with the cool temperature of the shower and the added effects from Mother Nature had Piper wishing this unexpected night would never end.

Ryan kissed her shoulder, moving his way across to her neck, then down to take one nipple into his mouth. Piper wasn't sure what else he had in mind, but her body was still humming and she didn't know how much longer she was going to have to wait.

Time to take charge.

She shoved him back and smiled. Placing a hand on his chest, she eased him back until his legs came in contact with the tiled bench. Ryan sank onto it and Piper settled one knee on either side of his hips.

Ryan leaned back against the wall. "This is a view I could get used to, as well."

Piper laughed. "You have a boob fetish."

"I'm a guy."

Piper started to sink down onto him, but Ryan gripped her waist and halted her progress.

"Condom?" he asked.

Piper closed her eyes and groaned. "I don't have any."

He nipped at her lips. "I've never gone without one and I have regular physicals."

"Same here," she panted. "And I'm on birth control."

His eyes sought hers. "I want to feel you. Only you."

"Please," she begged.

"I want to remember this, Piper. I don't want you to forget this moment."

Her eyes locked on to his. "As if I could."

She captured his lips as she sank down, consuming him in so many ways. He filled her, more than she'd initially thought he would and Piper took a moment to adjust.

"Okay?" he asked, his forehead resting against hers.

Piper nodded as she started moving, slowly at first, then faster. Ryan continued to grip her hips as his mouth found her breast. She braced her hands on the wall behind his head and pumped her body faster because another wave of glorious pleasure was building and she wanted to take him with her this time.

Piper shut her eyes, bit her lip, but nothing could hold back the scream as another climax took over.

Beneath her, Ryan stilled as he tilted his head back against the wall. The muscle in his jaw clenched and Piper rode out her pleasure with him. His body tightened and Piper had never seen a more glorious sight than Ryan giving in to total bliss and abandonment.

And when she wrapped her arms around his neck, rested her head on his shoulder, she let the cool shower beat down on her because she knew this night of passion was just getting started.

Twelve

Piper lay across her bed, sweaty, sated and sore. Mercy sakes, that man knew how to deliver on a promise. When he'd said he'd been thinking about intimacy with her for years she'd kind of laughed it off, but after that performance, she was inclined to believe him. That man had skills she'd never experienced before.

There wasn't a part of her body he hadn't touched either with his hands or his soft words. Piper would be lying if she didn't admit her heart had been just as involved as her body during their lovemaking last night. Getting tangled up with Ryan was something she certainly hadn't planned on, but there was no way she could've fought off the desire, the passion, any longer.

And now that her heart was becoming more immersed, she knew she had to watch every step she took in this new relationship. The last thing she could handle was losing his friendship. He'd been her rock, her sounding board and her fun-time friend for twenty years. Nothing could break her more than losing that solid foundation in her life.

The electricity still hadn't returned and she was going to have to fire up her generator so she could turn on her box fans or she'd end up in a cold shower again…not that the first round was bad.

She started to pull away from the dead weight of Ryan's

thick, muscular arm across her bare torso. She loved the feel of him on her, around her, in her. Who knew her best friend had such mad skills in the bedroom? No wonder all those buckle bunnies were traipsing after him at every event.

The man could ride without fear and never break a sweat. He was cool under pressure, but when it came to the bedroom, Ryan Grant was anything but laid-back. The man was in control, dominant and sexy as hell. The way he silently demanded affection… The way he so selflessly pleasured her over and over again… Piper was utterly ruined for any other man.

And how in the world could she ever go back to being just his friend? Yeah, that would never happen. No way could she look at him, talk to him, eat a meal with him and not recall the way he'd made her feel, the way he'd looked at her as he moved within her.

"Where are you going?" he mumbled, half his face squished into the wrinkled sheet.

"Just going to start the generator so I can get the fans moving some of this hot air."

"Why don't we go take another shower?" he said, eyes heavy and locking on to hers. "Or better yet, let's just go to my house. I probably have electricity."

"That was a nasty storm, Ryan. The streetlights were still out last night, so I imagine the town is out."

He lifted up onto an elbow and rested his head on the palm of his hand. "Yeah, but I live outside of town so maybe I didn't get hit as hard."

Piper eased up in bed, lacing her hand through his. "You have a problem staying here?"

In a swift move, he snaked his arm around her waist and pulled her back down. "Maybe I just want you in my bed."

The heat in his eyes this morning was just as intense as

she'd seen last night. She'd been worried that, come day-light, some of his enthusiasm for their newfound intimacy would've died down, but apparently not.

Yeah, she was so ruined for any other man. God help her.

"Don't make this weird, Red." He raked his thumb across her nipple. "We're just much better friends now."

"Well, I can honestly say I've never slept with a friend before, so this is uncharted territory for me."

"I've never slept with a friend before, either, but I'm sure as hell glad you were my first."

Piper laughed. "And here I didn't think you had any *firsts* left."

"I think you used up the last one." He chuckled, still fondling her breast. "I need you to know, I'm more than aware of how the media portrayed me through the years—my personal life on the road—but you surely know that I didn't sleep with every woman that slithered my way or that I was photographed with."

Piper held up a hand before he could speak. "We've been friends so long, Ryan, I know you're not one to sleep around. But I really don't want to hear about what you did or didn't do with those buckle bunnies."

He grabbed her hands, all joking aside as he searched her face. "No, it's important to me that you don't see me as some man-whore. I can count on one finger the number of one-night stands I've had on the road and I can count on my whole hand the number of women I've slept with… and that includes you."

Piper couldn't stop her gasp, nor could she stop her mouth from dropping open. "You don't have to say this."

"Yes, I do. I never cared what people thought about my sex life, the media will say what they want anyway." He squeezed her hands. "But I care what you think. I care now even more because of this."

Piper didn't want to delve too deeply into why it was so important for him to share all his bedroom romps now. She didn't want to think that maybe he was truly giving up the circuit and settling down. He'd made great progress with the school, which gave her hope that her best friend was indeed staying, but what if he got that itch to travel again? What if he decided that the adventure of home life wasn't enough?

What if he left like her father always had?

"Let's throw on the bare minimum of clothes and head to my place," he suggested, cutting into her thoughts. "It's quieter out there and there's more privacy. We can run naked through the house and no neighbors are around to see. Well, there are all the animals I have now, but they won't say anything."

Piper swatted his bare shoulder. "You're pathetic. I can't just be naked all day, Ryan. I have things to do."

"Like what? I know you're off today and with the electricity out, there's not much you can do on your house."

The man would tempt the devil himself. How could Piper say no when her body was already responding to him, already eagerly awaiting what talented moves he had yet to show her.

And in his bed? Piper would love nothing more than to wake up in his bed tomorrow morning, but how long would that last?

Her cell rang, breaking the intimacy.

"Let it go to voice mail," he told her.

"I can't, Ryan. It may be work or any number of people who need me. It would have to be important considering how early it is."

"I need you," he said, grabbing for her as she scooted off the bed. "I'll hold your place and I expect you to come back."

Piper smiled and went to her dresser to retrieve her cell. Cara's name popped up on the screen.

"Cara?" Piper answered. "Is everything okay?"

"It's fine," Cara told her. "I'm sorry to bother you so early, Piper."

"Is it Alex?" Piper asked, glancing across the room at Ryan who had now sat up in bed, the sheet pooling around his tanned waist.

"He's fine. I mean, he's the same," she clarified. "That's what's bothering me. I went to his house this morning, like I've been doing, to check on him. He's always been such an early riser, and I brought his favorite muffins. Anyway, after that bad storm, I was worried about him and I just keep hoping one morning I'll pop in and he'll tell me he's remembered."

Aware that she was standing completely naked, Piper crossed the room to her bath where she pulled her short, silky robe from the back of the door. Juggling the cell, she slid into the thin garment.

"Cara, it will take time," Piper assured her friend. "Don't be discouraged. You're doing everything you can to jog his memory."

"He has a wonderful life waiting on him," Cara went on. "I just want some answers. He's so frustrated and there's nothing I can do to help."

"Have you shown him more pictures?" Piper asked.

"We've looked at so many pictures. I'm at a loss now." Cara sighed. "I even asked him about having a barbecue with all of our friends in hopes that it would help to be surrounded by familiar faces, but he refused. He said he's just not ready for all of the questions and the pity. I understand that, but I just can't sit by and do nothing."

"You're not doing nothing, Cara. You're there every day. He's seeing your face over and over, and pretty soon he'll start having flashes of seeing you before the accident. And hopefully before long he'll remember what happened and we can put this nightmare behind us."

"I went pretty far in trying to jog his memory," Cara almost whispered. "When the pictures weren't doing anything, I…"

Piper waited, but her friend was silent. "Cara?"

"Never mind." Cara sighed. "I'm sorry to bother you, Piper. I just… I didn't know who to call and you've been so good to me through this. I have to be strong for him and occasionally I need to vent."

"I'm always here, Cara. Day or night."

"Thanks. I just needed to talk. I know we don't know each other really well, but I feel like we formed a bond after the accident." Cara sighed. "I guess I needed someone not so close to the situation. But Alex and I are going to get through this. I won't let him get away again. We have a life to plan together."

Piper grinned. "That's the kind of attitude you need, Cara. That strength will get you both through this."

Piper hung up and laid her phone back on the dresser.

"Alex okay?" Ryan asked.

Piper made her way back over to the bed. "He's the same. I think the lack of change is about to tear Cara down. She's really been so strong and holding it together. But there's only so much the poor woman can take."

Ryan reached for her hand and eased her down beside him. "She's got friends and family, and when Alex returns from whatever prison his mind is in, she will be fine."

"I hope so. She's so scared for him. She's not even feeling sorry for herself, she just wants to help him."

"I know another strong woman like that," Ryan said, toying with the ends of her hair.

God, her hair. She couldn't even imagine the mess it was in this morning after the shower, then air drying without product, then rolling around in the bed. Good thing Ryan was the man she'd woken up to. He'd seen her at her worst before and apparently he was fine with it.

Yes, there were perks to sleeping with your best friend. All the awkward moments were out of the way.

"If you keep looking at me like that, we won't make it to my house," he told her, his voice low, husky.

He pulled the silk ties of her robe until they slid loose, then he parted it as he ran his fingertips up from her abdomen to her breasts. Piper allowed the robe to slide back off her shoulders and land behind her on the bed.

"Who says we have to leave right now?" she asked. "I'm kinda hungry."

His eyes roamed over her chest and back up. "You have the best ideas."

Leaning back, Piper smiled. "Literally. I'm hungry."

She leaped out of bed, totally naked and not ashamed. He'd seen her, tasted her, why be shy now? Besides, she had plans for him later so getting dressed would be a waste of time.

Piper padded to the kitchen, knowing Ryan wouldn't be far behind. A naked female walking in the opposite direction? Yeah, he was a man. He'd follow.

As she pulled open the cabinet, a sensational, glorious thought crossed her mind. She turned to see Ryan in all his tanned naked cowboy glory standing directly behind her.

"Whatever naughty thought put that look in your eye, I like it," he said, grinning.

"Why don't you go back into the bedroom and wait for me." She shoved at his chest. "Or go into the living room. I'll start the generator and we can close those blinds."

He moved closer, stroking a hand down her face, her shoulder and the slope of her bare breast. "If you take too long, I'm coming after you and I won't care what room you're in."

Arousal shot through her and all she could do was nod. Yeah, he may say she had power over him, but since that first orgasm he'd given her on her porch, he pretty much had her trapped in a lust-filled haze and she wasn't sure she even wanted to get out.

"How about I go fire up the generator while you take care of whatever plans you have," he told her. "You have five minutes and I'll meet you in the living room."

He left her alone and Piper had to force herself to get back to the task she'd started before his heart-stopping nakedness nearly paralyzed her.

Turning back to the cabinet, she pulled out a variety of items. Piper wanted to explore a playful, fun side of sex with Ryan and hoped it would add to their pleasure.

Not surprisingly, she beat him into the living room and arranged her items on the old trunk she'd found at an antique shop. She smiled when he stepped into the room and took in her inventory, including his favorite food.

"If you're thinking what I think you are, I may have just died and gone to heaven," he told her.

"Get that fine butt over here, cowboy."

Feeling flirty and aroused, she couldn't wait to have playful sex. That, she could handle. It was the emotional, intense, slow sex that terrified her. Because she was hanging on by a very thin thread on a very slippery rope and it would only take one slip for her to fall headfirst in love with her best friend.

"I hope those mini marshmallows are for me."

She laughed. "You know I keep them here just for you."

"And what do you plan to do with them?"

Her eyes drifted down his lean, muscular body. "Lay on the couch and you'll find out."

Heat flared in his eyes as he did what she suggested. She knew he was loving every minute of this.

Once he was in position, all stretched out on the length of her sofa, she grabbed a handful of marshmallows and laid them one by one from the middle of his chest, down to his pelvic area.

"Don't move," she told him. "I'd hate to have to start over because one fell off."

His eyes darted to hers. "If these are my favorite, shouldn't I be eating them off of you?"

"You will." She went to her knees beside him, slid her tongue out and snatched the first one from his chest. "When I'm done."

His nostrils flared as she bent to suck off another one. Each time she snatched a marshmallow, he froze as if he were afraid to move, afraid she'd stop. By the time she got to the last one, he was near panting, his fists clenched at his sides.

Piper reached out to stroke him, but in a swift move, he was sitting up and looming over her.

"You're done," he growled. "Now get on the couch and let me return the favor."

Piper stared up at him in shock. "But I'd barely gotten started."

"And if you keep stroking me like that, we'll be done before I can have my fun."

Yeah, she had the control. They both knew it, which made her grin widen.

"I'll return the favor, Ryan." She leaned up, her mouth nearly touching his. "That's a promise and it'll happen when you least expect it."

"You'll be the death of me, Red. But I'll die a happy, satisfied man."

Piper laughed and squealed when he stood, hoisted her to her feet and nearly threw her on the sofa.

"Now it's your turn to see how well you can lay still."

Her body shivered at the promise, the anticipation. They'd always been competitive and she refused to let him win this little foreplay contest.

Ryan reached around, grabbed a handful of marshmallows and popped them into his mouth.

"That's not how you play," she told him, laughing.

"You play your way, I'll play mine."

Piper rolled her eyes. "Am I just going to lay here while you eat?"

His eyes roamed over her, heating her body just the same as if he'd touched her with his bare hands. "Hell, yeah, you are."

She realized her choice of wording may not have been the best, but the thought of Ryan between her thighs only made her all the more anxious.

"What else do we have here?" he said, glancing over at the trunk. "Oh, a little bit of chocolate sauce. This could be fun."

Piper stared at him as he placed one marshmallow at a time in a heart shape on her abdomen. The urge to squirm consumed her and he'd barely touched her. But she had to remain firm.

He popped the top of the chocolate sauce and slowly drizzled it in the outline of the heart.

"Hard to remain still, isn't it?" he asked, a naughty smirk spreading across his kissable mouth. "I promise to make it worth your while."

Piper shivered. She may just lose this little challenge, after all. But with the way his hands and mouth were roaming over her, she knew she'd still be coming out a winner.

Thirteen

"That's it," Ryan said encouragingly. "You've got him."

Will, a senior in high school, was just one of the boys participating in Ryan's program. He needed to get a feel for what worked, what didn't and what he could improve on before fully opening his school. This was a win-win for both him and the boys he had coming after school for a few hours a day.

Ryan climbed down off the chutes as Will headed for the gate. A ranch hand had herded the bull out of the arena already and was off to take care of the animals. Will had been trying his skills on several of the horses and broncs for the past week. From Will's performance today, Ryan was impressed by what he'd seen. This was a young boy who had been brought up learning the ropes and knowing how to handle most animals.

Ryan almost felt like a proud papa.

"You did really well," Ryan told the boy. "You're more than welcome to come out tomorrow even though it's Saturday. I'll be around if you'd like to continue your work."

Will nodded, adjusting his hat lower on his head. "Thanks, Mr. Grant. I'd like that."

Ryan slapped him on the back. "I've told you to call me Ryan. I really think you'll be a great asset to this school and I'd like to offer you a full-time position here for the summer once you're done with school."

Will's eyes widened. "That would be great, Mr.—uh, Ryan."

Ryan headed toward the tack room in the barn as Will moved toward the door. "I'll see you in the morning, Will."

Once he was alone in the barn, Ryan set his music to Metallica and attempted to unwind and relax. Nothing like a little vintage hard rock to round out his day. He usually didn't play music with anyone else here because no one appreciated his fine selection.

Well, he would play it around Piper, but she was special. She hated his music, and he found it amusing to drive her out of her mind as often as possible. And now that they'd shared a bed, numerous times, he'd found a new way to drive her out of her mind.

Barely a week had passed since the storm and since he'd brought her to his house to stay. Having Piper in his bed was exactly where he wanted to keep her. He wanted that extra layer of bonding and he knew she'd felt a connection being on his turf, too. She wanted to hide from any stronger emotions, but he wouldn't allow it.

As he was putting the rest of the equipment away, his cell vibrated in his pocket. Ryan pulled it out and checked the screen.

"Hey, Joe," he greeted his former roping partner.

"Ryan. What's up, ol' buddy?"

Taking a seat on the edge of the tack box, Ryan smiled. "Not much. Just got finished working with a boy who's helping with my school. There's some potential. Reminds me of me when I was a teen."

Joe sighed. "So you're really settling down there, huh?"

"I really am."

"I was hoping you'd be home for a bit and get the itch to get back out into the action."

Action? Yeah, he was getting all the action he could handle with Piper. The circuit didn't even compare.

"I'm staying in Royal," Ryan confirmed. "I'm pretty excited about opening the new school and settling roots in my hometown."

"You'll be great at it, Ryan."

The hesitation in his friend's voice had Ryan coming to his feet. "Joe? Something wrong?"

"I was hoping I could talk you into finishing this season with me."

"What?" Ryan asked, switching the phone to his other ear. "What happened to Dallas?"

"When Dallas replaced you he was on fire, but he broke his leg earlier this week when we were doing practice runs. Snapped his femur when he dismounted and landed wrong. We desperately need you back, man."

Finish the season? Put his school on hold for a little longer than anticipated?

Put Piper on hold?

"How soon would you need an answer?"

God, was he even contemplating this now that he was within reach of everything he'd wanted for his retirement? School, ranch…Piper.

"By tomorrow at the latest," Joe told him. "It would just be for a few more months. Then you can be out for good. You know I wouldn't ask if I didn't really need you."

"Why can't you ask someone else?"

Joe sighed. "I need the money, Ryan. I'm afraid if I don't win this championship we're going to lose our ranch."

Guilt weighed heavy on him. For a cowboy to lose his ranch, well, that was like taking the breath from his lungs. Ryan knew Joe had fallen on hard times recently with personal issues back home and there was no way Ryan could ignore his friend.

But this was a big step and one he'd really have to consider.

"I wouldn't have called if it hadn't been an emergency," Joe told him.

"I know." Ryan sighed. "Let me call you back."

"I knew I could count on you."

"I haven't said yes, yet."

"You will."

Joe disconnected the call and Ryan tossed the phone onto the tack box. Back on the circuit. It was like a drug pulling at him and he hadn't even realized he'd needed a fix. That craving for the adrenaline rush, the instant gratification of being part of a team, of winning, of conquering that damn bull that no one else could.

Every aspect of rodeo had always given him a high like nothing else…made him feel like he could do anything, gave him bragging rights that made him feel as though nothing could hold him back.

Ryan blew out a breath, cranked the heavy metal music even louder and headed outside to stack the hay bales. A little manual labor was what he needed to think, to really focus on what was best for him at this point in his life. But how could he focus on what was best for him when he now thought of himself as a team with Piper?

The late-afternoon sun beat down on him and Ryan reached behind his back and stripped his shirt off, hanging it over the post. Even though it was November, the weather was a bit on the warm side and he'd already worked up a sweat.

He pulled the worn leather gloves from his back pocket and slid them on and went to the stack of hay bales. One after another he tugged, tossed and stacked into the barn. In no time he'd gotten a good sweat worked up and his muscles were screaming. Unfortunately he was no closer to the answer Joe needed.

He'd been so confident when he'd decided to leave the circuit. He'd won nearly every championship, experienced the traveling, the ups and downs, broken bones and mouthfuls of dirt after being bucked. He'd been interviewed and flashed all over the television and every other media outlet.

When he'd walked away, he'd left knowing he'd dedicated years of his life to working, playing and living hard.

Ryan had left knowing the time had come to move on to another chapter, to settle down. Piper was a perk.

If Joe only needed him for the end of this one season, there would be no harm. Ryan hadn't exactly set a date for the school opening and he'd definitely be back by summer seeing as how it was only November. He'd be back by early spring at the absolute latest.

But was the choice to go just selfish on his part? Maybe a little, but he wasn't committing to staying on again or coming out of retirement. He was helping a friend in a desperate time. He knew Joe and Dallas had been winning and were close to the championship. If Ryan didn't step in and help Joe, all his friend's hard work would be for naught.

Ryan truly felt the pull, and not the pull to thrive on that adrenaline rush, but the pull to help his friend, to be able to do everything in his power to get that championship for him.

Another bale stacked and Ryan turned to see Piper holding the water hose, aiming it directly at him. The song in the background switched to Metallica's "The Struggle Within"...fitting for the abrupt turmoil.

He hadn't even heard her come up, which just indicated how loud he'd had his music and how deep in thought he'd been. He had no idea why she was here, but she had that rotten grin on her face and he knew he was in for it.

"I stopped by to see how the school was progressing, but then you were all shirtless and I thought maybe you could use cooling off." She tipped her head and her grin spread even wider. "Looking a little sweaty, cowboy."

He hooked his thumbs in his belt loops and grinned. "Try it. I guarantee you'll only get one shot before I'm on you and there will be repercussions for your naughtiness."

Piper bit her lip, then shrugged. "It's worth it."

The water hit him square in the chest, soaking him and sending water sluicing into his jeans. Ryan dodged the spray by making a hard right and running directly toward her. She'd just turned the hose back on him when he tackled her and sent her flying into a pile of hay. He wrestled the hose away from her and doused her.

That pale pink T-shirt she'd been wearing now molded to her every curve, outlining firm breasts and erect nipples.

Perhaps the torture was all on him, after all. Not that he would ever complain about seeing Piper in a wet T-shirt.

With hands up to protect her face, Piper laughed and came to her feet. Ryan let go of the nozzle, still holding on to the hose in case she decided to attack again.

"Give up?" he asked, staring directly at her chest and not caring if that was rude.

"I'll never admit defeat." She laughed as she walked toward him. "But you do look much cooler."

He tossed the hose aside and snaked an arm around her waist, hauling her against his chest. "I'm anything but cool."

Her eyes widened, then fell to his mouth. "Are we all alone in here?"

"Except for the animals, but I assure you, they don't care."

Ryan's hands slid up over her soaked shirt. When he

molded his hands around her breasts, she sighed, arching into him.

"And here I was just stopping by to see if you wanted dinner."

Ryan leaned forward, licked a droplet of water from her neck. "Yeah, I do," he whispered. "But I don't think we're suitable to be in public. Shame that."

He attacked her mouth. There was no finesse, no control. Only hot need to have her naked. Now.

There wasn't a time since they'd become intimate that he didn't want her. She looked like a walking fantasy right now and there was no way he could let her go without having her. The barn wasn't the most romantic place, but he'd pretty much killed the romance when he decided to have sex with her with blaring heavy metal for mood music.

Ryan backed her up to the saddle stand and eased her down to sit. In no time he'd pulled her shirt from her jeans and pried it up and over her head. The bra came next and then Ryan closed his mouth over one taut peak as Piper groaned and fisted her hands in his hair. Somewhere between the hose and the tackle he'd lost his Stetson.

The thought of being out in the open barn where anyone driving up could see them only added to his arousal. He needed her and everything else be damned.

Piper clutched at his shoulders, groaning as he licked, tugged and flicked her nipples with his tongue.

"Enough." She shoved him back, coming to her feet and reaching for his belt. "I want more."

"Here?" he asked, smiling at her control, her sudden dominance.

"Here, now and fast." She unfastened his wet jeans, then started tugging them down. "Think you can handle it, cowboy?"

Oh, he could handle it, but what he couldn't handle were

these damn wet jeans. The dead last thing he needed was restrictions for what he had in mind.

He kept his around his ankles and assisted her in ridding herself of her worn cowboy boots and wet jeans. That bright white thong was torn off in about a second and he spun her around.

"Brace your hands on the saddle," he whispered in her ear. "I've always wanted you like this."

"Then quit talking about it and do—"

He slammed into her from behind before she could finish her sentence. Yeah, tight and hot just as he'd imagined. Every single time with Piper was like the first. He never got used to the emotions, the euphoria that enveloped him. And he hoped to hell he never got used to how perfect they were together.

She leaned forward, tilting her hips higher, taking him deeper. Ryan clutched at her hips, afraid he'd bruise her if he held on as tightly as he truly wanted.

As he pumped in and out of her, he slid one hand up to palm a breast.

"Ryan," she panted. "Oh…"

That's right. His was the only name that would be on her lips if he had any say.

"You're so damn sexy," he said. "I can't get enough."

"Me, either."

Between her wet body bent over the saddle stand and her tight center, Ryan knew he was close. But Piper started jerking her hips faster, squeezing his hand tighter and within seconds she was contracting around him.

Ryan couldn't hold back another second. He pumped one last time and stilled. The climax shook his body, taking control as never before.

Beneath him Piper had rested her head on her arm and was still breathing hard.

When he'd finished trembling, he wrapped both arms around her waist and enveloped her body beneath his. He never wanted to be apart, never wanted this satisfaction to come to an end. But he had a decision to make and he feared her reaction wouldn't be in his favor.

"Did we make it out alive?" she muttered beneath him. "I'm pretty sure I had an out of body experience."

Ryan chuckled. "I feel honored I've made it into a cliché."

"God, that was…yeah."

"You feel so good," he told her, kissing her bare, wet shoulder. "Think we could just stay like this?"

"As long as you don't have anywhere to be or anyone coming for a visit."

"I do have a boy coming for training in the morning."

Beneath him Piper laughed. "I think he may get more schooling than he signed on for if he catches us like this."

Ryan eased up, pulling her with him. "You sure do look hot bent over a saddle stand, Red."

"You cowboys and your fantasies." She slid her arms up around his neck. "But I may have a fantasy or two of my own when it comes to you."

His hands slid down, cupping her bare rear end. "Feel free to use me for any and all fantasies from here on out."

Her eyes widened. "Are you…"

"I'm thinking long-term, Red. You know I want to settle with roots here. I've become a member of the Texas Cattleman's Club, I'm opening a rodeo school in the spring. I'm pretty happy with my life and I'm more than happy with the way we're heading."

"And where are we heading, Ryan?" she asked, her eyes searching his.

"I want to share our relationship," he told her. "We always seem to stay in."

"Because we're always naked," she told him with a smile. "Besides, you took me to Claire's last week."

"Yes, but we've been to Claire's as friends before. I want to take you as my girlfriend."

Piper's smiled widened. "I so wish there was another term for that. I mean, we are thirty and that sounds so high school. But I do love the fact you want to go public."

He kissed her softly, passionately, then pulled back. "Maybe public can wait till tomorrow. I'd rather work on some of those fantasies you had in mind."

Ryan led her to the tack room where he closed the door. He wanted to enjoy tonight. He wanted to spend hours of bliss with nothing between them.

Tomorrow he would tell her he'd made up his mind to rejoin the circuit for a few months to help a friend win the championship. He would try his damnedest to persuade her to come along with him and they could still be just as happy on the road.

And while all that sounded perfect in a dream world, Ryan knew he wouldn't be feeling so nervous about telling her if he thought she'd take the news well.

Yeah, his nerves didn't come from the thought of telling her; his unsettled worry stemmed from her reaction. Deep down he knew she would hate this news. But would she hate it enough to stay behind? Would she look beyond the fact he was leaving again and see what they mean to each other?

Morning would come all too soon and he'd have his answer.

Fourteen

Piper stretched. Muscles screamed, but her body had never felt better.

She glanced across the room to the small picture on Ryan's nightstand—a picture of the two of them as kids. Messy, dirty, holey jeans and cowboy hats. Piper smiled as she remembered that day. She'd wanted to impress Ryan and had convinced him to come to her house to meet her dad.

Walker Kindred had snapped a picture of the two of them in front of Piper's mare, Flash. Piper had never been more proud to be the daughter of a rodeo star. But that stardom had certainly come at a price and she and her mother had paid it.

Of course, she couldn't look at that picture and be sad. That was the first picture of her and Ryan together. All these years later he still had it, and in a frame, no less. She was well aware he had random pictures of them together, but knowing he felt this one was worthy of being the only one in his bedroom told her how special that moment was to him, as well. How special she was to him.

How could she deny her feelings? How could she pretend they were still just friends? The man practically worshipped her. He did everything for her, cared for her and had showed her what true friendship was all about. And isn't that how most couples started?

The intimacy with Ryan was amazing and she hoped their new, sexual relationship continued to grow. Dare she hope for something more?

He'd stated he was ready to settle down, ready to move on to the next stage of his life and he'd made it no secret he wanted to try with her.

A piece of her truly hoped this was headed toward something permanent, something…legal. Never before had she envisioned herself married. There were so many marriages popping up around town and she'd been thrilled for each and every couple, but had never once thought this would happen to her.

But now she teetered on the brink of daydreaming about a wedding. She'd want it outside, maybe in the fall with all the beautiful colors of nature surrounding them. A simple dress because she wasn't one to fuss over clothes.

Of course, the time and place didn't matter so long as Ryan was the man at the end of the aisle.

A giggle bubbled up within her. God, now she'd not only started envisioning weddings, she was on the verge of giggling. Could she act more like a teen girl?

But there was something special about moving to another level with her best friend. Piper hoped all married couples experienced a fraction of the happiness she had. Ryan was home, he intended to stay and he'd made an advance with her and their relationship that she'd been terrified of, but she was so glad she'd taken that leap with him.

Rolling over with a smile, she put her hand out and encountered a still-warm sheet. She glanced at the clock. Almost seven. Those rancher cowboys were always up so blasted early.

But the smell of coffee wafted through his house and Piper pulled herself out of bed. She snagged one of his plain white T-shirts from the top of a laundry basket in the corner of his room. After sliding into it, and relishing at the coziness, she padded barefoot down the gleaming hardwood hallway toward the kitchen.

From the doorway she saw him wearing nothing but those low-slung jeans that molded to his backside beautifully, holding a coffee mug and staring out at the barn. The golden sunrise in the distance brightened the room, almost as if a new promise for the day lay ahead for them. There was happiness sliding into her life where there had once been sorrow and void. Ryan had given her hope, had given her a reason to believe again.

Piper tiptoed forward, crossing the room silently, and wrapped her arms around his shoulders. She loved the sexy, masculine scent that always lingered on his skin. Whether it was his soap or cologne, she didn't know.

"Morning," she murmured against his neck. "Have you been up long?"

He reached up, holding on to her arm. "Not really. Couldn't sleep."

"You could've woken me up."

Turning in her arms, he reached to the side and set the mug on the small breakfast table. He wrapped his thick arms around her and pulled her against his bare chest, which had become her favorite place to rest.

"I didn't want to bother you," he told her. "Besides, if I'd woken you in bed and we were both naked, I think you know what would've happened."

Piper peered up at him with a grin. "Would that be so bad?"

He nipped at her lips. "Not at all."

When he eased back, Piper took in the crease between his brows, the tension in his shoulders, the near frown on his devastatingly handsome face. Something weighed heavy on his mind and he was trying to figure it out on his own. She wasn't having any of that.

"What is it?" she asked.

Ryan smoothed a hand over her hair, pushing the way-ward curls away from her face. A fruitless attempt considering her hair was a wreck in the mornings, but he seemed to be agitated or nervous about something. Being on edge was not a quality she'd ever known Ryan to possess, which told her what he hadn't yet…something was wrong.

"Ryan."

"You know I have strong feelings for you."

It wasn't a question, but he didn't sound thrilled about the announcement, either, so Piper just nodded.

"When I say deeper, I mean like I'm pretty sure I'm falling in love with you, Red. I don't take this lightly."

Piper's breath caught. She'd had a feeling, but to hear the words come from his mouth…

"Ryan—"

"Wait—" he held up a hand "—I just need to get this out and then you can have the floor and say anything you need."

Piper nodded and stepped back, giving him space. Apparently whatever he needed to say was going to be life-altering and she needed to be closer to the door…in case she had to make a hasty exit. If he was calling this off, she would be utterly broken.

"When I moved back home I was more than ready to start this school, to become an active member with TCC and to really put down roots in Royal." He raked a hand over his messy bed-head. "I even imagined this, between us. I knew if I could somehow take us beyond our comfort level of being best friends, I was confident we could have something special."

Piper really, really liked what he was saying, but for each second he spoke she waited on the giant "but" that would inevitably come. And if he dashed her dreams, if he was trying to break things off, she would be crushed, heartbroken and shattered. But she had to remain strong for now until she knew what she was facing. So help her, if he decided he'd changed his mind, she'd kick his ass for making her envision a future with him.

"And what we've found is far greater than anything I ever imagined, Piper." He met her gaze and stepped forward. "I want you to know all of that. I want you to understand the level of my feelings for you, the fact that I would die before I ever let anyone or anything hurt you."

Tears pricked her eyes and she blinked them away. She honestly couldn't tell if he was getting ready to propose, tell her he had a fatal disease or if he was breaking up.

"You're scaring me, Ryan. Just say what you need to say. The groundwork has been laid."

Ryan sighed, reaching for her hands and squeezing them. "Joe called me yesterday."

For a moment the name didn't hit her, but when it did, dread settled in the pit of her stomach.

"Your old roping partner," she said slowly. "I'm assuming he wants you back and that's why you had to tell me your feelings so I'd be all mushy and happy on the inside before you delivered this blow."

Okay, so maybe she was jumping the gun and letting her anger seep in just a wee bit. But from the look on his face, she knew she'd nailed it.

Oh, God. The hurt. That instant, piercing pain that enveloped her nearly knocked her to her knees. How dare he do this to her, to them? Especially knowing how she felt about the circuit. Was he seriously just going to jump back in and say to hell with everything else?

"You've got to be kidding." She slid her hands from his and crossed her arms over her chest. "You get one phone call and you're ready to just throw in the towel on everything? The school, your new home and the club? Us?"

"Hear me out before you jump to conclusions."

Piper needed to do something, needed to keep busy so

Ryan wouldn't see her hands shaking…from fear, from anger. She went to the cabinet and pulled down a mug.

"By all means," she said, pouring herself a cup of coffee. "Don't let me stand in the way of your dream. Carry on."

Okay, she was a tad snarky and she'd already put up a wall of anger around her, but damn it, she'd known this could happen. She was more than aware of his love of the rodeo and she'd seen how the circuit got in the blood and became more addictive than drugs. She'd seen firsthand how this damn sport destroyed her family and she would not lay back and play the victim if Ryan chose to leave. This was as much her fault for getting her hopes up, for trusting him when he'd told her time and time again that he wasn't her father.

When she turned and leaned against the counter, her gaze sought his over the top of her mug.

"Joe's new partner that replaced me broke his leg last week," Ryan started, holding her gaze. "They only need me to finish out the season. Two months tops. I don't intend to return permanently, Piper. I hadn't planned on this, either, but Joe needs an answer soon and I can't leave him hanging."

Piper nearly choked on her coffee. Damn, she hated black anyway, but she wasn't breaking the tension by crossing the room for the milk. She needed the anger that enveloped her because if she let go of it, all she'd have left to hold on to would be fear, anguish and a flood of tears she'd be damned if she'd let him see. One had already leaked out, but she'd remain in control for as long as possible. She was a strong woman; she'd lived through rejection before.

"And leaving everything else hanging is something you're comfortable with." She silently commended herself for the iciness she'd been able to lace through her tone.

"That's just it," he told her, stepping toward her. "I don't want to leave anything hanging. My school won't open until spring anyway and I was hoping you'd come with me."

Piper froze, clutching her mug. "You what?"

"I want you to come with me."

"Let me get this straight." She set the mug on the granite countertop behind her and turned back to him, coming to stand at her full height. "You want me to uproot a life I love here, friends I love and friends who need me, just so you can get a few last kicks in?"

"You're not uprooting, Piper. It's two months. And it has nothing to do with my kicks."

She poked his chest. "You're damn right I'm not uprooting. You say two months, but what you really mean is two months now and when next season rolls around maybe a few more then and before you know it, you've gotten sucked back in."

The muscle in Ryan's jaw ticked. Yeah, he may be angry but she was fuming.

"I'm not your father," he said through gritted teeth.

"From where I'm standing you're exactly like him."

Ryan shook his head, placing his hands on his narrow hips. "And that's been hanging between us this whole time, hasn't it? You've been waiting on me to go back. You've been waiting on me to screw up so you could throw your father back in my face. The one man who you trusted as a little girl, the one man who'd let you down. Well, if you want to play that card, fine. I can't stop you, but you damn well know I'm a man of my word, Piper, and when I say I'll be back, I will. It's up to you what you want to do with that information."

"You're right," she agreed. Piper cursed the lone tear that slid down her cheek. So much for control. "But for how long will you be back, Ryan? I can't fault you for loving the rodeo. I can't fault you for wanting to help your friend. But I can fault you for promising me to stay and then expecting me to be happy when you're not. I can fault you for pulling our relationship into something I'd only dreamed of and I can fault you for making me love you. Because I do."

Piper paused, swallowed and wiped at her damp cheek. "God help me, Ryan, I do love you. But I can't wait for you to decide if you're going to stay or go. And I can't just give up my job, my friends, and wait on you to make up your mind on what you truly want because I'm convinced you don't know."

"But I do, Red. I know what I want."

She smiled through the pain. "Yes, you do. It's just that you can't have it all at the same time, so you'll have to choose."

When he remained silent, the fullness he'd placed in her heart shattered and each and every shard sliced into her. Even as he stood with tears brimming in his eyes, she couldn't believe he wasn't backing down. Of course, neither was she, so they were at a standstill.

Pride…it was a fickle emotion that ruined lives.

Running a hand through her mass of curls, Piper nodded. "It's okay. I won't make you say it. I'll get my stuff and be on my way. Go ahead and call Joe."

Piper didn't wait on him to respond, to tell her she was wrong. The entire way back to the bedroom where they'd made love and shared dreams of the future, she waited on him to call her name.

But silence filled the house.

Fifteen

Today wasn't as bad as the past few days at work had been. At least that was a positive in Piper's life.

Alex still hadn't regained his memory. Her house renovations were at a standstill because, well, she'd been spending more and more time at Ryan's house and her priorities had shifted.

Ryan. Even his name made her ache. But she would not give in to the anguish. She'd known his leaving was a very real possibility even though he'd denied it adamantly. She'd seen it before, that confidence in retirement, but all it took was one simple phone call for the two men she'd loved to walk easily out of her life.

Oh, her father had claimed he'd be back, but at that point her mother had had enough and set the divorce in motion. It had been her father's "get out of jail free" card because the man had barely looked back.

Piper couldn't blame Ryan for going back to rodeo. That was the life he knew, craved, loved. After his mother passed, he'd escaped to the circuit and had never known any other way.

Staying home, founding a rodeo school for children was a wonderful idea, but in all reality he probably wasn't ready to hang up his rope just yet.

But by the time he decided to come back to Royal,

would she be available? Would she just keep waiting for a time that may or may not come?

There was no one else she'd ever gotten that close with. And if he chose to sell his ranch, nix the school plans and travel around the country again, Piper would survive. She'd hurt more than she'd ever known possible, but she'd live through it.

Piper pulled into her drive and sighed at the unfamiliar vehicle. A very shiny, very new-looking full-size truck with a nice set of wheels. Who was blocking her garage door? The cost of a truck like that would complete all her necessary renovations, that's for damn sure.

At least the roof was finished, as were the kitchen and bath. And finally, thank you, God, the A/C had been installed. All that was left on the inside was the trim work in the living room. Now she was slowly saving for new siding and stone, but that would be a while down the road.

That's it, she told herself as she grabbed her purse from the seat. Think long term about living in this little bungalow she'd always loved and not long term about Ryan because that window of opportunity had slammed shut when she'd rejected his offer to go on the road.

But that was a depressing thought for another time because there was a man on her porch swing, looking very much like he belonged there.

And it wasn't just any man. It was Walker Kindred, her father.

Piper squared her shoulders and tilted her chin as she hoisted her purse up onto her shoulder. She mentally prepared herself to face the man she used to call Daddy, yet hadn't seen in nearly fifteen years—glimpses on television didn't count.

As she approached the steps he came to his feet, slower

than how she'd remembered him moving, whether from age or caution, she didn't know.

She stared at him, unsure of what to say, and he stared right back. Obviously they were at a standstill, but if he had the courage to make it this far, surely he had the courage to start the conversation and explain what had brought him here after all this time.

Piper tried to tamp down the little girl inside her, the one who'd have given anything to have her father come to her. She was an adult now. She was tougher, but her father had come at a time when she was vulnerable. How many more blows could she take in such a short time?

She started forward, but froze when he spoke.

"You look beautiful."

Piper stopped, her foot on the bottom step. "Well, of all the things I expected you to say, that wasn't it."

He grinned. "I wasn't quite sure what I'd say, either. I had hoped something would come to me once I got here."

Piper remained silent again. She hated the awkward silence, hated that she didn't know how to act, how to feel around the man who'd given her life.

"I wasn't sure when you'd be home," he told her, taking off his white cowboy hat and toying with the edges. "I hope it's okay I waited on your porch."

Piper nodded as awkwardness settled between them. They may be family, but they were total strangers. Seeing as how she never thought this moment would come, Piper was at a loss for words. Well, seeing him brought back all the hurt, so she had words for him, she just thought it best to remain silent and not make this any worse.

Walker shook his head. "It's just so good to see you, Piper Jane. I guess while I was sitting here thinking, I just imagined an innocent teenager pulling up. I forget you're a grown woman."

"I won't get into the fact you could've seen me turn into that woman anytime you chose, but that's in the past." She crossed her arms over her chest, to keep the hurt from seeping in any further. So much for keeping those snarky words bottled inside. "What are you doing here?"

He took a step forward toward the edge of the porch. "I'm here to see you. I have some things to discuss. Is there a time that's good for you?"

Piper looked at him, really looked. His skin was pale, wrinkles fanned out around his eyes and he was thinner than she remembered.

No matter how he'd hurt her, he was her father. She was still reeling over Ryan's departure, so this was really sucky timing. Seriously, could she not catch a break?

"You can come in now," she told him. It's not as though she had a hot date this evening or any plans. "The house is being fixed up a little at a time, so be cautious in the living room. There are probably still some tools out and the trim is lying around."

After brushing past him, Piper unlocked the front door and gestured him inside.

"We can go into the kitchen to get away from this mess." She motioned toward the back of the house. "I can see what I have to eat if you're hungry."

Walker remained in her living area and shook his head. "I didn't come to impose, Piper. But we can talk in the kitchen."

Piper set her purse on the island and went to grab a bottle of water from the fridge. She needed to do something with her hands or he'd see they were not quite so steady. Déjà vu from the experience she'd had in Ryan's kitchen a few days ago.

"Want one?" she asked, holding the cold bottle up.

"No, thanks."

She untwisted the cap and took a drink. What she needed was a beer, but she'd save that for when her father left. She was off work tomorrow and she had every intention of getting good and drunk tonight. She may even sit and watch Lifetime movies just to torture herself further with one happy ending after another.

"I'm sorry this visit is a bit…strained," he told her, taking a seat at her small kitchenette. "I know you're wondering why I just showed up at your house unannounced after all this time."

Piper didn't say a thing as she waited on him to struggle with his own words. In the years she'd lived with him, she'd never seen her father be anything but strong and confident. Now he seemed not only worn and tired, but nervous and unsure.

"What I did, the way I went about handling the divorce and being a father to you, was wrong."

Piper clutched her bottle until the plastic cracked. "If this is—"

"No, Piper." He held up a hand, shaking his head. After tossing his hat onto her table, he continued, "This is something that's been years coming. It needs to be said and you need to hear it."

Nodding, she pursed her lips together. Apparently, Walker Kindred had some sort of guilt laying heavy on him, as well he should. And he was right—this apology was a long time coming.

"I was so caught up in being in the limelight, of being popular and at the top of my game, bringing in more money than we would ever need, I completely lost focus of what was important."

Piper glanced away. God, she was a coward. For years she would've given anything to hear her father say he was sorry, to confess that he was wrong. But now as an adult, she didn't care so much. There was a little girl deep inside her that would forever be scarred by not having her father around, yet seeing him on television smiling and waving to thousands of fans.

She hated being cynical and hard where he was concerned, but she honestly didn't know how to handle this unscheduled, uncomfortable reunion.

"So why are you here now?" she asked, bringing her gaze back to his.

"I have cancer."

Piper was so glad she was leaning against the counter, otherwise she would've fallen to the floor. She set her bottle behind her and wrapped her arms around her waist. Questions whirled around in her head.

She'd been wrong. The hurt could slice deeper. He may have neglected her, may have lived by his own selfish ways, but this was still her father and the word *cancer* brought on a whole host of emotions…namely fear.

She swallowed and held his gaze. "Tell me this isn't a deathbed confession."

Walker shook his head. "Not at all. Actually, I just finished my last chemo treatment and my doctors are confident I'll be perfectly fine."

A wave of relief swept through her. "Good. So you're here because you…"

He came to his feet and crossed the room to stand in front of her. "I'm here because when I was told I had cancer, I immediately thought of what I'd done with my life. The championships I'd won, the people I'd met, the bonds I formed on the road with crew and partners. But there was a huge void in the decades that played out in my head. You and your mother."

Piper cursed the tears that pricked her eyes. Damn vulnerability. Why couldn't she hold it together lately?

"I wanted to wait until I was finished with all of my treatments before I came to see you, to beg you for another chance. I know I missed important years, years I'll never get back, but all I can do is try to be a father now."

Piper sighed. That young girl who lived inside her, the one who'd grown up with a single mother, wanted to throw her arms around the man, take him at his word that he wanted to be part of her life, and forget all that had happened in the past.

But she was not only older now, she was more skeptical.

"It's not that easy. I want it to be—you don't know how much I do," she told him. "But that hurt, that pain that settled in when you left for good, it won't just go away because you were sick and saw the proverbial light."

God, she sounded harsh. She truly didn't mean to be, but how many times could she let her heart lay on the line only to have someone toss it aside for their own self-centered needs.

"I'm not asking for a miracle," he explained, his dark eyes searching hers. "I'll do what you need, go as slow as you like, to see if we can repair or even start fresh with a father-daughter relationship."

"Are you staying in Royal?"

"I'm staying at the small hotel just outside of town," he told her, sliding his hands into his jeans' pockets. "I checked in before I came here."

Piper was torn in so many directions, but she knew there was no way she could in good conscience let her father stay at a hotel. He'd extended the olive branch and now she had to decide whether or not to grab hold.

"We won't be able to get to know each other if you're at a hotel," she said, offering a small smile. "I have a spare room and it's even been freshly painted."

Piper couldn't believe big-time rodeo hotshot Walker

Kindred's eyes misted as a smile spread across his face. Hope speared through her at the thought that this might just work. Her father might finally be ready to be part of her life. Time would tell.

As it would with Ryan.

She sighed. One man at a time.

"I'd really like that," her father told her. "But I don't want you uncomfortable."

Piper shrugged. "I'm not uncomfortable."

"Did I ruin any plans for the night?"

She laughed. "Yeah, I was going to get drunk. Care to join me?"

"I'd love to, but I can't with the meds I'm taking." He smiled. "But I'd be happy to keep popping your tabs for you and work on a beer-amid out of your cans."

Piper laughed as hope spread through her. Maybe they could reconnect and maybe he'd stick through the holidays. Having her father for Thanksgiving would be an awesome gift.

A loud crash sounded through the house. Piper sprang out of bed, her bare feet slapping against the hardwood as she moved into the darkened hallway.

"Dad?" she called.

"I'm fine," he yelled back. "Sorry I woke you."

She followed his voice and found him coming to his feet in the living room. She flicked on the dimmer switch and left it turned down low so the glare from the bulb wouldn't blind them.

"What happened?" she asked.

He laughed, shaking his head. "I was trying to get to the kitchen for some water to take a nausea pill and I tripped over the sawhorse."

"God, I'm so sorry." She glanced at his plaid pajama

168 TO TAME A COWBOY

bottoms and navy T-shirt. Nothing appeared torn. "Did you hurt yourself?"

"I'm fine," he assured her, placing his hand on the wall for support. "I've taken harder hits falling off angry bulls."

Piper smiled. "Why don't you have a seat and I'll get that glass of water. Do you have your pill?"

He held up a large white pill. "I didn't lose it in the fall."

Laughing, Piper went to get a bottle of water from the fridge. She knew her father was weak from his treatments. She still couldn't get used to seeing him like this, almost frail and, well, older. The once-black hair was now silver and thin from the chemo, the wrinkles around his eyes deeper. The man had lived an entire life without her and now he was here to make amends.

One part of her was thrilled to have her dad back; another part was still skeptical he truly wanted a relationship with her. She couldn't hold back the excitement of getting to know her father again. If he decided to leave, she would be utterly crushed…again.

She honestly believed Walker was here because he loved her and wanted to work at a relationship.

Piper took the water back into the living room and grabbed a seat beside him on the couch.

"Here you go."

After taking his pill, he took another drink and screwed the cap back on. "Sorry again for waking you."

Piper waved a hand. "No problem. I haven't been sleeping that well anyway."

"Problems?"

She eyed him, wanting to laugh for the natural way he asked, but wanting to cry because he genuinely seemed to care and she'd always wanted that father-daughter bond.

"Sorry," he told her with a slight laugh. "I really have no room to ask."

"It's okay." On a sigh, Piper fell back against the cushions. "I'm having an…issue. Nothing I can't handle."

Insomnia, loss of appetite and random bursts of crying, then screaming into an empty room. Yeah, she was handling this breakup quite well. Like a champ.

"I know I have no right to pry," Walker said as he shifted to look at her. "But I'm more than happy to listen, and it's the middle of the night. Since you're not sleeping, we've got nothing else to do."

Piper looked at her father. Another sense of déjà vu settled in. Weeks ago she'd opened up to Ryan in the middle of the night. There was something about darkness that made it easier to open up, easier to not face reality and pretend that there was this special connection.

"I made a stupid mistake and fell in love."

Walker nodded as if he understood.

"And then I made an even stupider mistake and broke it off."

He lifted his brows. "Why was that?"

Piper glanced away, hating how shallow this was going to sound. "I couldn't handle his career decision."

"And what's his career?"

Bringing her eyes back up to his, she said, "Rodeo."

Walker Kindred ran a hand down his face and sighed. He shook his head and let out a laugh.

"God, Piper Jane. I just… I can't even think of what to say." He met her gaze and now hurt stared back at her. "I had no idea my actions would ruin your life."

"Why did you leave?" she asked, emotions clogging her throat. "Why did I never hear from you other than birthdays and Christmas?"

"I let my selfish ways lead my life." He eased back against the cushions, sliding one arm along the back of the sofa. "I wish I could tell you something more tragic, but I was not ready for parenting, or at least not ready for staying home every day, day in and day out. I begged your mother to take you on the road with me. I begged her to homeschool you, but that was selfish of me. Even if you two had joined me, I wouldn't have devoted the time and attention both of you needed."

Piper brushed her hair behind her ear. "I hate your answer, but I appreciate your honesty."

She toyed with the hem of her sleep shorts and wished she could've had her father around to talk to years ago. Even though she wasn't happy with what he told her, she knew he was speaking from his heart and he'd come to her for a fresh start. And honesty was the place to begin if they wanted a firm foundation for building any relationship.

"Who's the cowboy?"

Piper sighed. "Ryan Grant."

Walker's smile widened. "No kidding? Your childhood friend? That man tore up the circuit. It was a shame when he announced his retirement. Wasn't he opening a school or something?"

"A rodeo school for kids," she told him. "He already has most everything ready and had even asked one high school boy to come on full-time in the summer."

"Will he be home for Thanksgiving?"

Piper shrugged. "Honestly, we didn't discuss that."

"You're wishing you hadn't called it quits?"

Shaking her head, Piper groaned. "I don't even know what I wish. I really don't. I wish he hadn't made me fall in love. I wish he hadn't been so damn giving… I wish he hadn't left without even considering me… And I hate that I'm so selfish about it, but I wanted that love. I wanted him and the life he'd laid out for us."

Walker reached out to her cheek to wipe away a tear that Piper hadn't even realized had escaped.

"No man is worth your tears," he whispered. "Including me."

Piper wiped her eyes, hating the vulnerability she had no control over lately. "You're both worth my tears."

Walker started forward as if to hug her, but stopped.

Piper didn't ask, didn't care if she seemed vulnerable. It had been way too long since she'd felt the strong embrace of her father. She reached out, wrapped her arms around his broad shoulders and squeezed.

"Oh, Piper," he murmured as his arms enveloped her. "I've missed you."

Piper cried. Damn it, she couldn't be strong another second. She cried for the little girl who'd never really known her father. She cried for the woman who broke it off with Ryan. And she cried for the reunion she was having because, God help her, she wanted this to last. She wanted this relationship more than she thought possible.

"I love you, Piper," her father whispered.

Piper squeezed her eyes as tears slid down her cheeks. "I love you, too, Dad."

<u>Sixteen</u>

Only one night after the first show, Ryan was already restless. This was not the life he'd wanted, not the life he'd planned when he'd hung up his rope and chosen not to be a Header anymore.

Now he was in a hotel room, same hotel smell and same tacky decor as all the other countless ones over the years. But it had never bothered him before. When he'd sat in his rooms in the past, he'd either have a few beers with his partner or some other members of the circuit or they'd hit a honky-tonk and dance with some mighty fine ladies.

But there was only one lady tonight who he was thinking of. Only one lady who was occupying his time, his thoughts, his every breath. And being on the road was pure hell.

Nearly every second since he'd left, Ryan had wondered what Piper was doing, how she was feeling and if she would ever forgive him. Would she blow him off? Would she try to be all prideful and pretend he hadn't hurt her? Or would she light into him and let him know exactly how much she hated him?

Only seven more weeks until he would officially be done. He would be taking a break for the holidays but he doubted he'd be welcome in her home.

Pain sliced deep through him. Why hadn't he insisted

she come? Why hadn't he done something to make her see he wasn't brushing her or their relationship aside?

Instead of fighting, he'd watched her cry, watched her pour her heart out through tears and then turn and quietly walk out of his life.

What the hell kind of man did that?

A man who didn't think he'd truly lose the woman of his dreams. A small sliver of hope still lived within him that all was not lost, but he hadn't heard a word from her since he'd left. His cell was quiet and Ryan feared with each passing moment of silence, the wedge between them was growing wider and wider. Over the past several days Ryan had pulled out his phone to call her, but he always backed out because he was a coward. The thought of her rejecting him terrified him, so he thought it best to just let her think, let her have some space.

At last night's show, he'd not performed to the best of his abilities because his mind had been elsewhere. Joe would've been better off with another partner who was invested and had his head in the competition. Ryan had merely been filling a spot and nothing more.

Another first for him. Never in all his time on the circuit had he allowed a woman to come between him and the love of his job. No one had ever been important enough or worth the distraction. Distractions could get cowboys hurt; he'd seen it numerous times over the years and had sworn that would never be him.

Because he had to finish what he was doing, help secure Joe that championship cash so he could save his ranch because the man was too prideful to take a handout. But Ryan was going to try again because this scenario of trying to help was not working. Then when Ryan went home, he'd do so with a ring and a promise. He wouldn't leave Piper again.

Ryan was a firm believer that if something was supposed to happen, it would. And in his heart, he knew that he and Piper were not over. They'd hit a bump, one he'd placed in their path, but they would get over it together. If he had to carry her over it, they would make it.

He crossed to the wide window overlooking downtown Dallas and raked a hand through his hair. He should just call her. The worst she could do is tell him to go to hell and hang up, but he really didn't think she would.

He'd been the one to make this mess; the least he could do was try to smooth things over so it didn't get any worse.

Just as he pulled his cell from his jeans' pocket, someone knocked on his door. Confident it wasn't a buckle bunny, since he'd checked in under an alias, he moved through the room and checked the peep hole. His partner, Joe, stood on the other side.

Ryan slid the chain across and opened the door. "What's up?"

"There's a nice group of very interested ladies in the bar downstairs. We were all wondering where you were. Since I'm married, they aren't so interested in me."

It wasn't long ago that he would've been right down there with all of them. And even though the media played him out to be a total player, he truly wasn't. Other than one time he'd had a one-night stand, he'd never taken any wanna-be-cowboy-lovers back to his room.

And there wasn't a woman down there who could even compare to the one woman he was needing tonight. No woman would ever compare to Piper.

"I'm good," he told Joe. "I may turn in early, but I'll see you first thing in the morning."

Joe shook his head and laughed. "Dude, you've got it bad. Why the hell did you agree to come back? You're miserable."

"I wouldn't say miserable," Ryan countered defensively, resting his hand above his head on the door. "I screwed up today, but I'll be back in it tomorrow."

"Ryan, we were partners a long time. I know you." Joe settled his hands on his hips, staring directly into Ryan's eyes. "You don't have off days. You never have. Today was mediocre for some, but for you? I didn't know you could get sidetracked and you did. That right there tells me you don't belong here. Your heart has found somewhere else to be."

Ryan stared at Joe for a second, then busted into a fit of laughter. "Partner, are you watching too many talk shows and getting in touch with your feelings?"

Joe shrugged. "Maybe I don't want to see you throw something away just to win a championship."

"I don't care about winning," Ryan told his partner. "I care about getting that for you."

"When I called you, you never mentioned how fast or how deep your roots were already. I honestly assumed you'd be chomping at the bit to have another round on the circuit, even if there's only seven weeks left in the season."

Ryan nodded. "Probably had you called when I first left, I would've felt that way, but something changed when I went home. I know I went with every intention of starting a school for kids, but there was so much more than that."

He'd fallen in love.

Yeah, he could freely admit it now. He was spurs over chaps in love with Piper Kindred.

"Do I need to search for another partner?" Joe asked, a knowing grin spreading across his face.

Ryan nodded. "It might be best. I won't leave you until you have someone."

Joe nodded. "I'm going to miss you, man. But I've never seen you so unhappy doing something you love. Whoever this woman is, you must love her a whole lot to replace the rodeo."

Ryan laughed. "You remember the rodeo star from when we were younger, Walker Kindred? I'm in love with his daughter."

Joe's eyes widened. "Wow. Wasn't she your best friend in school or something?"

"Yeah. Now she's the woman I'm going to marry."

Joe smiled. "Good for you. We'll start looking for a new partner as soon as possible. If you have to fake an illness or injury to get out, I got your back, partner. Why don't you go on home? We have the next two days off and I'm sure I can ask Dillon to step up."

"Thanks, man." Ryan reached one arm out, pulling his friend into the male version of a hug, one arm around the neck with a hard pat on the back. "Now go tell the ladies I'm taken, as well. Introduce them to Dillon."

Joe lifted his brows. "I'm pretty sure he already went off with a lady earlier. But I'll break the news gently that you're off the market."

After Ryan closed the door, he was more anxious than ever to call Piper. But what if she shot him down? A phone call was so…impersonal. He didn't want to be a coward about this, but he also didn't want to take the easy route, either.

He was only in Dallas. Thankfully they weren't that far from Royal. He'd rent a car and drive. It was only six hours. Or he could check on flights. Surely there was something that would get him home soon. Even if he had to pay a private pilot—that would be the best money he'd ever spent.

But before he could approach her, he had to lay some groundwork. He wanted to be able to go to her with absolute certainty that what they had was real, was the beginning of a lifelong commitment.

* * *

Piper had never made Thanksgiving dinner. Having a dinner for one was so…depressing and a waste of time. But now that her father was back, she figured she'd better at least give it a try. If she botched it up, at least they could laugh and have a good story to tell later.

Walker had gone out to visit some old friends and Piper was juggling groceries while trying to get her key in the back door. Before she could turn the knob, the door flew open and Piper gasped.

"Ryan."

He reached out, taking most of her load from her hands. "I nearly gave up waiting on you to come home," he said, setting the bags on the counter. "How much food do you need here, Red?"

Piper stood in the doorway, still clutching her keys, staring at the one man she didn't think she'd see for at least two more months. Her heart pounded from the initial shock of someone in her house when she thought she'd be alone, but even more than shock was hope. Ryan was back for a reason and she hoped it wasn't just for a turkey dinner.

"What are you doing here?" she asked, totally ignoring his question.

He glanced in the bags and then turned to her, resting a hand on the counter. "Hoping to get you to cook for me."

Piper stepped inside, slowly, still shocked that Ryan was standing in her kitchen. Maybe he'd come back because he'd been injured.

"Are you hurt?" she asked.

"Actually, I am."

Her eyes raked over him, taking in his dark gray shirt and faded jeans, scuffed boots. "You look…" Hot as hell. "Fine."

Stepping closer, Ryan stood toe to toe with her and

grinned. "My heart is broken, Red. You took it when you walked out on me."

That very second tears burned her eyes. "I may have physically walked out, but you left us before I could leave you."

Ryan nodded. "That's a fair statement and one I'm sure you won't let me live down anytime soon. But I've come to the conclusion that I'll put up with you mocking me, so long as you let me back in your life."

"I want to make you suffer," she told him.

He reached for her, cupping her face between his strong hands. "I've suffered, Red. Believe me, I've suffered."

"What about the circuit? Are you just here for Thanksgiving?"

With the holiday being tomorrow, Piper didn't want to jump to conclusions, but neither did she want to give up hope.

Stroking her cheeks with his thumbs, Ryan shook his head. "I'm here for the duration if you'll have me."

A tear slipped over and she blinked the others back. "What about Joe and the championship?"

"I'll think of something," he told her. "If I have to pay off his debt, I'll find a way."

Piper closed her eyes. "Why now, Ryan? Why did you come back?"

"Because watching you walk away was one of the hardest things I've lived through. Because I was miserable without you and because you've gotten into my system. I was a mess out there because you were on my damn mind all the time. You were wreaking havoc on my work."

"So sorry," she said as she met his gaze and offered a half smile.

"You're not sorry, you're gloating." He held her gaze and opened his mouth a couple times before he finally spoke, as if he needed to gather the right words. "I can't be without you again, Piper."

Moisture filled his eyes. In all of their years as friends, she'd only seen him cry at the death of his parents.

"What will happen when you want to leave again? When you get the urge to have an adventure or if someone needs you?"

"First of all, being with you is adventure enough," he informed her.

A laugh escaped her.

"Second—" he nipped at her lips "—the only person that needs me is you."

Piper opened her mouth, ready to defend herself, but he laid a fingertip over her lips.

"And I need you," he murmured. "More than I ever thought possible."

Ryan rested his forehead against hers and sighed. "I'll resort to begging if I need to, Red. But for the love of God, tell me something. Tell me you forgive me or you'll think about it. Anything."

Piper smiled. "As much as I'd love to see you groveling, I'll cut you some slack."

"Does that mean you love me?"

She wrapped her arms around his waist and held on, not ready to let go anytime soon. "It means if you try to leave again, I'll castrate you."

Ryan picked her up, spun her around and kissed her. Hands-in-her-hair, devouring-her-lips, making-her-breathless-with-want kissed her. Yeah, they would have one hell of a reunion tonight.

"Uh, should I come back later?"

Piper jumped back. She'd been so caught up in the blissful moment she hadn't heard the back door open, nor had she heard her father step in. While she wasn't a teen, she was still embarrassed that he'd seen her getting hot and heavy with Ryan.

"Piper?" Ryan asked, glancing between her father and her.

She smiled. "A lot happened while you were gone."

Walker stepped forward, extending his hand. "From what I heard and saw, I think I should say welcome to the family."

Piper and Ryan laughed.

"He hasn't proposed, Dad."

Ryan shook Walker's hand. "No, I haven't. I think he just did it for me."

Stepping back and sliding his hand into his pocket, he pulled out a small box. Lifting the lid, he got down on one knee.

"I know you aren't one for mushy or traditional things," he started, "but I have to propose the right way."

Piper stared at the simple band of diamonds. Placing a hand over her mouth, she tried not to start crying again like some lovesick woman.

"I've loved you since you punched me in my face. I've never met anyone who cares for people the way you do. I'm not worthy of your love, but I'm asking for it anyway."

From the corner of her eye, Piper saw her father step back. The fact that he was present for the most important moment of her life was not lost on her. He had been absent for nearly everything, but now, when she was starting a new chapter, he was there.

"The band is flat because you work with your hands a lot, but we can get something else if you want."

Piper grabbed his hands and tugged until he came back to his feet to stand in front of her. "This is perfect," she told him.

"It's got diamonds all the way around and it's called a

Forever band." He removed the ring and slid it onto her finger. "I didn't want traditional, not for you. And forever seemed to sum up my feelings perfectly."

Piper stared down at the band on her finger and couldn't suppress her tears or her smile. She'd cried so much lately, but she didn't care. Ryan had come back to her and so had her father. All those tears were worth it.

"You were pretty sure of yourself, cowboy." She looked back up at him. "Coming here with a ring."

"I wasn't sure of myself. I was a nervous wreck. But I was sure of us."

Piper threw her arms around Ryan and whispered in his ear, "I love you. And when my father isn't looking, I'll show you just how much."

He wrapped his arms around her and whispered back, "Can you send him to the store for more groceries?"

"Okay," Walker said across the room. "I may be old, but I can still hear. You two need privacy. I'll just go…out. Somewhere. For a few hours. Um…yeah, I'll find some-where."

Piper laughed at her father's stuttering, his red face. "Seriously, Dad. You can stay. I love having the two most important men in my life here with me. Besides, I have no clue how to get started on preparing this Thanksgiving feast for tomorrow."

Ryan stepped back, unbuttoned his cuffs and rolled up his sleeves. "Well, Red, you're in luck. I used to help my mama in the kitchen and Thanksgiving was her specialty."

As they started preparing dressing and pies, Piper's heart swelled. In her tiny, remodeled kitchen they worked and she couldn't have been happier. Ryan and her father spoke of the rodeo. They'd traveled on two separate cir-cuits, but the level of respect was evident from both men.

"And you needed to help your partner?" Walker asked.

"Did he find someone to fill in already? Someone as good as you?"

Ryan shrugged as he continued to tear bread and throw it in the bowl for the stuffing. "He's no slacker. I just worry about Joe not getting that championship money."

"I'll give it to him," Walker said easily.

Piper spun around from the counter where she'd been pouring filling into a pie crust. "What?"

"I told you I worked my ass off and have more money than I know what to do with."

Piper's gaze shot to Ryan's, then back to her dad's. "Wow, um. That's great, Dad."

Ryan nodded. "If you're serious, Walker, then we'll split it, but it's not necessary for you to pitch in. I had already thought of just giving Joe the money so he could relax and not be so stressed and his family wouldn't have to worry anymore."

"Fine then." Walker smiled. "Damn, I'm glad I'm back home."

Piper knew in her heart Ryan was here to stay. The man hadn't been gone too long before he realized where his heart belonged and she was quite certain that had a friend not needed him to begin with, he never would've left.

Piper crossed the room and bent to hug her father. "I'm glad you're back, too. This will be the most memorable Thanksgiving ever."

Seventeen

Ryan closed and locked the bedroom door. He didn't know what had shocked him more today, that Piper had agreed to marry him or that her father was back and they seemed to be building a relationship. He'd give anything to have his parents back and he was proud of Piper for giving her father another chance.

She came out of the bathroom wearing a short, silky black gown that stopped at midthigh and had a deep vee in the front.

"God, I've missed your lingerie," he said.

Piper laughed. "As opposed to my sunny disposition and my snarky comments?"

"I've missed it all." He pushed off the door and started unbuttoning his shirt. "I never want to be away from you again."

Piper held his gaze. "On that we can agree. I was miserable and then when Dad came I was even more torn up. But you're both here, you're both in my life and I can't ask for more."

"I'm surprised you seem so comfortable with your dad. Did you two have a fast reunion?"

She nodded, holding on to the post of the bed. "He has cancer."

"My God, Piper." Ryan froze. "Is he okay? Are you?"

"I'm okay and so is he. He's finished his treatments and the doctors say he's well on his way to recovery. But he told me it made him realize what was important. At first I was angry that it took a potentially terminal illness to wake him up, but then I decided I had a second chance and if he was willing to try, then so was I."

Ryan shrugged out of his shirt, tossed it aside and made fast work of his boots, socks and jeans. Standing in only his boxer briefs, he crossed to her.

"I'm glad you've been in the mood for second chances lately."

She tipped her face up to meet his and smiled. "I'm not as hard as I used to be. I guess that's what love does to you."

He slid his hands around her waist and tugged her against him. "Say it again. I'll never tire of hearing you say you love me."

She looped her arms around his neck. "I do, Ryan. I love you so much that I was completely shattered when you left."

Ryan didn't want to focus on the negative and he sure as hell didn't want to think about the ass he'd been.

"Let's look forward," he told her, nipping her lips. "Let's pretend I wasn't a jerk and now that my priorities are in the right order, we can start planning our wedding. Because I can't wait until you are Mrs. Piper Grant."

A wide smile spread across her freshly washed face. "I love how that sounds."

His hands slid up her bare arms. Taking her thin straps, he eased them down. "I love how you dress for me," he whispered. "I love how I can peel you out of this in no time. And I love how you feel around me."

The straps rested on her biceps and she slipped her arms free. The material hung on her breasts until Ryan gave one swift tug and sent the garment to the floor with a whoosh. She stepped out of it and stood in front of him wearing nothing but his ring.

"You undo me, Piper." His eyes raked over her as he ridded himself of his briefs. "I'm nothing without you."

"Show me," she told him as she held out her hands and led him toward the bed.

He tumbled down on top of her, sinking into the plush comforter. Easing her legs apart, he settled between her hips.

Resting his elbows beside her head, he lifted his body slightly. Watching her face, her parted lips, her soft eyes, Ryan slid into her in a slow, deliberate move that had her arching her back and closing her eyes.

"Look at me," he whispered. "Always look at me, at us."

Her eyes locked on to his and he felt her love, her power, all the way to his heart.

Her ankles locked behind his back as her hips lifted beneath his. Ryan knew she wanted fast and rough, but he wanted slow and memorable.

Setting the pace he wanted, he leaned down, kissed her lips then slid his mouth down the column of her throat until he found one pert nipple. When he clamped his mouth around her, she tightened her grip with her knees on his sides.

Her hips pumped faster and Ryan lifted his head. "You're in such a hurry."

"And you're not moving fast enough," she told him.

Ryan smiled, turning his attention to the other breast as he eased in and out of her. But there was only so much control he had and, when she tightened around him, he knew she was close.

Reaching down, he slid a hand between them and touched

her in her most intimate area. In no time Piper stilled, her body tensed as she bowed and cried out his name.

There was no more beautiful sight than Piper beneath him, coming undone, with his name on her lips. And because he'd held back as long as he could, Ryan gave one last thrust and allowed his climax to overtake him, reveling in the fact this was just the beginning of the best days of his life.

When their tremors ceased, Ryan eased down on top of her, stroking her side and whispering, "I love you" in her ear because he never wanted her to doubt it again.

"Are we going to have a big wedding?" he asked, rolling over just enough so he wasn't squashing her. "I imagine all of our friends will want to come since they've invited us to theirs."

Piper laced her fingers with his and rested their joined hands on her flat stomach. "I never wanted a big wedding, but I suppose we need to invite all of our friends."

"Do what you want, Piper," he told her. "If you want to fly to Vegas, we'll fly there tonight. If you want to plan something, we'll plan it."

Ryan watched the play of emotions on her face. Her brows were drawn, but then her eyes widened and a wide smile spread across her face.

"I'm going to need a real wedding," she told him, turning her head to meet his gaze. "Nothing elaborate. We can marry at your ranch. I'd like it outside with our closest friends."

Ryan grinned. "Sounds good to me."

"And I want my father to walk me down the aisle."

Ryan searched her face and nodded. "He would love that."

Piper sighed, snuggling deeper against him. "Timing is everything and I believe he came back now for a reason."

Ryan wrapped his arm around her and pulled her close. There was nothing that satisfied him more than seeing Piper so happy, so content.

"I never thought I'd marry you," he whispered. "I always knew I loved you, but I never thought I actually had a chance at winning your heart."

Her face tipped up to his. "Oh, you won my heart, cowboy. Now you're going to have a long, long time with your prize."

Ryan kissed the tip of her nose. "Best prize I ever won."

* * * * *

"No, Maksim. I refuse your new deal."

"It's a proposal, Caliope."

She took a step back, then another, making him feel she was receding forever out of reach. "Whatever you want to call it, my answer is still no. And it's a final no. You had no right to think you can seek redemption at my expense."

"The redemption I'm seeking is for you. I'm offering you everything I can, what you just admitted you need."

"I only said you left at a time when I most needed you, not that I need you still."

Every word fell on him like a lash, their pain accumulating until he was numb. But after leaving her, how could he have hoped for anything different?

* * *

Claiming His Own
is part of the No.1 bestselling miniseries from
Mills & Boon® Desire™ —
Billionaires and Babies: Powerful men…
wrapped around their babies' little fingers

CLAIMING
HIS OWN

BY
OLIVIA GATES

MILLS
BOON

Published in Great Britain 2013
by Mills & Boon, an imprint of Harlequin (UK) Limited,
Eton House, 18-24 Paradise Road, Richmond, Surrey TW9 1SR

© Olivia Gates 2013

ISBN: 978 0 263 90490 1

51-1113

Harlequin (UK) policy is to use papers that are natural, renewable and recyclable products and made from wood grown in sustainable forests. The logging and manufacturing processes conform to the legal environmental regulations of the country of origin.

Printed and bound in Spain
by Blackprint CPI, Barcelona

Olivia Gates has always pursued creative passions such as singing and handicrafts. She still does, but only one of her passions grew gratifying enough, consuming enough, to become an ongoing career—writing.

She is most fulfilled when she is creating worlds and conflicts for her characters, then exploring and untan- gling them bit by bit, sharing her protagonists' every heart-wrenching heartache and hope, their every heart- pounding doubt and trial, until she leads them to an indisputably earned and gloriously satisfying happy ending.

When she's not writing, she is a doctor, a wife to her own alpha male and a mother to one brilliant girl and one demanding Angora cat. Visit Olivia at www.oliviagates.com.

To my brother. Thanks for being you. Everyone who's ever known you will understand just what I mean.

Prologue

Eighteen months ago

Caliope Sarantos stared at the strip in her hand.

It was the third one so far. The two pink lines had appeared in each, glaring and undeniable.

She was pregnant.

Even though she'd been meticulous about birth control, she just…was.

A dozen conflicting emotions frothed over again, colliding inside her chest. Whatever she did about this, it would turn her world upside down, would probably shatter the perfection she'd forged with Maksim. If *she* didn't know what to feel about this, what would he…

Suddenly her heart fired so hard, she almost keeled over.

He was here.

As always, she felt Maksim before she heard him. Her whole being surged with worry this time rather than welcome. Once she told him, nothing would remain the same.

He walked into the bedroom where he'd first taught her what passion was, where he continued to show her there was no limit to the intimacies and pleasures they could share.

His wolf's eyes sizzled with passion as he strode to-

ward her, throwing away his tie and attacking his shirt as
if it burned him. He was starving for her, as usual. But
what she'd tell him was bound to extinguish his urgency.
An unplanned pregnancy was the last thing he expected.

This might end everything between them.

This could be her last time with him.

She couldn't tell him. Not before she had him.

Desperate desire erupted, consuming her sanity as she
met his urgency with her own, pulling him down to the
bed on top of her, trembling with the enormity of having
him in her arms. His lips fused to hers, his rumble of vo-
racity and enjoyment pouring into her, spiking her arousal.
Before she wrapped herself around him, he yanked her
up, bent her over one arm, had her breasts jutting in an
erotic offering. Pouring litanies of craving all over her, he
kneaded her breasts, pulling her nipples into the moist heat
of his mouth, sucking with such perfect force that each
pull had her screams of pleasure rising. Then he glided a
hand over her abdomen until he squeezed her trim mound.

Just as she screamed again, he slid two fingers between
the slickness of her folds, growling again as her arousal
perfumed the air.

With only a few strokes, he had her senses overloading
and release scorching through her body in waves, from
his fondling fingers outwards. He completed her climax
with rough encouragements before he slid down her body,
coming between her shaking legs, spreading them over
his shoulders, exploiting her every inch with hands, lips
and teeth until she was thrashing again.

"Please, enough," she moaned. "I need you...."

He subdued her with a hand flat on her abdomen, his
face set in imperious lines. "Let me have my fill of your
pleasure. Open for me, Caliope."

His command had her legs falling apart, surrendering everything to him. He latched on to her core, drank her flowing essence and arousal until she felt her body would unravel with the need for release. As if he knew the exact moment when she couldn't take any more, he tongued her, and she cried herself hoarse on a chain reaction of convulsions.

Before her rioting breath had a chance to subside, he slid up her sweat-slick body, flattening her to the bed. Her breath hitched and her dropping heat shot up again as soon as his tongue filled her, feeding her his taste mingled with that of her pleasure. It was unbelievable how he ignited her with only a touch.

He fused their lips for feverish seconds before he reared up, his eyes searching hers, his erection seeking her entrance. Finding both her eyes and her core molten, he growled his surrender and sank into her.

She cried out at the first inevitable shock of his invasion, that craved expansion of her flesh as it yielded to his daunting potency and poured more readiness to welcome him.

He groaned his own agonized pleasure as he rose to his knees between her splayed thighs, cupped her hips and thrust himself to the hilt inside her, hitting that trigger inside her that always made her go wild beneath him.

Knowing just what to do to wreak havoc on her senses, he withdrew, plunged again and again until her breath became fevered snatches and she writhed against him, demanding that he end his exquisite torment. Only then did he give her his full ferocity, in ram after jarring ram, in the exact force and cadence she was dying for.

He escalated to a jackhammering tempo inside her until she shrieked, arched in a spastic bow, crushed herself to him as pleasure detonated her, undoing her to her very cells.

Through the delirium she heard him roar, felt his great body shuddering, his seed splashing against her intimate flesh, dousing the inferno that threatened to turn her to ashes. She held on to awareness, to him, until he collapsed on top of her, filling her trembling arms, before she spiraled into an abyss of satiation, hitting bottom bonelessly, consciousness dissipating....

She came back into her body with a gasp as, still fused to her, he rose above her, his breathing as labored as hers, his eyes crackling with satisfaction, melting with indulgence, his lips flushed and swollen with the savagery of their coupling. He looked heartbreakingly virile and vital, and he was...hers.

She'd never allowed herself to think of him this way... but he was.

Since she'd met him, Maksim Volkov had been hers alone.

Though she'd long known of him, the Russian steel tycoon who was on par with her eldest brother, Aristedes, as one of the world's richest and most powerful men, it had taken that first face-to-face glance across the room at that charity gala a year ago for a certainty to come to her fully formed. That he'd turn her life upside down. If she let him.

And she'd let him, and then some.

She still remembered with acute intensity how she'd breathlessly allowed him to kiss her within minutes of meeting, how he'd claimed her lips, thrust his tongue inside her gasping mouth, fed her the ambrosia of his taste, turned her into a mass of mindlessness. She'd never imagined she could feel anything so suffocating in intensity, so transporting in headiness. She'd never imagined she could need a man to take her over, to dominate her.

And within an hour, she'd let him sweep her to his presidential hotel suite, knowing that she'd allow him every intimacy there. It had only been on the way there in his ultimate luxury Mercedes that she'd regained enough presence of mind to tell him that she was a virgin, even when she'd been dreading that the revelation would end their magical encounter prematurely.

She'd never forgotten his reaction.

The banked fire in his eyes had flared again as he took her lips again in a kiss that was possession itself, a sealing of her surrender.

As he'd released her and before he'd set the car in motion, he'd pledged, "It's my unparalleled privilege to be your first, Caliope. And I'm going to make it your unimaginable pleasure."

And how he'd fulfilled his pledge. It had been so overwhelming between them, they'd both known that a one-night stand was out of the question. But because of the disastrous example of her own parents, then the disappointing track records of almost everyone she knew, she believed commitment was just a setup for anything from mind-numbing mediocrity to soul-destroying disappointment. She'd never felt the least temptation to risk either.

But wanting more of Maksim had gone beyond temptation into compulsion. The very intensity of her need had made it imperative she make sure their liaison didn't take a turn in the wrong direction.

To ensure that, she'd demanded rules, upfront and unswerving, to govern whatever time they had together. They'd be together whenever their schedules allowed. For as long as they shared the same level of passion and pleasure, felt the same eagerness for each other. But once the fire was gone, they'd say goodbye amicably and move on.

He had agreed to her terms but had added his own non-negotiable one. Exclusivity.

Stunned that he'd propose or want that, with his reputation as a notorious playboy, it had only made her plunge harder, deeper, until she'd lost herself in what raged between them. But all the time she'd wondered how long it could possibly last. Not even in her wildest dreams had she hoped it would burn that brightly for long, let alone indefinitely.

But it was now a year later and it kept growing more powerful between them, blazing ever hotter.

And she couldn't lose him. She *couldn't*.

But she had to tell him…

"I'm pregnant."

Her heart hammered painfully as even she was taken aback at her own raggedly blurted out declaration. Then more as silence exploded in its wake.

It was as if he'd turned to stone. Nothing remained animate in him except his eyes. And the expression that crashed into them was enough.

Any unformed hope she might have held—that the pregnancy might lead to something more for them—died an abrupt and agonizing death.

Suddenly, she felt she'd suffocate under his weight. Sensing her distress, he lurched off her. She groaned with the pain of separation as he left her body for what was probably the last time.

She sat up unsteadily, groping for the covers. "You don't need to concern yourself with this. Being pregnant is my business, as it is my business that I decided to have the baby. I only thought it was your right to know. Just as it is your right to feel and act as you wish concerning the fact."

His grimness was absolute as he, too, sat up, as if rising from under rubble. "You don't want me near your baby."

Did her words make him think that she didn't?

She forced out a whispered qualification through her

closing throat. "It is your baby, too. I welcome your role in its life, whatever you want it to be."

"I mean you *don't* want me near your baby. Or you as a new mother. I'm not a man to be trusted in such situations. I *will* give the baby my name, make it my heir. But I will never take part in its upbringing." Before she could gasp out her confusion over his contradicting statements, he carried on, "But I want to remain your lover. For as long as you'll have me. When you no longer want me, I'll stay away. You will both have my limitless support always, but I cannot be involved in your daily lives."

He reached for her, his eyes piercing her with their vehemence. "This is all I can offer. This is what I am, Caliope. And I can't change."

She stared up into his fierce gaze, knowing one thing. That the sane thing to do was to refuse his offer. The self-preserving thing was to cut him off from her life now, not later.

But she couldn't even contemplate doing that. Whatever damage it caused in the future, she couldn't sacrifice what she could have of him in the present to avoid it.

And she succumbed to his new terms.

But as the weeks passed, she kept bating her breath wondering if she'd been wrong to succumb. And right in believing the pregnancy would shatter their perfection.

She did sense his withdrawal in everything he said and did. But he confused her even more when he always came back hungrier than ever.

Then just as she entered her seventh month, and was more confused than ever about where they stood, her world stopped turning completely when Maksim just... disappeared.

One

Present

"And he never came back?"

Cali stared at Kassandra Stavros's gorgeous face. It took several disconcerted moments before she reminded herself her new friend couldn't possibly be talking about Maksim.

After all, Kassandra didn't even know about him. No one did.

Cali had kept their...liaison a secret from her family and friends. Even when declaring her pregnancy had become unavoidable, with Maksim still in her life, she'd refused to tell anyone who the father was. Even when she'd clung to the hope that he'd remain part of her life after her baby was born, their situation had been too...irregular, and she'd had no wish to explain it to anyone. Certainly not to her traditional Greek family.

The only one she knew who wouldn't have judged was Aristedes. Her, that was. He would have probably wanted to take Maksim apart. Literally. When he'd been in a similar situation, her brother had gone to extreme lengths to stake a claim on his lover, Selene, and their son, Alex. He'd consider any man doing anything less a criminal. His outrage would have been a thousand fold with her and his nephew on the other end of the equation. Aristedes would have probably exacted a drastic punishment on Maksim for shirking his responsibilities. Knowing Maksim, it would have developed into a war.

Not that she would have tolerated being considered Maksim's "responsibility," or would have let Aristedes fight her battle. Not when it hadn't been one to start with. She'd told Maksim he'd owed her nothing. And she'd meant it. As for Aristedes and her family, she'd been independent far too long to want their blessings or need their support. She wouldn't have let anyone have an opinion, let alone a say, in how she'd conducted her life, or the… arrangement she'd had with Maksim.

Then he'd disappeared, making the whole thing redundant. All they knew was that Leo's father had been "nothing serious."

Kassandra was now talking about another man in Cali's life who'd been a living example of "nothing serious." Someone who should also hold some record for Most Callous User.

Her father.

The only good thing he'd ever done, in her opinion, had been leaving her mother and his brood of kids before Cali had been born. Her other siblings, especially Aristedes and Andreas, had lifelong scars to account for their exposure to his negligence and exploitation. She'd at least escaped that.

She finally answered her friend, sighing, "No. He was gone one day and was never heard from again. We have no idea if he's still alive. Though he must be long dead or he would have surfaced as soon as Aristedes made his first ten thousand dollars."

Her friend's mouth dropped open. "You think he would have come back asking for money? From the son he'd abandoned?"

"Can't imagine that type of malignant nonparent, huh?"

Kassandra shrugged. "Guess I can't. My father and uncles may be controlling Greek pains, but it's because they're really hopeless mother hens."

Cali smiled, seeing how any male in the family of the incredibly beautiful Kassandra would be protective of her. "According to Selene, they believe you give them just cause for their Greek overprotectiveness to go into hyperdrive."

A chuckle burst on Kassandra's lips. "Selene told you about them, huh?"

Selene, Aristedes's wife and Kassandra's best friend, had told her the broad lines about Kassandra before introducing them to each other, confident they'd work spectacularly well together. Which they did. But they'd only started being more than business associates in the past two months, gradually becoming close personal friends. Which Cali welcomed very much. She did need a woman to talk to, one of her own age, temperament and interests, and Kassandra fulfilled all those criteria. Although Selene certainly fit the bill, too, ever since Cali had given birth to Leo, being around family, which Selene was now, had become too…uncomfortable.

So Kassandra had been heaven-sent. And though they'd been delving deeper in private waters every time they met, it was the first time they'd swerved into the familial zone.

Glad to steer the conversation away from herself, she grinned at her new confidante. "Selene only told me the basics, said she'd leave it up to you to supply the hilarious details."

Kassandra slid lower on the couch, her incredible hair fanning out against the cushions in a glossy sun-streaked mass, her Mediterranean-green eyes twinkling in amusement. "Yeah, I flaunted their strict values, their conservative expectations and traditional hopes for me. I wasted one huge opportunity after another of acquiring a socially enviable, deep-pocketed 'sponsor' to procreate with, to provide them with more perfect, preferably male progenies to shove onto the path of greatness, following my brothers' and cousins' shiningly ruthless example, and to perpetuate the romantic, if misleading, stereotype of those almighty Greek tycoons."

Cali chuckled, Kassandra's dry wit tickling her almost atrophied sense of humor. "They must have had collective strokes when you left home at eighteen and worked your way through college in minimum-wage jobs and then added mortification to worry by becoming a model."

Kassandra grinned. "They do attribute their blood-pressure and sugar-level abnormalities to my scandalous behavior. You'd think they would have settled down now that I've hit thirty and left my lingerie-modeling days behind to become a struggling designer."

Kassandra was joking here since at thirty she was far more beautiful than she'd been at twenty. She'd just become so famous she preferred to model only for causes now. And she was well on her way to becoming just as famous as a designer. Cali felt privileged to be a major part of establishing her as a household name through an innovative series of online ad campaigns.

Kassandra's generous lips twisted. "But no. They're still recycling the same nightmares about the dangers I must be facing, fending off the perverts and predators they imagine populate my chosen profession. And they're lamenting my single status louder by the day, and getting more frantic as they count down my fast-fading attractions and fertility. Thirty to Greeks seems to be the equivalent of fifty in other cultures."

Cali snorted. "Next time they wail, point them my way.

They'd thank you instead for not detonating their social standing completely by bearing an out-of-wedlock child."

A wicked gleam deepened the emerald of Kassandra's eyes. "Maybe I should. It doesn't seem I'll ever find a man who'll mess with my mind enough that I'd actually be willing to put up with the calamity of the marriage institution either for real, or for the cause of perpetuating the Stavros species. Not to mention that your and Selene's phenomenal tykes are making my biological clock clang."

Cali's heart twitched. Whenever Kassandra lumped her with Selene, it brought their clashing realities into painful focus. Selene, having two babies with the love of her life. And her, having Leo…alone.

"Being a single parent isn't something to be considered lightly," she murmured.

Contrition filled Kassandra's eyes. "Which you are in the best position to know. I remember how Selene struggled before Aristedes came back. As successful as she is, being a single mother was such a big burden to bear alone. Before her experience, I had this conviction that fathers were peripheral at best in the first few years of a child's life. But then I saw the night-and-day difference Aristedes made in Selene and Alex's lives…." She huffed a laugh. "Though he's no example. We all know there's only one of him on planet earth."

Just as Cali had thought there was only one of Maksim. If not because of any human traits…

But Aristedes had once appeared to be just as inhuman. In his case, appearances had been the opposite of reality.

Cali sighed again. "You don't know how flabbergasted I still am sometimes to see how amazing Aristedes is as a husband and father. We used to believe he was the phenomenally successful version of our heartless, loser father."

It had been one specific night in particular that she'd become convinced of that. The night Leonidas—their brother—had died.

As she and her sisters had clung together, reeling from the horrific loss, Aristedes had swooped in and taken complete charge of the situation. All business, he'd dealt with the police and the burial and arranged the wake, but had offered them no solace, hadn't stayed an hour after the funeral.

That had still been far better than Andreas, who hadn't returned at all, or even acknowledged Leonidas's death then or since. But it had convinced her that Aristedes, too, had no emotions...just like their father.

She'd since realized that he was the opposite of their father, felt *too* much, but had been so unversed in demonstrating his emotions, he'd expressed them instead in the support he'd lavished on her and all his siblings since they'd been born. But after Selene had *claimed him,* as he said, something fundamental had changed in him. He was still ruthless in business, but on a personal level, he'd opened up with his family and friends. And when it came to Selene and their kids, he was a huge rattle toy.

"So your father was that bad, huh?" Kassandra asked.

Cali took a sip of tea, loath to discuss her father. She'd always been glib about him. But it was suddenly hitting her how close to her own situation it all was.

She exhaled her rising unease. "His total lack of morals and concern for anything beyond his own petty interests were legend. He got my mother pregnant with Aristedes when she was only seventeen. He was four years older, a charmer who never held down a job and who only married her because his father threatened to cut him off financially if he didn't. He used her and the kids he kept impregnating her with to squeeze his father for bigger allowances, which he spent on himself. After his father died, he took his inheritance and left."

Cali paused for a moment to regulate her agitated breathing before resuming. "He came back when he'd squandered it, knowing full well that Mother would feed him and take care of him with what little money she earned or got from those who remained of her own family, those who'd stopped helping out when they realized their hard-earned money was going to that user. He drifted in and out of her and my siblings' lives, each time coming back to add another child to his brood and another burden on my mother's shoulders before disappearing again. He always came back swearing his love, of course, offering sob stories about how hard life was on him."

Chagrin filled Kassandra's eyes more with every word. "And your mother just took him back?"

Cali nodded, more uncomfortable by the second at the associations this conversation was raising.

"Aristedes said she didn't know it was possible for her not to. He understood it all, having been forced to mature very early, but could do nothing about it except help his mother. He was only seven when he was already doing everything that no-good father should have been doing while mother took care of the younger kids. By twelve he had left school and was working four jobs to barely make ends meet. Then when he was fifteen, said non-father disappeared for the final time when I was still a work in progress.

"Aristedes went on to work his way up from the docks in Crete to become one of the biggest shipping magnates in the world. Regretfully, our mother was around only to see the beginnings of his success, as she died when I was only six. He then brought us all over here to New York, got us American citizenships and provided us with the best care and education money could buy.

"But he didn't stick around, didn't even become American himself, except after he married Selene. But his success and all that we have now was in spite of what that man who fathered us did to destroy our lives, as he managed to destroy our mother. All in all, I am only thankful I didn't have the curse of having him poison my life as he did Aristedes's and the rest of my siblings'."

Kassandra blinked, as if unable to take in that level of unfeeling, premeditated exploitation. "It's mind-boggling. How someone can be so…evil with those he's supposed to care for. He did one thing right, though, even if inadvertently. He had you and your siblings. You guys are great."

Cali refrained from telling her that she'd always thought only Leonidas had been deserving of that accolade. Now she knew Aristedes was, too, but she felt her three sisters, though she loved them dearly, had been infected with a degree or another of their mother's passivity and willingness to be downtrodden. Andreas, sibling number five out of seven, was just…an enigma. From his lifelong loath interactions with them, she was inclined to think that he was far worse than anything she'd ever thought Aristedes to be.

But while she'd thought she'd escaped her mother's infection, perhaps she hadn't after all.

Apart from the different details, Cali had basically done with Maksim what her mother had done with her father. She'd gotten involved with someone she'd known she shouldn't have. Then, when it had been in her best interest to walk away, she'd been too weak to do so, until he'd been the one who'd left her.

But her mother had had an excuse. An underprivileged woman living in Crete isolated from opportunity or hope of anything different, a woman who didn't know how to aspire to better.

Cali was a twenty-first-century, highly educated, totally independent American woman. How could she defend her actions and decisions?

"Look at the time!" Kassandra jumped to her feet. "Next time, just kick me out and don't let little ol' kidless me keep you from stocking up on sleep for those early mornings with Leo."

Rising, Cali protested, "I'd rather have you here all night yammering about anything than sleep. I've been starving for adult company...particularly of the female variety, outside of discussing baby stuff with Leo's nanny."

Kassandra hugged her, chuckling as she rushed to the door. "You can use me any time to ward off your starvation."

After setting up a meeting to discuss the next phase in their campaign and to go over Cali's progress reports, Kassandra rushed off, and Cali found herself staring at the closed oak door of her suddenly silent apartment.

That all-too-familiar feeling of dejection, which always assailed her when she didn't have a distraction, settled over her like a shroud.

She could no longer placate herself that this was lingering postpartum depression. She hated to admit it, but everything she'd been suffering for the past year had only one cause.

Maksim.

She walked back through her place, seeing none of its exquisiteness or the upgrades she'd installed to make it suitable for a baby. Her feet, as usual, took her without conscious volition to Leo's room.

She tiptoed inside, though she knew she wouldn't wake him. After the first six sleepless months, he'd thankfully switched to all-night-sleeping mode. She believed taking away the night-light and having him sleep in darkness had helped. She now only had the corridor light to guide her, though she'd know her way to his bed blindfolded.

As her vision adjusted, his beloved shape materialized out of the darkness, and emotion twisted in her throat as it always did whenever she beheld him. It regularly blind-sided her, the power of her feelings for him.

He was so achingly beautiful, so frightfully perfect, she lived in dread of anything happening to him. She wondered if all mothers invented nightmares about the catastrophic potential of everything their children did or came in contact with or if she was the one who'd been a closet neurotic, and having Leo had only uncovered her condition.

Even though she was unable to see him clearly in the dark, his every pore and eyelash were engraved in her mind. If anyone had suspected she'd been with Maksim, they would have realized at once that Leo was his son. He was his replica after all. Just like Alex was Aristedes's. When she'd first set eyes on Alex, she *had* exclaimed that cloning had been achieved. Now their daughter Sofia was the spitting image of Selene.

Every day made Leo the baby version of his impossibly beautiful father. His hair had the same unique shade of glossy mahogany, with the same widow's peak, and would no doubt develop the same relaxed wave and luxury. His chin had the same cleft, his left cheek the same dimple. In Maksim's case, since he'd appeared to be incapable of smiling, that dimple had winked at her only in grimaces of agonized pleasure at the height of passion.

The only difference between father and son was the eyes. Though Leo's had the same wolfish slant, it was as if he'd mixed her blue eyes and Maksim's golden ones together in the most amazing shade of translucent olive green.

Feeling her heart expanding with gratitude for this perfect miracle, she bent and touched her lips to Leo's plump downy cheek. He gurgled contentedly and then flounced to his side, stretching noisily before settling into an even sounder sleep. She planted one more kiss over his averted face before finally straightening and walking out.

Closing the door behind her, she leaned against it. But instead of the familiar depression, something new crept in to close its freezing fingers around her heart. Rage. At herself.

Why had she given Maksim the opportunity to be the one to walk out on her? How had she been that weak?

She *had* felt his withdrawal. So why had she clung to him instead of doing what she herself had stipulated from the very beginning? That if the fire weakened or went out, they'd end it, without attempts to prolong its dying throes?

But in her defense, he'd confused her, giving her hope her doubts and observations of his distance had all been in her mind, when after each withdrawal he'd come back hungrier.

Still, that *had* been erratic, and it should have convinced her put a stop to it.

But she'd snatched at his offer to be there for her, even in that impersonal and peripheral way of his, had clung to him even through the dizzying fluctuation of his behavior. She'd given him the chance to deal her the blow of his abrupt desertion. Which she now had to face she hadn't gotten over, and might never recover from.

Rage swerved inside her like a stream of lava to pour over him, burning him, too, in the vehemence of her contempt.

Why had he offered what he'd had no intention of honoring? When she'd assured him she hadn't considered it his obligation? But he'd done worse than renege on his promise. Once he'd had enough of her, he'd begrudged her even the consideration of a goodbye.

Not that she'd understood, *or* believed that he had actually deserted her at the time.

Believing there must be another explanation, she'd started attempting to contact him just a day after his disappearance,

The number he'd assigned her had been disconnected. His other numbers had rung without going to voice mail. Her emails had gone unanswered. None of his associates had known anything about him. Apart from his acquisitions and takeovers, there'd been no other evidence of his continued existence. It had all pointed to the simple, irrefutable truth: he'd gone to serious lengths to hide his high profile, to make it impossible for her to contact him.

Yet for months she hadn't been able to sanction that verdict. She'd grown frantic with every failure, even when logic had said nothing serious could happen to him without the whole world knowing. But, self-deluding fool that she was, she'd been convinced something terrible had happened to him, that he wouldn't have abandoned then ignored her like that.

When she'd finally been forced to admit he'd done just that, it had sent her mad wondering…why?

She'd previously rationalized that his episodic withdrawal was due to the fact that her progressing pregnancy was making it too real for him, probably interfering with his pleasure, or even turning him off her.

Her suspicions had faltered when those instances had been interrupted by even-wilder-than-before encounters. But his evasion of her attempts to reach him had forced her to sanction those suspicions as the only explanation. Then, to make things worse, the deepening misery of her pregnancy's last stages had forced another admission on her.

It hadn't been anguish, or addiction, or needing closure.

She'd fallen in love with Maksim.

When she'd faced that fact, she'd finally known why he'd left. He must have sensed the change in her before she'd become conscious of it, had considered it the breaking point. Because *he'd* never change.

But if she'd thought the last months of her pregnancy had been hellish, they'd been nothing compared to what had followed Leo's birth. To everyone else, she'd functioned perfectly. Inside, no matter what she'd told herself— that she had a perfect baby, a great career, good health, a loving family and financial stability—she'd known true desolation.

It hadn't been the overwhelming responsibility for a helpless being who depended on her every single second of the day. It had been that soul-gnawing longing to have Maksim there with her, to turn to him for counsel, for moral support. She'd needed to *share* Leo with him, the little things more than the big stuff. She'd needed to exclaim to him over Leo's every little wonder, to ramble on about his latest words or actions or a hundred other expected or unique developments. Sharing that with anyone who wasn't Maksim had intensified her yearning for him.

Her condition had worsened until she'd started feeling as if he was near, as if she'd turn to find him looking at her with that uncontainable passion in his eyes. Many times she'd even thought she'd caught glimpses of him, her imagination playing havoc with her mind. And each time this mirage had dissolved, it had been as if he'd walked out on her all over again. Those phantom sensations, that need that wouldn't subside, had only made her more bereft.

Now all that only poured fuel on her newfound fury.

But anger felt far better than despondence. It made her feel alive. She hadn't felt anywhere near that since he'd left.

She was done feeling numb inside. She'd no longer pretend to be alive. She'd live again for real, and to hell with everything she...

The bell rang.

Her heart blipped as her eyes flew to the wall clock. 10 p.m. She couldn't imagine who it could be at this hour. Besides, anyone who came to see her would have buzzed her on the intercom, or, at the very least, her concierge would have called ahead to check with her first. So how could someone just arrive unannounced at her door?

The only answer was Kassandra. Maybe she'd left something behind. Probably her phone, since she hadn't called ahead.

She rushed to the door, opened it without checking the peephole...and everything screeched to a halt.

Her breath. Her heart. The whole world.

In the subdued lights of the spacious corridor he loomed, dark and huge, his face eclipsed by the door's shadow, his eyes glowing gold in the gloom.

Maksim.

Inside the cessation, a maelstrom churned, scrambling her senses. Heartbeats boomed in her chest. Air clogged in her lungs. Had she been thinking of him so obsessively she'd conjured him up? As she'd done so many times before?

Her vision distorted over the face that was omnipresent in her memory. It was the same, yet almost unrecognizable. She couldn't begin to tell why. Her consciousness was wavering and only one thing kept her erect. The intensity of his gaze.

Then something hit her even harder. The way he sagged against the door frame, as if he, too, was unable to stand straight, as enervated at her sight as she was at his. His eyes roamed feverishly over her face, down her body, making her feel he'd scraped all her nerve endings raw.

Then his painstakingly sculpted lips twitched, as if in... pain. Next second it was her who almost fell to the ground in a heap.

The dark, evocative melody that emanated from his lips swamped her. But it was his ragged words that hit her hardest, deepened her paralysis, her muteness.

"Ya ocheen skoocha po tebyeh, moya dorogoya."

She'd been learning Russian avidly since the day she'd met him. She hadn't even stopped after he'd left, had only taken a break when Leo was born. She'd resumed her lessons in the past three months. Why exactly she'd been so committed, she hadn't been able to rationalize. It was just one more thing that was beyond her.

But...maybe she'd been learning for this moment. So she'd understand what he'd just said.

I missed you so terribly, my darling.

Two

That was it. Her mind had snapped.

She was not only seeing Maksim, she was hearing him say the words that had echoed in her head so many times, waking up from a dream where he'd said just that. Then, to complete the hallucination, he reached for her and pulled her into his arms as he'd always done in those torment- ing visions.

But he didn't surround her in that sure flow of her dreams, or the steady purpose of the past. He staggered as he groped for her. His uncharacteristic incoordination, the desperation in his vibe, in every inch that impacted her quivering flesh, sent her ever-simmering desire roaring.

Then she was mingled with him, sharing his breath, sinking in his taste, as he reclaimed her from the void he'd plunged her in, wrenching her back into his possession.

Maksim. He was back like she'd dreamed every night for one bleak, interminable year. He was back…*for real*.

But he couldn't be. He'd never been with her for real. It had never become real to him. She'd accepted that in the past.

She wouldn't accept that anymore. Couldn't bear it.

No matter how she'd fantasized about taking him back a thousand times, that would remain an impossible yearn- ing. Too much had changed. She had. And he'd told her he never would.

The fugue of drugging pleasure, of drowning reprieve, slowly lifted. Instead of a resurrection, the feel of him around her became suffocation, until she was struggling for breath.

He let her go at once, stumbled back across her threshold. "*Izvinityeh*... Forgive me.... I didn't mean to..."

His apology choked as he ran both hands through hair that had grown down to the base of his neck. One of the changes that hadn't registered at first that now cascaded into her awareness like dominos, each one knocking a memorized nuance of him, replacing it with his reality now.

He looked...haggard, a shadow of the formidably vital man he'd once been. And, if possible, she found him even more breathtaking for it. That harsh edge of...depletion made her want to crush against him until she assimilated him into her being....

God... Was she turning into her mother for real? Is this the pattern she'd establish now? He'd leave without a word, stay away through her most trying times then come back, and without a word of explanation, say he'd missed her and one soul-stealing kiss later, she'd breathlessly offer him said soul if only he'd take it?

No way. He'd submerged her mind because he'd taken her by surprise, just when he'd been dominating her thoughts. But this lapse wouldn't be repeated.

Maksim was part of her past. And that was where she'd keep him.

Yet even with this resolution, she could only stare up at him as he brooded at her from his prodigious height, what was amplified now by his weight loss.

"Won't you invite me in?"

His rough whisper lashed through her, made her breath leave her in a hiss. "No. And before you leave, I want to know how you made it up here in the first place. Did you con a tenant to let you in, or did you intimidate my concierge?"

He winced. No doubt at the shrill edge in her voice. "I won't say these things are beyond me if I wanted something bad enough. And I certainly would have resorted to whatever would have gotten me up here. But in this case, I didn't have to con or coerce anyone to get my way. I entered with your pass code."

How did he know that?

She'd once thought it remarkable a man of his stature walked around without bodyguards and let her into his inner sanctum without any safeguards. She'd thought he'd trusted her that much.

But what if she'd been wrong about that, too? Had he just seemed trusting because his security measures were of such a caliber they'd been invisible to her senses?

It made sense his security machine dissected anyone with whom he came in contact, especially women with whom he became sexually intimate. Come to think of it, they probably collected evidence on his conquests to be used if they stepped out of line. He probably had a dossier on her every private detail down to the brand of deodorant she used. What if he...

"I once came here with you."

His subdued statement aborted her feverish projections. She stared up at him, unable to fathom the correlation.

"You inputted your pass code at the entrance."

If anything, that explanation left her more stunned. "You mean you watched me as I entered it, and not only figured out the twelve-digit code, but memorized it? Till now?"

He nodded, impatient to leave this behind. "I remember everything about you. Everything, Caliope."

With this emphasis, his gaze dropped to her lips, as if he was holding back from ravishing them with a resolve that was fast dwindling.

Her lips throbbed in response, her insides twitched…

He took a tight step, still not crossing the threshold. Which really surprised her. The Maksim she knew would have just overridden her, secure that he'd melt any resistance. Not that he'd ever met with that, or even the slightest hint of reluctance, from her. But that had been in another life.

"Invite me in, Caliope. I need to talk to you."

"And I don't want to talk to you," she shot back, struggling not to let that…vulnerability in his demand affect her. "You're a year too late. The time for talking was before you decided to leave without a word. I got over any need or willingness to talk to you nine months ago."

His nod was difficult. "When Leonid was born."

So he knew Leo's name, though he used the Russian version of Leonidas. He probably also knew Leo's weight and how many baby teeth he had. All part of that security dossier he must have on her.

"Your deduction is redundant. As is your presence here."

His hands bunched and released, as if they itched. "I won't say I deserve that you hear me out. But for months you did want to hear my explanation of my sudden departure. You wanted to so badly, you left me dozens of messages and as many emails."

So he had ignored her, let her go mad worrying, as she'd surmised. "Since you remember everything, you must remember why I kept calling and emailing."

"You wanted to know if I was okay."

"And since I can see that you are…" She paused, looked him up and down in his long, dark coat. "Though maybe I can't call what you are now *okay*. You look like a starving vampire who is trying to hypnotize his victim into letting him in so he can suck her dry. Or for a more mundane metaphor, you look as if you've developed a cocaine habit."

She knew she was being cruel. But she couldn't help it. He'd sprung back into her life after bitterness had swept away despondence and anger had cracked its floodgates. Feeling herself about to throw all her anguish to the wind and just drag him in after one kiss had brought the dam of resentment crashing down.

"I've been…ill."

The reluctant way he said that, the way his eyes lowered and those thick, thick lashes touched his even more razor-sharp cheekbones made her heart overturn again in her chest.

What if he'd been ill all this time…?

No. She wasn't doing what her mother had done with her father—making excuses for him until he destroyed her.

He raised his gaze to her. "Aren't you even curious to know why I left? Why I'm back?"

Curious? Speculating on why he'd left had permanently eroded her sanity. Her brain was now expanding inside her head with the pressure of needing to know why he was back.

Out loud she said, "No, I'm not. I made a deal with you from day one, demanding only two things from you. Honesty and respect. But you weren't honest about having had enough of me, and you would have shown someone you'd picked off the street more respect."

He flinched as if she'd struck him but didn't make any attempt to interrupt her.

It only brought back more of memories of her anguish, injected more harshness into her words. "You evaded me as you would a stalker, when you knew that if you'd only confirmed that you were okay, I would have stopped calling. I did stop when your news made the confirmation for you, forcing me to believe the depth of your mistreatment. You've forfeited any right to my consideration. I don't care why you left, why you ignored me, and I don't have the least desire to know why you're back."

His bleakness deepened with her every word. When he was sure her barrage was over, he exhaled raggedly. "None of what you just said has any basis in truth. And while you might never sanction my true reasons for behaving as I did, they were…overwhelming to me at the time. It's a long story." Before she could blurt out that she wasn't interested in hearing it, he added, almost inaudibly, "Then I was…in an accident."

That silenced her. Outwardly. Inside, a cacophony of questions, anxiety and remorse exploded.

When? How? What happened? Was he injured? How badly?

Her eyes darted over him, feverishly inspecting him for damage. She saw nothing on his face, but maybe she was missing scars in the dimness. What about his body? That dark shroud might not obscure that he'd lost a lot of his previous bulk, but what if it was covering up something far more horrific?

Unable to bear the questions, she grabbed his forearm and dragged him across the threshold, where the better lighting of her foyer made it possible for her to check him closely.

Her heart squeezed painfully. God… He'd lost so much weight, looked so…unwell, gaunt, almost…frail.

Suddenly he groaned and dropped down. Before fright could register, he rose again, scooping her up in his arms.

It was a testament to his strength that, even in his diminished state, he could do so with seeming effortlessness, making her feel as he always had whenever he'd carried her: weightless, taken, coveted, cosseted. The blow of longing, the sense of homecoming when she'd despaired of ever seeing him again, was so overpowering it had her sagging in his hold, all tension and resistance gone.

Her head rolled over his shoulder, her hands trembled in a cold tangle over his chest as all the times he'd had her in his arms like this flooded her memory. He'd always carried her, had told her he loved the feel of her filling his arms, relinquishing her weight and will to him, so he'd contain her, take her, wherever and however he would.

He stopped at her family room. If she could have found her voice, she would have told him to keep going to her room, to not stop until they were flesh to flesh, ending the need for words, letting her lose herself in his possession, and even more, reassure herself about his every inch, check it out against what she remembered in obsessive detail, yearned for in perpetual craving.

But he was setting her down on the couch, kneeling on the ground beside her, looking down at her as she lay back, unable to muster enough power to sit up. And that was before she saw something…enormous roiling in his eyes.

Then he articulated it. "Can I see Leonid?"

Everything in her, body and spirit, stiffened with shock. All she could say was, "Why?"

She was asking in earnest. He'd told her he wouldn't take any personal interest or part in Leo's life. She could find no reason why he would want to see him now.

His answer put into words what she'd just thought. "I know I said I wouldn't have anything to do with him personally. But it wasn't because I didn't want to. It was because I thought I couldn't and mustn't."

The memory of those excruciating moments, when she'd accepted that he'd never be part of the radical change that would forever alter her life's course, assailed her again with the immediacy of a fresh injury.

"You said you're not 'a man to be trusted in such situations.'"

A spasm seized his face. "You remember."

Instead of saying she remembered everything about him, as he claimed to about her, she exhaled. "That was kind of impossible to forget."

"I only said that because I believed it was in your and his best interest not to have me in your lives."

"Is the reason you believed that part of the...long story?"

"The reason *is* the story. But before I go into it, will you please let me see Leonid?"

God... He'd asked again. This was really happening. He was here and he wanted to see Leo. But if she let him, nothing would ever be the same again. She just knew it wouldn't.

She groped for any excuse to stop this from spiraling any further. "He's asleep...."

His eclipsed eyes darkened even more. "I promise I will just look at him, won't disturb his sleep."

She tried again. "You won't see much in the dark. And I can't turn the lights on. It's the only thing that wakes him up."

"Even if I can't see him well, I will...feel him. I already know what he looks like."

Her heart lurched. Had she been right about this security report? "How do you know? Are you having us followed?"

He stared at her for a moment as if he didn't understand. "Why would you even think that?"

Regarding him warily, she told him all her suspicions. His frown deepened with every word. "You have every right to believe the worst of me. But I never invaded your privacy. If I ever were to have you followed, it would be for your protection, not mine. And I had no reason to fear for your safety before, since associating with me would have been the only source of danger to you, and I kept our relationship a firm secret."

"So how do you know what Leo looks like?"

"Because *I* followed you."

Her mouth dropped open. "You did? When?"

He bit his lip, words seeming to hurt as he forced them out. "On and off. Mostly on for the past three months."

So she hadn't been imagining it or going insane! All the times she'd felt him, he had been there!

Questions and confusions deluged her. Why had he done that? Why had he slipped away the moment she'd felt him? Why hadn't he approached her? And why had he decided to finally do so now? Why, why, *why?*

She wanted to bombard him with every why and how could you, to have answers *now,* not a second later.

But those answers would take time. And though she might be her mother's daughter after all, she couldn't press him for them now. She couldn't deny him access to his son. Even without explanations, the beseeching in his eyes told her enough. He'd waited too long already.

She nodded, tried to sit up and pressed into him when he didn't move. His hands shot out to support her when she almost collapsed back, his eyes glazing as that electricity that always flowed between them zapped them both.

As if he were unable to stop, his hand cupped her cheek, slid around her nape, tilting her face up to his. He groaned her name as if in pain, as if warning her he'd kiss her if she didn't say no. She didn't. She couldn't.

As if she'd removed a barbed leash from his neck, relief rumbled from his depths as he lowered his head, took her lips in a compulsive kiss.

She knew she shouldn't let this happen again, that nothing had been resolved and never would be. But at the glide of his tongue against hers, the mingling of his breath with hers, she was, as always, lost.

She surrendered to his hunger as his lips and teeth plucked at her trembling flesh, as his tongue plunged into her mouth, plundering her response. Her body melted, readied itself for him, remembering his invasion, his dominance, his pleasures, weeping for it all. He pressed her back on the couch and bore down on her, restlessly moving against her, rubbing her swollen breasts and aching nipples with the hardness of his chest... Then, without warning, he suddenly wrenched his lips from hers, shot up on his knees, his eyes wide in alarm.

It took her hard-breathing moments to realize the whimper she'd heard hadn't come from her. *Leo*.

It took a few more gurgles for her to remember the baby monitor. She had a unit in every room.

This time when she struggled up, Maksim helped her. She didn't know if his hands were shaking or if hers were, or both.

He rose to his feet, helped her to hers then stood aside so she'd lead the way.

The unreality of the situation swamped her again as she approached Leo's room, feeling Maksim's presence flooding her apartment. The last thing she'd imagined when she'd last made that same trip was that in an hour's time, Maksim would be here and she'd be taking him for his first contact with her... With his... With *their* son.

She felt his tension increase with every step until she opened the door, and it almost knocked her off her feet.

She turned to him. "Relax, okay? Leo is very sensitive

to moods." It was why he'd given her a hellish first six months. He'd been responding to her misery. She'd managed to siphon it into a grueling exercise and work schedule, and to compartmentalize her emotions so she didn't expose him to their negative side. "If he wakes, you don't want him seeing you for the first time with this intensity coming off you."

She almost groaned. She'd said "the first time" as if she thought this encounter would be the first of many. When Maksim probably only wanted to see him once because... She had no idea why.

Unaware of her turmoil, grappling with his, he squeezed his eyes shut before opening them again and nodding. "I'm ready."

Nerves jangling, she tiptoed into the room with him soundlessly following her. She hoped Leo had settled down. She really preferred this first, and probably last, sighting to happen while he was asleep. The next moment, tension drained as she found Leo snoring gently again.

Before she could sigh in relief, everything disappeared from her awareness, even Leo, as Maksim came to stand beside her. Adapting to the dark room, she stared at his profile, her heart rattling inside her chest like a coin in a box. She'd never imagined he would...would... God.

His expression, the searing emotion that emanated from him as he looked down at Leo... It stormed through her, brought tears surging from her depths to fill eyes she'd thought had dried forever.

His face was a mask of stunned, sublime...suffering, as if he were gazing down at a heart that had spilled out of his chest and taken human form. As if he were beholding a miracle.

Which Leo was. Against all odds, he'd come into being.

And with all she'd suffered since she'd seen the evidence of his existence, she would never have it any other way.

"Can—can I touch him?"

The reverent whisper almost felled her.

He swung his gaze to her and she nearly cried out. His eyes! Glittering in the faint light...with tears.

Tears? Maksim? How was that even possible?

Feeling her heart in her throat, she could only nod.

After hard-breathing moments when he seemed to be bracing himself, he reached a trembling hand down to Leo's face.

The moment his fingertips touched Leo's averted cheek, his inhalation was so sharp, it was as if he'd been punched in the gut. It was how she felt, too, as if her lungs had emptied and wouldn't fill again. And that was before Leo pressed his cheek into Maksim's large hand, like a cat demanding a firmer petting.

Swaying visibly now, or maybe it was her world that was, Maksim complied, cupping Leo's plump, downy cheek, caressing it with his thumb, over and over, his breathing erratic and audible now, as if he'd just sprinted a mile.

"Are all children this amazing?"

His ragged words were so thick, so low, and not only on account of not wanting to disturb Leo. It seemed he could barely speak. And his words weren't an exclamation of wonder or a rhetorical question. He was asking for real. He truly had no idea. It was as if it was the first time he'd seen a child, at least the first time he'd realized how incredible it was for a human being to be so tiny yet so compact and complete, so precious and perfect. So fragile and dependent, yet so overpowering.

She considered not answering him. The lump in her throat was about to dissolve into fractured sobs at any moment. But she couldn't ignore his question, not when his gleaming eyes beseeched her answers.

Mustering all she had so she wouldn't break down, she whispered, "All children are. But it seems we are equipped with this affinity to our own, this bond that makes us appreciate them more than anything else in the world, that amplifies their assets, downplays their disadvantages and makes us withstand their trials and tribulations with an endurance that's virtually unending and unreasoning."

His expression was rapt as he listened to her, as if every word was a revelation to him. But suddenly his face shut down. The change was jarring, and that was before his rumble repeated her last word, reverberating inside her, fierce, almost scary.

"Unreasoning..."

Before she could say or think anything, he looked down at Leo for one last moment, withdrew his hand and stalked out of the room.

She followed, slowly, her mind in an uproar.

What was up with this confounding, maddening man?

What did he mean by all that? Coming here, the unprecedented show of emotions for her, that soul-shaking reaction at seeing Leo up close…and then suddenly this switch to predator-with-a-thorn-in-his-paw mode?

Was this what he'd meant when he'd said he wasn't a man to be trusted "in such situations"? Did he suffer from some bipolar disorder that made him blow hot and cold without rhyme or reason? Did that explain his fluctuations in their last months together? His unexplained desertion and sudden return?

She caught up with him in the living room. He stood waiting for her, his face dark and remote.

She faced him, anger sizzling to the surface again. "I don't know what your problem is, and I don't want to know. You came here uninvited, blindsided me into a couple of kisses and wheedled your way into seeing Leo. And now you're done. I want you to leave and I don't want you to ever come back or I…"

"I come from a family of abusers."

To say his out-of-the-blue statement flabbergasted her would be like saying that Mount Everest was a molehill.

Her mind emptied. There was just nothing possible to think—or to say—to what he'd just stated.

He went on, in that same inanimate voice. "It probably goes back to the beginnings of my lineage, but I only know for a fact that my great-grandfather was one, and that the disorder got worse with every generation, reaching its most violent level with my father. I believed it ran in my blood, that once I manifested it, I would be the worst of them all. That was why I never considered having any relationship. Until you."

She could only stare at him, quakes starting in her very essence, spreading outward. She'd lived for a year going crazy for an explanation. Now she no longer wanted to know. Not if the explanation was worse than his seeming desertion itself.

But she couldn't find her voice to tell him to stop. Not that he would have stopped. He seemed set on getting this out in the open once and for all.

"From that first moment," he said, his voice a throb of melancholy, "I wanted you with a ferocity that terrified me, so when you stipulated the finite, uninvolved nature of our liaison, I was relieved. I believed it would be safe as long as our involvement was temporary, remained superficial. But things didn't go as expected, and my worry intensified along with my hunger for you. I lived in fear of my reaction if you wanted to walk away when I wasn't ready to let go. But instead, you became pregnant."

She continued to stare helplessly at him, legs starting to quiver, feeling he hadn't told her the worst of it yet.

He proved her right. "As you blossomed with Leonid, I was more certain every day I'd been right to tell you I'd withdraw from your life eventually and never enter his. I found myself inventing anxieties every second you were out of my sight, had to constantly struggle to curb my impulses so I wouldn't smother you. I even tried to stay away from you as much as I could bear it. But I only returned even hungrier, feared it would only be a matter of time before all these unprecedented emotions snapped my control and manifested in aggression. That was why I forced myself to leave you before you had Leo. Before I ended up doing what my father did after my sister was born."

He had a sister?

His next words provided a horrific answer to her unvoiced surprise. "He'd been getting progressively more volatile. There were no longer days when he didn't hit my mother or me or both of us. Then one night, when Ana was about six months old, he went berserk. He put us all in the emergency room that night. It took my mother and I months to get over our injuries. Ana struggled for a week before she…succumbed."

Three

Maksim's words fell on Cali like an avalanche of rocks. She stood gaping at him, buried under their enormity. *His father had killed his sister. His* baby *sister.*

He feared he suffered from the same brutal affliction.

Was that what had overcome him back there in Leo's room? This "unreasoning" aggression toward the helpless?

Sudden terror grabbed her by the throat.

What if he lost control now? What if— What if…

As suddenly as dread had towered, it crashed, deflated.

This man standing across her living room, looking at her with eyes that bled with despondence she recognized only too well, having suffered it for far too long, wasn't in the grips of uncontrollable violence. But of overwhelming anguish.

He feared himself and what he considered to be his legacy. That fear seemed to have ruled his whole life. He'd just finished telling her it had dictated his every action and decision in his interactions with her. The limits he'd agreed to, the severance he'd imposed on them, had been prodded by nothing else. He'd thought he was protecting her, and Leo, from his destructive potential.

And she heard herself asking, "Did you ever hurt anyone?"

"I did."

The bitten-off admission should have resurrected her fears. It didn't. And not because she was seeing good where there was none, as her mother had done with her father. As his own mother must have done with his father, to remain with an abusive husband.

She only couldn't ignore her gut feeling. It had guided her all her life, had never led her astray.

The one time she'd thought she'd made a fundamental mistake had been with him. But his explanations had reinstated the validity of her inner instincts about him.

From the first moment she'd laid eyes on Maksim, she'd felt she'd be safe with him. More. Protected, defended. At any cost to him. That nobility, that stability, that perfect control she'd felt from him—even at the height of passion—had led her to trust him without reservation from that first night onward. It all contradicted what he feared about himself.

She started walking toward him and he tensed. It was clear he didn't welcome her nearness now, after he'd confessed his shame and dread to her. What must it be like for him to doubt himself on such a basic level? What had it been like for him believing he had a time bomb ticking inside him?

She had to let him know what she'd always sensed of his steadiness and trustworthiness. That it had been why it had hit her so hard when he'd left. She hadn't been able to reconcile what she'd felt on her most essential levels with his seemingly callous actions. Thinking she'd been so wrong about him had agonized her as much as longing for him had.

But she'd been right about him. As misguided as his reasons had been, he'd only meant to protect her and Leo.

He took a couple of steps back as she approached, his eyes imploring her not to come any closer, not just yet.

"Let me say this. It's been weighing on me since I met you. But if you come near me, I'll forget everything."

In answer, she stopped, sank down on the couch where he'd ravished her with pleasure so recently and patted the space next to her. He reluctantly complied.

"Those you hurt were never weaker than you are." It was a statement, not a question.

His hooded eyes simmered. "No."

"They were equals…" her gaze darted over the daunting breadth of his shoulders "…or superior numbers." His nod was terse, confirming her deduction. "And you never instigated violence."

"But I didn't only ward off attacks or defend the attacked. I was only appeased when I damaged the attackers."

"Were those times so frequent?"

He nodded. "My father left another legacy. A tangled mess in our home city. In the motherland, some areas are far from the jurisdiction of law, or the law leaves certain disputes to be resolved by people among themselves. The use of force is the most accepted resolution. I became an expert at it."

"So those times you hurt others, you were not only defending yourself but others. You did what had to be done."

"I was too violent. And I relished it."

She persisted. "Did you lose control?"

"No. I knew exactly what I was doing."

"A lot of men are like you…. Soldiers, protectors—capable of stunning violence, of even killing, for a cause, to defend others against aggressors. But those same men are usually the gentlest men with those who depend on them for protection."

His eyes grew more turbid. "I understood that mentally, that I had good cause. But with my family history, I feared it meant I had it in me…this potential for unprovoked vio-

lence. My passion for you was intensifying by the hour…
but my fear of myself came to a head one specific night.
It happened when I was waiting for you in bed and you
were walking toward me in a sheer turquoise negligee."

Her throat closed. She remembered that night. Only too
well. Their last night together.

She'd woken up replete from his tender, tempestuous
lovemaking to find him gone.

"I'd never seen you more beautiful. You were ripe and
glowing—your belly was rounding more by the day, and
you were stroking it lovingly as you approached me. What
I felt at that moment, it was so ferocious, I was scared out
of my wits. I'd put bullies twice your size in traction…or
worse. I couldn't risk having my passions swerve into a
different direction."

Needles pricked behind her eyes, threatening to dissolve down her cheeks at any moment. "You hid it well."

His eyes widened in dismay. "I didn't have to hide
anything. I never felt anything anywhere near aggressive
around you. But the mere possibility of losing control of
my passion carried a price that was impossible to contemplate."

He never said emotion. Did he use passion interchange-
ably, or was everything he felt rooted in the physical?

"You have to believe me. You don't have to look back
and feel sick thinking you'd been in danger and oblivious of it."

She shook her head, needing to arrest his alarm. "I
meant you hid that increasing passion. I never sensed that
you felt a different level from what you had always showed
me."

His nod was heavy. "*That* I hid. And the more I tried not
to show you what I felt, the more it…roiled inside me. And

if I felt like this when you were still carrying my child, I couldn't risk testing how I'd feel after you had him."

He must have been living a nightmare, worrying he'd relive what had happened with his father, reenact it.

A vice clamped her throat. "Abusers don't fear for their victims' well-being, Maksim. They blame them for provoking them, make themselves out to be the wronged ones, the ones pushed beyond their endurance. They certainly don't live in dread of what they might do. You're nothing like your father."

The pain gripping his face twisted her vitals. "I couldn't be certain, couldn't risk a margin of error."

"Tell me about him."

He inhaled sharply, as if he hadn't expected that request, as if he loathed talking about his father.

He still nodded, complied. "He was possessive of my mother to madness, insanely jealous of the air she breathed, suspicious of her every move. He begrudged her each moment alone or with anyone else. It got so bad he went into rages at the attention she bestowed on his children. Then came the day he convinced himself she was neglecting him on our account, because we weren't his."

"And that was when he…he…"

He nodded. "After he beat us to a pulp, he rushed us to emergency. On the day he was told my sister was dead, he walked out onto the street and let himself be run over by a truck."

God, the sheer horror and sickness, the magnitude of damage was…unimaginable. How had his mother survived, first sustaining the brunt of her husband's violence then suffering such an incalculable loss because of it? Had she survived? At least emotionally, psychologically? How could she have?

She finally whispered, "How—how old were you then?"

"Nine."

Old enough to understand fully, to be scarred permanently. And to have suffered intensely for far too long.

"And you've since been afraid you'd turn into him."

His eyes loathed the very thought that he might be so horrifically infected. She stopped herself from reaching a soothing hand to his cheek. Not yet. It wouldn't stop at a touch this time. And he needed to get this off his chest.

"Your mother didn't realize he was unstable before she married him?"

The loathing turned on the father who'd blighted his existence. "She admitted she'd seen signs of it while he was courting her. But she was young and poor and he was a larger-than-life entity whose pursuit swept her off her feet. She did realize he was disturbed the first time he knocked her down. But he was always so distraught, so loving afterward, that she kept sinking deeper into the trap of his diseased passion. It was a mess, a never-ending circle of fear and abuse. Then came Ana's unforeseen pregnancy."

Like hers, with Leo. Yet another parallel that must have poured fuel on his untenable projections.

"She thought of aborting her, terrified her pregnancy would trigger a new level of instability, as it did. The best thing he ever did was step in front of that truck, ridding her of his existence. But after all the harm he'd inflicted, it was too little, too late."

It was unthinkable what his father had cost them.

But... "Stepping in front of that truck might have rid her of his physical danger, but that he seemingly forfeited his life to atone for his sins must have robbed her of the closure that hating him unequivocally could have brought her."

His eyes widened as if she'd slapped him awake. "I thought I dissected this subject, and him, to death a million times already. But this is a perspective I never considered. You could be right. *Bozhe moy*...you probably are. That bastard. Even dying, he still managed to torture her."

There was no doubt Maksim loved his mother, felt ferociously protective of her. Would defend her to the death without a second thought. And this, to her, was more proof that he'd always been wrong to fear himself.

"But why did you even think you'd one day develop into another version of him? When you hate what he was so profoundly?"

"Because I thought hating something didn't necessarily mean I wouldn't become it. And the evidence of three generations of Volkov men was just too horrifically compelling. I learned about them later on, so they had no impact on shaping my life. I made my decision never to become involved with anyone that night Ana died. I didn't question my resolve for the next thirty years, never felt the need to be close to anyone. Then came you."

The way he kept saying this. *Until you. Then came you.* As if she'd changed his life. As if...he loved her?

No. He was being totally honest, and if this was how he felt, he would have confessed it.

"I left, determined to never come back, even when all I wanted was to stay with you...to be the first to hold Leonid, to be there every single second from then on for you and him. But I couldn't abide by the sentence I imposed on myself. I started following you, like an addict would the only thing that could quench his addiction. I had to see that you and Leonid were all right, to be near enough to step in if you ever needed me."

We needed you—I *needed you every second of the past year.*

But she couldn't say this. Not yet.

For now, he'd answered the questions that had been burning in her mind and soul. All that remained was one.

"What made you show yourself now, after you slipped away for months whenever I noticed you?"

This seemed to shock him. "You did? I thought I made sure you wouldn't."

"I still did. I...felt you."

The bleakness of dwelling on the tragic past evaporated in a blast of passion. She'd barely absorbed this radical switch when he singed her hands in the heat of his hands and lips.

Before she threw herself in his arms, come what may, he captured her face in his hands, the tremor in them transmitting to her whole body like a quake.

"That deal we made our first night," he groaned against her trembling flesh, "and the one I made when you told me you were pregnant with Leonid..."

A thunderclap went off in her chest. He wanted to reinstate them?

"I want to strike new deals. I want to be Leonid's father for real, in every way—and your husband."

Maksim watched stupefaction spread like wildfire over Caliope's exquisite face.

Bozhe moy...how he'd missed that face. The face sculpted from the shape of his every taste and desire, every angle and dimple the very embodiment of elegance, harmony and intelligence. How he'd longed for every lash and fleck of those bluer-than-heaven eyes, every strand of this dipped-in-gold caramel hair, how he'd yearned for every inch of that sun-infused skin and that made-for-passion body. And then came every spark of her being— every glance, every breath, her scent, her feel, her hunger.

His gaze and senses devoured it all, his starvation only

intensifying the more he took in. It wasn't only because he'd been deprived of her, or was maddened by the taste he'd just gotten of her ecstasy. He'd felt constantly famished even when he'd been gorging himself on all that she was.

It was why he'd distrusted himself so much, feared the intensity of his need. But everything had changed. He had.

As if coming out of a trance, Caliope blinked, then opened her lips. Nothing came.

His proposal had shocked her that much. Though her reaction was the only one he'd expected, it still twisted the knife he'd embedded in his own guts when he'd walked away from her.

She tried again, produced a wavering whisper. "You want to marry..." She stopped as if she couldn't say *marry me*. "You want to get married?"

He nodded, his heart crowding with too much.

Her throat worked, as if this was too big a lump for her to swallow. "Sorry if I can't process this, especially after what you just told me. What could have changed your mind so diametrically?" Suddenly those azure eyes that he saw in his every waking and sleeping moment widened. "Is this because of the accident you had? Has it changed your perspective?"

He could only nod again.

"Will you tell me what happened? Or will it take years before you're ready to talk about it, too?"

Unable to sit beside her anymore without taking her into his arms, he heaved himself up to his feet. He knew he had to tell her what she had a right to know. She stared up at him, a hundred dizzying emotions fast-forwarding on her face.

He braced himself against the temptation to sink back

over her, convince her to forget everything now, just let him give them the assuagement they were both dying for.

He balled itching hands, smothering the need to fill them with her. "I'm here to offer you full disclosure."

She sagged back against the couch, as if she felt she'd be unable to take the rest of his confessions unsupported.

He wanted to start, but found no way to put the emptiness and loss inside him into words.

"Don't look for a way to tell me. Just...tell me."

Her quiet words surprised him so much his heart faltered.

Despite their tempestuous passion, he'd never felt they'd shared anything...emotional, psychological, let alone spiritual. He'd wondered if it had been because of their pact of noninvolvement, or if there was simply nothing between them beyond that addicting, unstoppable chemistry.

But she'd felt his inability to contain his ordeal into expression, his struggle to find a way that would be less traumatic than what it had been in truth.

Had she always possessed this ability to read him, but hadn't employed it—or at least shown it— because it had been against their agreement? Or had he hidden his feelings too well, as she'd said, and succeeding in blocking her? Had she ever wished to come closer? If she had, why hadn't she demanded a change in the terms of their involvement? Or was she only now reaching out to him on a human, not intimate, level?

This last possibility made the most sense. She *had* shown him understanding he hadn't felt entitled to wish for, had argued his case against his own self-condemnation with reason and conviction. When all he'd hoped for was to make a full confession, to beg for her forgiveness, to ask for any measure of closeness to her and to Leonid that she'd grant.

Not that he'd abided by the humble limitations of his hopes. One glimpse of her and his greed had roared to the forefront. He'd wanted all of her, everything with her.

But now that she hadn't turned him down out of hand, he could dare to hope that an acceptance of his proposal wasn't impossible. But he couldn't press for one. Not now. Not before he told her everything.

He inhaled. "You remember Mikhail?"

She blinked at the superfluous question. For she knew Mikhail well. His only friend, the only one who'd known about him and Caliope.

Whenever they'd gone out with him, he'd felt she'd connected with Mikhail on a level she'd never done with him. He'd felt a twinge of dismay at the...ease they shared. Not jealousy, just disappointment that, in spite of their intense intimacy, this simple connection, this comfortable bond would always be denied them.

But he'd known there'd been no element of attraction. At least on her side. On Mikhail's— What man would not feel a tug in his blood at her overpowering femininity? But being his friend, and more, hers, had been Mikhail's only priority. And though Maksim had felt left out when those two had laughed together, he'd been glad she could share this with his friend when he couldn't offer her the same level of spontaneity.

Caliope's eyes grew wary. "How can I forget him? Though he disappeared from my life the same time you did, I like to think he became my friend, too."

"He did. He was." She lurched at the word *was,* horror flooding her eyes. He forced the agony into words that shredded him on their way out. "He died in the accident."

Her face convulsed as if she'd been stabbed. Then before his burning eyes, the anguish of finality gradually filled hers, overflowing in pale tracks down suddenly flushed cheeks.

He'd once delighted in the sight of her tears. When he'd tormented her with too long anticipation, then devastated her with too much pleasure. Her tears were ones of sorrow now, and those gutted him.

Suddenly confusion invaded her eyes, diluting the shock and grief. "You mean you weren't involved? But you said…"

He gritted his teeth. "I was involved. I survived."

Eyes almost black, she extended her hand to him.

She was reaching out to him, literally, showing him the consideration she'd said she didn't owe him. His chest burned with what felt like melting shards of glass.

Taking her trembling hand made the intimacies he'd taken tonight pale in comparison to that simple voluntary touch. With a ragged exhalation, he sagged down beside her again.

Then he began. "Mikhail was involved in extreme sports." She nodded. She'd known that…and had worried. "When I couldn't dissuade him to stop, I joined him."

Mikhail had left it up to him to tell her he shared his pursuits. He hadn't. The realization of yet another major omission on his part filled her eyes. Another thing he had to answer for.

He forced himself to go on. "I felt better about his stunts sharing them, so I'd be there if something went wrong. For years it seemed nothing could. He was meticulous in his safety measures, and I admit, everything he came up with was freeing and exhilarating. It also intensified our bond when I experienced firsthand what constituted a fundamental part of what made him the man he was. Then one day, during a record-setting skydive, my parachute didn't open."

The sharpness of her inhalation felt as if it had sheared through his own lungs.

Was she unable to bear imagining his peril, or would she have reacted the same to that of anyone?

It was at this moment that he realized. This woman he wanted with every fiber of his being, who had borne his only son... He didn't know her.

Not what affected her emotionally or appealed to her mentally, not what provoked her anger, what inspired her happiness, what commanded her respect.

Right now, her eyes were explicit, overflowing with dread, awaiting the rest of the account of what had changed his life forever...and had written the end of Mikhail's.

He exhaled. "Mikhail swerved to help me. We couldn't both use his parachute like in a tandem dive, as this was a record dive and our parachutes didn't have the necessary clips. We were fast approaching the point where it would be too late to open parachutes, and I kept shouting for him to open his own and I'd manage on my own. He wouldn't comply, forcing me to shove him away. But he dove at me again, grabbed me and opened his parachute."

Her hand convulsed over his. His other hand caressed her, shaking with remembered horror. "The force of the opening chute yanked him away. He miraculously clung to me with his legs, then managed to secure me. But our combined weight made us drop too fast, and we'd strayed far from our intended landing spot over a forest. I knew we'd both die, if not from the drop, then from being shredded falling through those trees. So I struggled away, praying that losing my weight would slow his descent and make him able to maneuver away. I struggled with my parachute one last time and it suddenly opened. It felt as if it was the very next second that I crashed into the top of the trees. Then I knew nothing more."

He stopped, the combined agony of what had come after and her reaction to his account so far an inexorable fist squeezing his throat. Her tears had stopped, but her eyes were horrified, her breath fractured.

He'd thought she'd only felt desire for him. Then when she'd become pregnant, he'd thought an extra dimension had been added to her feelings, what any woman would feel toward the man with whom she shared the elemental bond of a child.

But had she felt...more? Did her reaction mean she still did? How could she, after what he'd done?

The plausible explanation was that she'd react this way to anyone else's ordeal. He shouldn't be reading more into this. And he had to get this torture over with.

"It was dark when I came to. I was disoriented, not to mention in agony. Both my legs were broken—compound fractures, as I learned later—and I was bleeding from injuries all over my body. It took me a while to put together what had happened, and to realize I was stuck high up in a tree. It was so painful to move, I wanted to give up, stay there until I died of exposure. The only thing that kept me trying to climb down was needing to know that Mikhail had made it down safely."

Twin tears escaped from eyes growing more wary, as if she sensed there was much more to this account than just the catastrophic ending he'd told her about upfront.

"My phone was damaged, so I couldn't even hope anyone would follow its GPS signal. I could only hope Mikhail's was working, that he was okay or at least in much better shape than I was. I kept fading in and out of consciousness, and it took me all night to climb half the way down. Then it was light enough...and I saw him in a small clearing dozens of feet away, half covered in his parachute, twisted in such a position it was clear..."

The memory tore into his mind, blasted apart his soul all over again. His throat sealed on the molten lead of agony. And that was before Caliope sobbed and reached for him, hugging him with all her strength.

He surrendered to her solicitude, grateful for it as he felt the tears he hadn't known except when Ana then Mikhail had died, surge to his eyes. He hugged her back, absorbed her shudders into his, feeling her warmth flood his stone-cold being. She didn't prod him to continue, wanted to spare him reliving the details of those harrowing times.

But he wanted to tell her. He couldn't hold any detail or secret from her. Not anymore. He needed her to make a decision based on full disclosure this time.

"I finally made it to his side, but there was nothing I could do for him except keep him warm, keep promising I'd get him through this. But he knew only one of us could walk out of this alive. I'm still enraged that it was me." He inhaled raggedly as she tightened her arms around him. "He confessed he'd directed his parachute toward me, afraid he'd lose me in the forest. He reached me as I hit the trees and twisted us in midfall to take the brunt. He killed himself saving me."

A whimper spilled from her lips as she buried her face in his chest, her tears seeping through his clothes to singe him down to his essence.

"But he didn't die quickly. It was a full day before he… slipped through my fingers. I lay there with him dead in my arms as night fell and day came over and over, praying I'd die, too. I kept losing consciousness, every time thinking the end had finally come, only to suffer the disappointment of waking up again, finding him in my arms—and feeling as if he'd just died again. It was four more days before his GPS signal was tracked down." Another wrenching sob tore out of her, shaking her whole body. He pressed her head harder into his chest, as if to siphon her agitation into his booming heart. "I reached the hospital half-dead, and they spent months putting me back together. The moment I was on my feet again, I came here."

She raised tear-soaked eyes to him. "And followed me and Leo around." He could only nod. She bit her trembling lip. "How—how long ago was the accident?"

"Less than a month after I left."

The hand resting on his biceps squeezed it convulsively. "I knew it. I felt something had happened to you. It was what drove me insane when you didn't answer me. But when I heard you were closing deals, I thought it was only self-delusions."

"My deputies were responsible for the deals, under the tightest secrecy about my condition to guard against widespread panic in my companies or with my shareholders. Though you know now the accident wasn't why I didn't answer you. I intended to never respond, but I kept waiting for your calls, rereading your messages incessantly, compulsively. And the day you stopped…"

His arms tightened around her. He'd been counting the days till her due date, and when she stopped calling, he'd known she'd given birth. Knowing that she and Leonid were fine had been the only thing that had kept his mind in one piece. He'd kept hoping she'd start calling again after a while, at the same time hoping she never would. And she never had. She'd given up on him as he'd prayed she would. Yet it had still destroyed him.

"You kept saying, 'Just let me know if you're okay.' But what could I have told you? 'I'm not? Not physically and not psychologically? And would never be?'"

Her tears stopped as she pulled back to look earnestly into his eyes. "It isn't inevitable the abused became abusers, Maksim. And heredity is not any more certain. You've displayed none of your menfolk's instability, certainly not with me. Why should you believe you'd turn into a monster when the record of your own behavior doesn't support this fear in any way?"

"I couldn't risk it then. But everything has changed."

Contemplation invaded her incredible gemlike eyes. "Because you faced death, and lost your only friend to it? Did that change what you believe about yourself?"

He shook his head. "It wasn't facing my mortality that did it. It was that last day with Mikhail. He told me he didn't risk his life for me only because of what he felt for me as his best friend, but also because I was the one among the two of us who had others who needed me...you and Leonid, and my mother. He made me promise I wouldn't waste any of the life he'd sacrificed himself to save, to live for him, as well as myself. The more I thought of what he said as I recuperated, the more the hatred toward my father, and by extension myself, dissipated. I finally faced that my paralyzing fear wasn't a good enough reason to not reach out to you, the one woman I ever wanted, to the child you've blessed me with. And here I am. But I'll make sure you'll both be safe, from me...and from everything else in the world."

She pulled back in the circle of his arms, eyes stunned.

And he asked again. "Will you take me as your husband and father of your child, *moya dorogoya?* I want to give you and Leonid all of me, everything that I am and have to offer."

Her eyes... *Bozhe moy...* He'd never hoped he'd see such...emotion in them. Was all that for him, or was it maybe relief at the possibility of not being a single parent anymore?

Whatever it was, he hadn't told her everything yet.

He had to. It was the least he owed her.

He caught the hand that trembled up to his cheek, pressed his lips into its palm, feeling he was about to jump out of that plane again, without a parachute at all this time.

Then he did. "There's one last thing you need to know. I had a skull fracture that resulted in a traumatic aneurysm. No surgeon would come near it—as there's an almost hundred percent risk of crippling or killing me if they do—and no one can predict its fate. I can live with it and die of old age, or it can rupture and cost me my life at any moment."

Four

Maksim stared into Caliope's eyes and felt his marrow freeze. It was as if all life had been snuffed inside her.

He captured the hand frozen at his cheek. "I only told you so you'd know everything. But you don't need to be alarmed…"

She snatched her hand out of his hold, pushed out of his arms and heaved unsteadily to her feet, taking steps away, putting distance between them.

Without turning to face him, she talked, her voice an almost inaudible rasp. "You come seeking absolution and the sanctuary of a ready-made family, just because your crisis has changed your perspective and priorities. And you expect me to what? Agree to give you what you need?"

He opened his mouth, but her raised hand stopped his response, his thoughts.

She turned then, her voice as inanimate as her face. "Based on your own fears, you made the unilateral decision to cut me from you life without a word of explanation when I needed you most. And now you're back because you feel your life might end at any moment, and you want to grab at whatever you can while you can? How selfish can you be?"

When I needed you most.

That was what hit him hardest in all she'd said.

Had he been right just now, when he'd hoped she'd once felt more than desire?

He rose, approached her slowly, as if afraid she'd bolt away. "I never thought you needed me. You made it clear you didn't, only enjoyed me. It was one of the reasons I feared myself, since I started needing more from you than what you appeared to need from me. Had I known…"

"What would you have done? What would have changed? Would you have disregarded the 'overwhelming reasons' you had for leaving?"

He stabbed his hands in his hair. "I don't know. Maybe I would have told you what I just told you now and left it up to you to decide what to do. Maybe I would have stayed and taken any measures to ensure your safety."

"What measures could you have possibly taken against turning into the monster you feared you were bound to become?"

"I would have found a way. Probably some of the measures I intend to install now. Like telling Aristedes of my fears so he'll keep an eye on me. And having someone there all the time to intervene if I ever cross the line." He took her gently by the shoulders, expecting her to shake him off again. She didn't. She just stared up at him with those expressionless eyes that disturbed him more than any reaction from her so far. "I knew you had no use for the material things I offered, and I thought you didn't need anything else from me. Feeling of no use to you, then being unable to be with you, made me feel my existence was pointless. It wasn't conscious, but maybe I suggested that record-setting stunt to Mikhail wishing I'd self-destruct."

"Instead, you caused Mikhail's death. And ended up with a ticking time bomb in your head. A literal one, on top of the psychological one you feared would detonate at any time."

He hadn't expected cruelty. Not after she'd shown him such compassion. But her words were only cruel for being true.

His hands fell off her shoulders, hung at his sides. "Everything you say is right. But I am not after absolution, just redemption. I pledge I will do anything to achieve it, to earn your forgiveness, for the rest of my life."

"The life that can end at any moment."

Her bluntness mutilated him. Yet it was what he deserved. "As could any other's. The only difference between me and everyone else is that I'm aware of my danger, while others are oblivious to what's most likely to cause their death."

"But you're not only aware of a 'danger,' you're manifesting its symptoms quite clearly."

She must mean how much he'd deteriorated. He'd somehow thought this wouldn't be the point where she'd show no mercy.

"The aneurysm is a silent, symptomless danger. I'm far from back to normal because I didn't make any effort to get over the effects of my injuries and surgeries. But now I…"

"No."

The word hit him like a bullet. So harsh. So final.

But he couldn't let her end it without giving him a real chance. "Caliope…"

She cut him off again, harsher this time. "No, Maksim. I refuse your new deal."

"It's a proposal, Caliope."

She took a step back, then another, making him feel as if she were receding forever out of reach. "Whatever you want to call it, my answer is still no. And it's a final no. You had no right to think you can seek redemption at my expense."

"The redemption I'm seeking is *for* you. I'm offering you everything I can, what you just admitted you need."

"I only said you left at a time when I most needed you, not that I need you still. Which I don't. If you were thinking of me as you claim, the considerate thing to do was to stay away. The *last* thing Leo and I need is the introduction of your unstable influence in our lives. You had no right to force these revelations on me, to make those demands of me. And I'm now asking that you consider this meeting as having never happened, and continue staying away from me and Leo."

Every word fell on him like a lash, their pain accumulating until he was numb. But how could he have hoped for anything different?

In truth, he hadn't. He'd come here not daring to make any projections. Still, her coldness…shocked him. After baring his soul to her, he'd thought she'd at least let him down easy. Not for him, but because of who she was. He hadn't thought she had it in her to be so…ruthless. And for her to be so when he'd divulged his physical frailty—something beyond his control—was even more distressing.

It *had* been when he'd confided his medical prognosis that all the sympathy she'd been showing him had evaporated. And he had to know if his observations were correct. He hoped they weren't.

"Are you turning me down because you can't forgive me? Or because you don't want me anymore? Or…are you simply put off by my unstable physical condition?"

"I don't need to give you a reason for my refusal, just like you gave me none for your disappearance."

"I had to tell you the full truth, so you'd make an informed decision…."

"Thanks for that, and I have made such a decision. I expect you to abide by it."

He tried one last time. "If you're refusing because of my condition, I assure you it will never impact you or Leonid. If you let me be your husband and father for Leonid, you will never have anything to worry about in my life…or death."

"*Stop it.* I said no. I have nothing more to say to you."

He stared into those eyes. They smoldered with cold fire. Whatever compassion she'd shown him *had* been impersonal. Maybe only an expression of her anguish over Mikhail's loss, and she'd been sharing it with the one other person on earth who truly understood. Whatever she'd felt for him in the past he'd managed to kill, and in his current damaged state, everything he offered her now wasn't only deficient, but abhorrent to her.

And he couldn't blame her. It was his fault that he'd dared hope for what he'd never deserve.

He watched her turn stiffly on her heel, heading to the door. She was showing him out.

Following her, every step to that door felt as if it was taking him closer to the end. Depriving him of the will to go on. Like when he'd walked away from her before. But this felt even worse.

She held the door open, looking away from him as he passed her to step out of her domain, an outcast now.

He turned before she closed the door behind him, his palm a deterrent against her urgency to get rid of him.

Her gaze collided with his in something akin to…panic?

The next moment, what he'd thought he'd seen was gone, and she flayed him with stony displeasure at his delaying tactics.

But he had to ask one last thing.

"I'm not surprised at your rejection," he said, his voice

alien in his own ears, a despondent rasp. "I deserve nothing else. But will you at least, on any terms you see fit, let me see Leonid?"

Cali collapsed in bed like a demolished building.

She'd held it together until she'd closed the door behind Maksim, then she'd fallen apart. She'd barely reached the bathroom before she'd emptied her stomach.

But that hadn't purged her upheaval. A fit of retching, the likes of which she'd only suffered once before, had wrung her dry until she felt it would tear her insides up, until she'd almost passed out on the bathroom floor.

She'd dragged herself to the shower after the storm of anguish had depleted her, to dissolve in punishingly hot water what felt like even hotter tears.

She'd told Maksim no. A harsh, final no.

Now her every muscle twitched, her stomach still lurched.

The blows had been more than she could withstand. From the moment she'd found him standing on her doorstep to the moment he'd told her that he...he...

Her mind stalled again, to ward off that mutilating knowledge, swerved again to the lesser shocks. His unexpected return, the reason he'd left...then his proposal.

The first time he'd made it, her only reaction had been numb disbelief. It had been something she'd never visualized, not in her most extravagant fantasies of his return.

But by the time he'd told her everything and proposed again, her response had progressed from incredulity to delight. Acceptance wouldn't have been far behind.

Then he'd told her. Of his aneurysm. That he could be gone in a second. At any second.

And memories had detonated, with all the brutality of remembered devastation. Of what it had been like to love someone so much, to find out he had a death sentence hanging over his head then to lose him in unbearable abruptness.

Just the thought of repeating the ordeal had panic sinking its dark, bloody talons in her brain…and wrenching the life out of her.

Terror had manifested as fury. At him, for what he'd done to himself, and at fate, for taking Mikhail's life and blighting his with this sentence. And she'd lashed out at him.

Her harshness had only intensified at his disappointment.

Had he expected she'd be insane enough to say yes? Did he have no idea what it would do to her? Or how she felt at all?

She'd thought he'd felt her deepening emotions, and that had been why he'd left. But as it turned out, he'd been totally oblivious to her feelings, had just been focused on *his* needs and fears.

But she'd loved him when he'd been her noncommittal lover. How much more profoundly would she love him if he became her committed husband? She'd barely survived losing him to his seeming desertion. Losing him for real wouldn't be survivable.

Out of pure self-preservation, she'd told him no.

But she'd said yes to something else. To his seeing Leo.

She couldn't deny him his child. Especially now.

But now that she'd defused his need for redemption, without the influence of honor-bound obligation, he'd probably see Leo, awake this time, and realize that having a child in his life, even peripherally, was every bit as repugnant as he'd originally thought. Then it would just be a matter of time before he disappeared again.

This time she'd be thankful for his desertion.

Soon was all she could hope for. For no matter how brief his passage through her life would be this time, she had no hope it would be painless.

The next day, at 1:00 p.m., she'd just finished feeding Leo lunch when the bell rang. She almost jumped out of her skin and her heart stumbled into total arrhythmia.

Maksim. Arriving at the exact minute she'd asked him to. Though she'd been counting down the moments since he'd left last night, his actual arrival still jarred her.

She plucked Leo from his high chair, hooked him on her hip and smiled at him indulgently as he yammered in his usual gibberish, enthusiastically pointing out things all the way to the door.

Though she walked very slowly, feeling if she went any faster she'd fall flat on her face, Maksim didn't ring the bell again. She could imagine him, patiently waiting for her answer the door. Maybe even expecting her not to. And with every step the temptation rose. To renege on her word, to ignore him until he went away for good.

But she couldn't do it. She only hoped he'd quench his curiosity, or whatever it was that made him want to see Leo. In a worst-case scenario, if he asked for a role in Leo's life, what he'd discarded before Leo was born, she'd be willing to negotiate. She really hoped he'd end up wishing not to be involved.

Drawing a breath, she smiled down at Leo once more, holding him tighter as if to prepare him for this meeting that she feared would change his life forever.

Then she opened the door.

Maksim towered across the threshold, his sheer physical presence and size overwhelming her as it always did. He looked as if he'd had as sleepless a night as hers, haggardness making him even more hard-hitting to her senses.

He was wearing light clothes for the first time ever, light beiges and cream, and it only made his gorgeousness overpowering.

She felt his agitation, but not because he was exhibiting it. He was containing it superbly, emanating equanimity, to observe Leo's acute response to moods. His eyes met hers briefly. Resignation at her rejection tinged their gold, along with the intensity that always made her every nerve burn. Then his eyes moved to Leo. And what came into them…

If she'd thought he'd looked moved when he'd beheld the sleeping Leo, now that he met his son's eyes for the first time, what stormed across his face, radiated from him was…indescribable. It was as if his whole being were focused on Leo, every fiber of him opening up to absorb his every nuance.

And Leo was looking back. As rapt, as riveted.

He wasn't used to other people, seeing even her family infrequently. With strangers, he usually buried his head in her bosom, watching them like a wary kitten from the security of her embrace. Leo had been his most uncertain around Aristedes, the most intimidating person he'd ever seen, until he'd gotten used to him. He should have reacted most unfavorably to Maksim, as he was even more daunting than Aristedes.

But it was just the opposite. His fascination with that huge, formidable, unknown being who was looking at him as if nothing but him existed in the world was absolute. It was the first time he'd reacted this openly, this fearlessly to anyone. It was as if he felt Maksim was different from everyone else. To him. She could almost *taste* their blood tie. It emanated from each of them, its influence instant and inextricable.

Suddenly, Maksim moved closer, intensity crackling from his eyes, making her instinctively press against the wall. When this squeezed a high-pitched gurgle from Leo, she rubbed her son's back soothingly and opened her mouth to tell Maksim not to test Leo's uncharacteristic acceptance.

Next second Leo squeaked again, but it was an unmistakable sound of delight this time. Then his six-toothed smile broke out.

Her nerves fired in surprised, agitated relief. But that was nothing to that smile's impact on Maksim. He looked as if a breath would blow him off his feet as he looked down at Leo's rosy-cheeked grin.

Then, as if touching priceless gossamer, he reached a hand that visibly shook to feather a caress down Leo's expectant face. Though he'd touched him before, it had been while Leo had been unaware. Now that same gesture, with Leo's sanction, became momentous. She watched it as it was given, received, felt as if a bond was being forged right before her eyes, felt caught in its cross fire, in the density of its weave, tangled in its midst.

"*Bozhe moy,* Caliope, how did I never notice how astounding children are? Or is it really because he's our son that I think him such a miracle?"

Her heart quivered at the ragged wonder in his voice, the agonized delight gripping his face. The hushed reverence in which he'd said "our son."

She had no words to answer his question, which wasn't one really, just this spontaneous venting of wonder she'd so many times longed to share with him. He was doing it with her now.

"Can I hold him?"

The rough, tentative whisper had tears squeezing out from her very essence.

It was as if he was asking for something so huge, he had little hope he was truly worthy of it. Yet he still braved

asking, even as he looked as if he feared it was tantamount
to asking her to relinquish a vital organ to him.

She shook her head as he turned his eyes to her. "It's
not up to me. If he allows it, you can."

Maksim nodded as his reddened eyes tore from her
face to Leo's, asking his baby for the privilege of his trust.

"Can I hold you, *moy malo* Leonid?"

My little Leonid. He talked to him as if he'd understand,
at least the gentleness in his entreaty.

Next second, Maksim's sharp inhalation synchronized
with hers. Leo held out his arms, hands opening and closing, demanding him to hurry and do what he'd asked for.

Maksim looked down on his hands, as if not sure what
to do with them, before he swallowed audibly, raised his
eyes to Leo and reached out to him.

A shudder shook through Maksim's great body as Leo
pitched himself into his arms, as he received the little re-
silient body with such hesitancy and agitation.

A whimper escaped her. Leo hadn't hesitated, hadn't
needed her encouragement before he threw himself at
Maksim. Leo *had* recognized him. There was no other
explanation.

Then she saw what snapped her control. Tears filling
Maksim's wolf's eyes, accompanying a smile she'd never
thought to see trembling on his lips, one of heartbreaking awe and tenderness. Her tears wouldn't be held back
anymore.

They arrowed down her cheeks as she leaned against
the wall so she wouldn't collapse, watching this meeting
unfold between the two people who made up her world.
Both father and son were so alike, so absorbed in their
first exposure to each other, she felt her heart would shatter with the poignancy of it all.

Maksim held Leo with one arm, his other hand skimming in wonder over him. Leo allowed it all, busy exploring his father in utmost interest, groping his face, examining his hair and clothes. Maksim surrendered to his pawing, looking more moved with every touch than she had thought possible.

In the past, she'd never imagined this meeting would come to pass, so had never had any visualization of it. Even when she'd promised to let Maksim see Leo last night, she'd refused to anticipate his reaction, let alone Leo's. Any projection would have created dread or expectation, and she hadn't been able to deal with either. But this surpassed anything she could have come up with, couldn't be as transient as she'd hoped. It certainly wouldn't end here, at her door.

So she whispered, "Come in, Maksim."

Caliope had given Rosa, Leo's nanny, the day off in anticipation of Maksim's visit. Not that she'd thought he'd stay more than an hour or two. He'd again defied all her expectations.

In those two hours, he'd lost his inhibitions around Leo, made himself at home in her private domain and slotted effortlessly in her routine with her baby. The rest of the day flowed in a way she couldn't have dreamed of, in increasing ease and enjoyment.

There *were* many moments of tension throughout the day, seething with suppressed sensuality, but Leo's presence relieved those, his avid delight in Maksim drawing both of them back to the unit they formed around him.

Every now and then, Cali realized she was bating her breath. Expecting something to go wrong, to fracture the harmony that reigned over their company. But nothing did.

Maksim was at first uncertain what to do except let Leo do whatever he pleased with him. She soon had to warn him that he should firmly yet gently stop Leo if he went too far or demanded too much. Her son was still testing his boundaries, and he must be taught the lines he should never cross. Even with Maksim passing through their lives, she wouldn't have him upset the balance she'd gone to so much effort to establish, even if he didn't mean to.

Expecting Maksim to argue, he surprised her by bowing eagerly to her directive and doing everything to implement it.

She found herself looking at him so many times during the day, wondering how he could have ever feared himself. She couldn't imagine him being anything but that stable, indulgent, endlessly patient entity. Had his father ever possessed any of those qualities, and then lost them?

She couldn't believe that. Someone so volatile could never feign or experience such stability even for limited times. With every moment that passed, she became certain of one thing: whatever else he was, Maksim was not his father's son.

Leo on the other hand, was that and then some. She began to see even more similarities than those that had tormented her during the past year. Facial expressions, head tilts, glances, even grins— Now she saw actual ones from Maksim.

And Maksim was something else, too. An incredibly quick study. In doing anything for Leo, he obeyed her instructions to the letter and carried them out meticulously. Then came diaper-changing time.

He insisted on accompanying her for the unpleasant chore, stood aside watching her intently. A few hours later when that chore had to be repeated, he insisted on relieving her of it. Believing he'd balk at the…reality of Leo's diaper, she was again stunned as she watched that force of nature changing it without as much as a grimace of distaste, and with the earnestness and keenness that she'd seen him employ in negotiating multibillion-dollar business deals.

In between, he'd jumped into the fray to do everything for Leo. Even when she started doing something for Leo by force of habit, it was Leo who stopped her, demanded that his new adult slave do it instead.

She more than once began to tell Maksim to temper his enthusiasm, that he'd soon burn out at this rate. But every time she had to remind herself that it wouldn't hurt to let him indulge the novelty. Which wouldn't last long…

After feeding Leo the dinner she'd taught him how to prepare, he sat down on the ground with his son and let him crawl all over him, like a lion would let his cub.

Soon, Leo started to lose steam until he climbed on top of Maksim and promptly fell asleep on his chest.

Maksim lay there unmoving, unable to even turn his eyes toward her as she sat on the couch inches away from him.

Her lips twitching, even as her throat closed yet again, she took pity on him. "You can move. Nothing could wake him up now." When he didn't answer, she talked in an exaggeratedly loud whisper, "You *can* talk, you know?"

His whisper was barely audible. "Are you sure?"

"Certain. After six months of sleeping in fifteen-minute increments, until I thought I was destined for the insane asylum, he started sleeping like a log through the night."

He still whispered, "You mean I can rise and take him to bed and he still wouldn't wake up?"

"You can juggle him in the air and he wouldn't wake up."

It was still a while before he risked moving, and he still did it with the same caution he would employ defusing a bomb. It was so funny—especially since it seemed beyond him to do anything else—it had her dissolving in laughter.

He at last did rise, but still walked in slow motion all the way to Leo's cot, with her giggling in his wake.

But with the click of the door of Leo's room, she was dragged back to the terrible reality. That Maksim was here temporarily, that she had refused anything more with him for the best of reasons. And that she was on fire for him... and he clearly felt the same. She could feel his eyes boring into her back, his hunger no longer kept in check by Leo's presence.

And she had to deny them both.

He followed her in silence to the door, not even saying good-night as he exited her apartment.

She shook with relief and disappointment as she started to close the door, but he turned, his eyes the color of cognac as they brooded down at her.

"Can I have another day, Caliope?"

Her heart jumped with eagerness. But she couldn't heed it. She had to say no. It was the sane thing to do.

Today had come at a bigger price than she'd expected, the day's perfection the worst thing that could have happened to her. Another day together would definitely compound the damages.

But this man, who stood imploring her for another day with his child, had already lost so much—and continued to live with such pain and uncertainty. She'd always known Maksim could be trusted with her, and he'd proved that he could be trusted with Leo. She'd already told him a final no to anything between them. But Leo was his child, and he hadn't abandoned him as she'd believed.

Anyway, the perfection was bound to falter. Leo was a handful, was bound to wear him out. Maybe not in another day, but soon. And when Maksim pulled back to the position he'd originally wanted to occupy in his life, Leo would be too young to remember his transient closeness for long.

She'd be the one wrestling with need and dread. But how she felt wasn't reason enough to deny him his child, for as long as he needed to be close to him.

Fisting her aching hands against the need to reach out and drag him back in, she nodded in consent.

He still waited, needing a verbal affirmation.

Knowing she was going to pay for this in heartache but unable to do anything else, she whispered, "Yes."

Five

Cali had given Maksim the day he'd asked for.

But there had been one problem. He'd asked for another.

She'd granted him that, too, promising herself it would be the last. But she'd ended *that* day by agreeing, breathlessly, to let him be with them yet another day. Then another. And another.

Now it was ten weeks later. And Maksim had become a constant and all-encompassing presence in her and Leo's lives.

And with every passing minute she'd known she was causing them all irreparable damage by letting this continue. But she hadn't been able to put a stop to it, to go back to her status quo before Maksim's return.

She hadn't been happy, but she'd been coping well. But with Maksim sharing in Leo's day-to-day life with her, shouldering everything she allowed him to and offering more than she'd ever dreamed possible, she realized how much she'd been missing out on. She feared that his… completion was already indispensable.

She knew she'd always have the strength to go it alone if need be. But she no longer wanted to be alone, couldn't bear to think how it had felt when she had been, or to imagine how it would be again if she lost Maksim.

And she had to face it. She was insane. For letting him

invade and occupy her being and life again. And now that of Leo, who woke up every day expecting to see Maksim, and more often than not going to sleep in his arms. She kept placating herself that no matter how dependent on his presence Leo had become, he was far too young to be affected in any permanent way if Maksim was no longer there for any reason.

But where *she* was concerned, it was already too late.

Even if Maksim was gone tomorrow, she had dealt herself an indelible injury with these ten weeks in his company.

Though she hungered for him with a ferocity that had her in a state of perpetual arousal, without the delirium of their sexual involvement, she was levelheaded enough to appreciate so much more about him than ever before. She constantly discovered things about him that resonated with her mentally, commanded her respect for the man and human being, when previously she'd only had esteem for the businessman. He'd told her he was discovering those things about himself right along with her.

He, too, hadn't imagined he could possibly be with her without touching her, that he could be satisfied with just talking to her, discussing everything under the sun, agreeing on every major front. Even when they argued, it was stimulating and exhilarating, and he never tried to browbeat her into adopting his views or attempted to belittle hers. He listened more than he talked, seemed to like everything she had to say and admired all her choices and practices, whether in business or with Leo.

And she regularly found herself wishing he didn't, wishing he antagonized her or exasperated her in any way. How could she break free when he was being this all-around wonderful? She'd rather he started overstepping his limits and infringing on her comfort zones. It

would be so much better if he became obnoxious or entitled. Or just anything that gave her reason to fear his
existence in her life or to instigate a confrontation where
she could cut him off.

But damn him… He didn't.

Worse still, it was no longer only her and Leo who'd
been snared in his orbit. Her family and friends had entered the unsolvable equation, too.

Yeah, she'd told them. She'd had to. There'd been no
hiding his presence in her life this time.

When pressed for details, she'd only said that they'd
had an affair, he'd been involved in a serious accident and
the moment he was back on his feet he'd come to see Leo.

Even with this dry account, their reactions to unmask-
ing Maksim as Leo's father had been varied and extreme.

The women were stunned, delighted—not a little
envious—and confused. They considered Maksim *the*
catch of the millennium and couldn't imagine how she
wasn't catching him, when he seemed to be shoving himself in her grasp.

The men thought she was plain bonkers that she wasn't
already Mrs. Volkov, or at least putting the Volkov tag
on Leo.

Selene, who had her own millennial catch and a similar history with him, thought it was only a matter of time
before Maksim and Cali reached their own happy ending.
It was Kassandra who had the most astute reading of the
situation, convinced that there was so much more to the
situation than her friend was letting on.

On the other end of the spectrum was Aristedes's reaction. After systematically interrogating her and finding out that Maksim had known about Leo from the start
and had still left, nothing else had made an impression on
him. Not that Maksim was back, or that he was offering

her and Leo full access to his assets, name and time. That year she'd struggled alone had been unforgivable in his book. And no matter what Maksim was doing to rectify his desertion now, it would never wipe the slate clean. It was only after threatening to cut him out of her and Leo's lives that she was able to obtain a promise that Aristedes wouldn't act on his outrage.

"Did Maksim tell you he came to see me yesterday?"

The deep voice roused her from her reverie with a start.

Aristedes. He was standing right before her.

She hadn't even noticed he'd walked into his expansive living room, where she'd come to take a call then stolen a few moments alone before dinner got underway. She replayed what he'd said and her heart clenched with dismay.

Maksim *hadn't* told her.

Throat suddenly parched, she could only shake her head in negation. What had Maksim done now?

Aristedes sat down beside her. "He wanted to 'chat' before we met for the first time in a family setting."

Aristedes and Selene were hosting one of their now-frequent family dinners, and her sister-in-law had insisted Cali invite Maksim. Cali had at first turned down the invitation. It was one thing for them to see him in passing with her. But to have a whole evening to investigate him up close?

When Selene wouldn't take no for an answer, Cali had been forced to tell her that Maksim would eventually exit her and Leo's life, and she preferred that he didn't become even more involved in it, making that departure even more difficult and unpleasant. Selene had only argued that if Cali indeed wanted Maksim's withdrawal, what better way to help her achieve that goal than by exposing him to her meddling Greek family? One evening of them en-

croaching on him would be the best way to convince him
to make a hasty exit.

Just because she'd known Selene would persist until
she got her way, Cali had grudgingly accepted. Not that
she had any hope whatsoever that Selene's scenario would
come to pass. From the evidence of the past ten weeks, she
was convinced Maksim would endure mad dogs shredding him apart to be with her and Leo. What was some
obnoxious intrusion compared to that?

Maybe she *should* sic Aristedes on him after all.

Though she doubted even the retribution of her almighty Greek brother would do the trick. Not only was
Maksim powerful enough to weather any damage Aristedes might inflict on him, she had a feeling he'd relish
submitting to his vengeance. He'd probably consider it a
tribute to her and to Leo, a penance for the time he hadn't
been there for them.

"Aren't you going to ask what he said?"

She glowered at Aristedes. "I'm sure you'll inflict the
details on me. Or else you wouldn't be sitting here beside
me. You do nothing arbitrarily."

"My opinion of you is confirmed with each passing
day." Though his tone was light, there was a world of emotion in his steel-hued eyes. Fury at the man they were discussing, protectiveness of her, amusement at her glibness
and shrewdness as he scanned her soul for the truth he
knew she was hiding. "You remain the most open-faced,
inscrutable entity I've ever known. When you want to hide
something, there's just no guessing it. I've known you had
a secret for over two years, but even when I investigated, I
came up empty-handed. How you hid something the size
of Maksim, I'll never know."

"You investigated me?"

At her incredulous indignation, his nod was wry and

unrepentant. "You think I'd leave my kid sister guarding a secret that implacably without worrying?"

"You mean without interfering." She scowled at him. "So what were your theories? That I was involved in some criminal activity or a victim to some terrible addiction?"

"Would that have been far from the truth? Weren't you involved with a dangerous scoundrel and, from the uncharacteristic behavior and length of your involvement, seriously addicted to him?"

Aristedes was one astute and blunt pain in the ass.

But she couldn't let one thing pass. "Maksim was never a dangerous scoundrel. As for my so-called uncharacteristic behavior with him, just ask any woman and she'd tell you that *not* being involved with him when I had the chance would have been incomprehensible, not the other way around."

Aristedes pursed his lips, clearly not relishing hearing her extol Maksim's attractions to women, starting with her.

"However irresistible you thought he was at the time, Maksim Volkov is certainly the last man I would have hoped you'd get involved with. He's not happily-ever-after material."

She snorted. "Isn't it fortunate then that I'm not, either?"

"And you still had a child with him."

"Something that I certainly didn't plan, and never considered pretext for a happy ending."

He lifted one formidable black brow. "So how do you define your situation right now? Where do you see this going?"

"Does it have to go anywhere? I would have expected you of all people to have the broadmindedness not to squeeze everything into the frame of reference of social mores. People can share a child without anything more between them."

"But that's not what Maksim thinks. Or wants."

God, what *had* Maksim told him?

Suddenly, it hit her. Aristedes, that gargantuan rat, was herding her with his elusive comments and taunts to goad her into asking what Maksim had said to him.

She skewered him with a glare that said she was onto him.

His storm-colored eyes sparked with that ruthless humor of someone who knew he always got his way.

"So…does your man like seafood?"

She blinked at the abrupt change in subject, at his calling Maksim "her man."

Then she slapped him on his heavily muscled arm. "I'm starting to think I liked you better when you were a humorless iceberg. Even when you developed a sense of humor, you wield it as a weapon."

"You mean he doesn't like seafood?"

The blatant mock-innocent pout earned him another whack.

He huffed a chuckle. "Just this time, I'll take pity on you, because I'm big that way…" She raised her hand threateningly, and he backed away, hands raised in mock defense. "…and because your deceptively delicate hand has the sting of a jellyfish." Her heart quivered as he paused. Then he exhaled dramatically. "*Nothing.* He told me a big, fat load of nada. You coached him well."

Her heartbeats frittered with the deflation of tension, with lingering uncertainty. Aristedes could be pulling her leg to make her spill info. She wouldn't put anything past him in his quest to get to the bottom of her situation with Maksim.

"He came offering his own version of what you told

us," he added. "Nothing more. He said he wouldn't make any excuses for leaving, that if I saw fit to punish him for it, he would 'submit'—*his words*—to any measures I exacted." He smiled sardonically, looking as if he relished the thought of taking Maksim up on his offer of a good, old-fashioned duel. "Then he went into great detail about how committed he was to Leo, and that if you agreed, he wanted to give him his name—but even if you didn't, the two of you have every right to all his assets, in life and death."

Her heart felt it had squeezed to the size of crumpled-up wrapper. "That's plenty more than what I told you."

Aristedes shrugged, looking annoyed, evidently disagreeing. "He didn't give me one drop of info on what happened between you in the past, no comment on what's going on in the present and zero projections for the future."

"What do you find so hard to line up in your head in an acceptable row? We had a…liaison, it resulted in a pregnancy then it ended. Now he's back because he wants to own up to his responsibilities toward his child, and he wants to be on good terms with the mother of his son."

Aristedes twisted his lips, his eyes wry. "He wants to be on the most intimate of terms with said mother. And don't even bother denying that. I'm a man who knows all the symptoms of wanting a woman so much it's a constant physical ache. I see my symptoms in him." He exhaled his displeasure with her. "Alas, I'm not as good a reader of women, and of you, I'm hopeless. That said, I still feel your answering attraction. So what's the problem? Is it your anti-marriage-or-long-term-commitment philosophy?"

She wanted to grab and kiss him for that way out. "Yes."

"Liar."

At his ready rebuttal, she shrugged. "You can think whatever you like, Aristedes. Bottom line is, I'm an adult, contrary to your inability to see me as one, and the way things stand between me and Maksim right now is the way I want them to be. When it's over…"

"Is this why you're so averse to letting him close?" he pounced, eyes crackling with danger. "You think he'll walk out on you again? Like our father? If he does that, I promise you, I'll skin him alive."

"Why, thanks for the lovely mental image, Aristedes. But no thanks. If he walks away, it's his right. Those were the terms of our liaison from the start. And then if he decides it's better for him not to be around us anymore, it certainly would be better for us not to have him around. So…give it a rest, will you? Let me conduct my life the way I see fit, and don't make me sorry I invited him here, or that I told you he's Leo's father in the first place."

"You didn't tell me. One glimpse of him all over you, with Leo all over him—his spitting image—outed you. It would have taken an imbecile not to put two and two together."

"You'll be one if you interfere, as I'll brain you."

"Any new reason you're threatening my husband with lobotomy?" Selene chuckled, striding toward them. "Just asking, since I happen to be very fond of his brain just the way it is."

Suddenly, terrible images cascaded in her mind's eye. Of Maksim, with his head cut open, surgeons exposing his brain…

"So what did he do now?"

Cali blinked as the overwhelming whoosh receded enough to let her hear the last snippet of Selene's question.

Exhaling her agitation, she grabbed the other woman's hand. "Your husband's doing the same thing you're doing. You both want to observe me and Maksim together—to judge the extent of our relationship and to try to influence its direction. And both of you will stop it right here, or I'll take Leo and leave and you can examine and probe Maksim on his own all you like. Then you won't see me again until you promise to behave."

Selene's other hand covered hers soothingly. "Hey, relax. We won't do a thing."

Selene turned gently warning eyes to Aristedes, asking his corroboration. As always, he immediately relented, this vast…adoration setting his steely gaze on tender fire. It was amazing to see this unstoppable force submitting, out of absolute love and trust, to his beloved's lead like this.

Maksim had been giving her the same reverent treatment.

And here he was now, entering the huge room, flooding it with his indomitable vibe and setting her perpetually racing heartbeat hammering. To compound his impact, he wasn't only laughing with his companions—her closest family and friends—he was holding Leo to his side, as if he was enfolding the heart that existed outside his body.

Seeing them together was, as always, the most exquisite form of torture.

Though Leo was his miniature replica, on closer inspection, she was in there, too. Maksim had pondered just yesterday that Leo made them look like each other. Her first reaction had been that this was preposterous, as they were as physically different as could be, but after catching a glimpse of all of them in a shop window, she'd had to admit he was right. Leo was the personification of everything they both were, as if the fates had mixed them up into a whole new being made of both. He did somehow make them look alike.

Maksim was preceded by his now-biggest fan, Leo's nanny. In the past ten weeks, Rosa had come to believe, right along with Leo, that the sun rose and set with Maksim and at his command.

When Cali had whimsically commented that Rosa had been struck by an acute case of hero worship, she'd looked at her disbelievingly and only said, "And you wonder why?"

Cali watched Maksim murmuring earnestly to Leo, as if agreeing on something confidential. She knew he was convincing their son to let Rosa take him, as he had something to do where no babies were allowed, then he'd be right back with him.

She didn't know who was more reluctant to leave the other: Leo, as he rubbed his eyes and grudgingly went into Rosa's arms, lips drooping petulantly, or Maksim, who looked as if he was relinquishing his heart to her. Rosa swept Leo away as all the nannies were taking the kids to Alex and Sofia's domain while the adult guests converged in the dining room.

Maksim turned and snared her in his focus across the distance. It was a good thing she was still sitting or his devouring smile would have knocked her down.

He prowled toward her like the magnificent golden-eyed wolf that he was, coming to escort her to dinner. She gave him a cold, clammy hand and rose shakily to her legs. He was glowing…for lack of another more accurate description. With vitality and virility.

In the past ten weeks he'd bounced back from his wraithlike state by the day, as if being with her and Leo had reignited his will to live, as if it infused him with limitless energy and was a direct line to a bottomless source of joie de vivre. He'd transformed back under her aching eyes to a state that even surpassed his previous beauty and vigor.

As he pulled the chair back for her at the table, she

could feel the combined scrutiny of everyone present on her, almost forcing her down under its weight.

As soon as they all settled into their respective seats, Selene beckoned to the caterer to start serving dinner. There was absolute silence as the first course was served, everyone's eyes busy studying both Cali and Maksim. Cali pretended to stir the creamy seafood soup, while acutely aware of Maksim as he sat beside her, taking everyone's examination in total serenity.

Praying that they'd all start eating or talking—or doing anything other than counting her and Maksim's breaths—she heaved a sigh of relief when Melina, sister number one, her second-oldest sibling after Aristedes, finally broke the silence.

"So Maksim…" Melina was looking at him in awe and perplexity, no doubt wondering how her little sister had such a man in her life at all, let alone have him willing to jump through hoops for her and his son. "You're a steel magnate."

Maksim put down his spoon respectfully, inclined his head at Melina. "I work in steel, yes."

"How's *that* for understatement?" That was Melina's husband, Christos. He was…crass, mostly with Melina, and that was what Cali called him, instead of Chris. "Volkov Iron and Steel Industries is among the world's top-five steel producers and is the leader in the Russian steel sector."

Maksim turned tranquil eyes to Christos. "Your information is up to date."

Christos looked very pleased with himself at Maksim's approval. "Yeah, I've been reading up on you. I'm very impressed with the dynamic growth you've achieved through the past decade that stemmed from continuing modernization of your production assets and adoption of state-of-the-art technology, not to mention integration into the global economy. And with the economic and marketplace difficulties in Russia, that's even more remarkable."

"And that means you're a multimillionaire, right?" That was Phaidra, sister number two.

Christos snorted. "Multi*billionaire,* Phai, like our Aristedes here. Maybe even a bigger one, too."

"You mean you don't know our exact net worth already, Christos, to decide who's…bigger?" Aristedes mocked.

Christos grinned at him, clearly still flabbergasted that he was in the presence of such men as his brother-in-law, and now his sister-in-law's "man," as Aristedes had called Maksim. "It's hard to tell when you two megatycoons keep exchanging your places on the list."

"But we're talking an obscene amount of money in either of your cases." That was Thea, sister number three, the youngest of her older sisters. "But all talk of mind-boggling wealth aside, are you going to give Leo your name?"

And Cali found her voice at last. "Oh, shut up, all of you. Can't you control your meddling Greek genes and try to keep your noses out of other people's business, at least to their faces?"

"You mean it's okay if we gossip about you behind your backs?" Thea grinned at her.

Cali rolled her eyes. "As long as I don't hear about it, knock yourselves out."

"If only you gave us straight answers," Phaidra said, "we wouldn't have to resort to any of this."

Melina nodded. "Yeah, do yourselves a favor and just surrender the info we want and you can go in peace."

Cali let her spoon clang into her bowl. "Okay, enough. I didn't invite Maksim here so you can dissect him and…"

"I don't mind."

His calm assertion aborted her tirade and had her mouth dropping open as she turned to him.

"What are you *doing?*" she whispered. "Don't encourage them or they'll have you for dinner instead."

"It's all right, Cali. Let them satisfy their...appetite. I'm used to this. Russian people aren't any less outspoken or passionate in their curiosity to find out the minute details of everyone around them, whether relatives or strangers. I feel quite at home."

"You mean they're as meddlesome and obnoxious? God, what kind of genes have we passed down to Leo?"

Aristedes cleared his throat, his baritone soaked in amusement. "Just letting you know that we can hear this failed attempt at a private aside. And that the soup is congealing."

Cali relinquished Maksim's maddeningly tranquil eyes and turned to her equally vexing brother. "Oh, shut up, Aristedes." Then, she rounded on the rest of them. "And all of you. Just eat. Or I swear..." She stopped, finding no suitable retribution to threaten them with.

"Or what, Cali?" Thea wiggled her eyebrows at her. "You're going to pull one of your stunts?"

Phaidra turned to Maksim. "Did she ever tell you what she used to do when she was a child when we didn't give in to her demands as the spoiled baby of the family?"

Maksim sat forward, all earnest attention. "No. Tell me."

From then on, as her siblings competed to tell Maksim the most "hilarious," aka *mortifying,* anecdote about her early years, the conversation became progressively livelier. Maksim was soon drawing guffaws of his own with his dry-as-tinder wit, until everyone was talking over each other and laughing rambunctiously. Even Aristedes got caught up in the unexpectedly unbridled gaiety of the gathering. Even she did.

It was past 1:00 a.m. when everyone got up to leave, hugging Maksim as if he were a new brother. Then Cali waited with Aristedes and Selene as Maksim went to fetch Rosa and Leo. He came back carrying everything, to Rosa's continued objections, with a sleepy Leo curled contentedly in his embrace.

As thanks and goodbyes were exchanged, she watched the two towering male forces shake hands and almost laughed, sobbed and stomped her foot all at the same time.

Aristedes's glance promised Maksim that live skinning if he didn't walk the straight and narrow, and Maksim's answering nod pledged he'd submit to whatever Aristedes would inflict if for any reason he didn't. The pact they silently made was so blatant to her senses, as it must be to Selene's, that it was at once funny, moving and infuriating.

She barely held back from knocking their magnificent, self-important, terminally chivalrous heads together.

They left, and after dropping Rosa off, Maksim drove back to Cali's apartment. In her building's garage, he enacted the ritual of taking her and Leo up, shouldering all the heavy lifting, and accompanying her to put Leo in his crib. Then without attempting to prolong his stay, he walked back to the door.

Before he opened it, he turned to her, his eyes molten gold in the subdued lighting. "Thank you for this evening with your family, Caliope. I really enjoyed their company."

She could only nod. Against all expectations, she'd truly enjoyed the whole thing, too. And it just added another layer of dismay and foreboding to their situation.

"They all love you very much."

She loved them, too, couldn't imagine life without them. She sighed. "They're just interfering pains with it."

"It's a blessing to have siblings who have your best interests at heart, even if you have to put up with what you perceive as infringements." Maksim sighed deeply. "I always wished I had siblings."

Her heart contracted so hard around the jagged rock she felt forever embedded inside it.

Did he mean what…?

Before the thought became complete, forming yet another heartache to live with, he swept her bangs away, his gaze searing her as it roamed her face.

She thought he'd pull her into his arms and relieve her from her struggle, end her torment, give her what she was aching for.

He didn't. He only looked at her with eyes that told her how much craving he was holding back. And that he wouldn't act on it, except with her explicit invitation.

Then he said, "Will you come to Russia with me, Caliope?"

Six

Maksim saw the shock of his request ripple across Caliope's face. This had come out of the blue for her.

It had for him, too.

He could feel an equally spontaneous rejection building inside her, but he couldn't let her vocalize it.

Her lips were already moving when he preempted her. "My mother lives there. It would mean the world to her if she could see her grandson."

At the mention of his mother, the refusal she'd undoubtedly been about to utter seemed to stick in her throat.

She swallowed, the perfection of her honeyed skin staining with a hectic peach. "But...Russia!" He waited until the idea sank in a bit further. Then she added, "And you're proposing...we go right away?"

Relieved that he'd stopped her outright refusal in its tracks and that they were already into the zone of negotiation, he pressed his advantage. "It would be fantastic for her to attend her grandson's first birthday."

It took a moment before the significance and timing of that milestone hit her with their implications.

And she exclaimed, "But that's two weeks away."

"A trip to Russia shouldn't be for less than that."

"But if it's for Leo's birthday, we can leave a day or two beforehand."

He bunched his hands into fists, or he would have reached for her, crushed her against him, kissed her senseless until she said yes to anything he asked.

He held back, as he now lived to do. "I know she would appreciate as much time with Leo as possible, and I'm sure she'd love to prepare his birthday celebration and host it in her home."

That made her eyes widen. "Her home? Not yours, too?"

"I don't live with her, no."

That seemed to derail her meandering train of thought, bringing that gentle, curious contemplation he was getting used to to the forefront. "Then where *do* you live? I never got around to asking. When you're not traveling on business and staying in hotels?"

"If you're asking if I have a home, the answer is no."

He almost added he'd only ever wished for a home with her. The only home he wanted now was with her and Leo.

He didn't. She'd already told him she wouldn't be his home. And she had every right to refuse to be. Her first and last duty was to protect herself and Leo from his potential for instability and premature expiration. He should be thankful—he *was* thankful she was allowing him that much with her, and with Leo. He shouldn't be asking for more.

Not that what he should feel and what he *did* feel held any resemblance. He went around pretending tranquility and sanity when he was going insane with wanting more.

Considering his answer about having no home a subject ender, she resumed her unease about the original one. "This is…so sudden, Maksim…and I'm not prepared. I have work…."

"Most of your work is on the computer, and you can work anywhere. And I'll make sure you regularly have the peace and quiet you need to."

"But Leo…"

"He'll be with me while you work, and with my mother. And she has a *lot* of help. And we'll take Rosa, too."

The peach heat across her sculpted cheekbones deepened. "Seems you have this all figured out."

It was all coming to him on the fly. But it didn't make it any less ferocious, the need that was now hammering at him to whisk her away, to rush her and Leo to his mother's side, to connect them before he…

Exhaling the morbid and futile thought, he shrugged, hoping to look calm and flexible about the whole thing, so he wouldn't scare her off. "Not really. I only thought of it right now."

Her gaze became skeptical. "You mean you didn't plan to eventually take Leo to see his grandmother before?"

The strangest thing was that he hadn't. Now, as she confronted him with the question, the truth suddenly dawned on him. "No, I didn't. I no longer plan anything ahead."

Her pupils expanded, plunging her incandescent heaven-hued eyes into darkness. No doubt remembering why he didn't.

He hadn't brought up his condition since he'd admitted it to her. But as Caliope's and Leonid's closeness infused him with boundless energy and supercharged his life force, he'd almost forgotten all about it. He felt so invincible now that most times he couldn't believe there was anything wrong with him. But he *had* been told it was a silent danger.

Now her unspoken turmoil was more unbearable than sensing that ticking time bomb she'd said he had inside his head. He had to take her thoughts away from this darkness.

The only way he knew how was to give her back the control that his condition, something so out of anyone's control, deprived her of. "Or I still make plans, but only in work. With you and Leo I can't, since it's not up to me to make any plans."

As he'd hoped, the terrible gloom that had dimmed her vibe lifted, as her thoughts steered away from the futility.

She lowered her eyes while she considered her verdict, and that fan of lashes eclipsed her gaze and hid her thoughts. His lips tingled, needing to press to their silken thickness, closing those luminous eyes before melting down those sculpted cheeks, that elegant nose, to her petal-soft lips. Just looking at those lips made his go numb with aching to crush them beneath his, with clamoring to tangle his tongue with hers, to drain her taste, to fill her needs. For he could feel them, and they were as fierce as his. But he knew she wouldn't succumb to them. The price was too high for her, when she had Leo to think about.

He understood that, accepted it. He could barely function with suffering it, but he'd known that if he pushed through the boundaries she needed to maintain, she'd slam the door in his face. And he would put up with anything to have whatever she would allow him of herself, of Leonid.

But now that the idea had taken root, it was no longer about him. It was about his mother. And he decided to use this as a point of persuasion, since it was true.

A finger below Caliope's chin brought her now-turbid gaze up to his. "I didn't feel I had the right to ask this before, when I thought my admission into your lives would be short-lived. I couldn't risk letting my mother know of Leonid only to lose him again when I lost my unofficial visitation rights. If you feel you're not going to end those, or that even if you do you wouldn't cut my mother off from Leonid's life by association, let me take you to meet her."

"Maksim…don't…"

At her wavering objection, he pressed on with his best argument. "I always thought nothing could possibly make up for what she'd lost and suffered. But if there's one thing that can heal her and make it all up to her, it's Leonid."

She hadn't been able to say no.

How could she have when Maksim had invoked his mother?

She actually felt ashamed he'd had to, that she hadn't been the one to consider the woman and her right to know Leo, her only grandson. She'd known Tatjana Volkova was alive, but she'd shied away from knowing anything more about her. What Maksim had told her of his mother had been so traumatic she'd avoided thinking of her so she wouldn't have to dwell on what the woman had gone through. It had to have been so much worse than what her own mother had suffered, though *that* much less abusive experience had undeniably altered her own attitude toward life and intimacy. She had too much to deal with what with her situation with Maksim, and she couldn't add to her turmoil by introducing more of Tatjana's sufferings into her psyche.

But not only was Leo Tatjana's only grandchild, she was the only grandparent he had. He had a right to know her, just as Tatjana had more right to him as his grandmother than any of Cali's own family.

There had been no saying no to Maksim in this. Nor could she have played for more time. The timing was very significant. A first birthday was a milestone she couldn't let his mother miss. And she'd also bought his argument of going there ahead of time and letting Leo's grandmother share the joy of preparing that event.

This meant that she didn't have time to breathe as she threw together a couple of suitcases for the two weeks Maksim had said they'd stay. And the very next morning, she found herself, along with Leo and Rosa, being swept halfway across the world, heading to a place she'd never been or ever thought she'd be: Maksim's motherland.

The flight on his private jet had been an unprecedented experience. She was used to high-end luxuries, from her own financial success, and Aristedes's in-a-class-of-its-own wealth. But it was Maksim's pampering that went beyond anything she could have imagined. She squirmed at how much care he kept bestowing on them. Though he remained firm when needed with Leo, seamlessly keeping him in check with the perfect blend of loving indulgence and uncompromising discipline.

So she couldn't use spoiling Leo as a reason to demand he dial down his coddling, and he insisted that since she and Rosa were responsible adults, his efforts wouldn't spoil *them* and they should just sit back and enjoy it.

She couldn't speak for Rosa, but he was definitely wrong in her case. He was spoiling her beyond retrieval, taking her beyond the point where being without him would be impossible.

And self-destructive fool that she was, she'd only put up a token resistance, as halfhearted as all those other instances over the past ten weeks, before finally surrendering to his cosseting and reveling in his attention and nearness.

And now here she was. In Russia.

They'd landed in a private airport an hour ago. They were now in the limo that had been awaiting them at the jet's stairs, heading toward his mother's home. Rosa and Leo were in the limo's second row, while she and Maksim sat in the back.

And to top it all off? The city in Northern European Russia that they were now driving through was called Arkhangel'sk. *Archangel.*

How appropriate was that? For it to be the hometown

of the archangel who was sitting beside her and acting the perfect guide?

"The city lies on the sides of the Dvina River near its exit into the White Sea…" he pointed at the river they were driving along "…and spreads for over twenty-five miles along its banks and in its delta's islands. When Peter the Great ordered the creation of a state shipyard here, it became the chief seaport of medieval Russia. But in the early eighteenth century, the tsar decreed that all international marine trade be shifted to St. Petersburg, leading to the deterioration of Arkhangel'sk. The decree was cancelled forty years later, but the damage was done and Baltic trade became more relied on."

Her gaze swept the expansive stone sidewalk running by the river, trying to imagine how the city had looked all those centuries ago when Russia was an empire. She had a feeling it hadn't changed much. It had an authentic old-world vibe to it, echoes of long enduring history in every tree and stone and brick forming the scene.

"So did Arkhangel'sk's economy revive at all before *you* put it back on the map?"

Clearly gratified with her interest on his account, he nodded. "It did somewhat, at the end of the nineteenth century when a railway to Moscow was completed and timber became a major export. And until fifteen years ago, the city was primarily a center for the timber and fishing industries."

Her gaze melted down his face as she marveled yet again at his beauty, at the power and nobility stamped on his every feature. "Until you came along and turned it into the base for Russia's largest iron and steel works."

His lips twisted. "That implies that I switched its historical focus from timber and fishing to steel, when I only added that industry to the existing ones."

"And revived and advanced the other two beyond recognition." His dismissive shrug was another example of how he never took any opening to blow his own horn. She persisted. "I've been reading up on your contributions here. People no longer say this city is named after the archangel Michael, who'd been designated as the city's protector centuries ago, but after your nickname here as its current and far more effective benefactor."

His eyes glowed. Not with pride at his gargantuan accomplishments, which he treated with a pragmatic, almost indifferent matter-of-factness. His gratification seemed to be on account of her investigating said accomplishments and finding them—and him—worthy of admiration. It seemed to be her own opinion that counted to him, far more than what he believed of his actual worth.

This explicit reaction, whenever she lauded his actions or complimented his character in any way, always left her with a knot in her throat and a spasm in her heart.

To realize he needed her validation was at once delightful and heartbreaking. She'd lost so many opportunities to show him her appreciation during their year together, when she'd been so busy hiding the extent of her emotional involvement that she hadn't given him his due in fear he'd suspect it and it would change everything. Now that she had stopped pretending that she didn't see his merits and freely expressed her esteem, they were in this impossible situation....

She turned her eyes to the scenery rushing by her window, of that resplendent subarctic city draped in a thin layer of early November's pristine snow, and saw almost none of it as she wrestled with another surge of regret and heartache.

After an interval of silence, Maksim resumed his narration, continuing to captivate her with anecdotes of the city and region.

Then they turned onto a one-way road flanked by trees, their dense, bare branches entwining overhead in a canopy.

"We're here."

Her heart kicked into a higher gallop at his deep announcement.

This was really happening. She was going to meet Maksim's mother, and spiral further into the depths of his domain.

Swallowing the spike of agitation, she peered out of the window as they passed through thirty-foot-high, wrought-iron gates adorned with golden accents into a lushly landscaped park. She'd been to stunning palaces that had parks of this magnitude before, but those had been tourist attractions. She'd never seen anything like this that was privately owned.

The park seemed endless, nature weaved into the most delicate tapestry. Cut-stone passages wound through parterres of flowers and trimmed hedges, meeting at right or diagonal angles, with marble statues situated at each intersection, and lined with myrtle trees formed into spheres or cones and huge mosaic vases before converging on a circular pavilion.

"This is the French 'stage' of the park," Maksim said. "Then in the late eighteenth century, the Russian nobility's taste changed, explaining the zone we'll pass through next."

As soon as the limo left the pavilion behind, Cali saw what Maksim meant. There was a dramatic change in the park to something even more to her liking than the perfect geometry she'd just seen. An English landscape garden, an idealized version of nature, with winding paths, tunnels of greenery, picturesque groves of trees, lawns and pavilions, all with that dusting of snow, turning it into a winter wonderland.

She turned her eyes to him, awed. "This place is… breathtaking. Did you buy it for your mother when you started your steel business here?"

"No, this is where I grew up."

Her mouth dropped open at that revelation. "This is your family estate?"

That tight shrug again, which she by now knew indicated a subject he was loath to discuss. "It's a long story." His tone suddenly gentled. "The estate is called *Skazka,* by the way."

She repeated the word slowly. "*Skazka.* Fairy tale. How appropriate. This does look like the setting of one."

"Maybe a horror tale. At least in the past." A shadow crossed his face as he referred to the time when his father had been alive. "Now it's just the place my mother considers home." His eyes brightened. "But you never told me you knew any Russian. *Skazka* isn't a common word, which can only mean you know more than the basics."

She'd kept it to herself so far, had just savored understanding his spontaneous exclamations and endearments.

Feeling it was time to come clean, she attempted a grin. "I started learning it when we first…" she cleared her throat awkwardly "…started seeing each other."

His gaze lengthened, heated, as if he was seeing a new facet to her and it sent his appetites flaring.

She expected him to try to draw a confession that she had learned Russian for him. But, as always, she couldn't predict him.

One finger feathered her cheek in a trail of fire, his eyes also burning as they mimicked its action. "So you understood everything I've been saying to you." She nodded, and an enigmatic expression entered his eyes. Then he broke contact and gestured straight ahead. "And here's the mansion."

She tore her gaze to the place that had been the setting for the life-altering ordeal that had put him on a path of self-destruction, causing that chain reaction that might *still* succeed in detonating their lives.

The massive building was imposing, majestic. Built in the architecture of a summer country house in the neo-classical style with Grecian influences, it was so huge she thought it must house dozens of rooms. Plastered planks painted in soft beiges and cream comprised the exterior facade. The columned portico had a wide ramp leading to the front door, for cars now, but it must have been for carriages with horses back in the time it had been built. She could almost see a scene from that era as a carriage arrived, with servants rushing out the front doors to hold the horses while guests descended.

As soon as the limo stopped at the front door, Maksim stepped out, and she waited as she'd learned to for him to come around and open her door for her. He covered the fast-asleep Leo securely, then carried him out in his car seat.

In a few minutes, they were walking from the biting cold into the mansion, where it was perfectly warm. Drinking in her surroundings, Cali stared up into a vestibule with a thirty-foot ceiling with walls painted to resemble marble and columns to reflect the porticos.

Without stopping, Maksim led them to a reception room with an ornate fireplace and an oven decorated in colored tiles, with the rest of the decor and furnishings displaying the artistic traditions in Russia at the time the mansion had been built. Everything looked as if had been just finished, which could only mean Maksim had had this place restored to its original condition.

And she again wondered how and why he had, when this place held nothing but horrific memories.

She shook away the speculations as Maksim led them in silence to another reception room, decorated with tapestries depicting the scenes from the parks. Between the tapestries, tall windows looked out onto the lake and gardens. And at one of those windows, with her back to them, clearly unaware of their silent entry, there she stood.

Maksim's mother.

The woman in her late sixties was very tall, which meant she'd been even taller as a young woman, much taller than Cali. This must be where Maksim had inherited his prodigious height. Or maybe he had from both parents. Tatjana Volkova looked like a duchess from the time of the tsars, with her thick dark hair held up in a sleek, deceptively simple chignon, and her statuesque figure swathed in a flowing, cream-colored pantsuit, with exquisite lace accents at the collar and cuffs.

"Mamochka."

Cali jumped at the word, the most loving form of mother in Russian, murmured with such fathomless tenderness in Maksim's magnificent voice.

It had the same effect on his mother, who suddenly lurched and swung around at the same time and stood facing them for a moment of paralysis that echoed Cali's. Then she exploded in motion.

Cali stood beside Maksim, unable to breathe as the woman streaked toward them, marveling at the fact that she was looking at the older, female version of Maksim.

Then she was in her arms, being hugged with the fervor of a mother who at last had her long-lost daughter in her arms.

Cali surrendered to the older woman's need to express her emotions physically. She felt her hugs were fueled by a long-held belief she'd never have more than Maksim in the world, and Cali was the reason she now had more—a grandson.

When Tatjana finally withdrew, she still held her by the shoulders, her hazel eyes, a slightly darker hue of Maksim's, shining with tears. "Caliope, my dear, thank you so much for coming to see me. I can't tell you how much I appreciate it. I'm so sorry to drag you all the way here. I wanted to fly to you as soon as Maksim told me of you and Leonid, but my son insisted you'd be the ones who came to me."

"You fear flying, *Mamochka*," Maksim said. "And there was no reason to put you through that, even in my company."

Cali nodded. "You mustn't do anything you're uncomfortable doing. Leo can handle flying, and it's my pleasure to come to you."

Tatjana only grabbed her and kissed her again, and her eyes filled more as she drew away. Then she transferred her gaze to Maksim, or more specifically, to what he was carrying: Leo.

"*Bozhe moy,* Maksim… *On vam, kogda vy byli yego vozrasta.*"

My God, Maksim… He is you, when you were his age.

Cali's swallowed that ball of thorns lodged in her throat, tears sprouting in her eyes. The anguished joy that gripped Tatjana's face was shearing in intensity, just like Maksim's had been, hitting her again with the power of that same instant connection to Leo.

She knew Leo had people who loved him, all her family. But Maksim and Tatjana were the only two who would love him more than life itself, just like she did.

She touched Tatjana, running a soothing hand down

her slim arm, her voice not as steady as she hoped. "Wake him up."

"I can't…. He looks so peaceful…like an angel."

Cali's lips trembled on a smile. "And he'll be a devil if he sleeps any more. He's been asleep most of the trip and in the car, and if he doesn't wake up now, he won't sleep tonight. And between you and me, I'd really rather not have his rhythm thrown out of whack. So go ahead, wake him up."

Tatjana's wiped away her tears. "Will you do it? I don't want him to get startled, finding a stranger rousing him."

Cali decided to heed Tatjana's worry. She wanted this first meeting to go perfectly, so why risk initial discomfort?

But she had a better idea, something Tatjana would appreciate seeing far more: Maksim waking his son up.

She looked at Maksim, her request explicit in her eyes. The flare of thankfulness in his almost blinded her.

Then he put the chair on the ground, crouched to his haunches beside Leo, kissed his forehead and cheeks, then crooned to him in the most loving, soul-stirring voice, *"Prosypat'sya, moy lyubimaya…* Wake up, my beloved Leonid."

Tears burned at the magnitude of love that poured from Maksim. She knew Leo basked in it, awake and asleep, thrived with it more daily, becoming progressively happier…stronger. She also loved how Maksim always talked to him in both English and Russian, making sure Leo would grow up speaking both fluently. He also urged her to speak in Greek to Leo, so their son would be raised with every facet of his heritage. Though Greek didn't come naturally to her, since she'd lived only six years on Crete before Aristedes took them to America, she did what he asked. And Leo was already trying out words in all three languages.

Leo stirred, stretched noisily as he blinked up sleepily at his father. Maksim's heart was in his smile as he gently caressed his son's downy head, delight radiating out of him as Leo reached out and clung around his neck, burying his face into his chest.

She heard a sharp sob, thought it was her own. It never ceased to overwhelm her, the depth of the bond both man and son had developed in the past weeks.

But it was Tatjana who was now crying uncontrollably. Anxiety crept up Cali's spine that Leo would see his grandmother for the first time like this, and might react to Tatjana's tears like he had to hers when she'd once let him see them.

But Maksim didn't seem worried as he scooped up an immediately alert Leo and approached his mother, talking to him in this soft, confidential way he reserved only for him. "I want you to meet someone who loves you as much as I do."

She could swear Leo understood, even nodded his consent; then he transferred his attention to the weeping woman.

Cali bated her breath, her nerves tightening in expectation of Leo's reaction. For long moments as Maksim brought him within arm's length of Tatjana, Leo just gazed at her as her sobs increased and her tears poured thicker, his watchful eyes gleaming with curiosity, his rosebud mouth a wondrous O.

Then she whispered, *"Ya mogu derzhat' vas, moy dragotsennyye serdtsa?"*

Can I hold you, my precious heart?

Leo looked at her extended arms, a considering look coming over his face. Then he swung his gaze to Maksim, then back to Tatjana, as if noticing the resemblance and realizing who Tatjana was. Then his smile broke out.

Next moment, he pitched himself from Maksim's arms and into Tatjana's. With a loud gasp, the older woman received him in trembling arms, hugging him fiercely, her sobs shaking him and her whole frame. But Leo only squealed in delight and hugged her back.

He'd apparently recognized that her tears weren't ones of misery but of joy, and reacted accordingly, with the pleasure of being the center of attention and the pride of being the source of such overpowering emotions.

Cali found her tears flowing freely, too, then found herself where she yearned to be every second of every day... in Maksim's arms, ensconced against his heart.

She looked up at him, to catch his reaction, and found him looking down at her, his eyes full.

He held her tighter to his side. "*Spasiba, moya dorogoya.* Thank you, for Leo...for everything."

Her tears poured faster as she sank into his embrace, having no words to express her own gratitude—for him, for this, the family she and Leo suddenly had. And mingling with all that joy was the dread that this would only be temporary. His eyes told her no words were needed, that he understood her upheaval. Then hugging her more securely, he turned his loving gaze to his mother and child, clearly savoring those poignant moments.

She leaned against his formidable shoulder and wondered how this would end.

And when it did end, since nothing this good could possibly last, would she survive it?

Seven

Maksim sighed as he gazed out his bedroom window.

Not that it was really his, just the suite he occupied when he stayed here. The one he'd had as a child he'd turned into part of a living area his mother used for her weekly gatherings with her various public-work committees. His mother had given Caliope and Leonid the suite across from him.

He'd almost moved out when she had.

Being in constant proximity to Caliope during the day was something he could relish…and withstand. During the nights, to feel her so close, to visualize her going about her nightly routines was sheer torture.

That first night, he'd lain in bed imagining he could hear her showering, feel the steam rising to shroud her lush body, the lather sliding tantalizingly over her every swell and into her every dip, the water sluicing over her curves, washing suds away. Then he'd seen her drying her hair until it cascaded around her smooth shoulders in a glossy mass, applying lotion to her velvet flesh, slipping into a silky nightgown, sinking into bed between the covers with a sigh of pleasure. All those things he'd so many times done for her as she'd surrendered to his ministrations, as he'd pampered her, indulged her, possessed her all through that magical year. Exquisite pleasures he'd never have the privilege of having again.

He'd woken up aching, wrecked, intending to hole up somewhere on the far side of the mansion. But she'd exited her bedroom suite at that same moment, a smile of pure joy flashing at the sight of him, and he'd known. He'd put up with any level of frustration and agony for the possibility of a moment like this.

The last time he'd stayed here had been six months ago, when he'd finally succumbed to his mother's fretting and had come visiting her. He'd tried everything to put off that visit, hating to let her see him in his condition back then.

She'd been horrified when she'd laid eyes on him, but she'd thought he was just desolate over Mikhail's death. He'd let her think that. It had given her hope he'd eventually climb out of the abyss of despair and regain his health. He hadn't even thought of telling her the truth.

Then a miracle had happened. He'd reached out to Caliope, and though she'd refused to let him back into her own life, to bestow her intimacy on him again, she'd let him into her precious family unit with Leo. Beyond all expectations, she had given him a closeness he'd never thought possible to have with her, or with anyone else after Mikhail.

She'd become his friend, his ally, when before she'd only been his lover. Every minute with her made him realize how much he'd been missing—with her, in life. He couldn't help but keep envisioning how much deeper it could all be if she let him cross that final barrier into passion once more.

But he would never ask for it. What she continued to give him was enough, more than enough. The past ten weeks had been a heaven he'd never dared dream existed, or that he would ever be worthy of having anyway. He still couldn't believe it was really happening.

But it was. He was beholding it in the gardens his suite overlooked. They were talking, laughing and reveling in being together. Caliope. Leonid. And his mother. Everything that made his heart beat, that formed his world and shaped his being.

For the past two weeks, he'd often found himself overwhelmed with so much emotion, so much gratitude, he had to force himself to breathe. Both Leonid and Caliope had taken to his mother as he could have only hoped they would. Leonid's instant attachment had been the far less surprising one. That sensitive, brilliant baby had recognized his mother for what she was to him, and as an extension of the father he had accepted and claimed from the very first instant. But it was Caliope's delight in his mother that sometimes threatened to crush his heart under its significance.

During one of their intimate fireside chats, she'd confided that she'd never really had a mother. Her own had been a shadow by the time Caliope was born, and had died when she'd been not yet six. Now it felt to Maksim as if in his own mother she'd found that maternal presence and influence she'd never known she'd missed, let alone craved. While it also felt his mother had found the daughter she'd lost in Caliope.

To crown the perfection, tomorrow was Leonid's first birthday. He'd had only the last three months of that first precious year, and he ached for every minute he'd wasted, lost, not been there for Caliope and his son. But he would be there for them both from now on. Till his dying day.

Although he lived every second with them as if it would be his last, he prayed that day wouldn't come anytime soon. Nevertheless, he'd put everything in order for all of them, just in case. And now that he had the peace of mind that Cali and Leo's future was secure, he could focus on making plans as if he'd live forever. He now had every reason to hope he would live as long as humanly possible. He'd never felt more alive or robust. His energy levels were skyrocketing, and he continued to grow more vigorous with each passing day, as if his will to live had come into existence. Before Caliope and Leonid, he'd only had a will to survive, to decimate obstacles and reach the next level, then the next. But all that hadn't amounted to living. Not without them filling his heart and making it all worthwhile.

He sighed again at the sight of them, let it permeate his soul with its sheer beauty and magic.

How he loved them all.

He didn't know how long he remained standing there, hoarding yet more priceless memories, before he roused himself. He had plans for today and he'd better get going so he'd have time to see them all through.

He rushed down to the gardens, and as he approached the trio, they turned to him, eager to see him. And he wondered again how he could possibly deserve all that.

But if he never had before, he would now. And he'd revel in every single second of their blessings and give them back a thousandfold, until he'd given them all that he was.

His gaze went first to his mother. In spite of all the ordeals she'd suffered, she'd always remained strong, stable, even, most of the time, amazingly sunny. But now… Now she radiated *joy*. And it was all thanks to Leonid. And Caliope.

His gaze moved next to Leonid. That little miracle that always had his insides melting with a million emotions, half of them sublime and the other half distraught. He wondered again how parents survived loving their children and worrying about them this much. But he was learning how, with Caliope's constant support and guidance. This again led him to wonder how his father had been able to hurt him. He'd rather have his arms hacked off before he even upset Leonid.

Yes, he was now certain. He had none of his father's sickness. And not because his ordeal had reconfigured him. He just didn't have it in him. All his dread now was from external sources. Life had so many dangers, it suffocated him at times to think of Leonid being exposed to any of them.

But even with the constant fears that had become part of his consciousness, he wouldn't change a thing. He wanted nothing but to be Leonid's father, to give him the safest, happiest, most adjusted and accomplished life.

He'd left looking at the center of his universe, the spark of his existence, for last. For she was where his gaze would stay, where his heart would lie down to rest. Caliope.

How was it possible that she was more beautiful every time he beheld her?

Her radiant smile rivaled that of the bright Russian autumn sun. Her naturally sun-kissed complexion glowed with vitality in the cold, her caramel-gold hair gleamed and undulated in the tranquil breeze and her azure eyes were incandescent with warmth and welcome. Her lips, flushed and dewy, spread to reveal those exquisitely uneven white teeth in that smile that splintered his heart with its beauty. He hardened all over, as he always did when he even thought of her, which was almost constantly. Now, with her so close in the flesh, warding off the blow of longing was nearly impossible.

Then Leonid threw himself at his legs, looking up at him, demanding his full attention.

He swooped to pick him up, groaning as Leonid's total trust and dependence inundated his heart. He almost succumbed and followed the pattern they'd established, the daily activities that included their quartet—or quintet, with Rosa.

But today would be Caliope's. She'd been here two weeks and had barely seen anything beyond the estate's boundaries. He wanted her to explore his motherland, experience it with him, share a part of him that she hadn't so far. And when she did, she'd make this land a true home for him. Up till now he'd only considered it his birthplace and base of operations.

He looked up from kissing Leonid to find her and his mother gazing at them with their hearts in their eyes, savoring the picture they made together, father and son.

He kissed the top of Leonid's head again. "*Moy dorogoy,* I have to take your *mamochka* on a sightseeing tour that you won't appreciate just yet, so you have to remain here with your *babushka,* Tatjana, and *nyanya,* Rosa, until we come back. But I promise you, tomorrow is all yours, birthday boy."

Caliope's smile faltered. "He can come. I'm sure he'll like it. He likes everything we do together...."

Khorosho. Good. He'd feared she'd say a point-blank no to the tour. But she only didn't want to leave Leonid behind.

Caliope turned to his mother, and to his hyper senses, there was a hectic tint to her smile. "We can all go. It would a lot of fun with all of us together. I'll go get Rosa."

Ne tak khorosho. Not so good. This was even worse than saying no. She was trying to get out of being alone with him.

Before he could think how to say he wasn't trying to get her alone in front of his mother, said mother intervened.

"I need Rosa while I see to last-minute details of tomorrow's celebration. And you two *will* leave me something to do on my own. And *you,* Caliope, need to see something outside the boundaries of my retreat. Leonid would get bored to tears in tourist attractions and he'd turn your outing into a struggle for all of you." She snapped Leonid out of his arms and almost ran away before Caliope could react, calling across her shoulder over Leonid's gleeful shriek, "Off you go. Shoo."

Caliope gaped after his mother's retreating back for a moment before she turned on him, eyebrow raised.

"You planned this, didn't you?"

His lips spread at her half accusing, half amused expression. "With my mother? No. She's just quick on the uptake. So quick it seems she's been impatiently waiting for me to act your proper host for longer than she could bear."

Her eyes twinkled turquoise with teasing. "If she has been, why didn't she give you a nudge?"

"She's the most progressive mother on the planet and would never interfere in my life. Not that I make it easy for her to be so restrained. My only drawback in her idolizing eyes is my lack of social skills."

She sighed as she fell in step with him. "I used to think so, too. But turns out you're not so bad."

He sighed, too. "I'm trying to recover from a lifelong atrophy of those skills."

"Your recovery has been phenomenal, then. Seems you can't do anything but superlatively."

His heart boomed. He'd become addicted to her praise, when he'd never before cared what anyone thought about him.

Overwhelmed with gratitude that she had forgiven him to the point that she acknowledged his efforts to change for the better, and praised each instance of success, he took her supple hand and raised it to his lips.

At her audible gasp, Maksim immediately broke contact, afraid she'd consider this a breach of their unspoken pact. He couldn't risk spoiling the spontaneity she'd miraculously developed with him.

Pretending an easy smile, he hoped to dissipate tension. "I'm honored by your opinion of my efforts, *moya dorogoya.*"

He couldn't stop calling her *my darling.* But she probably thought he meant the milder *my dear,* since he used it with Leonid, too. But they were both his darlings. His only loves.

Still, he kicked himself for succumbing to the need for any physical expression of his emotions when her answering smile wasn't as open as it had previously been. Injecting as much artificial ease into his own, he handed her into his Maserati, then filled her silence with his usual commentary on the areas they were passing through.

At her insistence, after he took her to the major landmarks of the city, he swung by Volkov Iron and Steel Industries headquarters and factories. It felt as if he were seeing it through her eyes, his view of it colored by her appreciation. She told him she'd never seen anything so advanced and extensive. As usual, her approval was what counted most to him.

As the sun started to decline, and while they approached the final man-made attraction he had on his list, she suddenly turned from watching the road to him.

"You haven't told her."

His mother. About the accident. It wasn't a question.

He still answered. "No."

"I'm not prying," she said. "But Mikhail came up yesterday and it was clear she didn't know you were involved in the accident. I just need to know what you told her so I won't say anything wrong if the subject crops up again."

After parking the Maserati, he turned to her, needing to make one thing clear. "You can never pry. It's your right to know anything and everything about me."

Some deeply moved, if stunned emotion swept in her eyes, darkening them.

She didn't already know that she had every right to all of him? Or was it that she didn't want to have that right, since she'd already said she wouldn't take all of him?

He forced himself to smile. "But thanks for your concern. I told her the same story, just took myself out of it. She loved Mikhail as a son, and she suffered his loss almost as much as I did. I just couldn't make it even worse than it is."

"So she doesn't know about…"

It was the first time she'd alluded to his aneurysm, even though she seemed unable to bring herself to name it. That she had brought it up must mean it had been on her mind. As, of *course,* it must have been. Then she held up a hand, asking him not to answer.

But he did. "No, she doesn't know about my…condition."

Her sigh was laden with what sounded like pained relief. "I'm glad you didn't tell her. She's so happy now."

"And it's all thanks to you."

She shook her head. "It's all thanks to Leo."

"And you. I know when my mother is being her usual gracious self and when she is emotionally involved. I can tell she considers you a daughter, not only her grandson's mother."

Those incredible eyes he wanted nothing but to lose himself in gleamed with tears. "Isn't it too early for that?"

"Time has nothing to do with how you feel about someone."

Her slow nod was an admission of how time hadn't factored into what they'd felt about each other from the first moment.

Out loud she only said, "You're right. And I'm glad you think she feels like this, since I feel the same about her. It's the best thing for Leo, to have his family in such accord. I believe he senses it and is thriving on it."

"It's the best thing for you. And for her. You two deserve to have this special connection, regardless of any other consideration, and I can only see it growing deeper by the day." Her nod was ponderous this time, then conceding. To stop himself from swooping on those serious lips, he said, "Now for our last stop in my guided tour, the oldest building in Arkhangel'sk."

In minutes, they were entering the main tower of Gostiny Dvor—The Merchant Court—and Caliope was, as usual, inundating him with questions.

It delighted him how engrossed she was. She already did know a lot about his homeland, as much as could be gleaned from the internet, but she kept asking things only a native would know, to deepen and personalize her knowledge.

He kept answering as they walked through the massive and long complex of buildings. "This place was the raison d'être of Arkhangel'sk in the late seventeenth and eighteenth centuries. During that time, Arkhangel'sk handled more than half the country's exports. As we Russians like our buildings grand, the lofty status of the city back then necessitated building something imposing. It took a team of German and Dutch masons sixteen years to build it. And this turreted trading center was born to become the nexus of all trade between Europe and Russia."

As they entered another section, answering another of her questions had him elaborating on the place's history.

"Yes, everything arrived or left from this network of depots. Luxurious European textiles like satin and velvet were imported, while flax, hemp, wax and timber were exported. But after Peter the Great conquered the Baltic coastline and moved the capital to St. Petersburg, most foreign trade was rerouted and the Arkhangel'sk trade center was abandoned. But by the mid-twentieth century, at the height of communist decay, many of the buildings here followed suit in deterioration and were demolished. After the fall of the Soviet empire in the latter half of the century, the crumbling place was elected to house a local-history museum, but for a long time restoration was never completed due to lack of funds."

"Until you, Arkhangel'sk's archangel, waved your magic wand—" she spread her arms in an encompassing movement "—and restored it to its former and current glory."

He blinked in astonishment. "How do you find these things out? I'm sure they're not on the internet."

She gave him a self-satisfied look. "I have my ways."

Unable to stop, he traced that mischievous dimple on her right cheek. "You have your ways…in everything."

For a long moment, he thought she'd reach up and drag him down for the kiss he knew she was burning for as much as he was.

But she turned away, pretended to look around before returning her gaze to him, with her desire under control. "So are you planning on feeding me, or are you out to make me lose the weight I've put on with Tatjana's mouth-watering feasts?"

Suppressing his own hunger, he fell into step with her as they exited the complex, grinning down at her. "I'm definitely feeding you. There can't be enough of you for me."

Before the heat that flared in her eyes reduced him to ashes, she suppressed it. "There definitely is enough of me, thanks. So take me somewhere with a weight-conscious menu."

He raised an eyebrow at her. "Seafood?"

She burst out laughing. As his other eyebrow joined in his perplexity, she spluttered, "Long story."

On their way to the restaurant, she told him of Aristedes's seafood-related teasing of her during that dinner. He laughed at her account, and they kept laughing all through their meal, about one thing or another. It was amazing how much had changed between them, yet how much remained the same.

They lingered over their meal for hours; then he took her driving outside the city until they reached the nearby Severodvinsk. On its outskirts, he parked the car in the best possible spot, then waited, a smile dancing on his lips in anticipation of Caliope's reaction.

For a while there was none. She was engrossed in discussing Leonid's birthday, expressing her delight that Maksim was flying her family and friends out for the celebration. Then she suddenly stopped and swung her gaze around to stare out of the windshield.

"The aurora!"

His lips spread as she squealed in excitement, sat up straight, eyes wide with wonder, as she, for the first time, witnessed nature's own light show and fireworks.

He watched her as she started swaying with every change in the celestial lights. The glowing curtains undulated as if raining from the heavens in emerald shimmers tinged with cascades of rubies and sapphires and laced with diamonds. They seemed to be dancing to an unheard rhythm, the same one that had caught Caliope and was moving her body with every sweeping arch, with every wave and curl of light moving across the sky, punctuated with sudden rays shooting down from space.

It was a long while before she could tear her eyes from the spectacle. "I've heard how the aurora was spectacular, seen photos and footage of it, but nothing conveyed even one iota of its reality. It's…beyond description."

He nodded, overjoyed at her enthrallment. "That it is. But it's more spectacular than usual tonight. It must have decided to put on an unprecedented show just for you."

She pulled one of those delicious comical faces. "Yeah, sure. It's all on account of the exceptionally clear sky or stronger solar winds…or some other factor."

"Granted, that's the scientific explanation. But why now, and so suddenly? It didn't start showing off until you took notice and started watching."

"Then what are you proposing? That the wavelengths of my delight boosted the magnetic waves causing this phenomenon?"

"Thought waves are electric and magnetic. Why not?"

She pondered his question, her eyes pools reflecting the myriad emissions before she smiled and sighed. "Yeah. Why not? I am enchanted enough to cause it to show off for me."

She sank back in her seat to continue watching the magnificent display, sighed again then suddenly turned to him, face flooding with dismay. "Leo would have loved this! He would have freaked out!"

"It'll still be here for the next three months. We'll bring him another time, after making sure he sleeps during the day so he'll be awake for the show. Tonight I wanted you to relax and enjoy yourself, be yourself, not Leonid's mother."

She relaxed back in her seat, her dainty lips twisting. "You make it sound as if I have no life outside him."

"You only have work. You have no recreation, no fun."

"Look who's talking!"

"I looked, and I didn't like what I saw. Neither of us has to work that hard anymore."

"Who's working hard? I've barely worked since... Well, since you came back. And come to think of it, neither have you."

"I *have* almost ground to a halt for the past three months," he admitted. "But I thought you were working as hard as ever to make up for the times we spent together."

"Are you for real?" She pulled another of those adorable faces. "Apart from the daylong outings and the ton of indoor activities you always plan, it's a miracle I've had time to bathe."

That image of her bathing, the very thing he'd tormented himself with this morning, hit him between the eyes—and in the loins. But the tenderness that she aroused in him was just as fierce. He wanted to give her everything and ensure her fulfillment in every way.

"You only had to tell me I was interfering with your ability to work."

"And what would you have done?" Her eyes gleamed with challenging mischief. "Don't tell me you would have come less frequently for shorter durations. I think it was beyond you to do that. I actually thought it quite a feat that you didn't set up camp in my living room to be with Leo around the clock."

"It wasn't only Leo's side I could barely leave, *moya dorogoya.*" All traces of levity fled at his rasped confession. "But I would have made sure your work never suffered. Don't you know by now that I'll do anything to ensure that you have everything you need, want or aspire to in your life?"

Her eyes became black wells ringed in azure fire as she bit her lower lip, nodded. She knew he meant it.

But did she know *she* meant everything to him?

He opened his mouth to tell her that, that he loved her, worshipped the dirt beneath her feet. But the look in her eyes stopped him. She looked almost…lost. And professing his feelings to her would put her in an even more untenable position.

So he said nothing, just took her hand and leaned back in his seat, pretending to watch the magical manifestation across the sky. Soon she followed suit, and they spent another hour watching in silence until she asked him to take her home.

Maksim stood beneath the stinging, scalding jet of water, willing his senses to subside, his arousal to lessen enough so he wouldn't burst something vital. Like his aneurysm.

Not funny, Volkov. He knew physical stress had nothing to do with the possibility of that ticking bomb in his head going off. If it ever decided to go, it would, just like that. Now it was his heart that might race itself to a standstill.

Caliope had wanted him tonight. He could tell with every fiber of his being that she'd been craving him from that first night. But tonight, being alone and free from distractions, her hunger had almost killed him. Up till the moment they'd parted ways in the hallway.

If he pushed, if he went to her now, snatched her up into his arms and marched back to his suite, he knew she'd go up in flames in his arms. She'd beg him to take her, plunder her to sobbing, nerveless satiation.

But he couldn't. It wouldn't mean anything if she didn't seek him as she once had, out of her own free will and full choice. So though he craved her desperately, would do just about anything to have her, he couldn't take her power away like that.

Which meant he'd live in hell for the rest of his miserable life—one that he could only pray would be long, for Leonid's sake—and try to find a way to withstand the torture of her nearness.

It was no use now. His body remained clenched under the unremitting barrage of yearning that neither punishingly hot nor cold water had ameliorated. He rinsed the hair she'd told him she loved long, combed it back out of his eyes with his fingers, reliving the times she'd done that, until he couldn't bear the phantom sensations of her hands running through...

"Maksim."

He squeezed his eyes tighter. He kept hearing her voice calling him. As she used to—intimate, hot, hungry.

"Maksim."

There he went again. But this time, it sounded so...real.

Knowing he'd kick himself for being a wishful fool, his eyes snapped open to make certain. And through the heavy spray and the misted glass of the cubicle...there she was. *Caliope.*

As if from the depth of a dream, he pushed the door open.

And she was really there. Standing framed against the closed, ivory-painted door in a satin-and-lace nightgown and robe a darker shade of her eyes, just like he'd imagined in his fantasies.

His senses rioted so violently, he almost charged her. But he had to wait for her to tell him what she wanted.

For soul-searing moments she stared at him, her eyes briefly leaving his to skim over his body, wincing as she saw the evidence of his accident in his fading scars, then gasping at the sight of his arousal, before returning to his face.

He could barely hear her whisper over the still-pounding shower. "I couldn't wait any longer."

Then she moved, strode toward him, picking up speed with every urgent step. With the last one she threw herself against him under the gushing spray of water.

He almost lost his balance with her hurtling momentum and barely steadied them, looked down at her in pure astonishment. Was this really happening?

In answer to his silent disbelief, she climbed him, winding herself around him, twisting in his arms, forcing him to press her against the marble wall.

His hand behind her head and his arm at her back took the impact at the last second. They remained like this for endless moments, panting, their bodies and gazes fused. And he saw it all written all over her face, in the depths of her eyes: memories, longing, hunger…everything.

Then her hands were stabbing into his hair as he'd been yearning for them to minutes ago, grabbing his head by its tether and dragging his lips down to hers. She wrenched at them, and when he only surrendered to her fervor, paralyzed under the onslaught of her feel, the disbelief at her actions, she whimpered in frustration, bit his lower lip, hard.

A guttural growl rumbled from his gut as he dropped her to her feet and tore the clinging wet ensemble off her body. Then she was naked against him. She crushed her swollen, hard-tipped breasts against his chest, rubbed her firm belly feverishly against his steel erection.

Before his mind overloaded, he dropped to his knee to rid her of her last barrier, that wisp of turquoise lace. But as he started worshipping the feast of her long-craved flesh, her hands were again gripping his hair, pulling him back up to his feet. Straining against him, climbing him again, trembling all over now, she clamped her legs around his buttocks and sobbed, streams of tears flowing with the water sluicing over her face.

"I need you inside me…now, Maksim, *now*."

"Caliope, *moya serdtse*…"

He didn't recognize the voice of the beast who'd growled this to her, proclaiming her his heart. He was abruptly at the end of his tether, no more finesse, no more restraint. She'd demolished his control with her distressed demand.

Fusing their mouths together, he flexed his hips, his manhood nudging her entrance, and went blind with the sledgehammer of pleasure as her hot and molten core opened for him. Passion roared as she surrendered fully, all of her shuddering apart for his invasion, his completion.

But as he began to ease himself inside her, she bit down hard on his lip again. "I can't *bear* slow or gentle. Give me all you have, all your strength and greed. Devastate me, *finish* me."

He would have withheld his next heartbeats than deny her what she needed. Holding her gaze that shimmered with tears, he stabbed his girth inside her, hard and fierce. Her hot, honeyed flesh yielded to his invasion as he watched greedily the shocked wonder and pained pleasure slashing across her magnificent face, squeezing out of her in splintering, ravenous cries.

He bottomed out in her depths with that first ferocious plunge, dropped his forehead to hers, groaned deep and long at the severity of sensations. "Caliope, at last, *moya dusha,* at last…"

"Yes…Maksim, do it, take everything, do it all to me. I missed you so much, I've gone insane missing you…."

Unable to hold back anymore, he rammed into her, that unbearable tightness still the same sheath of madness he remembered, even after she'd given him Leonid. The impossible fit, the end of his exile, coming home inside her, sent him out of his mind. He withdrew and rammed back again and again, turning her cries to squeals, then shrieks.

She thrashed against him as her slick flesh clamped around his length with a force he was only too familiar with, had craved to insanity. The herald of her orgasm. He knew what it would take now to give her an explosive release, wring her voluptuous body of every last spark of sensation and satisfaction.

He built the momentum of his thrusts until he was jackhammering inside her in frantic, forceful jabs. Her convulsions started from the farthest point he plunged, constricting her whole body around him, inside and out. Her shrieks became one continuous scream, stifling as bursts of completion raged through her.

He withstood her storm until she'd expended every shudder and tear, then he finished her as she'd always craved him to, impaling her beyond her limits, nudging the very core of her femininity, releasing his agonized ecstasy there, in one burst after another of scorching pleasure.

She sagged in his arms, nerveless, replete. He, too, could barely stand, so sank down, containing her. It felt as if she had been made to fit within him, as if he had been made to wrap around her.

His mind was a total blank as his tongue mated with hers in a languid, healing duel. He'd thought he'd starved for her taste. He'd been wrong. He'd shriveled up and expired. Drinking from its very fount was a resurrection.

A long, long time later, he relinquished her lips to gaze down at her. Her head fell back against his shoulder, her eyes drugged with satisfaction.

Then those lips he'd kissed swollen moved, and that beloved voice poured out in a heartbreakingly tender melody.

Then he realized what she'd said.

"Will you marry me, Maksim?"

Eight

Maksim stared at Caliope's flushed face and intoxicated eyes and wondered if his mind had finally snapped.

If he'd been able to think at all about what her coming to him meant, he wouldn't have dared to hope for more than her finally accepting him as a lover again. So he couldn't be hearing what he wanted to hear. Since he hadn't wanted to hear *that*.

This meant…this was real. She meant it.

One question expanded to fill the world. But he couldn't ask it just yet. He had to take her out of here.

Coordination shot from the one-two combo of satiation and shock, he turned the water off, then scooped her up. He stepped with his armful of replete woman outside the shower, dried her then carried her to bed. She surrendered to his ministrations like a feline delighting in her owner's cosseting.

Coming down beside her on the bed, entwining their nakedness, sweeping her beloved flesh in caresses and her face in kisses, he asked the one thing left in his mind.

"Why? What changed?"

She pulled back to stare into his eyes. And the change in hers startled him. They looked somber, sorrowful.

"Don't…*bozhe moy,* please don't. I can't bear you to feel a moment's distress. I don't need explanations. I don't need to know anything more than that you're here in my arms."

She cupped his face in her hands, her eyes beseeching. "But I need you to understand why I said no, why I held you at arm's length the past three months." She paused, inhaled a shuddering breath. "It was because of Leonidas."

Her dead brother, the one she'd named Leonid after.

Feeling her revelations would hurt her, he didn't want her to go on. But he also sensed that she needed to unburden herself. He turned his lips into the palm caressing his face and nodded, encouraging her to continue.

She did, sharing with him the intensely personal loss for the first time. "I never told you much about what happened, because we didn't delve into each other's private lives before, then because it remained too painful even when we did. Leonidas was…was the closest to me in age, and in everything. My only friend. My Mikhail." He ran soothing hands down her back, fortifying her when she faltered. She went on, her voice subdued. "He, too, was into extreme sports, though the extreme exertion variety. He was competing in a decathlon when he suffered a severe fracture in his left knee. During treatment, it was discovered the fracture had tumors behind them, in his tibia and femur around the joint—what he'd long thought was overtraining pain. After investigation, it was found to be an extremely malignant form of osteosarcoma."

His heart convulsed. He now knew where this was probably going. He hugged her closer, as if to ward off the desperation she'd felt for the sibling she'd loved most in the world.

"We told everyone his surgery was to fix his fracture. Only I knew it was a tumor-resection, limb-salvage surgery. But he was already in an advanced stage with metastasis to the lungs. We were told with aggressive treatments he had about fifty percent chance of survival. I talked him into going for it, since he was otherwise healthy and could withstand treatment, and I'd be there with him every step of the way. He agreed and I moved in with him, and we went through the cycles of treatment, which he weathered as best as could be expected."

Her eyes started to overflow with remembered despair, her whole body buzzing with the desolation of reliving the ordeal. "But a year later, another tumor was found, and this time there would have been no way to salvage his leg. And his survival rates had also plummeted. As we left the hospital, he told me he wanted to be on his own for a while, would come home later. But in two hours, I was contacted by the police. He'd just had a fatal car crash."

It was agonizing to see the shock in her eyes as if it was fresh, as if she relived the loss all over again.

"I…I thought I had more time with him. But he was suddenly gone, and everything I'd been bottling up since the discovery of his cancer and during his agonizing treatments—the pain, the fear, the constant anxiety—came crashing down on me. It was such a devastating blow, knowing it had all been for nothing. For months I didn't know that I'd ever rise from beneath the rubble. Then I met you."

When she'd detailed the emotional abuse her mother had gone though at the hands of the father she'd never seen, he'd thought this explained her no-strings-attached position on intimacy when they'd met. But this revelation gave a far deeper dimension to her mindset at the time. She'd met him in the aftermath of this life-changing loss, must have been reeling, needing closeness yet dreading it.

Remorse tore into him again, fiercer than ever before. "And I exposed you to more distress, especially when I deserted you, and then came back offering you more angst and uncertainty."

Her tears abruptly stopping, a look of urgency and conviction replaced the despondency on her beloved face. "No, Maksim. I see now that your problems did seem insurmountable to you back then, and I no longer think telling me about your past at the time would have led to us working things out. We both had to go through all this to know ourselves better, and to find out what we mean to each other, for better or for worse."

Still feeling unworthy of her love and forgiveness, after all that he'd put her through, he pulled away and sat up. "I understood why you said no to my proposal. I was too much of a risk, on every front, and you had your priorities right. But I didn't imagine you had such personal injury and dread to fortify your rejection. Now that I know, I can't understand why you've suddenly changed your mind about us."

She sat up, too, a goddess of voluptuousness, her breasts full and lush, her waist nipped, her thighs long and sleek, her hair gleaming silk around her polished shoulders. His body roared, forcing him to snatch the covers to hide his engorged erection, angry at his reaction when he should be tending to her emotional needs.

But she pressed her softness into his hardness, palm spreading over his heart, turning arousal to distress.

"There's nothing sudden about it," she murmured against his chest. "I refused you that first night because I thought I could go back to my old life, raising Leo alone without you. But I couldn't act on my conviction and I let you in, and there's no changing that you are part of our family, part of *us,* now. *Ya lyublyu tebya...nye magoo zheet byes tebya....* I love you and I can't live without you, Maksim. So will you marry me, *moy lyubov?* You've already claimed me as yours."

Hearing her calling him her love, admitting his claim to her heart, her life, was beyond endurance.

What had he done?

He had craved her nearness and passion, but he hadn't thought she'd open herself so completely to him like this. He'd only ever wanted the best for her, and Leo.

"What if you were right to refuse me? What if the worst thing that ever happened to you is when I insinuated myself into your lives? What if something happens to me...?"

She stemmed the flow of his doubts and trepidations in a desperate kiss. "I already loved you with everything in me *before* you left. It was why your departure devastated me. And I've loved you more with each moment since your return. If anything happens to you now, whether we're married or not, it would shatter me just the same. So really, all I've been achieving by keeping you away is depriving us of all the intimacy only we can give each other, and having the pain without the pleasure."

His whole body stiffened as if under a barrage of blows. To imagine her in pain was unendurable. He'd wanted to love her, but he hadn't wanted her to suffer the agony of loving him to the same degree, to live in fear for him.

As if realizing the trajectory of his thoughts, she tugged on his hair to bring him out of his surrender to recriminations. "As you said that first night—nobody knows how long they'll live, or how long they'll have with someone. All we can do as finite humans is take whatever we can whenever we can and make the best of it. And you are the best possible *everything* that has ever happened to me. You're also the best father I've seen or imagined, surpassing even Aristedes."

The delight of her adulation, the dread of her dependence, sank into his heart with joy and terror.

But he'd created this impossible dilemma. She already loved him as much as he loved her, and he would hurt her whether he gave her the closeness and commitment she now craved or if he maintained their status quo. He'd been a fool not to realize how risky this all was, to think they could share so much without dragging her down into the well of addiction with him. He'd done this to her, and could only now give her whatever she wanted. Every single second of his life, every spark of his being.

What she already had total claim to.

Now she needed his corroboration. And for him to provide a distraction from all this overwrought emotion.

He forced a grin to his lips. "Better than the legendary Aristedes, huh? And you're not biased at all, of course."

An impish grin overlapped her urgency, transforming her face. "Not one tiny bit. He's a close second, granted, but you're the unapproachable number one." She pushed him on his back, coming to lie on top of him, pressing her hot length to his every inch. "So since it would be for better or for worse between us from now on, whether I marry you or not, 'not' is only pointless denial. So I again ask you, *moy serdtse*. Marry me."

He gazed up at her adoringly, unable to do anything anymore but risk living with constant worry and dread for the pleasure and privilege of any time they could have together.

"*Pozhaluista, moy lyubov...* Please, my love, say yes."

How could he say anything else? "Yes, *moy dusha,* yes.... I'm all yours to do with as you please."

He rose beneath her and swept her around until he was pressing down on her between her eagerly spreading legs.

Tears of happiness glittered as she arched, opening herself for his domination. "As soon as possible?"

"How about tomorrow?" He delivered the words into her lips as he thrust inside her, going home.

The shock of his combined proposition and invasion tore a cry from her depths.

With ecstasy shuddering across her face, she wrapped herself around him, taking him deeper, and moaned, "Yes."

Caliope still couldn't believe it.

She'd gone to Maksim's room last night without thinking.

She'd just been unable to stay away anymore. None of what had happened—their intimacies, her confessions, her proposal—had been in the least premeditated. Not only hadn't she thought of impassioned arguments to convince him to marry her beforehand, she hadn't even first convinced *herself.* She'd just gone to him, and had taken this life-altering step.

But then her fate had changed forever the moment she'd met his eyes across that reception hall three years ago. There'd always been no going back. The only difference now was that she was finally at peace with it, wouldn't settle for anything less.

If she couldn't be with him, she wanted nothing at all.

She passed by one of the ornate mirrors studding the walls of the mansion and met her own eyes. And winced.

Could it be more obvious that she'd barely survived a night of wild possession with that incomparable Russian wolf?

Everything about her was sore and swollen; even her hips swayed in a way that said she'd been plundered. As she'd begged him to when he'd attempted gentleness. She'd wanted him to dominate and devastate her. And how he had.

They hadn't slept at all, but who needed sleep? The rush of his lovemaking would keep her awake and going for a week straight. She felt as energized and as alert as she'd ever been. But it had only been after making love to her for the fifth time that they'd finally taken a breath not laden with delirium, and she'd started having qualms about saying yes to his proposition of an immediate wedding.

Fearing their anniversary would be supplanted by Leo's birthday, she'd proposed they keep their guests here for a few days and then have their wedding at the end of the week.

But he'd insisted that they didn't need a specific date every year to celebrate their marriage, since he'd be celebrating with her every single day. And she'd believed him.

So they were having their wedding today.

At 6:00 a.m. sharp, he'd gone to prepare everything and she'd given him carte blanche to do whatever he saw fit. She had no demands, only wanted to have the freedom of showing him that he was her everything. And to announce their bond to the world.

She'd seen tears fill his eyes before. But last night, they'd flowed. Hers had flooded in response, then deluged when he'd asked *her* to tell the world, starting with his mother.

He wanted her to be the one to give his mother what he knew would be the best gift anyone could give her, after that of Leo. A wife for her son. A daughter-in-law. A daughter, period.

And she had a six-thirty meeting with Tatjana at the chamber where they'd planned on holding Leo's birthday party, and where they'd now also have their wedding. Leo had practically been the one to pick the setting in the dance hall or "hall of mirrors". His delight in its painted ceilings and ornate, mirror-covered walls had been so explicit, he'd had them stay there at least an hour a day, as he pranced on top of tables in front of the mirrors, turned upside down to see himself from all different angles and rolled on the ground to stare at the ceiling. It was also the setting for a most important milestone. He'd taken his first steps there a couple of days after they'd arrived in Arkhangel'sk.

He'd chosen well, since it was the mansion's largest and most decorated room. But with the list of people Tatjana had invited, seemingly all the citizens of Arkhangel'sk, they'd need more than that space. Maybe even *all* of the mansion.

Her feet almost leaving the ground, she rushed through said mansion, feeling again as if she'd stepped back in time, all the time half expecting she'd meet figures from the era of the tsars.

It almost seemed an anachronism that the people she did meet, those who worked on the estate and on Tatjana's myriad community projects—all part of her continuous efforts to act as the community's uncrowned queen—were all jarringly modern.

She smiled left and right to everyone she met, almost running the last steps as she entered the dance hall.

The sight that greeted her had her heart doing its usual jig. Tatjana and Leo were perfect together. She was grateful every minute she'd agreed to come here, to give them all this rich and unique relationship. Rosa, an integral part of the family now, was also having the time of her life here, and apparently finding the love of her life, too, in Sasha, Maksim's chauffeur/bodyguard.

Could things get more perfect?

As soon as she thought that, her heart quivered with trepidation.

Could anything be this perfect…for long?

"Caliope, *moya dorogoya!*"

Tatjana's cheerfulness jerked her out of those dark thoughts, and she ran to her and to Leo.

For the next fifteen minutes, Tatjana didn't give her the chance to say much of anything as she supplied her with every minute detail of the birthday-party preparations, then solicited her opinion on changes in the color schemes, menu and seating plans.

Leo soon got bored, and Rosa took him away to what Maksim had transformed into every child's wonderland.

Then Tatjana was sweeping her along to her favorite sitting place, the grand living room. It was studded with paintings and decorations that felt like a documentary of the long history and glory of the Volkov family. Something Maksim had never mentioned.

As much as he was copious with his information about the country and the region, he'd been stingy with family details.

From what he'd told her of his father and grandfather, she understood his reluctance. She'd at first thought it wasn't a good idea to know more than she already knew. But now she felt she needed to glean as much information as possible in order to know him from every facet. She'd tried to broach the subject many times, but he'd always ingeniously escaped giving any details.

But here she was, with the one other person who could supply her with the knowledge she needed. Not that she had one single idea how to introduce the topic. If she asked outright, it would appear as if she was prying into matters Maksim hadn't seen fit to share with her. Which, of course, she was.

But what was she *thinking?* She should be telling Tatjana of the wedding, not trying to get her to spill the Volkov family secrets!

Tatjana offered her a plate of *pirozhki,* mouthwatering pastries filled with potato and cheese, with a side bowl of *smetana,* delicious sour cream that Russians used copiously.

Cali reciprocated by handing her tea, then began, "Tatjana…"

Clearly not realizing that she was cutting her off, Tatjana said, "Maksim didn't tell you much about his father, did he? Or about my marriage to him? Beside it being an abusive relationship that ended horrifically?"

Whoa. Had she been thinking of it so intensely she'd telepathically conveyed her burning curiosity to Tatjana?

She could only shake her head.

Tatjana sighed. "It pains me that he can't forgive or forget."

Cali put down the *pirozhki,* suddenly finding eating impossible. "Is it conceivable to do either when such wrongs have been dealt? I wondered how you survived when he first told me. But now that I've seen you, I know you're the strongest person I've ever known, and you can weather anything. And from the way you talk about your late husband, I can sense that *you,* at least, have forgiven him. And I wonder how you did it."

"I want to tell you how so you can understand Maksim better. But I have to tell you my life story to explain."

Cali nodded, even the slight movement difficult.

Tatjana sighed again. "I first saw Grigori when I was twenty and he was twenty-nine. I was working in one of the timber factories here when he came with his father, the city's governor, to learn the ropes of the position he would occupy, which would place him on his father's and grandfather's paths, as high-ranking Soviet officials. I was struck by him, and he was as struck by me."

She paused for a brief moment before continuing. "But all talk of equality in communism aside, a poor factory worker and a young man from what was considered the new royalty in Soviet Russia was an impossible proposition. But he moved heaven and earth, and fought his father and family long and hard to have me. Though I was at times disturbed by his intensity, I was hopelessly attracted to him. And he did seem like a fairy tale come true to the girl I was then."

She took a sip of tea, encouraged Cali to do the same. Cali gulped down a scalding mouthful, on the edge of her seat, the feeling that she'd plunged into a past life and another era intensifying.

Tatjana went on. "Then we were married. But for years, I couldn't conceive. Everyone kept pushing him to leave me, as not only was I inappropriate but barren. I think he thought it was him who was barren, and he grew progressively more morose, especially as his positions kept getting bigger and his responsibilities with them. It was five years after we got married that I became pregnant. I think he always had unreasonable doubts that Maksim wasn't his."

Was that what had driven him to abuse his wife and son? He'd believed she'd betrayed him to conceive, then saddled him with the fruit of her infidelity to raise as his own?

"Not that his abuse started only then. It just started to become a pattern." So much for that theory. The bastard had already been an unstable monster. "But it was a terrible time all around. We were passing through the worst phases of the Cold War, and the situation of almost everyone in Russia was dismal. Having a husband who slapped me around, but otherwise gave me, and my family, everything, seemed like such a tiny quibble in comparison to those who had no homes or jobs or food. And I was inexperienced for my age, having been totally sheltered living here, so I didn't know any better."

Just like Cali's mother. It made her again realize just how much women today took for granted in all the rights and powers they'd gained in the past fifty years.

"After the birth of Maksim, Grigori was promoted to become the vice governor, a position he soon realized he was totally unsuited for. But he couldn't admit that or risk dishonoring his father—and himself—forever. He knew what happened to those they considered inadequate in the hierarchy. He struggled, and it only got worse as time went by. Reports of his mistakes and investigations into his failures began to accumulate, and he began to disintegrate."

Cali had to bite her tongue. If the older woman thought she'd make her sympathize with the weak bastard who'd scarred Maksim, and almost had made him destroy what they'd had and had now regained by a sheer miracle, she had another think coming!

Unaware of her venom, Tatjana went on. "He started to take it out on me more often, but as Maksim grew bigger and began to stand up for me and antagonize him for what he did to me, he turned his wrath on him. I believe he was more convinced every day that Maksim couldn't hate him like that if he was his. Then, in spite of all my measures, I got pregnant again. I thought of terminating the pregnancy, but ultimately didn't have the heart to and was forced to tell Grigori. His paranoia increased, but he didn't fully break down until he was fired from his position, just five months after Ana was born. We were given a month's notice to vacate this residence for his replacement. On the day we were set to leave, he went berserk, accusing me of being the reason for all his ill fortune, that I blighted him with my two bastards and…the rest you know."

Oh, she knew. And now hated Maksim's father all the more. Try as she might, she just couldn't understand how Tatjana managed to remain this adjusted, considering everything she'd endured.

Tatjana sighed. "Now comes the part about me and Maksim. We came out of the hospital to find no home

and no family, as my parents had died and I had no siblings, and Grigori's family wanted nothing to do with us.
He'd made a lot of enemies here and so much of his failures were snowballing." She sighed again, remembered
sadness tingeing her face. "The whole place seemed to be
going to hell. I worked any job I could find, and my darling Maksim was with me every step of the way, studying, working, doing everything for me that grown men
couldn't. I don't think I would have survived without him.

"Then the Soviet Union collapsed and it was mayhem
for a long while. I was almost afraid Maksim had turned
to crime when he kept coming home covered in cuts and
bruises. But he was actually defending the helpless here
against the criminals who were exploiting them. And instead of working in a job in the industries here, he wanted
to introduce something new to the region, so he could rule
it. He chose steel. But he needed to learn the process from
the ground up, so we went to Magnitogorsk, the center of
steel industries in Russia. He made a living for us right
away, then kept soaring higher every day. By the time he
was in his mid-twenties, he'd already become a millionaire. He took us back here to set up Volkov Iron and Steel
Industries and bought me this place."

Caliope had given up trying to hold back the tears.
Imagining Maksim as a young boy, then teenager, then
young man, as he struggled through the most unforgiving
of social, political and financial circumstances, fending
for his mother and all who needed his superior courage
and strength and intellect, surmounting any difficulties
and coming out not only on top but as such a phenomenal
success, was beyond awe inspiring.

To think he was hers was still unbelievable.

But another thing was incomprehensible. "Why did

you want to reclaim the place where you'd both suffered so much?"

Tatjana's eyes, which were so much like Maksim's, melted with tenderness. "Because my main memories here consisted of being with my beloved son. And my parents until they died. And after the loss and the pain began to fade away, I needed those precious memories back."

"But what about Maksim?" Cali said. "Doesn't your staying here make it hard for him to spend time with you?"

"I do know that the good memories with me don't make up for the horrible ones for him. But it's not only family nostalgia that made me wish to be back here. I have a responsibility to the people here, who stood by me at my worst times, and whom Grigori's mismanagement had harmed. I wanted to provide as many jobs and do my part in developing the community on a cultural and social level as Maksim was doing on an economic one."

This explained so much. Everything, really. She now finally and fully understood how he'd become the man she loved and respected with all her soul.

And now it was time to give Tatjana the wonderful news.

But Tatjana wasn't finished. She put her cup down and reached for both of Cali's hands, her eyes solemn. "I know Maksim always carried within him the fear that he might manifest his father's instability, but I assure you, Caliope, Maksim is nothing like his father or his menfolk. He'd been tested in the crucible of unendurable tests and had remained in control and never exhibited his father's volatility, not for a moment. In fact, he becomes more stable under pressure." Fierce maternal faith crossed Tatjana's face and her voice filled with urgency. "So you have absolutely *nothing* to fear. Maksim would rather die than raise a hand against anyone weaker, let alone those whom he loves and who depend on him."

Cali was the one who squeezed Tatjana's hands now, soothing her agitation. "I know that, Tatjana. I'm certain of it as much I'm certain that I'm alive."

"Then why won't you marry him?" Tatjana cried.

So that was what this was all about? Her future mother-in-law selling her on the idea of marrying her son?

Joy fizzed in her blood as her lips split in a grin that must have blinded Tatjana.

"Who said I won't? I'm marrying him...today!"

Nine

After announcing to Tatjana the wedding would be that very same day, and after the older woman had gotten over her *very* vocal shock, she hadn't even attempted to talk her into a postponement to give them time to prepare. According to Maksim's mother, this was three years overdue and they weren't putting it off one second longer. And then they still had twelve hours. *Plenty* of time in the hands of someone versed in preparing celebrations.

Of that Cali was sure. Between Maksim and his mother, who'd each separately promised her a wedding to rival those of the tsars, she knew they could make anything come true.

Not that she cared about what the wedding would be like. She only wanted her family and friends here to see her exchange vows with Maksim, even in her current jeans and ponytail if need be. All that truly mattered was becoming Caliope Volkov...

Caliope Volkov. She liked that. No. She *loved* that. And she loved that Leo would become Leonidas Maksim Volkov. His doting father had said he'd grow into a fearsome man, both lion and wolf.

Though she was considering changing Leo's name to Leonid, as Maksim called him. To give tribute to Leonidas yet at the same time pay proper homage to Leo's heritage. Maksim had refused that categorically, saying that he'd stop calling him Leonid if she thought he preferred it, that he just found it more natural to say. He wanted her to honor her brother and best friend, and was honored that she'd named his son after him.

When they couldn't reach a compromise, he'd suggested they leave it up to Leo to choose when he grew older.

Not that this was a time to think of names. Now it was time to be swept into the whirlwind of preparations.

"So your man is so stingy, he wants to squeeze one major and another monumental event into one?"

Cali rushed out of the bathroom at hearing the deep teasing voice, squealing in pleasure at finding Aristedes and Selene and their two kids standing on her suite's doorstep.

Though she was already so tired all she wanted was to collapse in bed and snooze for ten hours straight, she hurtled herself at the quartet, deluging them with hugs and kisses.

As she carried Sofia and cooed to her how her auntie had missed her and how her cousin Leo couldn't wait to have someone his age around, Aristedes continued his mockery.

"I've heard of double birthdays or weddings, but a baby birthday and the wedding of said baby's parents? That's new."

Selene nipped his chin in tender chastisement. "You are *not* going to start playing the nitpicking brother-in-law."

Aristedes turned indulgent eyes to his wife. "That's my kid sister over here. You bet I'm going to watch that Russian wolf's every breath and hold him accountable for her every smile. And if I see as much as one tear…"

Selene curled her lips at him. "You mean like the rivers you made me cry once?"

He narrowed his eyes, clearly still disturbed that he'd caused her pain for any reason. "That was before we married."

Selene arched one elegant, dark eyebrow at him. "And now you're walking the line because I have not one but three hulking, overbearing Greek brothers watching your every breath and holding you accountable for my every smile."

"If you think those brothers of yours have *any*..."

"Down, Aris." Selene dragged him down for a laughing kiss. "That was just me teasing you to make you lay off Maksim." At his harrumph, which said he took severe exception to any allusions—if even in jest—that her brothers could *ever* influence his behavior, especially concerning her, she turned to wink at Cali. "He still has humorless blackouts. But I'm working on him."

"You've done a miraculous job so far." Cali giggled, fiercely happy to see how adored her eldest brother was by the woman who owned his heart. "Before you, we didn't think he had humor installed at all. We didn't think he was human!"

"Like your man, you mean?" Aristedes twisted his lips, hugging Selene more securely, his eyes darting to keep track of Alex, who'd climbed Cali's bed and was playing with the articles on her nightstand. "He was established as an arctic Russian robot of the highest order."

Selene chuckled. "Seems we'll discover that your man and mine are twins separated at birth."

Cali burst out laughing. "Just substitute Russian for Greek and anything you say about one could well be describing the other."

Aristedes pursed his lips, not quite mockingly this time.

"Good news for your man is he finally did the right thing. And he wore you down in record time, too."

"You're wrong on both counts, since I was the one who asked him to marry me, and three months felt like forever."

A lethal bolt of lightning burst in Aristedes's steel eyes. "You mean you were the one trying to pin him down to a commitment all this time?"

She held up a placating hand. "First, 'down, Aris,' like Selene just said. Second, there is no pinning down involved. We both want this with every fiber of our beings. Third, he asked me to marry him the first night he came back and I turned him down, but he proceeded to dedicate his life to me and Leo anyway. Then just yesterday, I faced it that we have no life without him. But knowing he'd never ask again, so he wouldn't pressure me, I had to propose this time."

Still looking unconvinced, Aristedes growled under his breath. "This had better be the truth, Cali."

Did he suspect she had their mother's victim affliction? The very thing their sisters had, to one degree or another?

She held his eyes reassuringly. "It is. I don't have a blind-eye-turning bone in my body."

His eyes bored into hers as it to gauge the veracity of her claim. Then he inhaled. "As long as you're sure…"

"I am." She handed him Sofia, who'd nestled into her neck and gone to sleep, and ran to fetch Alex. Once she had him carrying both of his children, she turned him around toward the door. "Now I'll borrow your wife and you go fetch me Melina, Phaidra, Thea and Kassandra, too."

"You called?"

The cheerful voice was Thea's. The next second, she had appeared in the doorway, followed by everyone Cali had just named. They were all wearing the same dress that was sculpted over Selene—an incredible sleeveless creation with an off-shoulder décolletage, nipped waist and flowing skirt in powder-blue, supple satin embroidered with gold thread. Which meant they were serving as her bridesmaids. The ever-present lump in her throat expanded.

"How's that for fast service?" Kassandra chuckled.

"You're mind readers." Cali pounced on them and dragged them in, before turning back to Aristedes. "You go see what Maksim has planned for you during the ceremony, but behave or I'll sic Selene on you." Aristedes gave a sigh of mock resignation, dropping a kiss on her cheek, then another on Selene's lips.

Before he walked away, she clung to him. "Is he here?"

His lips thinned. "Andreas? I would have skinned him alive if he didn't come."

She winced. "You have a thing for skinning alive men who don't perform to your standards, don't you?"

He exhaled. "Lucky for him, I won't have to this time. He wasn't coming when it was only Leo's birthday, but as per his words, 'not even a bastard like him would miss his kid sister's wedding.'"

Not exactly the enthusiasm she would have hoped for from her older brother, but all that mattered was that Andreas was here. Everyone was here.

Her eyes filled, her chest tightened. As it seemed was her natural state these days.

Aristedes kissed her again. "Now hurry and be a ready bride so I can give you away. And ladies, don't get so carried away dressing her up that you lose track of time and keep us waiting too long."

"We don't *have* long," Cali wailed as she closed the door to drown out the sound of his infuriating chuckling, then turned to the grinning women. "Wait until you see what Maksim sent me for a wedding dress. I'm afraid to even…approach the thing, let alone wear it. And to think I sent away those stylists and beauticians Maksim hired to help me get ready, thinking I can manage."

Selene smiled. "Based on his similarity to Aris, I bet he has them standing by in case you change your mind."

"He did send in plan B." Melina pointed at herself.

Phaidra nodded. "Yep. He barely saluted us before almost chasing us here so we'd run to tend to your needs."

"But what were you thinking sending professionals away, you silly girl?" Thea scolded. "Since when do you know the first thing about makeup and hairdressing, when you never use any with your disgustingly perfect coloring and hair?"

Cali sighed as they approached the dressing room. "Your all-too-kind compliments aside, that's why I didn't want their services. Makeup and a hairdo would make me look different, and I don't want Maksim to find a woman he doesn't know walking down the aisle to him. Then I saw the so-called wedding dress and its accessories and almost fainted. Here…" She turned on the dressing room's lights. "You'll see what I mean."

Everyone blinked and their jaws dropped.

But it was Kassandra, of course, who recognized what that masterpiece was.

Her exclamation reverberated in the spacious room. "That's Empress Alexandra Feodorovna's dress!"

Yep. Maksim had gotten her the dress of the freaking last tsarina of Russia. She'd recognized it from her extensive research into his motherland's history.

Kassandra shook her head in disbelief. "It has to be a replica. That V-shaped satin inlay in the bodice below the embroidery was red in the original. This one's is—" she swung her dazed gaze to Cali "—the exact color of your eyes."

Cali's eyes misted again at the lengths he'd gone to at such short notice. "I thought so at first, but couldn't figure out how he could have had a replica made in under ten hours. The more plausible, if more insane, explanation is that he had the original customized to me."

"But…but—he couldn't have!" Kassandra looked faint with even imagining this. This would be tantamount to sacrilege to the designer in her. "That dress, if it's the real thing, is a…a *relic*. He couldn't have tampered with it for any reason. And how could he have gotten his hands on it at all? God, Cali, just *who* is this man you're marrying?"

"A very, *very* influential man, m'dear," Selene retorted.

But Kassandra was rushing to closely examine the dress in openmouthed shock and wonder and was joined by the others.

Selene remained beside Cali. "For your ears only, Cali, since the ladies are overwhelmed enough, I wouldn't put obtaining such an artifact past Maksim. Literally anything is possible with our one-in-a-billion men."

Kassandra turned stricken eyes to them. "It's done ingeniously, but I can detect where the azure inlay overlies the original red. It is *the* dress."

Cali shuddered. "So I was right to fear touching it."

Thea scratched her head. "Apart from its pricelessness, how do you put it on? I don't see any zippers or buttons."

"It does seem as if there is no way to get into it," Phaidra agreed.

"Oh, of course there is." Kassandra waved their stymied perplexity away with the assurance of an expert. "And it's a good thing you declined putting on makeup, Cali. I would have had an ulcer dreading you'd smudge this one-in-history masterpiece." She picked up the extremely heavy dress reverently, her eyes eating up the details before turning to the others. "You ladies sit down over there—" she indicated the brocade couches on the other side of the room "—while I get Cali into this, and we'll get this show on the road."

Selene curtsied. "You're the boss here, Kass."

Melina bowed before Kassandra with arms stretched in mock worship. "She is the goddess, you mean. She conjured those bridesmaid's dresses in Maksim's demanded shade for all of us in under three hours!"

Imitating their sister, Thea and Phaidra bowed to Kassandra, who touched their gleaming heads in mock magnanimity, before they all burst out laughing.

Sobering a bit, Kassandra said, "Seriously, I couldn't have gotten everything done on *that* short a notice. I made the final selections, but it was Maksim's magic wand that had the dresses adjusted and flown in to your doorsteps in time."

As Cali's eyes welled and her sisters swooned over her groom's gallantry, Kassandra shooed them away again.

Clearly delighted to not have to handle Cali's wedding artifact, to sit down and watch as if they were in a fashion show, everyone hurried to comply with Kassandra's directives while Cali rushed after her to the changing room.

Ten minutes later, she stood gaping at herself. It was a good thing she'd declined a professional hairdo and makeup. With only the dress, she looked totally transformed. The white satin masterpiece molded to her like an extension of her. The bodice opened on a plunging off-the-shoulders oval décolleté, pointing into a sharp V at the nipped waist. The long sleeves opened longitudinally at the armholes and flowed down, folding back to expose her arms whenever she moved them. The skirt was bell shaped in the front with a detachable ten-foot train at the waist that folded softly at the back with pleats of tulle.

The bodice below the décolleté, with that newly installed azure-satin inlay, was embellished in prominent silver flower wreaths, and the borders of the sleeves and train, as well as the middle of the bodice and skirt, were all embroidered in complex golden garlands. A panel of gold velvet traveled down the midfront with pearl and diamond buttons, and the *kokoshnik,* the headdress that stood for a veil, was exquisite snow-white lace worked with the same designs.

Cali let out a ragged breath, still hardly believing her own eyes. "I don't think I could have gotten into this thing if you weren't here, Kass."

"I trust Maksim will know how to get you out of it?" Kassandra chuckled, then frowned in alarm. "Do you get how we put it on you to instruct him if he runs into trouble? If he gets frustrated being unable to peel it off you and damages it, I'd…"

"Yeah, have an ulcer."

"Ulcer is for makeup smudges," Kassandra scoffed. "For an actual tear? Nothing less than an aneurysm."

Cali's heart slammed painfully against her ribs.

Of all the things to mention, why would Kassandra say this specifically? Was this more than a coincidence? The fates telling her something through her unwitting friend…?

Just how ridiculous was she being? People blurted out things like this all the time. It was she who was hypersensitive to it.

Her smile wavered as she met the other woman's eyes in the mirror. "Shall we let my sisters be the ones to help with the headdress and accessories?"

"Yeah, they can help with all the indestructible articles. And let's have Phaidra twist your hair up like her own hairdo. It'll suit you and the accessories perfectly."

Even in her lingering dismay, she smiled at Kassandra's

protectiveness of the dress, which only a true artist would feel toward an irreplaceable work of art.

The others' reaction to her appearance confirmed that she looked like a totally different woman. Her sisters, especially Melina, as her eldest sister, went all teary eyed at the sight of the baby of the family looking like an empress, and basically *becoming* an empress of the new world, since her groom was an emperor of industry and commerce.

As they gathered around her, Kassandra stopped them from hugging her so *their* makeup and perfume wouldn't stain the dress. Teasing Kassandra about her new obsession, they started adorning Cali in the jewelry Kassandra insisted *had* been that particular dress's, especially the breathtakingly ornate crown of white gold, pearls and diamonds.

Then it was time. To marry Maksim.

She rushed out of the suite as fast as the dress allowed her with the rest behind her, trying to help her with her train, then giving up because she needed no help at her speed, since it flew behind her on the marble floors of the mansion.

They had to pull her back at the entrance of the dance hall so she wouldn't spill in. She forced herself to walk in as if she weren't a mass of excitement and screaming nerves.

And she found herself stepping into a place she felt she'd never seen before. It had been transformed into a scene from the most sumptuous times of imperial Russia. The paneled-in-gold walls gleamed under the combined lights of the crystal and gold-plated metal sconces hanging between them and the spotlights that were directed toward the thirty-foot painted ceiling, reflecting on the scene to drench it in magical golden glow.

Against each side of the length of the gigantic rectangular hall, endless tables were set, leaving the rest of the elaborate hardwood floor empty, with only an aisle running down its middle. The tables were covered by an organza tablecloth with the symbol of the estate—a cross between a phoenix and an eagle with its wings spread—repeated in a pattern throughout. Tatjana had told her that the extravagant sets adorning the tables came from a service of Sevres porcelain Napoleon Bonaparte had given to Tsar Alexander. There were only about three hundred people seated there, with the rest of the guests attending the reception/birthday afterward.

Among those, she looked for one person first. Andreas.

It was actually hard to believe he'd come for her wedding, when he hadn't for Leonidas's funeral.

She didn't look long. He stood out in the bright, festive scene, emanating his own deep shadows. He wasn't sitting with the rest; he was standing almost at the entry, apart, alone. And, as always, he looked like a barely leashed predator, his black hair and eyes matching the darkness he exuded.

He met her eyes across the distance, didn't smile. Then he raised his hand and placed it flat over his heart.

Her nerves jangled. She loved Andreas but had never figured him out—or if her emotions were reciprocated, if he even felt anything for anyone. This simple gesture somehow told her everything he'd never said. He did love her—and probably loved the rest of his siblings, too, just in his own detached, unfathomable way.

Unfortunately, she couldn't stop to savor this rare moment, had to relinquish his gaze, move on.

Tatjana captured her focus next. She was at the middle of the table to the left, looking majestic in an elaborate gold-satin dress that she believed belonged to one of Russia's grand duchesses. Rosa, in something sumptuous from Tatjana's wardrobe, was standing behind her, with an enthralled Leo in a vivid blue-and-gold miniature of an adult costume, looking so absolutely adorable her heart flailed in her chest.

She kept her eyes averted from the end of the hall. She knew Maksim was there, flooding the hall with his over-powering presence, permeating her cells with his influence. She wanted to keep him for last. There would be no looking anywhere else after she laid eyes on him.

Aristedes, in his resplendent tuxedo, strode toward her, smiling into her dazed eyes as he took her arm.

As they walked down the royal-blue-satin aisle, spread on both sides with white-and-gold rose petals, he said, "Your man throws a mean party in record time. At least I hope he does, and this isn't how he intended to celebrate a one-year-old's birthday."

She wanted to explain that this was all new, but had no more breath. Only her feet remained working on autopilot. For she had finally looked down the aisle. At Maksim. It was a miracle she remained erect.

With every step closer he came into clearer focus, in-ducing more tremors into her limbs and heart.

He was wearing the adult-size version of Leo's costume, imperial clothes, though she failed to pinpoint its origin. His shoulders and chest looked even more imposing than usual in a midthigh coat in vivid blue, the same hue of the inlay in her dress but many shades darker. It was embroi-dered exquisitely with gold thread and cord in a horizon-tal repetitive pattern, each ending where golden buttons closed the coat down his massive chest. At his hard waist it opened down to reveal white gold-embroidered satin pants gathered into navy-and-tan leather boots.

And then she looked up at his face, and that was when she almost fell to her knees.

The mahogany hair that now rained down to his shoulders was scraped away from his leonine forehead and gathered back into a ponytail, the severe pull emphasizing his rugged bone structure, the lupine slant of his eye and the sensual hardness of his lips.

He looked way more than heart-stopping. And he looked…hungry. She felt him devouring her from afar, felt her body readying itself for his possession, didn't know how she'd survive the time until she could have him again.

Then they reached him where he stood on the draped-in-satin, five-step platform, and Aristedes unhooked his arm from what she realized had been her spastic grip.

He held out his hand to Maksim, who gripped it in a firm handshake, then drew him into one of those sparse male hugs. Cali heard their brief exchange.

"Make her happy, Volkov," Aristedes said. *Or else* was conveyed clearly.

It was lucky she hadn't applied makeup or she would have ended up a streaked mess when she heard Maksim's answer.

"I live to make her happy, Sarantos."

The two most important men in her life parted with a final look of understanding. Then Aristedes placed her hand in Maksim's and stepped down.

Everything from the moment her groom took her hand onward went by in a dreamlike blur.

Maksim tucked her to his side as if he were afraid she'd disappear as an ornately dressed minister started reciting the marriage vows first in Russian, then in English. After she'd recited them after him in a fugue, another man stepped forward, took the minister's place and recited vows in Greek.

No longer able to manifest surprise or to deal with these spikes in emotion, she only looked up at Maksim, love and gratitude flowing from her eyes. He hugged her tighter, his eyes smoldering with passion so fierce it singed her soul.

After they'd exchanged their own vows, and he'd kissed her senseless, he held her swooning mass to his side as he gestured to someone in the distance. In moments, Rosa came rushing up the platform with Leo popping with excitement in her arms. He threw himself at both of them, but it was Maksim who had the coordination to catch him.

Holding both of them to his heart, he addressed the guests.

"Every man lives searching for a purpose in life. If he is blessed, he finds it and can dedicate his life to it. I have been blessed beyond measure. I give you my purpose, my blessings, the owners of my heart and soul and everything that I am and have. My bride, the love of my life, Caliope Sarantos Volkova, and my son and heir, Leonidas Sarantos Volkov."

Everyone stood as one, cheering and raising their glasses in a toast to the family, and Cali broke down at last, burying her face into Maksim's chest, sobbing, while Leo jumped up and down in his father's embrace and screeched in elation, as if realizing that this was a momentous moment in all their lives.

The out-of-body feeling she'd been experiencing only deepened as the celebrations continued, merging the wedding with the birthday. Maksim took her to salute their guests before heading outside the hall, where she found the rest of the mansion *was* spread with tables for the attendees, with the children converging on Leo's wonderland.

She thought she laughed with her family, chattered in Russian with Tatjana's acquaintances, joked with Maksim's business associates who wanted to know how she'd melted that iceberg. She believed she joined in dancing the *khorovod,* the Russian circle folk dance, which her family eventually turned into the *pidikhtos,* Crete's version of the dance.

Then she was hugging and kissing endless bodies and faces, the only ones she'd remember later being her family, especially Andreas, who promised he'd come visit her... sometime.

Then she was held high in Maksim's arms, swept through the mansion to a wing she hadn't been in before. As she peeked over his shoulder, she found Kassandra and Selene running to keep up with his urgent strides. A beaming Kassandra explained with gestures that they were coming to get her out of the dress. Seemed she'd taken Maksim aside and convinced him to recruit her for the chore.

Inside a suite that Maksim had lavishly prepared for their wedding night, he reluctantly set her down on her feet, thanked Kassandra and Selene then whispered in her ear that he'd be waiting for her inside and strode away.

After a giggling Kassandra and Selene helped her out of the dress, Kassandra worshipped it back onto its hanger and Selene gave her a package that had been waiting on a coffee table. Then with one more hug, both ladies disappeared, leaving her standing in her lacy underwear and high-heeled sandals.

Cali's hands shook as she opened the package, which Maksim must have commissioned Kassandra to get for her. Inside was the most luxuriously erotic getup she'd ever seen.

Trembling all over with anticipation, she substituted it for her underwear, a dream of brilliant pearl-white stretch lace and satin that cupped her breasts into a deep cleavage and showcased the rest of her to the best advantage.

Unable to wait to see its effect on Maksim, she teetered inside, wishing he hadn't changed into anything himself, since she'd spent the whole evening dreaming of stripping him out of that costume. Yet part of her was also wishing that he *had* already disrobed, since she couldn't wait until she had his flesh beneath her hands and lips.

She entered a bedroom that was spread in gold and azure and lit with what must be a thousand candles. Maksim was at the far end with only those white pants on. His whole body bunched at the sight of her, like a starving predator who'd just spotted the one thing that would slake his hunger.

She almost fell to her knees when he rumbled, *"Moya zhena...nakonets."*

My wife. At last.

Maksim watched the incandescent vision that was his bride. He'd spent the previous night drowning in her. Instead of sating him, it had only roused the beast he'd been keeping on a spiked leash, fueling his addiction to searing levels.

He'd felt her equal craving all through the wedding, her impatience to continue making up for fifteen months of separation and starvation. He'd intended to drag her into the depths of passion the moment she walked in, give her what she needed, invade her, finish her, perish inside her.

Then she had glided in, and he'd called her his wife... and only when he'd said it had it fully registered.

She was his *wife*.

And what he felt now was...frightening. So much so it brought his old fears crashing down on him, paralyzing him.

But after her own moments of paralysis, when he didn't go to her, she started walking toward him, looking... celestial. It almost made him regret asking her friend to get her something made to worship her beauty. Her friend had chosen *too* well.

Then she was against him, running feverish hands and lips over his burning flesh, her eyes eating him up, her body grinding against his, pulling him down to the bed, taking him on top of her. Opening her legs for his bulk, undulating beneath him in a frenzy, she demanded him inside hers, riding her, pleasuring her, fulfilling her.

Her hands tangled in the string tying his hair back, almost tore at it as she tugged at his scalp, the exquisite pain lashing at his barely contained fervor.

Then her fingers bunched into his hair and she brought his head down to hers, his lips fusing with the fragrant, warm petals of her flesh to breathe a white-hot tremolo into his depths. *"Moy muzh."*

His every nerve fired. *My husband.*

And to have her say it in Russian. That she'd learned the language, and that well, for him…the gratitude he felt was at times…excruciating.

Spiraling, he tried to rise off her, to ration his response. But her pleading litanies to hurry, to take her, now, now, were like hammers smashing his control. Her beloved body quivered beneath his, her cherished face shuddered.

It was too much. He wanted too much. All of her. At once.

His growl sounded frightening in his ears as he sank his teeth where her neck flowed into her shoulder. She jerked and threw her head back, giving him a better bite. He took it. He was a hairbreadth from going berserk.

Then as she gazed up at him through hooded eyes, she made any attempts at curbing his passion impossible. "Show me how much you want me, Maksim." Her voice reverberated in his brain, dark and deep. Wild. "Brand me as yours, seal our lifelong pact, give me everything… take everything."

With a grunt of surrender, he freed her silky locks

from the high chignon he'd longed to demolish all evening, pulled her head to the bed for his devouring. She bombarded him with a cry of capitulation and command.

He rose to free himself from the confines of his pants, to tear that tormenting figment off her, then hissed in relief when he found her wearing nothing beneath it. His fingers slid between the lips of her core before dipping inside her, finding her flowing with readiness.

Blind with the need to ride her, he locked her thighs over his back, drove her into the mattress with a bellow of conquering lust and embedded himself inside her to her womb.

They arched back. Mouths opened on soundless screams at the potency of the moment. On pleasure too much to bear. Invasion and captivation. Completion. New, searing, overpowering. Every single time.

His roar broke through his muteness as he withdrew. She clutched at him with the tightness of her hot, fluid femininity, her delirious whimpers and her nails in his buttocks demanding his return. He met her eyes, saw everything he needed to live for. He rammed back against her clinging resistance, his home inside her. The pleasure detonated again. Her cry pierced his being. He thrust hard, then harder, until her cries stifled on tortured squeals.

Then she bucked. Ground herself against him. Convulsed around him in furious, helpless rhythms, choking out his name, her eyes streaming with the force of her pleasure.

He rode her to quivering enervation. Then showed her the extent of his need, her absolute hold over him. He bellowed her name and his surrender to her as he again found the only profound release he'd only ever had with her, convulsing in waves of pure culmination, jetting his seed into her depths until he felt he'd dissolved inside her.

Even as he sank into her quivering arms, he was harder than before. Which didn't matter. He had to let her sleep.

He tried to withdraw. She only wound herself tighter around him, clung to him.

"There will be more and more, soon and always." He breathed the fire of his erotic promise into her mouth. "Rest now. You've been awake for forty-eight hours, and I've taxed you in every possible way beyond human endurance."

She breathed her pleasure inside him, thrust her hips to take him deeper inside her. "I can only sleep if you stay inside me. I can't get enough of you, *moy dorogoy muzh.*"

"Neither will I of you...ever." She was driving him deeper into bondage. And he wouldn't have it any other way.

He drove back into her and she pulsed her sheath around him until he groaned. "Tormentress. Just wait until you're rested. I'll drive you to insanity and beyond."

In response to his erotic menace, she tossed her arms over her head, arched her vision of a body, thrust her breasts against his chest and purred low with aggressive surrender. Still jerking with the electrocuting release, he turned her, brought her over him, her shudders resonating with his.

"Give me your lips, *moya zhena.*"

As she gave him what he needed, her lips stilled while fused to his, exhaustion claiming her.

As she finally surrendered to slumber, totally secure and trusting in his arms, he knew.

His resurrected fears were totally unfounded. Even through the inferno of lust, tenderness and giving had permeated him. His feelings weren't forged in selfishness and dependence but fueled by the need to enrich her life, be the source of her fulfillment. His pleasure lay here, in being hers.

He took her more securely into his containment and surrendered to their union on every level. And to peace.

For the first true time in his life.

Ten

Cali stretched in the depths of utter bliss.

She wanted to never surface, to lie here on top of her Great Russian Wolf forever.

For the past four months since their wedding, she'd gone to sleep like that, after nights of escalating abandon.

But she had to wake up. She'd promised Tatjana to spend the day with her. At least she thought she had. After a night of mind-scrambling pleasure at Maksim's hands, she wasn't even sure where she was.

She actually had to open her eyes to make certain they *were* back in Russia. They'd just come back last night after a taking-care-of-business, apartment-buying stint in New York.

She'd thought this mansion had become her home, but then she'd also felt at home on their first night in their new NYC apartment. If she hadn't been certain by then, she was now. Anywhere Maksim was would always be home to her.

She propped herself up with palms flat over his chiseled chest to wallow in his splendor.

Unbelievable. That *did* just sum him up. And every moment of every day with him. She sometimes still did find herself disbelieving this was all really happening,

wondered if it was possible she'd ever get used to his...
their perfection.

But then why should she? How *could* she get used to
this? Nope. It was *im*possible. There was nothing to do,
and nothing she *wanted* to do, but live in a state of perpetual wonder.

Just looking at him had her heart trying to burst free
of its attachments and her breath refusing to come until
she drew it mingled with his beloved scent. So she did.

At the touch of her lips on his, he smiled in his sleep
and rumbled, *"Lyublyu tebya."*

She caught the precious pledge in an openmouthed kiss.

He instantly stirred, dauntingly aroused, returned the
kiss then took it over.

She gasped with pleasure as he swept her around, bore
down on her. "Love you more, Maksim."

"There's no way you love me more, *moye serdtse.* I've
waited all my life for you, knew it the moment I saw you."

She arched up, opening herself for him. "Same here."

He rose on his knees and positioned himself at her molten entrance, held her immobile by her hair for his passionate onslaught, the way she loved him to. *"Nyet,* I'm
older, so I don't only love you more, I've loved you longer."

She cried out with the searing pleasure of his words
and his plunge into her body. Their hunger was always
too urgent at first. It took only a few gulps of each other's
taste, a few unbridled thrusts to have them convulsing in
each other's arms, the pleasure complete.

After the ecstasy he drove her to demolished her completely, he twisted to lie on his back and draped her over
him again, a trembling blanket of sated flesh.

A sigh of contentment shuddered out of him after the
burst of exertion and satisfaction.

She raised an unsteady head to savor his beauty. "You're

feeling quite smug, aren't you? You think you've claimed the More and Longer Loving title for life, don't you?"

"If this ruffles your feathers too much, I can be persuaded to grant you equal billing in the 'More' category. The 'Longer' one, alas, is an unchangeable fact of time. Being the spring chick that you are, you just don't have the creds."

She drove her hands into the thick, mahogany hair that now fell past his shoulders at her demand, tugged sharply, knowing he loved it when she played rough. "Do you know what happens to condescending wolves, even the one-of-a-kind specimens?"

He stretched beneath her languidly, provocation itself. "*Da*...they get punished, with even more love and pleasure."

"Damn straight." She swooped to devour those maddeningly seductive lips, took him over this time, tormented and inflamed and owned every inch of him until she had him begging her to ride him. And she did. Hard and long, until they both almost shattered with pleasure.

Afterward, tingling with aftershocks, she let him haul her to the shower, where they spent an indeterminable time leisurely soothing and pampering each other.

They'd just exited the bathroom guffawing as he chased her to tickle her when a knock came on the door.

She bolted away from Maksim's groping hands and started jumping into her clothes. "Leo! Hurry, put something on."

He picked up his jeans, his smile unfettered. "Our son has an impeccable sense of timing. He lets us feast on each other in peace, then comes to join in for playtime."

She prodded him along and he shoved himself with difficulty into his jeans, wincing and muttering that only *un*dressing was safe with her around.

Her wide grin of triumph elicited a growled promise of retribution as she rushed to the door.

As soon as she opened it, Leo bolted inside without even looking at her. She laughed. The wily boy was pre-empting her, wasn't risking her telling Rosa to take him away for now. And he was after his daddy anyway, his biggest playmate and fan.

She exchanged a few words with Rosa, setting up the day, then turned to her men, delight dancing on her lips at the sight they made together.

Leo was popping up and down with arms stretched up for his daddy to pick him up. Maksim was standing above him, looking down at him.

Her smile faltered. The sense of something wrong hit first. What it was registered seconds later.

It was the way Maksim was looking down at Leo… as…as if…

As if he didn't know him.

Even worse, it was as if Maksim wasn't even aware *what* Leo was, where or who *he* was…

A bolt of ice froze her insides wholesale. Her heart exploded from the rhythm of serenity to total chaos.

"Maksim…?"

His eyes rose to her and what she saw there almost had her heart rupturing. Horror. Helplessness.

Then he collapsed…like a demolished building. As if every muscle holding him up had snapped, every bone had liquefied.

"Maksim!"

Her scream detonated in her chest and head, its sheer force almost tearing them apart. Hurling herself across the room, she barely caught him, slowing down his plummet before he keeled over Leo, desperation infusing manic strength into her limbs.

Shuddering, she crumpled with Maksim's insupportable deadweight to the ground, barely clearing Leo, who'd frozen to the spot, eyes stricken, fright eating through his incomprehension by the second. Any moment now he'd realize this was no game. Any moment now Maksim would...would...

She screamed for Rosa, a scream that must have rocked the mansion, bringing Rosa barging into the suite in heartbeats.

She heard herself talking in someone else's voice, rapid, robotic. "Get my phone, take Leo away, keep everything from Tatjana for now, get Sasha. *Go*."

She'd lived through a dress rehearsal of this catastrophe a thousand times in her mind. Leaving nothing up to chance, Maksim had coached her in the exact measures she'd take in case the worst happened. This constant dread had been the only thing polluting her psyche, eating away at her stamina. But the more time that had passed without even the least warning signs, the more she'd hoped it would never come to pass.

But it had. It *had*.

His aneurysm had ruptured.

Keeping her dry-as-rock eyes on Maksim's wide-open, vacant ones, she speed-dialed Maksim's emergency medical hotline. As per the plan, they assured her a helicopter would be there within minutes. The specialists he'd elected to handle his case would be waiting at the medical center of his choice.

Then she waited. Hit bottom, went insane over and over, waiting. Her heart had long been shredded, but it kept flapping inside her like a butchered bird only because Maksim's heart still beat powerfully beneath her quaking arms. The rest of him was inert. Feeling his vigor vanished, his very *self* extinguished, was beyond horrifying.

Those eyes where his magnificent, beautiful soul resided had emptied of everything that made him himself. Then it got worse.

At one point, something came across them, something vast and terrible spreading its gloom, eclipsing their suns. Something like anguish. No...regret. Then his lips moved in a macabre parody of their usual purpose and grace. His voice was also warped, sending more gushes of terror exploding through her.

She thought he said, *"Izvinityeh."*

Forgive me.

Then his eyes closed.

And she screamed and screamed and screamed.

She didn't stop screaming, she thought, until the medics arrived. Once there was something to do, solid steps to be taken, a switch was thrown inside her, shutting down the hysteria of powerlessness. And the rehearsed drill took her over once again.

She talked to him all the time they installed their resuscitation measures on the short flight to the state-of-the-art medical center he'd erected in the city. She told him all the good news she could—that his vitals were strong, that he had gone into shock and his whole body was flaccid, but he wasn't exhibiting any hemiparesis, which would indicate neurological damage. She told him she was there and would *never* leave his side, that he had to fight, for Leo, for his mother. But mainly for her.

She couldn't live without him.

Then they arrived at the hospital and the perfectly oiled machine of intervention he'd put in place months ago took over. She ran beside his gurney as he was taken to the O.R., but the doctors, as per his orders, wouldn't let her scrub in or watch the surgery from the gallery.

Unable to waste time arguing, she succumbed, but wouldn't be convinced to go to the waiting area. She collapsed in front of the O.R. where the man who embodied her heart and soul would be cut open, where he would struggle to stay alive. She had to be as close as possible. He would feel her, and she would be able to transfer her very life force unto him to keep him alive, to restore him.

And she wept. And realized that she'd never truly wept before. *This* was weeping, feeling her insides tearing, her psyche shattering, her very being dissolving and seeping out of her in an outpour that could never be stemmed. Only Maksim, only an end to his danger, could stop the fatal flow.

In the unending torment of waiting, she registered somewhere in her swollen, warped awareness that Aristedes and Selene had come. Their very presence reinforced the horror of what she already knew, counting the minutes since Maksim had been taken into the O.R. He'd been in there for over twelve hours.

After failing to make her get off the ground, they'd sat down there beside her, respecting her agony, trying to absorb it in the solidarity of their silence.

"Mrs. Volkov."

That voice. She'd know it among a million.

Maksim's neurosurgeon.

She shot up to her feet. But her legs had disappeared. With a cry of chagrin, she collapsed back down. Aristedes caught her, Selene shooting up to help him support her.

The moment she could feel her legs again, she pushed them away and staggered to Dr. Antonovich. This was hers alone to hear, to bear. Just like Maksim was hers alone.

Dr. Antonovich talked quickly as she approached him, as if afraid she'd attack him if he didn't. "Mr. Volkov made it without incident through surgery. He's in intensive care now, where he will stay for the next two weeks as we monitor him."

Alive. *He was alive.* He'd survived this catastrophe that had been casting its dreadful shadow over their lives.

But… "What—what is his condition now?"

Dr. Antonovich attempted to take her arm, to support her as she swayed. She shook her head, needing only answers, facts.

Nodding with understanding, he began quietly, "During his last checkup six months ago, the aneurysm had still been located where attempts to approach it would have caused serious brain damage or even death. But in the interim, it had expanded downward, which at once caused it to rupture, and enabled us to try a new kind of treatment through a noninvasive, endoscopic trans-nasal approach. I'm happy to report the aneurysm has been totally resected and the artery fully repaired."

She absorbed the information rabidly. But it still didn't tell her what to expect next. "What about prognosis?"

"Since his aneurysm was posttraumatic, Mr. Volkov has no underlying weakness in his vessels, and the possibility of recurrence is nil. While that is great news, it was the rupture of the original aneurysm that we had worried about. To tell you the truth, with Mr. Volkov's general condition in the months after his accident, I had little hope he'd survive a rupture. The last time he came in six months ago, he'd shown little physical progress. But the man I operated on today was the most robust person I've ever seen. If I had to hazard a guess, I'd say you're the reason behind his miraculous improvement."

Maksim had said that. That she and Leo were a magical elixir, that being with them—with *her*—had revitalized him, gave him new capacities and limitless strength.

It had been why she'd let her guard down, believing nothing would happen to him.

"What does his general condition have to do with his prognosis?" she choked out.

"Everything. Apart from the neurological condition after rupture, it's what decides the prognosis. As a surgeon who deals almost exclusively in cerebral accidents, I almost never give optimistic percentages. But with Mr. Volkov in superb physical condition, if the next two weeks pass without incident, I believe he has an over ninety percent chance of making a full recovery."

She pounced on him, digging her shaking hands into his arms. "What can I do? Tell me there's something I can do."

He extricated himself gently, took her arm. "You can keep on doing exactly what got him to this state of superb health. And once he clears the sensitive postoperative period, both of you can forget about this uncertain phase of your lives."

She stopped, the tears that hadn't slowed during their conversation flowing faster. "Wh-when can I see him?"

The surgeon ventured a faint smile. "Mr. Volkov has instructions firmly in place about every possible development of his condition. You and anyone you indicate are to have full access to him, night or day, as long as there is no medical reason not to. You can even stay with him in ICU."

She grasped his arm again. "I—I can?"

The man nodded. "He funded the whole hospital, and keeps upgrading it at our request with the latest technology. The only thing he ever asked for in return was that, if he ever needed our services, we would arrange for you to stay with him while he recuperates, if that was what you wanted...."

And she broke down, the agony of loving him and fearing for him, demolishing her. "I want... God, oh, God... I want...I want nothing else in the world...*please.*"

The first three days, Cali stayed by Maksim's side around the clock, counting his breaths, hanging on to the exact shape of his heartbeats and brainwaves. There was no change whatsoever. His vitals remained strong and steady, but he didn't regain consciousness.

The only reason she didn't go berserk was that the doctors insisted he was sleeping artificially. He'd been sedated to give his brain the chance to recover during this sensitive phase, when awareness would tax it. Dr. Antonovich was being extra careful, as she'd begged him to be, even if it freaked her out of her mind to see her indomitable Maksim so inert.

It was amazing how perfect he looked. The noninvasive technique had left his hair untouched, and it appeared as if he were sleeping peacefully, whole and healthy.

On the fourth day, they let him wake up. For one hour in the morning and another in the evening.

That first time he opened his eyes, she almost died of fright. The blank look he gave her had nightmares tearing into her mind. Of amnesia...or worse.

Then his gaze filled with recognition. Before jubilation could take hold, gut-wrenching emotion surged to the surface and the tears that constantly flowed gushed. She kissed him and kissed him, telling him she loved him, loved him, loved him, that she'd always, *always* be beside him, would never, ever leave his side, and that it was only a matter of time before they had their perfect life back.

He made no response as she talked and talked until she was terrified *he* couldn't talk. At last he told her he was just tired, then listlessly turned his head away and closed his eyes. She didn't think he slept, just kept his eyes shut. Until they'd come and put him under again.

When she'd pursued Dr. Antonovich with her report of his first weird waking episode, he said it was natural for Maksim to wake up groggy and not all there. When she insisted he'd been neither, just…blunted, he'd gone on to explain the obvious, that the brain was an unpredictable organ and she'd have to play it by ear, let him go through his recovery in his own pace and not worry, and mostly not let him feel her anxiety.

Determined to take the surgeon's advice, she told herself that anything she felt was irrelevant. Hard facts said Maksim was neurologically intact. And that was far more than enough. If it took him forever to bounce back from this almost lethal ordeal, it would be a price she'd gladly pay.

And he did bounce back, faster than his surgeon's best hopes. The two weeks in ICU became only one, with everyone, starting with Tatjana and Leo, coming to visit during his waking hours at his request. He was transferred to a regular suite and the sedation was confined to the night hours; then even that was withdrawn. By the next week, the surgeon saw no reason to keep him in hospital, discharged him with a set of instructions for home care and follow-ups, but gave him a clean bill of health.

But Maksim was subdued, only exhibiting any spark around his mother and son. With them he was almost his old self. Cali kept telling herself she was imagining things, and that even if she wasn't, there was a very good reason for this.

He was depleted, out of sorts, had just survived a near-fatal medical crisis and must be shaken to the core. But he couldn't show any of this to Tatjana and Leo. He hadn't even told his mother of his condition in fear of worrying her, and would now do anything to reassure her of his return to normal. He also wouldn't risk scarring Leo's young and impressionable psyche by allowing any of his post-traumatic stress to rise to the surface around him.

But around her? He could let his true condition show without having to bear the effort of putting on an act, and he could count on her to understand.

And she did understand. She only missed him. *Missed* him.

He was there but not there. He talked to her, especially when others where around, and she did feel his gaze on her sometimes, but the moment she turned to him, starving for connection, he looked away and sent her spiraling back into deprivation.

But she would persevere. Forever if need be. That was her pledge to him.

For better or for worse. For as long as she lived.

Three months after Maksim's discharge from the hospital, Cali's resolve was starting to waver.

Instead of things getting better, if even slightly, they only got worse.

The proof had come two weeks ago, when Dr. Antonovich had given him the green light to resume all his normal activities without reservations. It was as if he'd released him from a prison he'd been dying to break free of. He'd hopped onto a plane and gone on a business tour...alone.

He *had* called regularly during the past two weeks to reassure them, but called her own phone only when his mother didn't pick up. Even when he did, he said nothing personal, let alone intimate, just asking about Leo or asking her to put him through.

On the day he was supposed to come back, she'd run

out of rationalizations. There was no escaping the one possible conclusion anymore.

He was avoiding her.

And for the first time since she'd laid eyes on him, she dreaded seeing him, meeting his gaze. Or rather having him escape meeting hers again.

Just minutes later, he walked into the living room, where they were all gathered waiting for him. And the sight of him felt like a stab through her heart.

He'd lost weight since his crisis, understandably. But it wasn't only that his clothes hung around him that hurt. It was what felt like a statement that he'd withdrawn his emotional carte blanche to her.

He'd cut his hair.

It was now even shorter than when she'd first seen him across that reception hall—almost cropped off.

She felt catapulted back in time, only worse. Back then his eyes had smoldered with hunger; now they only filled with heaviness.

She still rushed to join in welcoming him, only to feel the white-hot skewer in her gut turning when he slipped away from her embrace, pretending to answer Leo's demand for his attention. She sat there with the talons pinning her smile up for Tatjana's and Leo's sake, sinking into her flesh and soul with every passing moment, until Leo fell asleep and Tatjana excused herself for the night. With just a curt good-night, Maksim walked out, too.

And she reached breaking point.

She had to know what was wrong or she'd lose her mind.

Forcing herself to follow him, dreading another brush-off, she approached the suite he'd moved to since he'd gotten out of hospital, with the excuse that he was suffering from bouts of insomnia at night and didn't want to disturb her.

Tiptoeing in, she found him sitting on the edge of a chair in the sitting area, his elbows resting on his knees, his cropped head held in his hands, his large palms covering his face. His shoulders, now looking diminished, were hunched over, his whole pose embodying the picture of defeat.

Her heart did its best to tear itself out of her chest.

A burst of protectiveness welled up inside her, had her running toward him, desperately needing to ward off whatever was weighing him down. His head snapped up at her approach, and for moments, she saw it. The unguarded expression of...torment.

Crying out with the pain of it, she hugged him fiercely, withdrawing only to hold his face in trembling hands, rain kisses over his face, his name a ragged litany, a prayer on her lips.

After only moments, he pulled away, his hands clamping hers, taking them away from his face. Her heart twisted in her chest at his clear and unequivocal rejection.

"I'm not ready for this."

This. Her nearness? Her emotions? What was...*this?*

She pried her hands from his warding grip, the sick electricity of misery that had become her usual state erratically zapping in her marrow. "Dr. Antonovich said you might suffer from some mood swings for a while."

He heaved up to his feet. "I'm suffering from nothing."

"This was a major trauma and surgery in your most vital organ. It's only expected you won't bounce back easily."

"He gave me a clean bill of health. There's nothing wrong with me. Just because I'm not up for sex doesn't mean I'm malfunctioning."

It felt like he'd backhanded her.

Was that how abused people felt? Would a physical blow have hurt more?

"I didn't say that," she choked. "And I'm not asking for sex or expecting it. I just want to…"

"You just want to touch me and kiss me. You want me to show you intimacy and emotion, what I showed you from the time I came back till the aneurysm ruptured." His voice hardened. "I tried to show you that I don't want any of that anymore, but you won't take a hint."

"It's all right. I understand…"

"You don't," he bit off. "You don't *want* to understand."

She swallowed back the sobs, unable to bear his harshness, which she'd never before been exposed to.

Then she remembered. "Dr. Antonovich said there was a chance for some personality changes…"

"There are no changes. This is me. The *real* me."

His growl fell on her like a wrecking ball. A lightning bolt of understanding.

"You mean it wasn't the real you before? Since your accident? Since you came back?"

He made no answer. And that was the most eloquent one.

"You mean when you left me, it was because you wanted nothing more to do with me? Then you had the accident, and thinking you'd die any moment made you vulnerable, made you need intimacy, to reaffirm your life? Or even worse, that aneurysm was pressing on your brain, causing your radical personality change. And once it was treated, you reverted to your real self, the self that didn't love me, that left me without a backward glance?"

The dismal darkness in his gaze said he hated hearing that. Because it was true. Because he felt terrible about it, but couldn't change it. He couldn't force himself to love her when he no longer felt anything.

His love for her had been injury induced. Now that he'd been fixed, he'd been cured of it.

She still had to hear him say it. "Do you want me to leave?"

His eyes were suddenly extinguished, as if everything inside him had just turned off, died. "I…think it would be best."

She'd hoped…until the words had left his mouth.

Her whole being lurched with agony so acute she caved under its onslaught; her face, her insides, all of her felt like a piece of burned paper crumbling in a careless hand.

One thing was still left unsaid. Not that it would change anything. It just had to be said.

"I'm…pregnant."

He nodded as if he, too, barely had enough life force to sustain him. "I know."

So he knew. Nobody had noticed as she'd lost so much weight. But he knew her intimately…as he no longer wanted to know her. As he seemed unable to contemplate knowing her.

"What I told you over two years ago stands."

About supporting her and his child. His *children* now.

She'd be a single parent now, not to one but two children. After she'd known what it was to share a child with him.

And she wailed, "Why did you ever come back? Why didn't you just leave me in my ignorance of what it could be like?"

He wouldn't look at her as he rasped, "I can't change the past, but this is better for the future, Caliope. I know you don't need anything, but you and…the children would still have everything that I have, and would have all my support in any way you'll allow. If you still let me be Leo's father, and the new baby's when it's born, you don't have to see me, too. In fact, I'd rather you didn't."

And the heart that had already been shattered was pulverized. "Did you *ever* love me, Maksim?"

He sat down heavily in his chair, throwing his head back, squeezing his eyes. "Don't dredge everything up, Caliope. Don't do this to yourself."

"I have to. I must make sense of this or I'll go insane."

He opened his eyes, looked at her with a world of dejection and said nothing.

No. He'd never loved her.

There was nothing more to say. To feel. To hope for.

She turned and walked away.

At the door, she felt compelled to turn back.

Strange how he still looked like the man she loved. The man who'd loved her. When that man had never existed.

"Since you told me of your aneurysm, I lived in fear of losing you. Now that I have, I'm only glad I didn't lose you to death. Even though I feel like a widow."

And she said goodbye. To the man who never was. To happiness and love and everything hopeful and beautiful she'd never have again.

Back in her suite, she stepped into the shower cubicle and stood limply beneath the powerful spray as the water changed from punishingly cold to hot, shudders spreading from her depths outward.

She squeezed her eyes, needing tears to flow, to release some of the unbearable pressure. None came. She'd depleted every last one and would forever be deprived of their relief.

Waves of despair almost crushed her, shudders racking

her so hard until she could no longer stand, and she sank in an uncoordinated heap to the cubicle's marble floor.

She lay there for maybe hours.

At last she exited the shower, dressed, packed her bags, gathered a bewildered Leo and Rosa and swept them back to New York.

Eighteen hours later, she entered her old building's elevator. She'd sent Leo with Rosa for the night.

She was…finished, didn't want to expose her son to more of her anguish. He'd felt it all through the flight, had fussed and wailed most of it. He must have also felt she was taking him away from his daddy.

Not that she would. Maksim would come for Leo, and she'd let him see him every day if he wanted. Despite everything, one thing was undeniable: Maksim loved his son. It had nothing to do with whatever he felt…or rather, *didn't* feel for her. That father/son bond hadn't been the aneurysm's doing, so it had survived its removal.

It was her love that had been so superficial, so artificial, it had vanished at the touch of a scalpel.

The ping of the elevator lurched through her. She stumbled out, walked with eyes pinned to the ground. She'd have to sell the apartment. Too many memories with Maksim here. She had to purge him from her life. If she hoped to survive.

Then she raised her eyes…and he was there.

He'd been sitting on the ground by her door, was now rising to his feet. Her legs gnarled together. And he was there, stopping her from plummeting to the ground.

Her eyes devoured him for helpless moments before common sense kicked in. "Leo… He's not with me…."

"I know. I'm here to talk to you."

And she panicked, pushed frantically out of his support-

OLIVIA GATES

ing arms. "No. No, no, *no*. You can't keep reeling me in, shredding me apart, throwing me out then doing it again. I won't let you do this to me. Not again. Not ever again."

Caliope's words fell on Maksim like fists dipped in ground glass...smashing into his heart and brain.

But he had to do this. He had to make her understand.

Taking the keys from her limp hands, he opened her door, urged her inside. "I have to talk to you, Caliope. After this, you'll never have to see me again."

The defeat and despair in her eyes made him wish again that he'd died on that operating table.

"It's you who doesn't want to see me, Maksim. You've reverted to your true nature, but I'm the same person who's always loved you, who can't stop loving you. I wish there was some medical procedure that would keep me from feeling like this, but if there were, I couldn't have it, because of Leo and the baby. You said you'd rather not see me again, and you were right. I *can't* see you again. Just thinking of you makes my sanity bleed out. Just looking at you makes my blood congeal inside my arteries with grief. If you want your children to have a mother and not a wreck, you won't let me see you again."

He deserved all that and more. But he had to do this.

He caught her arm as she turned away. "I left you once without explanations. I have to explain this time."

"I don't want your explanations. I don't care *why* you're killing me. It won't change the fact that you're killing me all the same."

He groaned, "Caliope..."

She stepped away unsteadily. "Okay, that was over the top. I am too strong to shrivel up and die. I will regain my equilibrium and go on. For myself as well as for my children."

His hands fisted, cramping with the need to reach for her. "This is what I want you to do. To move on, to forget…"

"You don't get to tell me what you want anymore," she cried out, strangled, shrill. "You don't get to pretend you care about what happens to me. I don't want to move on, and I don't want to forget. It if weighs on your conscience, I can't help you there. The man I love exists here—" she thumped her chest hard with her fist, face shuddering, eyes welling "—and here." Another jarring punch against her temple, her whole frame quaking with the rising tide of misery. "*He's* in my senses and reflexes, *he's* part of my every cell. Even if you're not him anymore, you can't take *him* away from me, so the new you can feel better…"

His own torment burst out of him on a butchered groan. "I was aware all the time after I collapsed, Caliope."

That brought her tirade to an abrupt end.

He went on. "All through the trip to the hospital, up to when they forced you, per my orders, to stay out of the O.R. I saw, *felt everything. I was mutilated* by what it did to you when I collapsed. I've never seen anyone so…wrecked, known someone could suffer so totally, so horrifically. And I realized that I'd done that to you. I've been far more selfish than you once accused me of being, involving you in this doomed relationship, where I get to have the happiness and blessing of your love as long as I live, only to leave you with the anguish of my loss and the curse of my memory."

Tears still cascading down her cheeks, she gaped at him.

"Dr. Antonovich might say he's over ninety percent certain I'm fully recovered, but there is still a percentage I'm not. And I can't bear making you live in constant dread waiting for me to collapse again, and maybe this time not making it...or worse."

Her tears suddenly stopped. Everything about her seemed to hit pause.

Then a cracked whisper bled out of her. "You mean you did love me? And never stopped?"

There was no way he could stop the admission now. "I've loved you from the first moment I saw you. I don't think I can stop loving you, even if they remove my whole brain."

This time her voice was more audible as her eyes became fiercely probing. "And you decided it was better for me to lose you while you were still alive? That's why you pulled away after your surgery, to build up my resentment toward you, so that if you eventually died it wouldn't hurt me as much?" His nod was wary, the dreadful feeling he'd botched this whole thing creeping up his spine. "Then why did you follow me here? Wasn't my leaving what you were after?"

His breath left him in a strangled rasp. "I've been trying to make you opt for saving yourself. I wanted you to walk out angry and indignant, intending to put me behind you. But you were *demolished* instead, without any hope of getting over me. *Bozhe moy*...the last things you said, about going insane not knowing...about feeling like a widow. What you said now...about loving me no matter what..."

He felt totally lost, no longer knowing what he was here to do or how he could possibly get her to save herself.

He tried again. "I couldn't leave you without an explanation again. I couldn't bear letting you keep on thinking I didn't love you. I love you so much, love our family and our lives together, I can't breathe with it most of the time. But I *can't* expose you to heartbreak of this magnitude again."

A long, full moment dragged by, then her murmur sounded more like the Caliope he knew. "One final question. If I were the one who got injured or crippled, would you abandon me?"

"Caliope, *nyet*..."

She plowed on. "If you knew I would possibly die at any moment, would you give up one single day with me now, live whatever time I had left apart from me to save yourself the anguish you'd feel if I died while we were in utmost closeness?"

Feeling his brain simmering, his eyes filling with acid, he protested, his voice a ragged, broken moan. "I'd give my very life for any time at all with you. For a month. A day. An *hour*. And nothing would ever take me away from your side if you love me, no matter what."

"Something *is* taking you away, when I love and need you, right now. You. You're the one who keeps depriving me of you."

And he realized. He hadn't only spoiled his mission, he'd closed the trap shut behind him...and her.

"*Bozhe moy*, Caliope, dying or worse, living crippled, is far preferable to me to hurting you. But whatever I do, I'll end up hurting you, and I thought..." He exhaled roughly. "I no longer know what I thought. Everything worked out in my mind when I was trying to drive you away...then I saw and felt the reality of your pain, and knew it wouldn't just end if I made you leave..."

He stopped, stared at her helplessly, loving her so much it overpowered him, defeated him.

And she gently drew him to her, clasping him into heaven, her supple arms sheltering him, taking him away from all his fears and uncertainty. "Then just accept your fate, Maksim, being mine for the rest of our lives, however long that will be. Just be ecstatically happy and humbly thankful, like I am, for every second we have together. Stop trying to save me future pain and only hurting me now and forever. Start loving me again and let me breathe again."

And just like that, every last shackle of anxiety snapped and every insurmountable barrier of dread came crashing down.

He surged around her, crushed her in his arms. "I can never stop loving you. I *won't* stop loving you even when I stop breathing. You are my breath, in my every cell, too. My heart beats to your name, my senses clamor for your being. I am yours, and I beg you to never let me go."

Her tears flowed again, this time of joy, of healing, drenching his chest, cleansing his soul. "I've never once let you go, mister. I've been clinging to you with all I have, but you're the one who keeps leaving every time your misguided chivalry and skewed self-sacrificing tendencies act up."

"If I ever stray again, out of any new bout of stupidity, club me over the head and drag me back into your embrace."

Her lips trembled in a smile of such acute love, he dropped his head in her bosom and let his tears flow.

Her hands shook over his head, sifting through his now bristly, short hair. "Mmm... I can and will carry out the clubbing part, but you're no longer a good candidate for being dragged back where you belong. No hair."

His laugh choked in his crowded chest. "That hair is growing back, waist length if you like."

"Ooh, I like." She leaned back in the circle of his arms. "And I want, Maksim, and need...and crave. Three months without you has taken me through all the stages of starvation."

"Can I dedicate the next thirty years to rectifying my major crime of three months of tormenting you in vain?"

She clung around his neck. "Make it fifty and you're on."

Feeling he'd just closely escaped an eternal plummet into hell, he swept her to bed, where he reunited them flesh in flesh, never to be sundered again.

And this time he knew that any lingering anxiety would only serve to intensify their union, make them revel in and appreciate each second they had together even more. If this wasn't survivable, who cared? Life itself ended, but this, their love, never would.

When the storm of passion had abated after a long night of wild abandon, he rose over her, caressing her from buttock to back, marveling in her beauty, wallowing in her hold over him. "Can we go retrieve our little lion cub now?"

She arched sensuously, the very sight of contentment. "Oh, yes. He's desolate without his dada. And Maksim..."

"Da, moy dusha?"

"If our baby is a boy, I want to name him Mikhail. If it's a girl, Tatjana Anastasia."

He buried his face in her neck, groaning, "You'll really kill me with too much love."

"I want to make you live like you never did."

And he told her what he'd once thought and never put it into words to her. "You do. Without you, I existed. With you, I'm alive, alight. I don't think I'll ever find enough ways to thank you for that, to show you how much I love you."

"When you weren't showing me you love me by leaving me, you did wonders."

Feeling beyond humbled by her blessing, he cupped her precious cheek. "For showing me the good inside of me, for giving me the best of everything, for loving me even when I made it impossible, for never giving up on me until I got it right…I promise you, you've see nothing yet."

His own personal pieces of heaven shone with tears and adoration. "I'll hold you to that. And I'll hold on to you. I'm never letting you go again."

"Never again, *moya zhena, moya dusha,*" he pledged. "Never, my wife, my soul. This time, forever."

* * * * *

A sneaky peek at next month...

Desire™

PASSIONATE AND DRAMATIC LOVE STORIES

My wish list for next month's titles...

In stores from 15th November 2013:

☐ It Happened One Night – Kathie DeNosky

& The Diplomat's Pregnant Bride

– Merline Lovelace

2 stories in each book - only £5.49!

☐ Her Return to King's Bed – Maureen Child

& A Billionaire for Christmas – Janice Maynard

☐ The High Price of Secrets – Yvonne Lindsay

& Second-Chance Seduction – Kate Carlisle

Available at WHSmith, Tesco, Asda, Eason, Amazon and Apple

Just can't wait?

Visit us Online

You can buy our books online a month before they hit the shops!

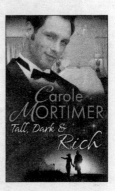

Meet The Sullivans...